# PRAISES
## AN AME

"**Conklin bases his well-realized historical novel on Black AAU heavyweight champion Norvel Lee.** The author's depth of research is apparent in the detailed chronicle of Lee's life, . . . The author displays a deep understanding of his lead character's biography, and provides convincing exploration of his life circumstances, from his segregated childhood to his WWII service; his development as an athlete; and his civil disobedience in the face of Jim Crow laws."

—*The BookLife Prize*

**Book Review:** Botetourt boxer Norvel Lee won landmark desegregation case

—*The Roanoke Times, book review by George Kegley, February 20, 2021*

"**This man, Norvel Lee, is my husband's uncle.** I've always heard snippets of what a powerhouse of a man he was. Now I have great details about him and I am very moved. He was an Olympic gold medalist in boxing, had a distinguished military career which included being a Tuskegee Airman. He was also an educator, a businessman, and a family man. Each of those titles holds SO many accomplishments within it, I can't possibly list it all here. All I can say is what a legacy this man left behind. Norvel Lee is the finest example I have read of what all people should strive to be. He did his best and always looked forward. Read this book. You will be the better for it."

—Audra Russell, author of *Blood Land*

### Olympic Gold Medal Journey and an Amazing Man

"The path to becoming an Olympic gold medalist is always intriguing. Is it destiny or is it drive? In the case of Norvel Lee you can argue that it was both. Or is it that drive leads to destiny? That is something to ponder after reading this well-researched book about a gentleman who excelled on boxing's world stage. If you love to read about what makes an Olympic athlete or you love the strategy of amateur boxing, you will definitely enjoy this book. And after reading about what Norvel Lee does after winning the gold medal, you will definitely appreciate the man."

—Lisa Telles, Communications Consultant (Author's note: Lisa is the daughter of John Boutilier. "Bout" as he was known makes notable appearances in the book.)

**An astounding man captured so timelessly**

"It is truly astounding to believe that everything captured in this novel is authentically about one great man, a man who should've been more well known before this masterpiece and deserves nothing but acclaim and recognition. Conklin so tirelessly retold Norvel Lee's life events in such a genuine way it's hard to believe he wasn't there with him during all these moments. This book reads like a remarkable work of fiction, so smooth and entrancing, it goes beyond words to express how inspirational and touching this extraordinary man's life was . . ."

—Victoria Whitehead, *Vinevoice*

"**I enjoy biographies**, especially those of people whose lives have not necessarily been lived in the spotlight. So I began this having never heard of Norvel Lee nor am I particularly interested in boxing. However, I can only give my highest recommendation to others to read this book. It tells the amazing life story of a man who came from humble beginnings and rose to become an Olympic hero and so much more. He was a man who kept hold of his integrity, his honour . . . often in the face of racism, discrimination and hostility. The book has a gentleness about the retelling in stark contrast to what I was expecting given it is set in the sport of boxing, but it becomes only more powerful because of that approach. . . I finished the book with a sense of indebtedness to people like Norvel Lee, who overcame so many barriers and did it with such humility and grace. The measure of a good book is the footprint it leaves on you after reading and without a doubt, this certainly does."

—Mrs. Rj, *Goodreads* UK reviewer

"**I went into this book blind, knowing nothing about Norvel Lee**, or boxing really, but I was very pleasantly surprised. It's actually an incredibly fitting read for what's going on in the country right now, to read an inspirational true story about a Black man faced with unimaginable adversity that fights (literally) through it to do amazing things. I'm a big believer that reading biographies of people like Norvel is an effective way to gain perspective on issues of the world, and life in general. Great read."

—Corrine Cassels, *Goodreads reviewer*

### A really well done biography

"Before reading *NORVEL*, I had no idea who Norvel Lee was . . . but I'm glad that I now know what an amazing person he was. The book is well-written . . . well-researched, and the subject matter is engrossing. Norvel was a hero of the civil rights era (his arrest and subsequent court case resulted in a landmark civil rights decision), a Tuskegee Airman, a WWII vet, a gold medal boxing winner, and that's literally not even half of what he was . . . I recommend it."

—Andrew Rivas, *Amazon reviewer*

"**Kenneth Conklin does a great job** spinning the story of Norvel Lee. The biography does more than introduce and cover the Tuskegee Airman and Olympic boxer. He paints a picture of history and how Lee changed the world. Most biographies are dull and read like school history books. Conklin's historical account of Lee is neither dull nor boring. His mastery of words will have readers eager to learn more."

—Mark Smith, *Goodreads reviewer*

"**So inspiring.** Oh my goodness. I cannot describe how inspiring this man's life was. This book was very well written and respectful and really made you feel like you were there, every painful step of the way. If you need something to help pick you up, read this book."

—Catherine, *Goodreads reviewer*

"**I went into this book not knowing anything about Norvel Lee.** I finished it with feelings of great respect for such an honorable man. He achieved so much it's inspiring. I think readers will relate to this humble man who excelled at everything. It's certainly poignant storytelling at its best and captures and relates what Norvel Lee was capable of achieving -- from the smallest endeavors to becoming a champion. I definitely feel this is a must read if you're someone who likes stories that tug at the heart strings."

—Kelly McDonough, *Goodreads reviewer*

### Great Man, Great Book!

"*NORVEL: An American Hero* is an awesome account of the life of Norvel Lee. Kenneth Conklin put together a masterpiece, from cover to cover. The book is well-written throughout. The historical pictures add perspective and a healthy dose of class. Norvel Lee has the chips stacked against him from the start; chips that would have debilitated lesser men. He overcame stammering and racism to become the greatest man I had never learned of. Throughout his life, he stayed busy fighting for what was right. When he lost, he simply took his fight to the next biggest opponent, and won! Mr. Lee stayed busy for his entire life; doing everything from teaching kids boxing to fighting for civil rights. Reading about Norvel Lee's schedule inspired me to do more with my life. The world needs to know the story of Norvel Lee, as told by Conklin. I wholeheartedly recommend to middle schoolers to 100-year-olds!"

—Dean Vargo, *Amazon* reviewer

### An inspiring amazing read

"This is an extremely well-written and researched book about Norvel Lee. He has many accomplishments including being an Olympic gold medalist, serving in the military, and being a devoted family man. He goes through a lot in his life to achieve his goals and dreams, including dealing with racism and a speech impediment. It was fascinating learning about his life journey and I was glad to learn more about an inspiring life. A very enjoyable read."

—Kris Woo, *Amazon Reviewer*

### A beautiful book

"Amazing!! To think that Norvel originated in Gala, Virginia, and became such a success in life. A humble, talented man who was a human being who cared for others more than himself. Thank you to the author for the research that you did and the beautiful book that resulted from that research. For those of you who have not read this book, just get it – you'll be so glad you did."

—*Amazon reviewer*

**"Readers experience the dialogue** as if Conklin was there several decades ago hiding around the corner with a tape recorder."
—*BookTrib*

# NORVEL

BY

KENNETH F. CONKLIN

Chapin Keith Publishing

Copyright © 2020 by Kenneth F. Conklin LLC

All rights reserved

Grateful acknowledgement is made to:

The United States Olympic and Paralympic Committee for permission to use the photo of the 1952 USA boxing team.

The Sports Museum Finland for permission to use photos from the *The XV Olympiad Official Report, Helsinki, 1952.*

Publisher's Cataloging-in-Publication Data

Names: Conklin, Kenneth F., author.

Title: Norvel / Kenneth F. Conklin.

Description: Includes bibliographical references. | Daleville, VA: Kenneth F. Conklin LLC, 2020.

Identifiers: LCCN: 2020901350 | ISBN 978-1-7344807-4-0 (Hardcover) | 978-1-7344807-2-6 (Paperback) | 978-1-7344807-3-3 (ebook)

Subjects: LCSH Lee, Norvel L. R.--Fiction. | African American boxers--Fiction. | Boxers (Sports)--Fiction. | Boxing--United States--History--20th century--Fiction. | United States--Race relations--History--20th century--Fiction. | Olympics--History--Fiction. | Educators--Fiction. | United States. Army Air Forces--History--Fiction. | African American air pilots--History--Fiction. | BISAC FICTION / Historical / General | FICTION / Sports | FICTION / African American / Historical

Classification: LCC PS3603.O5343 N67 2020 | DDC 813.6--dc23

This work of fiction is based on true events. Names, characters, places, and incidents derived from those events are the product of the author's imagination or are used fictitiously.
Cover and book design by Asya Blue

Front cover photo: Norvel Lee displaying his fighting form to his students.
UPI TELEPHOTO - 7/15/59

Back cover photo: Norvel Lee and Leslie Jackson driving around Washington.
*Ebony* – 2/1/51

First Paperback Edition

Visit the author's website at www.kennethfconklin.com

*In respectful memory of Georgia Meadows, Roger Terry, and all of the dedicated Jim Crow era teachers.*

# PROLOGUE

## *January 4, 1949—Alleghany County Courthouse, Covington, Virginia*

Judge Earl L. Abbott convened the Alleghany County Circuit Court to rule on a case regarding an incident that occurred on September 14, 1948, at the train station in Covington, Virginia.

On that day a man boarded the Chesapeake & Ohio's daily train No. 310 from Covington to Clifton Forge and took a seat in the area reserved for white passengers. An employee of the train asked him to move to the section set aside for "colored" travelers, but the tall, muscular man refused.

The Alleghany County sheriff, summoned by employees of the C&O Railroad Company, came onto the train and ordered the man to move to the colored section. Again, he refused. The sheriff then told him he would either have to take a seat in the colored section or get off the train. The man left the train, went to the ticket office, canceled his trip to Clifton Forge, and purchased a ticket for transportation from Covington to Washington, D.C. He reboarded the train and sat down in the same seat. The sheriff placed him under arrest for violating Virginia Code 3983, which stated that refusing to sit in segregated seating was a misdemeanor.

The man was booked and held in jail until a $250 bond was arranged later that day. On October 7, he was convicted of the misdemeanor by Alleghany County trial court Judge R. E. Dyche and fined $5. The man appealed the decision.

Now, with Judge Abbott presiding, the Commonwealth of Virginia, represented by T. Moore Butler, Esquire, presented its case by calling a series of witnesses, including C&O Conductor S. L. Lockhart, Brakeman R. H. Brisendine, and W. P. Henderson, the sheriff of Alleghany County. Their collective testimony supported the facts that a Negro man had boarded a train in Covington, Virginia, traveling the short route to Clifton

1

Forge, Virginia, and took a seat in the white section of a segregated passenger railcar. Additionally, it was shown that the conductor, Mr. Lockhart, had observed him in the white section the previous day going to Covington.

After Butler presented the Commonwealth's case, Martin A. Martin, a Black attorney from the civil rights law firm of Hill, Martin, and Robinson of Richmond, Virginia, was asked to present the argument for appeal. He called his only witness, the defendant, to the stand.

Dressed in a double-breasted gray suit and a reserved dark necktie resting on a crisp white shirt, the man walked with an athlete's quiet grace to the front of the courtroom. After being sworn in, he took a seat at the witness stand. Mr. Martin, slight and conservatively dressed, approached him, a congenial smile on his face.

He looked at his client and asked, "Your name is Norvel Lee?"

Lee responded, "Yes, sir, it is."

"Where do you live, Mr. Lee?"

"Uh, uh," said Lee, trying to compose himself, "I live in Washington, D.C., now."

"What are you doing there in Washington?"

"Uh, uh, I am a student at Howard University," Lee said, trying not to stammer.

"Where is your original home?"

"My uh, uh, original home is Eagle Rock, Virginia."

"Where is that?"

"It is out from Clifton Forge about ten miles."

Martin paused and looked at the scattered observers seated in the courtroom. "And have you been attending Howard University during the recent session?"

"Yes, sir, I have," Lee responded.

"How long had you been back in Virginia at the time this incident happened, on September 14th?"

"I had been here about fourteen days," Lee stammered.

"Where had you been prior to that time?"

"I had been overseas, in Europe."

"What part of Europe?"

"London," Lee said proudly, squaring his shoulders.

Mr. Butler interrupted them, saying curtly, "I don't see the materiality."

Judge Abbott responded, "I know he wants to get in the record what he is doing."

"When you got on the train, where did you sit?" Martin continued.

"I sat in the white section of the car. Uh, uh, at that time, the sign was turned so I couldn't see but about half of the white section and half of the colored section."

"Were there any other people in there?"

"Yes, sir, four white people and one colored fellow."

"What did you say about the sign?"

"I said the sign was tilted about halfway between the 'Colored' and 'White.'"

"Then what happened?"

"A young fellow came on the train and asked me to move back in the back section of the train. He first asked me if I had a ticket, and I said I had, and he asked me to move back, and I said I wouldn't."

In further questioning, Martin showed the brakeman had asked Lee to move and later the sheriff came on with another deputy and the conductor. At that point, Lee went back to the station, got a refund on the ticket to Clifton Forge, and bought a ticket to Washington, D.C. Lee sat in the same seat he'd been sitting in before. Again, the sheriff asked him to move back. He refused, and the sheriff arrested him.

Martin wrapped up the case for the defense by introducing the ticket Lee purchased as evidence that Lee's intent was to travel to Washington, D.C., that day.

Butler began the Commonwealth's cross-examination by casting doubt on Lee's testimony regarding his plan to travel to Washington, D.C., the day he was arrested. He asserted Lee actually planned to go home to Eagle Rock after the train stopped at Clifton Forge.

Butler continued his cross-examination. "And you were advised on the day before by the conductor that you were not permitted to ride in the white section?"

"Yes."

"So on September 14th, 1948, when you got in the white section, you did it deliberately, knowing that it was a violation of the rules of the railroad?"

"I sat in that section," Lee said firmly.

"I say you did it deliberately, knowing it was a violation of the rules of the railroad?" Butler said in a louder voice.

"I sat in the white section."

"Didn't anybody make you sit there? You did that because you were determined to sit there, regardless of the rules?"

"No."

"Why did you do it? Why didn't you go back in the section that was provided for you?"

"Both seats were the same."

"You knew you were not supposed to sit there in that section?"

"Uh, uh, at that time, the sign was turned both ways."

"The brakeman got on there and advised you. You knew it then, didn't you?"

"Yes, sir."

"Why didn't you go back in the colored section? Why didn't you do that?"

Norvel Lee was quiet, a look of confident defiance on his face, staring directly at Butler.

Frustrated, Butler turned and looked at the judge.

Judge Abbott turned to Lee and said, "Go ahead and answer the question."

Lee looked intently into Butler's eyes and said, "I didn't think it was necessary."

After further questioning, Butler again accused Lee of deliberately breaking the law and returned to his desk.

Judge Abbott asked Martin if he intended to redirect the witness.

Martin said yes and returned to the witness stand. After establishing that another Black man was sitting under the sign and was not asked to move, he paused for a moment.

Looking empathetically at Lee, Martin asked, "Do you know why they were running you down?"

"No," Lee said, appearing anxious.

"And you say you didn't see them do anything to this other colored fellow?"

"No, sir."

"Did they say anything to him, either the sheriff or conductor or brakeman? So that the reason they were after you was because you had just come back from overseas on a boxing tour with the United States Olympic Team?"

Butler jumped out of his seat and said, "I object to interposing something in the record by coming in the back door with something he can't come in the front door with."

Judge Abbott said, "It doesn't make any difference."

Martin turned to Lee and asked, "Do you know whether, if the reason the people were after you and let that other colored fellow sit in that same compartment, was the reason you had just come back from overseas with the Olympics?"

Judge Abbott jumped in and said, "I sustain the objection."

"Exception!" exclaimed Martin. He turned to Lee, noting, "You are a colored fellow with the Olympics?"

"Yes, sir."

"I have no further questions, Your Honor," Martin said.

Butler then questioned Sheriff Henderson, who stated that the other Black man did move to the colored section.

Martin, then, in a brief re-cross, asked Henderson, "If Norvel Lee had been a white person, he would not have been asked to move, would he?"

Henderson said, "I don't guess I would ever have been called around there, if he was."

"In other words, he was asked to move from that compartment because he was colored?"

Sheriff Henderson said, "Yes, sir."

After Henderson and Butler had returned to their seats, Judge Abbott simply said, "All right, I find the defendant guilty as charged in the warrant, and fix his punishment at a twenty-five-dollar fine."

Martin stood and asked, "Will Your Honor suspend the sentence and let us take an appeal?"

"Yes, continue on the same bond."

Later, outside the white granite Alleghany County Courthouse in the brisk January day, the slight Martin and much larger Lee stood talking.

"Son, you did a good job in there," Martin said. "The NAACP is going to take the case from here. I do not believe we will need you to be present for any further appeals."

"Yes, sir, thank you," said Lee, humbly.

"You appear older than the average college sophomore," said Martin. "What were you doing before you started at Howard?"

"I was in the service during the war," said Lee, adding, "U.S. Army Air Corps."

"Did you get into the war itself or serve here stateside?" asked Martin.

"I was in the South Pacific," said Lee.

"Is that where you picked up boxing?"

"No, sir, I started boxing at Howard, but I helped out as an assistant on a colored boxing team in Manila. I learned about the sport then."

"It seems you learned well," observed Martin, "seeing as you were part of the London Olympics."

"Yes, sir."

"I graduated from Howard University. It looks to me like you have every potential of being one of us out in the world doing good, one step at a time," Martin said sincerely. "I want you to go on back to Howard and study hard, and let your passions guide the path you take. You hear me, son?"

"Yes, sir."

"Some advice though," Martin continued, "and I know it's difficult, but see if you can get some help for your speaking difficulties."

Norvel Lee said, "Yes, sir. I will."

# CHAPTER 1

## *A Tuesday afternoon in May 1937—Gala, Virginia*

The rickety truck backfired as it bumped along the dirt road on its way to the Rising Mount Zion Baptist Church. Riding in the bed of the old truck were ten elementary school children. The driver, who also served as pastor of the church, drove them each school day to and from the two-room elementary school for the colored in nearby Eagle Rock. As the truck sputtered along, two twelve-year-olds, Eddie and Joe, were relentlessly mocking Norvel Lee, also twelve.

Eddie looked at Joe and shouted, "Ah, ah, ah, ah, ah, ah!"

Joe turned to Norvel and grimaced at him, then broke into exaggerated laughter.

Eddie stared at Norvel and again said in a mocking voice, "Ah, ah, ah, ah."

Dolores, a year older, piped up and said, "Eddie Jones. That's not nice. Lil' Norvel cain't help it. God made him like that for a reason."

The younger children sat quietly, their mouths agape.

Eddie and Joe continued their bullying while Norvel sat, determined not to react. Then as the truck pulled into the area beside the church building, Norvel rose from his seat and started to flail at Eddie with his fists.

Dolores screamed shrilly, "Boys! Quit it!"

Joe and Eddie hammered back at Norvel and then shoved him out of the truck onto the ground. The younger children jumped off the truck and started running off in the direction of their nearby cabins. Eddie and Joe pointed and laughed at Norvel, then swaggered away.

The pastor also walked away, ignoring the ruckus. Dolores leaned down over Norvel and said, "This don't mean diddly-squat. Those boys should know there be a day y'all gonna rise up above 'em. They just don't know any better."

Norvel's face and arm were bleeding from the fall. Sniffling, he got to his feet. His father was leaning against a tree, looking intently at him.

James Jackson Lee, or "Jack," was a serious man of few words. Tall and muscular, his constant scowl made him seem unapproachable to his children. He was often away from home as a laborer on the railroad in Clifton Forge ten miles north, or twelve miles farther at the train yard in Covington. When he wasn't at the railroad, he might be working in the nearby fields, tinkering with a car, or doing chores at the church. If there was any time for recreation, he played the card game pinochle with friends.

Only when Jack was with his wife, Georgiana, did his face soften. At age eighteen he'd spotted her picking flowers in a field in Gala while he was on a labor crew putting down railroad track. In the early 1920s, working for the railroads provided a reliable source of income for Blacks.

Norvel wanted desperately to avoid his father after he picked himself up off the ground, but his father just stood there staring him down. Jack held up his large hand and motioned for Norvel to come over.

Norvel reluctantly walked slowly over, scared about what his father might do, even though Jack Lee had never used physical punishment except for occasionally giving the kids a light paddle on the rear. But he had a reputation among his fellow laborers as being tough and no one to tangle with.

Jack put his hands on Norvel's shoulders and said sternly, "Son, we Lees don't get treated like that. Lees are to be respected, and I don't care if it's your pals or the boss man who isn't treatin' you right. You hear me?"

"Uh, uh, uh, yes, sir," Norvel said, trembling.

"You're a boy now, but soon you'll grow to a man. Your mother won't want me sayin' this, but sometimes you have to fight for respect. You know what I'm sayin'? I'm gonna show you how to do it."

Father and son walked down the path toward their cabin up on Big Hill, their shoes crunching on sticks left over from the harsh winter. When they came to a clearing, Jack told Norvel to stand facing him.

"Watch me."

Jack planted his feet, slightly bending his knees. He pointed his left shoulder toward Norvel, who copied him.

"Now hide your chin with your shoulder like this. It won't feel right, but just practice standin' like that. Your left hand is now closest to the person tryin' to hit you, but you can jab with it and push him away. Your right hand is free. You'll see you can hit someone real hard with it."

Norvel tried it, jabbing with his left hand, copying his father's movements.

"Okay, now hit my hand with your right fist as hard as you can," Jack said.

Norvel unleashed a surprisingly powerful right hand into his father's fist.

"You got it! You keep doing that, those boys will learn a lesson. Never forget you're a Lee, and no one musses with a Lee."

"Yes, sir," said Norvel, looking up at his father respectfully.

The next day, at an obscure clearing along the creek, Jack hung a potato sack filled with dirt, leaves, and straw from a thick branch of a white oak. He showed Norvel how to move around the makeshift bag, jabbing with his left hand and punching with his right. Every day of the spring and summer of 1937 Norvel practiced these techniques. That fall in school anyone who attempted to bully him about his stammer quickly learned to stop.

# CHAPTER 2

## *March 1942—The Academy Hill School for Negroes, Fincastle, Virginia*

During his sophomore year, Norvel had often stayed after school to help his high school teacher grade tests and prepare for the next day's classes. Roger Terry taught grades 9 through 12 at the two-room high school in Botetourt County's seat, Fincastle. Terry spent most of his day going from the room for grades 9 and 10 to another room for grades 11 and 12. This left little time for tending to administrative tasks. He was relieved when Norvel agreed to help.

Terry's ancestors had been in Botetourt County since the time of slavery. They had helped to form the various houses of worship in the area. He and his two sisters not only were influential in the churches but also became educators. From the time Academy Hill was designated as a school for older Black students, Terry was their teacher. Norvel was the most academically motivated student he encountered. During the past year, Norvel had earned straight A's. Norvel also had a natural curiosity about astronomy. He frequently asked questions about space travel, speculating how long it would take to fly to the moon. He never missed a day of school.

Norvel enthusiastically accepted Mr. Terry's request for help. It was an acceptable excuse to avoid the demanding physical labor his father expected when he arrived home on the bus. When he was done helping his teacher, Terry drove him the twenty miles back home. At times, Jack Lee fixed Terry's old Ford when it needed work. During the drive back to Gala, Norvel listened to Terry's instructive stories and related his own dreams and ambitions.

Under most circumstances, Norvel would have been teased about being a teacher's pet, especially with his pronounced stammer. But his affable nature and physical size kept the bullies away.

On this day, while finishing up their work, Terry said, "Son, a few months ago you and Bernie were asked to take a test put out by the government. I didn't know what it was except they asked the county to recommend two colored boys to take it. I coordinated with the Board of Education, and the two of you were selected."

"I uh, uh, remember," said Norvel, looking up from the test he was grading. "The test was hard, but it got me thinking about a lot of things, even though my head was spinning."

Terry chuckled. "It was supposed to. They called it a 'psychological screening test.' The government is trying to select colored candidates for a special program."

"What kind of program?" Norvel asked, now fully alert.

"They didn't tell us, but a while back I heard about an Army unit that's training colored boys to fly. I checked, and I'm sure that's what this test was about."

"They're letting us fly airplanes in the Army?"

"That's what I understand," Terry said as they walked out to the car. "I asked around and found some newspaper stories about it, too. In the First World War there were several military units for us. It was segregated like now; we were encouraged to serve but they wouldn't let us be pilots. They didn't think we'd be good at controlling the airplane."

Terry drove his old Ford up Botetourt Road on the warm late afternoon. Colorful sunflowers and lilies bloomed alongside the road and birds were busy gathering twigs from the roadside bushes to build their nests.

Terry said, "Well, two years ago President Roosevelt's wife, Eleanor, went down to an Army airfield in Tuskegee, Alabama. You know about Booker T. Washington, don't you?"

"Yes. Mama gave me a book about him. He was born a slave on a farm over in Franklin County, near here. I read a speech he made called the "Atlanta Compromise." And he was the leader of the Tuskegee Institute, a colored teachers college."

"It's to your credit you know something about him. Next year you'll be taking a Negro History class, and Booker T. Washington will be one of the main topics. What did you think of the Atlanta Compromise?"

Norvel thought a moment and then said, "Uh, uh, it was probably the right thing to do at the time because it helped get the colored some basic education, but I think we need to be more aggressive like the NAACP is now. I don't understand why we can't go to school with white people. Why don't the white folks want to be with us?"

"Son, it's complicated," Terry said, shrugging his shoulders. "It's unnecessary in my opinion, but here in the South they can't seem to forget we were all slaves. Anyhow, at Tuskegee the first lady took a flight with a colored pilot, Chief Anderson, who was in an experimental program to see if we could learn to fly airplanes."

Terry frowned, "I don't know why they thought we couldn't fly an airplane. You drive it like you would a car. Mrs. Roosevelt has always been an advocate for us. When she returned from her flight she told the press that Anderson could really fly. That's all it took—the colored pilot training program was off and running."

Norvel asked, "Do you think I can get into this program? I'd like to try to be a pilot."

"That's the reason we're talking about this. The test results came back, and you're qualified to apply for flight training."

"What about Bernie?" asked Norvel.

"No, he didn't qualify. You're the only one from the county that did."

Norvel looked at Terry and said, "Then I want to be a pilot. What do I have to do?"

"I have forms for you to fill out. You'll then need two recommendations, and I can provide one. The other one will have to come from a member of the board of education, but that won't be a problem because the superintendent who helped pick you as a candidate will approve it. But you have to be an adult to join, or get permission from your parents. Knowing them, that may be difficult. When will you be eighteen?"

"The 22nd of September."

"Well, I know your mother won't want you doing this, and I under-stand that. She wants you to get your education done and then do something locally."

Norvel crossed his arms and gazed out the window. "But I already know everything I'm gonna learn here. I want to learn something new."

"Patience, son. You'll get your chance."

The next day, after the other students had boarded the bus, Terry and Norvel sat at one of the tables that served as desks.

Norvel said, "Mr. Terry, uh, uh, I want to join the Army Air Corps and be a pilot."

Terry said, "After you turn eighteen in September, you will have the choice of doing just that."

Norvel said, "I want to do it now. If I can't get Mama to sign off, my father will do it. He'll understand."

"Your father's not going to do anything your mother doesn't want," Terry said.

"Well, I want to try it anyway. Do they have to sign something?"

Terry got up and opened a drawer in his desk, took out some papers, and brought them to Norvel.

The two-page document was called a "Record of Military Processing." In addition to requesting his personal information, it had a section with "Parental/Guardian Consent for Enlistment," which included language about the applicants not being induced or coerced into joining. It also stated clearly that the parents were relinquishing all legal responsibility to the government, and that they had not been given any compensation for permitting their son to enlist.

The following Sunday after church, Norvel sat on the front porch of their little home with his mother, his suit too tight because of a recent growth spurt. His sister, Edna, was looking at the lilacs along the road. Jimmy was still with their father, who was taking care of some church business. Jimmy, now thirteen, took advantage of opportunities to be with his dad when he could. Normally, Jack took Norvel for errands. But today Norvel was anxious to be with his mother.

"What's that you have?" she asked, looking at the papers Norvel was holding. Raven-haired like her mother, she was thin, with a nimble ease in her movements. Her birth name was George Anna Ray, after her father and mother, but she was known by all as Georgiana.

Norvel said, "You know our country is in this big war, and a lot of the boys we know have gone into the military. Now they've selected me for a special program to train to be a pilot. I want to learn to fly an airplane."

Georgiana gave him a pained look. "Oh, Norvel baby, they aren't gonna let you do that. They don't let people like us fly planes."

"No, you don't understand," said Norvel, smiling. "They already chose me. Mr. Terry had me and Bernie take a special test, but I'm the only one they selected. But since I'm not eighteen yet, you and Dad must sign this form so I can go."

"What about your schooling? I'm not gonna sign anything to send you off to kill people, or have them kill you. Not only don't I want that, God doesn't either. And I bet they won't really let you fly. You'll end up cleaning or cooking things for white pilots, wasting that smart brain till there's nothing left of it 'cept 'Yes, sir.'"

"But I have to do this! They picked me! I've learned everything my school has to offer. I want to go see the world!"

"Oh, baby," she said, her eyes filling with tears. "For now, your world is right here. You're a smart boy; you should be thinking of what college you'll be going to, so you can be a teacher or preacher. That's what will make me and Dad proud of you."

"Mama, you're going to be proud of me. I've outgrown this place!"

"I'm not gonna sign that form! And don't go to your father, cause he won't either." Georgiana got up from her chair and stomped into the house, leaving him sitting, staring out at the yard.

Norvel sat on the porch for a while, and then walked the several miles back to the church. He felt suppressed and smothered.

*They don't understand there's a big world out there. I can do a lot in that world,* he thought, *if only they'd let me.*

Inside the church Jimmy, his father, and several other men were standing in the aisle talking. Jimmy watched Norvel walk down the aisle, seeing that his brother's normally confident stride was subdued.

Like Norvel, Jimmy was academic and curious about people, but he wanted to be different than his older brother. Physically, he did not have Norvel's height or bulk. He also wanted to make his mark elsewhere, and decided to attend school in Clifton Forge instead of Academy Hill. In order to attend he was required to live in Alleghany County, so during the week he stayed with an uncle who lived there, but he was always in Gala for weekends for church services with his family. His mother insisted that all four of the children—Norvel, Edna, James, and George—attend together.

Jack turned to Norvel and said, "I'm gonna need you'n' Jimmy's help hauling some crops in from Jones's field. You two go get your work clothes on and get ready."

"Dad," Norvel said, "the uh, uh, Army wants me to be an airplane pilot for them, but Mama is saying I can't go. She won't sign these papers."

"If she won't sign, then that's it," Jack said. "Now go get dressed for work. I need your help."

Norvel looked at his father, was about to say something, but instead walked slowly back to the house with Jimmy to change his clothes.

The next week Norvel told Terry he was correct when he said his parents wouldn't let him join the Army. He told Terry that as soon as he turned eighteen, he would sign the papers himself. Norvel planned to keep busy during the intervening six months by working on his grandfather's farm in Amherst County, an hour's drive away.

For the past three years, as soon as school was let out for the summer, Norvel and Jimmy would ride a noisy pickup truck to the red clay dirt family farm. The ground was difficult to keep tilled, but also had its benefits. Properly furrowed, it yielded rich crops of corn, hay, and tobacco.

Norvel and Jimmy stayed at the Amherst farm during the week and returned to Gala for church on Sunday. When working in Amherst, they welcomed the break from the daily ritual at home, including having to gather around in the evening while Mama read Bible verses for what seemed like an eternity.

In mid-August, they returned to Gala to harvest the nearby popcorn fields for the local farmers. The field was only a mile's walk from home up along the banks of Mill Creek, where popcorn stalks poked high into the air. Some of the stalks were six feet tall, nearly Norvel's height.

Norvel and the other workers, mostly his friends, would fill trailer upon trailer with the harvested husks, which were hauled over to an ancient wooden hut to dry out. After a week or so, they would shell a few of the husks and bite into them to see if the kernels were still chewy. If they were, then the husks needed to dry for a few more days. If not, the workers would shell the entire batch, making room in the hut for the next batch of husks. To keep busy, Norvel also loaded railroad cars at the small train station in Eagle Rock—hard, sweaty work in the summer heat.

Soon after the beginning of the new school semester, the day after his eighteenth birthday, Norvel handed the signed enlistment papers to Terry and said, "I want to enlist in the Army Air Corps if I can train to be a pilot at Tuskegee. Will that test, uh, uh, I took still get me in?"

Terry said, "I believe it will. Are you sure about this? And what will your parents think?"

"I'm not going to tell them until I know I'm going," Norvel said.

"Okay, my advice is to tell them, but that's up to you. I'll sign this application and hand it over to the superintendent for his signature. Then he'll send it to the Army," Mr. Terry said. He added, "I'm proud of you, Norvel."

It took some time for the paperwork to make its way through the Army channels, but in May 1943, Norvel received orders to report for duty in Richmond on July 21.

Following Edna's turn at saying grace at supper that evening, Norvel announced, "I know what I'm about to say you won't be pleased with, but I am proud to inform you I have joined the Army. I leave the middle of July."

Jack and Georgiana paused and looked at each other. Jack took a deep breath. "We thought this might happen when you turned eighteen."

Georgiana asked grimly, "Are they going to teach you to fly airplanes?"

"Yes, I'll be going to Tuskegee for the training."

"And then what?" Georgiana asked.

"Time will tell—maybe some more training—or if the war hasn't ended maybe they'll send me overseas," Norvel said, his voice steady but his eyes flashing with excitement.

His young brother George and sister Edna remained silent, wondering what this turn of events would mean for themselves. Jimmy was in school that week.

Jack said, "Norvel, we understand and are proud of you. You will be missed here, but we know it's your time to see what the world has in store for you."

Georgiana said, "It's all part of God's plan. I know it is. But I still want you to find a way to get your college education. Will you promise me that?"

"Yes, I promise."

When Jimmy returned to Gala over the weekend, Norvel broke the news to him. Jimmy appeared to take the information in stride, but Norvel knew his brother would want to understand how this turn of events would affect his day-to-day life.

On July 20, Norvel dressed in a suit for the nine-hour train ride to Richmond. Georgiana dabbed a handkerchief to her moist eyes, and Jack was clearly struggling with his emotions when they arrived at the Clifton Forge train station. They walked to the boarding platform, Norvel carrying his small bag of clothes and a few books, where the C&O was waiting to begin its daily journey. Norvel hugged his mother, shook hands with his father, and then turned and walked through the door designated for "colored passengers." His parents watched him step onto the train as it started to move slowly away from the platform. Jack and Georgiana stood silently, watching their firstborn go out into the world, and probably to war.

That evening Norvel realized Richmond was the largest city he'd ever seen. The streets bustled with activity. He saw a traffic light for the first time. He was mesmerized by the downtown railway system made up of trolleys ferrying passengers about. Each car was connected to a long pole attached to an overhead wire feeding the cars with electric power. Norvel heard the electricity sizzle from the wires as the cars traveled through the busy streets.

The next morning Norvel stood at attention in the meeting hall that served as the enlistment center for colored troops. He was wearing the dark suit his mother had purchased with the money she'd stowed away, replacing the one he had outgrown. The money came from the sewing and laundry services she provided to local families.

Norvel and each of the other eighteen new recruits was handed a mimeographed sheet of paper. In unison with the rest of the inductees, he said, "I, Norvel LaFollette Ray Lee, do solemnly swear that I will support and defend the Constitution of the United States against all enemies, foreign and domestic; that I will bear true faith and allegiance to the same; and that—uh, uh—I will obey the orders of the President of the United States and the orders of the officers appointed over me, according to regulations and the Uniform Code of Military Justice, so help me God."

When they finished reciting the oath, a lieutenant said, "Congratulations, Privates. You are in the Army now. You will get outfitted in your uniforms and onto the bus that will take you down to Fort Benning for your basic training."

# CHAPTER 3

## *October 1943—Moton Field, Tuskegee, Alabama*

Norvel was excited to finally begin flight instruction. He'd spent the first eight weeks enduring boot camp at Fort Benning, Georgia, where the Army indoctrinated new recruits, Black and white, separately. While there he was subjected to an intense regimen of exercise, forced marches, weapons instruction, and sets of lessons regarding proper Army behavior.

The next four weeks at the Tuskegee Institute attending ground school were much more interesting for Norvel. During classroom instruction he learned about the aerodynamics of airplanes, vital airplane performance factors, critical decision-making, and basic navigation.

He was now at nearby Moton Field, getting ready for an introductory flight on a North American Aviation AT-6. Originally introduced in the mid-1930s, the AT-6 was the standard for training military pilots. Norvel was told to sit in the first of the two tandem seats. The rear seat had an identical set of flight controls that could, if necessary, override those of the front. The instructor sat in the rear seat. He was the pilot for this first flight.

Lieutenant Daniel James, who was informally known as "Chappie," explained that the front seat was designed to give the student pilot a feel for what it would be like to sit at the controls of a fighter plane, albeit without the speed and with more forgiving control.

When Norvel strapped himself into his seat, he felt as if he were sitting on a perch. Through the plexiglass windshield he saw a chromatic green view of the outside world. His legs stretched out on either side of the control stick, and his feet rested in giant trays that held the rudder pedals. Under his left arm, he saw the primary controls he had become familiar with during ground school. On his right were the radio and other electronics. In front were instrument dials to indicate altitude, ground speed, and engine performance.

Chappie settled into his seat, and soon Norvel heard simultaneously a whine and a growl from the front of the plane, then what sounded like a deep cough as thick black smoke moved past his elbows into the cockpit. The growl grew in intensity as the engine came alive, and the propeller in front of the nose began to turn. Finally, the smoke in the cockpit subsided.

They began to slowly move down Moton Field's single runway. Norvel's vantage point allowed him to see the runway on the left and right but not down the middle. He thought there must be something wrong because it seemed the plane was moving too slowly to get off the ground. But to his amazement, they easily lifted up and were in the air as he watched the world below fall away.

*I'm flying! Like a bird, I'm flying!*

During the next several weeks, Norvel learned to pilot the AT-6 and operate the instruments, until he could fly without help from Chappie. He also learned that each type of aircraft had its own idiosyncrasies and the AT-6 had some peculiar ones. If he focused on lifting the tail gently when he reached takeoff speed, the plane would take off on its own, easily. But if he moved the tail up too abruptly, the plane would lurch to the left and refuse to leave the ground. He also learned the AT-6 can easily stall at certain combinations of speed and bank angle. The combinations were consistent, however, and Norvel learned them quickly.

One day Chappie came to him and said, "Norvel, I believe you have mastered this phase of pilot training. To advance to the next level you will need to earn your wings by completing a solo mission. You have proven to me you are ready for it. Do you agree?"

"Yes, sir," Norvel said excitedly. "You won't be with me?"

"No," said Chappie. "This will be a true solo mission. You will be in radio contact with the tower. Rest assured, though, this will be basically a takeoff and a landing after you have circled the field a few times."

"Yes, sir," said Norvel. "I'm ready."

The next day Norvel was alone in the cockpit when he started the engine and taxied the AT-6 to the end of the runway.

"Texas 43, ready for takeoff," Norvel said into the radio.

"Cleared to take off, Texas 43," crackled the voice from the speaker.

Norvel released the brakes and placed his heels firmly on the deck. He then advanced the throttle smoothly to the appropriate stop. He held the stick slightly back of the neutral position in order to keep the tail down. He knew that engine torque would tend to pull the plane to the left, so he pointed the plane toward a spot on the horizon to the right of the nose. As the plane increased its speed down the runway, he kept it lined up by correcting the rudder position with his feet while easing the stick forward. When the plane reached takeoff speed, it easily left the ground.

"Texas 43, climb to two thousand," said the voice from the speaker.

"Climbing to two," Norvel confirmed.

Norvel adjusted the trim tabs to put the plane on a normal climb path and pulled the hydraulic lever to raise the wheels. When the altimeter showed he had reached two thousand feet, he adjusted the flaps to level the plane and began a left turn by adjusting the rudder.

Norvel spoke into the microphone, "Texas 43, uh, uh, at two thousand and coming around."

The radio responded, "Roger, Texas 43, maintain your altitude and circle Moton until you receive further instructions."

Norvel said, "Roger."

When Norvel neared completion of the third lap, the radio crackled again. "Texas 43, prepare to land."

Norvel responded, "Descending to one thousand," adjusted the flaps, and throttled back the speed to 120 knots.

Coming around the runway for the final time, he throttled back even more and lowered and locked the wheels. The plane descended to eight hundred feet as he adjusted the flaps again.

Norvel announced on the radio, "Landing checkoff list complete."

The radio crackled back, "Texas 43, cleared to land."

"Cleared to land," Norvel responded.

*Cleared to land,* Norvel said to himself.

The flight path was now parallel to the runway and his plane was at five hundred feet and 90 knots.

Norvel put the AT-6 into a power glide, reducing the speed to 80 knots. Turning toward the end of the runway, he maneuvered the plane such that it intersected the landing line at one hundred fifty feet, the perfect position. Then Norvel guided the plane to a spot on the first third of the runway and adjusted the attitude for a three-point landing by gradually pulling back the throttle. The plane hesitated over the ground for a moment, but as Norvel continued to ease back the throttle, the three wheels touched the ground. The AT-6 slowed, and Norvel taxied it back to the hanger, where he could see Chappie and many of his fellow cadets waiting for him. Norvel was the first of his class to solo.

"Congratulations," said Chappie. "You are officially a Tuskegee Airman. Welcome to the club."

Chappie handed him a pair of metal wings to pin on his uniform. Norvel grinned proudly while his classmates gathered around, shaking his hand and giving him pats on the back.

Earning his wings qualified Norvel to advance to the next level of training: formation flying. During that training he would learn the discipline of flying in formation, including taking up attack and defensive positions.

The advanced training was conducted at the Tuskegee Army Air Field (TAAF), ten miles from Moton. TAAF was built in 1941 specifically for training Black pilots. It was there that the pilots would learn to fly the P-47 Thunderbolt or P-51 Mustang, the planes the 332nd Fighter Group, made up entirely of Tuskegee Airmen, were using to escort bombers over Italy and Germany. Norvel was determined to become a 332nd Fighter Group pilot.

To learn the techniques of formation flying, Norvel was teamed with another newly minted pilot, John Porter from Cleveland, Ohio. The plan was to become accustomed to flying in a formation with the AT-6, then learn to fly the P-47 and practice air warfare formation tactics.

One of the planes was designated the Lead and the other the Wing. The Lead pilot is in command of the formation. The second pilot, designated the Wingman, is in charge of his own aircraft and ultimately responsible for its safe operation, but in the context of the formation is subordinate to the Lead. During the training, Norvel and Porter were each to take their turn as Lead and Wingman.

After a day of classroom work regarding protocol, Norvel and Porter made plans for their first flight together. The instructor designated Norvel as the first Lead and assigned their flight a call sign—Echo. Norvel, as required of the Lead, gave the preflight instructions, which included weather reports, assigned radio frequencies, and the operational plan. In this case the plan was for Norvel to take off, and as soon as his wheels left the ground, for Porter to follow him down the runway.

Both pilots climbed into their planes, unaccompanied by the instructors. They started their engines and taxied to the end of the runway.

Norvel, after making sure Porter was in place behind him, said into the microphone, "TAAF Tower, Echo ready for takeoff."

"Cleared to take off, Echo."

Norvel moved the throttle forward, and the AT-6 began moving down the runway. The plane took off, climbing to two thousand feet in accordance with the flight plan.

In a few minutes Norvel became aware of Porter's AT-6 slightly below and behind him on his right side.

Porter's voice came over the radio, "Echo Lead, Echo Flight here."

"Roger, uh, uh, Echo Flight," responded Norvel. "Hold your position."

"Roger Echo Lead, Echo Flight holding position."

Both pilots adjusted their throttles to maintain the agreed-upon speed of 140 knots.

After a few minutes Norvel informed the control tower: "Uh, uh, Echo Lead, uh, uh, executing one uh, uh, eighty."

The radio crackled, "Please confirm, Echo Lead."

Norvel said again, "Executing one-eighty."

The two planes circled the field several times before returning to the base.

Over the next few weeks, Norvel and Porter continued to fly increasingly complicated formations together, taking turns at Lead and Wingman. When Norvel was Lead, there were several more episodes of troublesome stammering when he was delivering the commands over the radio.

One morning in early February 1944, Norvel was ordered by the TAAF Commander, Captain Noel Parrish, to report to headquarters.

Norvel stepped into Parrish's office and saluted.

"At ease, cadet," said Parrish. "I've asked you to step in here so I could personally inform you that we are not going to continue your training as a pilot. I have met with the instructors and other observers, and we all are impressed with your dedication, commitment, and piloting skills. However, your speech deficiencies will not serve an air squadron appropriately during wartime conditions."

Norvel, masking his disappointment, simply said, "Yes, sir."

"We do believe, however, that you have the aptitude to serve as a leader in the Army. I've recommended you for officer training at West Point Military Academy. I have been in communication with Congressman Woodrum, your Virginia congressional representative, whose recommendation is required."

"Yes, sir. Thank you."

In a few weeks, however, Norvel learned his appointment was rejected. He learned that his actual chances of gaining acceptance at West Point were quite remote because there were only four Black enrollees at the time.

Norvel sent letters home weekly, sometimes more frequently. In his final letter from Tuskegee he cloaked his disappointment by simply saying he had completed his training and was looking forward to his next assignment.

By early March the class of qualified cadets he had trained with had graduated from the Tuskegee program and were assigned to the 332nd Fighter Group in Europe. Norvel and the others who did not qualify were sent to Keesler Field near Biloxi, Mississippi, for an eventual assignment in aircraft ground support.

Shortly after arriving at Keesler, Norvel was standing in the bustling line for supper when the man behind him said, "You must be a new arrival."

Norvel chuckled and said, "I am. Got in a few days ago."

"Robert Jackson Jr., from Leesburg, Virginia," he said, shaking Norvel's hand.

"Norvel Lee, also from Virginia—Gala," replied Norvel.

"Where the heck is Gala?" asked Jackson.

"Oh, down in the Blue Ridge Mountains. Closest town is Eagle Rock. Next closest is in the next county, Clifton Forge."

Robert and Norvel quickly became friends. In each other, they recognized a kindred spirit. Although they shared Virginia roots, their experiences growing up were quite different. While Norvel was raised in a rural atmosphere, where his family survived by working at various day-labor jobs, the Jacksons were a well-established family in Leesburg. Robert's father, the senior Robert Emmett Jackson, was a longtime popular employee at the local general store owned by a German, J. F. Whitmore. All the residents, Black and white, shopped there. The Jim Crow laws were in place but were not aggressively enforced. The neighborhood where the Jacksons resided included both Black and white families.

The bunk beds in the barracks for the Blacks at Keesler were tightly bunched so that all of the young troops would have a place to sleep and store their few personal items. Norvel's bed was at one end of the building, but he often went over to Jackson's to talk.

"What are you going to do when you get out of the service?" Robert asked during one of their chats.

"Don't know yet. My mother expects me to become a teacher near home, but I'm not sure about that," Norvel answered. "She would be happy if I and my siblings pursued a career in education. She wasn't too pleased I landed in the service. How about you? What are you going to do?"

Robert said, "I'm going to get out of this Army as soon as I can and see if I can get into Howard University."

"I've heard of it, but where is it?" Norvel asked.

"It's in Washington, D.C.," Robert said. "It's the best university that's especially set up for us."

Norvel nodded, absorbing the information, but thinking Tuskegee might be more to his liking.

Norvel noticed a photograph on a table next to Robert's bed and asked, "Is that your family?"

"Sure enough," said Robert, picking up the picture and pointing to each individual in it. "That's my mother and my father, and my sister Leslie. The little one is my baby sister. She has the same name as my mother, Margaret, but we all call her Weekie. Sometimes I think she believes she's just one of the guests living there because my folks are always taking in boarders. Weekie doesn't seem to realize that Leslie is her sister, especially with the age difference between them."

"Well, it's a nice-looking family there," Norvel observed. "Two sisters—are you the oldest?"

"Leslie's about the same age as you, almost two years older than me," Robert said. "She's a ball of fire. Growin' up, we'd call her little Napoleon 'cause she's very short but always takin' charge of somethin' or other. She normally has many activities in motion. Gettin' libraries to donate their old books to children in need is one of her pet projects."

"Maybe when we're back in Virginia I can meet them sometime."

"They'll enjoy meeting you, my friend," Robert said, and then, looking to make sure no one else was listening, added quietly, "I've heard some of us may be leaving soon. Maybe to the Pacific."

Three weeks later, their barracks were emptied and all three hundred thirty men were put on a train that took them west to San Diego, California. Norvel and Robert stuck together the best they could, providing a sane voice for one another in an otherwise chaotic atmosphere.

Finally, in October 1944 at the Navy's San Diego Base, the men were told to line up alphabetically by last name. There were only two other men between Norvel and Robert. Then a white officer started counting the troops, starting with the A's. Seagulls were flying around squawking while scavenging for food. When the officer reached the person standing behind Jackson, he ordered in a loud voice for the rest of them to move in formation over to another part of the assembly area. Jackson looked back at Norvel with a questioning look on his face until an officer ordered him to attention and to look straight ahead. Norvel stared in the direction of his friend for several minutes until he was marched away.

Norvel and the remainder of the troops in his group were put on buses and taken up the California coast to another Navy facility at Port Hueneme, north of Los Angeles. They were further divided until Norvel and a few others eventually found themselves on a transport ship to the Solomon Islands.

# CHAPTER 4

## *A Thursday afternoon in November 1947— Howard University, Washington, D.C.*

Norvel was jumping rope at the Howard University gymnasium while waiting to take his turn at the punching bag. His boxing gloves were lying on the wooden floor beside him. He was hoping at this workout session he would finally be able to meet Barnes, the boxing coach. The other boxers had told him Thursday afternoon was the most likely time to encounter Barnes.

Norvel started his freshman year at Howard in September, just before his twenty-third birthday, and soon after sought out campus recreational activities as a break from academics. The activity that interested him was intramural sports, possibly baseball, which he was introduced to in the Army while on standby with his maintenance crew. But he learned Howard's baseball program wouldn't begin until the following term.

Fortunately, on his first visit to the campus gym, Norvel noticed a sign on the wall stating Pugilists Only. Walking over to examine the area, he observed a red square boundary line painted on the hardwood floor and a rack containing boxing gloves, jump ropes, and weights. Hanging from a support beam was the punching bag for which he was now waiting his turn.

Eighteen months earlier, in Manila, Norvel was asked to fill in as assistant manager to the Black boxing team. His job was to help the coach keep the rambunctious group of young men organized. From the experienced boxers, he learned the importance of physical conditioning. Norvel was already an expert at jumping rope, an activity he perfected growing up in Gala, but this assignment exposed him to the punching bag, shadowboxing, and sparring with an opponent. He learned that boxing wasn't a sport of flailing away at an adversary, but one that involved sizing up and then exploiting an opponent's weaknesses while capitalizing on one's own strengths. The conditioning and the strategic aspect of the sport appealed to him. At one point the coach of the military team, while watching one of the boxers spar with Norvel, told him he thought he had the natural talent to be a boxer himself. Norvel brushed off the comment at the time.

Norvel began visiting the gym most afternoons, carrying a small bag containing a change of clothes, sneakers, and boxing gloves. Several members of the boxing team would also be there. If the punching bag was in use, Norvel would wait his turn by taking a jump rope from the rack and start moving it gracefully around his body. Norvel's pigeon-toed stance made quite the spectacle as he stepped over the rope each time it whirled by his feet. After several days, the other boxers began to acknowledge him, providing him a turn at the punching bag as if he were a member of the team. The other boxers, seasoned from their many years of competing in youth organizations and far more experienced than Norvel, were impressed with the sheer power Norvel displayed while pounding the bag.

Although Norvel wasn't sure he wanted to commit to boxing, the other members of the team suggested he ask Coach Barnes for a spot. Two of the members, Monte Hickman and York Van Nixon, thought he should be considered because if the Howard team had a weakness, it was in the heavyweight category.

As Norvel was finishing up his training routine Coach Barnes finally came strolling in. Short in stature compared to the young men he coached, Barnes began talking with Van Nixon. Norvel couldn't hear what was being said, but noticed Van Nixon pointing at him. A moment later, Coach Barnes asked Norvel to join them.

"Son, York here informs me you want to try out for our boxing team," Barnes said, with a hint of aloofness in his demeanor.

"Uh, uh, yes, sir," said Norvel.

"And where else have you boxed?" he asked.

"Well sir, uh, uh, I haven't boxed formally anywhere yet. I sparred a little in the service, but it wasn't anything official. But I've been practicing a lot. The fellas here have been watching me."

"So I've heard. You've impressed them. But here's the way it is, son. We already have a team put together. Every person on our team has experience. They've been doing this since they were in the junior programs, where they proved themselves. Each person here was recommended to me because of their boxing experience and reputation. You must understand that until this very moment, I've never heard of you."

Norvel lowered his head and said, "Yes, sir, I, uh, understand and respect that. I was just wondering if you might give me a tryout anyway."

Coach Barnes said, "It just wouldn't be fair to the others. We have a full complement. But maybe you can try to get some experience and we can look at you next year. You're welcome to use our facilities, such as they are, if you'd like."

"Thank you, sir," Norvel said.

"Good luck to you, son," Barnes said as he turned away to talk with the team members.

Several days later, Norvel went to the Founders Library on the Howard University campus, where he knew he would be able to find Dr. Henderson. He was hoping to get some advice on how to get more attention from the boxing team.

Dr. Edwin Henderson was in his mid-sixties and the health and education director for the Washington, D.C., segregated schools, and a renowned Howard graduate. He was often on the campus of his alma mater and was known as an active supporter of physical education and sports. He was also a strong organizing voice within the National Association for the Advancement of Colored People (NAACP). Even though Henderson was more involved with basketball, Norvel had heard he was also attempting to integrate the Golden Gloves, a national amateur boxing organization. Norvel spotted the distinguished-looking scholar-athlete at a table on the second floor. He was intently studying the open pages of a book while taking notes.

Norvel stepped up to the table. When Henderson looked up from the book, he said, "Sir, excuse me. Uh, uh, I would like to make an appointment with you to get some advice."

"Son, please sit down with me, and we can talk now," Henderson said kindly.

Norvel took a seat.

"First, tell me your name."

"Thank you, sir. My name is Norvel Lee. I'm a freshman here."

"You appear somewhat older than most freshmen," Henderson observed. "How old are you?"

"I'm twenty-three. I went into the service after high school, during the war," Norvel said. "My obligation to the service was satisfied a year ago April, too late to enroll last year. So I went home to Virginia and worked with my father, helping out the family."

"Did you go overseas?" Henderson said.

"Yes, sir, I did. I was assigned to the 93rd Infantry Division after getting trained as a pilot at Tuskegee. I earned my wings there, but they wouldn't let me go ahead and be a pilot because of my stammer. So I was on a maintenance crew with the 93rd. We went to mop up at Bougainville Island which is part of the Solomon Islands near New Guinea."

"Gee, son," exclaimed Henderson. "That is way out in the South Pacific, isn't it?"

"Yes, sir," answered Norvel. "I was in the 93rd because it was for the colored and that's where they decided to send us."

"What was it like, pretty rough?" asked Henderson.

"For some it was, but I was fortunate," Norvel said. "I spent my time helping our captain keep things organized. We were mostly waiting for the next wave of planes to come in so we could get them ready to go again."

"Looks like you survived well enough to be accepted here. What can I help you with?"

"While I was in the Army, I got acquainted with boxing," said Norvel. "I helped with an Army Air Corps boxing team after Joe Louis came to see us overseas. He put on an exhibition with one of my fellow soldiers there who was a boxer. I got to meet Mr. Louis. He was real nice and inspirational. And, like me, he stammered. I figure if he could be successful, so could I."

Henderson smiled and said, "Well there is a resemblance. Go on."

"I want to know how I can pursue boxing more seriously. I've been practicing over at the gym, and the fellas seem to like what they see. I went to see Coach Barnes and he said I can use the facilities, but the team is set."

"Knowing the coach, he probably turned you down because he didn't discover you. I know how to get his attention. I suggest you get involved with the local Golden Gloves. Mr. Drake over at the Apollo Athletic Club is in charge of the Golden Gloves program in D.C. He's interested in helping me get other races accepted at the local organization. I'm guessing he'll like having you there."

Dr. Henderson paused and then added, "We're attempting to get the Uline Arena to host the regional championship early next year, but they also would have to accept all races. It's an uphill battle with Mr. Uline, who is very set in his ways. But we're giving it our best."

Norvel knew of the Uline Arena. It had been established during the war as an ice arena but had become a general D.C. sports venue for basketball, hockey, and now, apparently, boxing. Mike Uline built it next to the company he founded that distributed ice around the greater D.C. area. His business was established when iceboxes were used to keep food fresh in homes, before refrigerators were common.

The following Saturday, Norvel walked the two miles to the Apollo Athletic Club at H and 6th Streets NE, carrying a duffel bag with his boxing gloves and workout clothes. Norvel entered the front door of the building and walked over to the counter.

"Only wagers still open today are those out at Santa Anita," said a man, not looking up.

Norvel said, "Oh, I must be in the wrong place. I'm here to see Mr. Drake."

The man motioned to a door to the right of the counter, and Norvel went to open it.

To his right was an open room with a roped-off regulation boxing ring, several punching bags, and numerous weights. Two men in boxing clothes were in the room working out. On his left was an office with its door slightly ajar. Norvel tapped lightly on the door and peered into the small room. Sitting at a desk was a man in his late forties, in an open-collar dress shirt, reading some papers.

Without looking up, the man mumbled, "Yes?"

"Uh, uh, excuse me, sir," asked Norvel. "Would you know where I could find Mr. Drake of the Golden Gloves?"

"Well, that's me," the man said, looking up from his paperwork. "What can I do for you?"

"Thank you, sir. I'm Norvel Lee. Dr. Henderson at Howard University told me I should talk with you about joining up with the Golden Gloves program."

"Did Ed tell you I was looking to get more colored boys to join up?" asked Drake. "He's been agitating for that, and I said I would. But I told him I might need some help convincing you boys to come over here."

Norvel smiled. "He didn't have to convince me. I wanted to join the Howard team, but Coach Barnes wouldn't look at me because he already has a full team. He told me if I got some experience, he might look at me next year. When I spoke with Dr. Henderson about it, he suggested, uh, I come to see you."

In the early 1940s, the Apollo Athletic Club was open to whites only. Its reputation had been established in Golden Glove circles by a local, Jim Hubbard, who went on to become the U.S. Navy's welterweight champion in 1945. Although he was a native of Washington, D.C., he did not return after leaving the Navy, settling in Oklahoma instead.

In 1946, Glenn Drake took over management of the Club. He moved it to its current space, renting the back unused section of the building and providing access to all races. The front area contained a presumably illicit bookie operation. All walks of life came and went from the building. Some made their way into the back room to observe the boxers when a match was in progress.

Noticing that Norvel had boxing gloves and a change of clothes with him, Drake said, "I see you have the right tools with you. If you have time I'd like to see what you've got."

After changing into his gym attire in the small locker room, Norvel stepped into the facility. He saw Drake waiting for him and the two young boxers practicing. One, about Norvel's size, was throwing jabs at the punching bag; the other was performing bicep curls with a hand weight.

Drake said, "Hey, Curly, I'd like to watch Norvel Lee here throw a few punches at the bag. I will appreciate you giving it up to him for a few minutes."

Curly, a young white man sporting a butch haircut and facial scars, reluctantly stepped aside. Norvel nodded a thank you, stepped up and established his proximity to the bag by poking at it with his left hand and then his right. He then started moving lightly on his feet and sending left- and right-handed jabs into the bag. He continued moving around the bag, his jabs turning into punches whose thuds resounded around the room. At one point, he let go a flurry of lefts and rights while quickly completing a three-sixty around the bag.

Drake finally said, "Well, Norvel, you look like you know what you're doing there. I'd like to see you spar with someone. How about you and Curly go a round or two in the ring."

As Norvel was nodding his agreement, Curly looked at Drake and said, "I ain't goin' to go up against no niggah! No, siree."

"You afraid he'll get the best of you?" Drake said, goading him. "If that's the kind of man you are, then go pack your things and move on somewhere else."

Curly said, "I'm not afraid, certainly not of someone like him."

Norvel was already in the ring dancing around, ignoring the conversation.

"You better get used to this. You know I'm trying to bring more colored and other races in here so we can get this chapter open to all talented boxers, not just whites. Now get in the ring and show Norvel what you've got."

Curly got into the ring, smiling menacingly and started moving toward Norvel. They exchanged a few body punches when suddenly Norvel unleashed a powerful combination of a right jab and then a quick left to Curly's midsection, sending him to the mat. Norvel stood there calmly as Curly picked himself up off the ground and moved back toward Norvel again. Norvel moved around as Curly made a couple of wild attempts that missed; then Norvel again caught Curly in the midsection, sending him back to the mat, this time groaning.

Drake stepped in and said, "Okay, men, I've seen enough."

Norvel went over to Curly and offered his hand. Curly reached up and allowed Norvel to pull him up. Curly looked at Norvel, gave a slight nod, and left the room.

During the following months, Norvel kept busy by staying absorbed in his freshman classes. His declared major was engineering, but those first-year classes consisted of the normal requirements. The engineering degree also required him to take Chemistry and Calculus, which he enjoyed. Math and the sciences always came easy for him.

Norvel spent thirty minutes every day jumping rope in either the Howard University gym or, when he had time, the Apollo Athletic Club. After jumping rope, he would spend another thirty minutes on the punching bag. After a few weeks he befriended several boxers at both venues who eventually became sparring partners.

In early 1948 Drake set up several interclub bouts to see if Norvel was ready to be entered into a sanctioned event. The first match-up was against Lloyd Johnson, a brash nineteen-year-old who during the previous year, while still in high school, had been a regional Golden Gloves champion. Johnson was planning on joining the Air Force, and Drake was trying to convince him to reconsider. He wanted the Apollo Athletic Club to make another good showing in the upcoming Golden Gloves championship.

Johnson was his ace. And Drake wanted to see how Norvel would handle himself against an experienced, highly confident opponent.

Ringside at the Apollo Athletic Club on a cold, damp January afternoon, a small group of boxers and other interested people gathered to watch the match between Johnson and Norvel. The onlookers were for the most part white, except for York Van Nixon from the Howard boxing team and eighteen-year-old Jim Finley. Norvel had started providing some guidance to Finley, who had been hanging around the Club recently. Finley relished the attention.

Norvel and Johnson stepped into the ring and quickly shook hands. Norvel noticed Johnson was slightly taller than him, with long muscular arms. Johnson turned and waved at the onlookers, who assumed he would have an easy time with Norvel.

When Drake rang the triangle that served as the bell, Johnson moved confidently to the center, taunting Norvel to come at him. Both men danced around. Johnson's long reach kept Norvel from landing many punches. Most were just glancing blows or were swatted away by Johnson. Likewise, Johnson was not able to cause any damage because Norvel had adopted the classic boxer's stance with his left foot forward, right foot in back with the heel raised and diagonal to his left. He distributed his weight evenly and slightly bent his knees. Norvel's elbows pointed down with his gloved hands up in front of his head. He kept his feet in motion, with his right hand alternating between probing and fending off Johnson's overtures. The first two of the planned three rounds were about the same; each boxer sizing up the other. Drake was surprised at Norvel's poise. At the end of the second round it became clear Johnson was becoming frustrated. He expected he would have been able to land something by this point. He heard some caustic murmuring from the onlookers.

Between rounds Norvel thought, *I need to take some chances. Maybe I can let him think he can get me, and he'll give me an opening. He's not going to hurt me.*

When Drake rang the triangle signaling the start of the third round, both boxers moved to the center of the ring. Norvel positioned his arms higher, exposing more of his belly and ribs. He watched Johnson's eyes size up the new stance and then attempt to go at Norvel's midsection with a left-and-right combination of punches. But Norvel unleashed a devastating left hook that connected solidly with Johnson's now unprotected head, just below the right temple. Johnson fell forward into Norvel's arms and then slid to the ground. While Norvel hovered over the groaning Johnson, waiting for him to get back up, Drake stopped the fight.

The onlookers, including Van Nixon, were stunned. The result was totally unexpected. Finley just stood there, admiring his mentor.

Norvel quickly established himself as the dominant heavyweight boxer at the D.C. Golden Gloves by easily outclassing several other aspiring local heavyweights.

Also in January 1948, Dr. Henderson and Glenn Drake convinced the *Washington Post* to withdraw their sponsorship of the Uline Arena if it would not open up its events to races other than white. Mike Uline finally relented. The newly integrated Golden Gloves held their regional tournament on Friday, February 6.

Norvel was Drake's entry in the heavyweight division, matched against Baltimore's John Gwalthney, another collegiate boxer. A capacity crowd of eight thousand filled the Uline Arena to watch the regional championship for the various weight divisions.

Norvel felt energized by the large, boisterous crowd. He could hear the rise and fall of their cheers and groans as the lower-weight bouts took place. He saw his opponent enter the warm-up area only thirty minutes before their heavyweight match, the final one of the evening.

Gwalthney picked up a jump rope, saw Norvel, and came over to introduce himself. Norvel saw that he was several inches shorter but stockier. Norvel knew from Drake that Gwalthney was a popular person in local Golden Glove circles. He had an affable smile and an understated, confident way about him. Norvel felt nervous anticipation as he also grabbed a jump rope and began getting loose.

Ten minutes before his fight, Drake came down to bring Norvel to the ring. They walked under the bleachers, where the sound of stomping feet and muffled cheering was not only heard, but felt.

Norvel was walking briskly, causing Drake to remark, "You seem nervous. I guess that's understandable, seeing this is your first official fight."

Norvel continued his brisk strides and said, "Well, uh, uh, I don't know what I was expecting, but I didn't think about a loud, noisy crowd. Guess I'm just excited about it."

"As soon as the bell sounds, you will shut them out of your mind and you'll be concentrating on your opponent. You're going to be fine."

They emerged from under the stands. Norvel noticed the spotlights on the ring and the distinct smell of cigar smoke in the air. The referee motioned to Norvel to climb up and through the ropes at one corner of the ring. In a few minutes a cheer arose from the stands as Gwalthney appeared at the opposite corner.

The referee called both men to the center of the ring. A man in a suit with a microphone joined them, looked out at the crowd, and spoke: "Ladies and gentlemen! This is the heavyweight and concluding fight of this year's local Golden Gloves Championship."

The crowd cheered as the announcer's words reverberated throughout the arena.

"From Washington, D.C., representing the Apollo Athletic Club, is Norvel Lee."

A polite applause ensued.

"And from just up the road in Baltimore, Maryland, John Gwalthneeeee."

Many in the crowd cheered and applauded enthusiastically.

*Just focus* thought Norvel. *Don't worry about the crowd. They don't matter—just focus.*

When the bell sounded to start the first round, Norvel immediately took the fight to Gwalthney, coming forward and stunning him with a left hook that drew blood from his nose for the remainder of the round, and on and off throughout the fight. Norvel kept coming forward, landing jabs on a surprisingly immobile Gwalthney, and nearly dropping him with a body punch in the second round that caused him to double over in visible discomfort.

While waiting for the bell to start round three, Norvel watched Gwalthney's coach give him a pep talk while waving his arms vigorously for emphasis. Norvel looked at Drake, Norvel's corner man, who simply gave him a thumbs up. In the meantime, Gwalthney's fans were yelling enthusiastic words of encouragement to him.

*He will have to knock me out to beat me, and that's not going to happen.*

The third round seemed to light a fire under Gwalthney, who sprang urgently out of his corner and rocked Norvel with left punches with some right crosses mixed in before dancing out of countering range. As the round wore on, Norvel chased him down and landed many jabs before Gwalthney could protect himself. Gwalthney continued to box smartly for short spurts, but it was sporadic.

When the bell sounded, signaling the end of the three rounds, each boxer retired to his respective corner to wait for the results. Norvel felt he performed well enough to win but prepared himself for the contrary if that was the case.

The announcer returned to the center of the ring and signaled both boxers to come forward. He said in a loud, resonant voice, "Ladies and gentlemen! For the heavyweight match just completed we have a unanimous decision."

The announcer took Norvel's arm and said, "The winner and the local Washington, D.C. Golden Gloves heavyweight champion: Norvel Lee!" He raised Norvel's arm up into the air.

Norvel stood there taking in the moment while the crowd clapped and cheered. For most in attendance, this was an upset.

*Wow! I can't wait to let home know!*

The next day Norvel wrote a letter to his parents letting them know of his boxing success, but he put equal emphasis on his studies and how engaged he was with them. The evening Jack and Georgiana received the letter, they included words of gratitude for their son's accomplishments in the supper-time blessing.

About the same time, Howard University's boxing team also established itself as a force to contend with. The 1947–1948 team consisted of twenty-two boxers representing all the weight classes. The team had its best year in the Colored Intercollegiate Athletic Association (CIAA). Had Henry Cochrane won his championship match in the heavyweight class, Howard would have won the CIAA championship, but Cochrane lost in a split decision.

After the Uline Arena Golden Gloves event, Drake asked Norvel to join him in his office. He said, "Young man, you are a surprise to everyone, including Coach Barnes."

"How so?" asked Norvel.

"Coach Barnes prides himself in being able to identify for himself the boxers he selects for his team," said Drake. "But here comes Norvel Lee, someone he has never heard of, who asks for a spot on the team. He turns you down. Now you, a Howard student, join Golden Gloves and perform probably better than anyone on his team. But the Coach, from what I understand, still wants to see how you do over the long run before he admits that you should be on his team."

Norvel shrugged his shoulders, thinking, *what do I have to do?*

"So through some political maneuvering within the confines of Howard University, I've been able to get a sponsorship from Howard University for you to represent the D.C. Golden Gloves at this year's Olympic Trials."

Norvel stood quietly for a moment, pausing, not knowing what to say. He finally smiled and said humbly, "Thank you, sir. Uh, uh, I don't know what else to say except that I will do my best."

Drake said, "I know you will. Norvel, the point of this is to get you more experience. We are also thinking if you are boxing at the national level outside the CIAA, Barnes will have no choice but to put you on the team next year."

Norvel thanked him again.

*The Olympics! Me! They want me to try for the Olympics. But what about my education? I'm going to have to concentrate on both. I promise I will, Mama!*

Later that evening, Norvel again wrote a letter to his parents. Not mentioning the Golden Gloves, he explained that Howard University was sponsoring him for the U.S. Olympic Trials. He wanted to assure his mother that it was a sanctioned school activity. He understated his excitement.

Drake entered Norvel into the trials for the upcoming Olympics, planned for London during the summer. Baseball had also started, and Norvel earned a spot as a reserve outfielder on the Howard team. But although he enjoyed the camaraderie of his teammates, his focus was more on his studies and the upcoming Olympic Trials.

# CHAPTER 5

## May 19, 1948—Griffith Stadium, Washington, D.C.

N orvel was on the heavyweight card at Washington's Griffith Stadium in a subregional Olympic trial officially representing the Apollo Athletic Club. Other members of the Howard boxing team were astonished that this person, who by now was a familiar face at their modest training facility, was trying out for the Olympics. Norvel maintained a nonchalant attitude with the other boxers while enjoying the attention. York Van Nixon needled him by telling him not to expect to make the big leap from the Olympics to becoming a member of the Howard University boxing team.

His opponent, Eddie Grant from Maryland, was a locally known experienced fighter whom Drake had seen fight. Grant was about the same age and size as Norvel. He was also Norvel's first Black opponent. Those in attendance expected Grant to have an easy time.

Drake told Norvel to expect a fighter acting like he was the center of attention at a barroom brawl but to watch out for Grant's powerful right hand. His style was to lower his head and keep swinging until someone fell. When Norvel first spotted Grant across the ring, he was reminded of a boy back home who had unsuccessfully tried to bully him.

From the opening bell Norvel's goal was to show Grant that he wouldn't be the usual opponent. He danced around the ring, flicking jabs at him. He moved so quickly that Grant couldn't counter or reach him. The noise from the crowd, expecting a quick knockdown, became a murmur.

During the second round Grant tried to fight his way inside, but as he did Norvel slugged a left to the top of Grant's head and danced away. Norvel anticipated when the reputed bully would try to move forward and then zinged him with his own powerful right. The fight continued in this manner until Grant's eyes were puffy from the barrage.

By the third round Norvel noticed that Grant, constantly blinking his eyes, was slow and plodding. So instead of dancing away as he did in the first round, Norvel planted his feet and began to land hard rights. Grant, the brawler, stood there taking the onslaught. Fortunately, the bell sounded, ending the bout. The judges awarded all three rounds to Norvel.

After absorbing Drake's compliments about how well he was able to adapt his strategy to his opponent's style, Norvel told him that having advance information on Grant was a key factor informing him how to handle the fight. Norvel thought to himself, *I may not have the experience of these other fellas, but I'll be smarter. I'll just keep movin' to my left when they think I'm goin' right.*

Norvel received a letter from his mother wishing him well in his upcoming final exams and hoping that his boxing activities weren't interfering with his studies. She also said that she and Jack were looking forward to the summer break and having him home to help out in the popcorn fields. Christmas was the last time he had visited Gala and, admittedly, he was missing home also.

The following week the Region 3 trials were held at Philadelphia's Municipal Auditorium. The semifinals and finals were both scheduled for May 25. Glenn Drake accompanied Norvel to the event, taking the train the day before from Washington, D.C's Union Station to Philadelphia's 30th Street Station. Each of them took a bed at a local hostel.

Norvel's first opponent was the heavily favored C. Louis Duncan, nicknamed "Bruiser," from Richmond, Virginia. Duncan was the National Negro Intercollegiate heavyweight champion.

The large auditorium, which could seat sixteen thousand people, was about three-quarters full for the afternoon bouts. Norvel felt calm, however. His demeanor was quietly resolute when he arrived at the locker room.

When Norvel entered the ring, he looked across to the opposite corner at his opponent. Duncan was taller, twenty pounds heavier, and carried a menacing scowl. Norvel concluded Duncan's look was where the Bruiser moniker came from. Drake had told him earlier that Duncan was actually a classic stand-up boxer. Drake also said he thought Norvel's best strategy was to keep on the move.

When the bell sounded, the boxers moved out of their corners cautiously, testing each other's range and readiness with some measured jabs. Norvel felt good. He imagined he was in the outfield playing baseball while he moved fluidly around Duncan, as if he were trying to field a line drive. Both men traded punches throughout the round, but Norvel felt his were more impactful and hoped the judges would notice the same.

Drake was Norvel's corner man, attending to him between rounds. At the end of the first round, as he toweled Norvel off, Drake said, "Good going. You got him that first round, impressively. Keep it up."

Norvel took in Drake's assessment and prepared to continue jabbing and moving around his opponent, if that's what it took to win. But as the second round was under way, Norvel saw a different, more determined Duncan. He saw a look of pure anger in his opponent's eyes — a deep-seated anger. Somehow, even while continuing to move, Duncan was able to land power punches to Norvel's rib cage. One such blow almost caused Norvel to lose his feet, but he was able to recover and protect himself before Duncan unleashed another combination of punches.

*Where did all this come from? He's completely different than before. I need to keep my balance and regroup!*

Norvel anticipated an attempted head shot and ducked just as the bell sounded, ending the second round.

*That was close!*

Norvel noticed Drake didn't give him any between-round advice. *I know what to do, and he knows it. This Bruiser doesn't know what's comin' now!*

Norvel practically leapt out of his corner at the beginning of the third and final round. He went right at Duncan and unleashed a furious combination of left and right punches—the left to the body and the right to the head. Then he reversed the order. Norvel felt quick and in control, and all Duncan could do was try to protect his body the best he could. By the time the round ended, Norvel was awarded the victory with a 2-1 decision. The next day the *Philadelphia Inquirer* reported that Lee "scored a surprising victory."

Later that evening, Norvel's opponent was hometown favorite Earl Matthews of Philadelphia, before a standing-room-only crowd. Buoyed by the sound of the crowd, although they were rooting for his opponent, Norvel scored another 2-1 victory. The same article reported, "Unmatched in fury, Lee was tipped over for no count in the second round. Rallying strongly in the last round, Lee floored Matthews for 'nine' with a sizzling left. Matthews came up punching, but was staggered by Lee's rapid-fire, two-fisted assault when the final bell sounded."

The victory over Matthews earned Norvel a quarterfinal slot for the national trials in Boston on June 28.

Norvel returned to Washington. A week later, the Apollo boxing gym was crowded with onlookers, mostly other boxers, wanting to see Norvel up close. Drake interrupted the workout session and requested that he come to his office. With a towel wrapped around his shoulders, Norvel came into the cramped space, ignoring Drake's offer for him to sit down.

"Stand if you must," said Drake, grinning. "Your fans have to stand to see you."

"Oh, uh, I don't know if 'fans' is the right word," said Norvel. "They're mainly just curious."

"Nope, they're definitely fans," said Drake. "The accolades are pouring in. And look at the mix of people out there. Blacks and whites. Eddie Henderson is elated. His goal of all races being included in amateur athletic pursuits is being realized."

"Yes, sir," said Norvel, smiling. "Glad I could help move things along. Just came along at the right time, I guess."

"Well, it is all about timing, Norvel," said Drake. "Just as I did in Philadelphia, I'm going to accompany you on this trip to Boston. I believe Coach Barnes may make an appearance there also."

Norvel's eyes widened.

"Between Barnes and myself, and some of our other contacts, we're going to do what we can to assess the competition you may face. You're entering the big leagues at the national level. These boxers are not only talented but also very experienced, especially with their ability to adjust their style to their opponents. We want you to be well equipped with information before you get into the ring against them."

Norvel said, "Thank you. I can use all the help I can get."

*Do all boxers on the national level get this kind of attention? If so, what will they say about me? Not much, I reckon.*

"We do know of a heavyweight boxer who garnered much attention earlier this year," continued Drake. "Coley Wallace is his name. His fame came when he controversially defeated an up-and-coming Italian, Rocco Marchegiano, who developed a reputation for having a devastating knockout punch. The fight occurred in March for the national Golden Gloves Championship. My guess is if you are going to make the Olympic team, you'll have to go up against him at some point."

"Why was the decision controversial?" Norvel asked.

Drake said, "I heard Wallace beat him fair and square, but the fight took place before Wallace's hometown crowd in New York. Marchegiano's Boston fans and Italians from New York started claiming it was biased. For fifteen minutes boos filled Madison Square Garden and debris rained all over the ring."

"And won't, uh, uh, I face this Marchegiano fella?" asked Norvel.

*I want him,* Norvel thought. *If he's the one to beat, I want him.*

"No, he's injured. He hurt his hand knocking out his opponent in the national Golden Gloves tournament in New York. I should have entered you in it, but we only had enough money to put you in these trials."

In the meantime, the final examinations for the spring term at Howard were complete and Norvel was receiving letters from his mother asking when they could expect him home. Norvel explained in a letter that he would be there after the Olympic Trials were completed at the end of the month. He expected to be home for the Fourth of July.

On June 26, Norvel and Drake took the train to Boston's North Station, located beneath Boston Garden, where the trials would take place. Coach Barnes was not able to join them, but was hoping to get to Boston in time to see Norvel. They checked into a hostel that was within walking distance of the arena.

This was Norvel's first time in Boston. He was taken with the distinct Bostonian accent, when he heard members of the hostel insert "ah" while saying words normally ending with an "r" sound.

In the morning Norvel attended services at a nearby church and afterward went on a conditioning run. The route took him down Commonwealth Avenue, onto Massachusetts Avenue across the Charles River on Harvard Bridge, around the MIT campus, and then back along the north side of the Charles River to the Longfellow Bridge. Then he ran back across the Charles River and into the Old North End of Boston. Later, after returning to the hostel, Norvel wrote a letter about his time in historic Boston and mailed it home the next morning.

Norvel looked forward to experiencing Boston Garden. Designed specifically for boxing, it had opened in 1928 with a capacity of thirteen thousand spectators. The noise of the crowds was said to be deafening. The Gardens was where the Boston Celtics basketball team played their home games, using the acoustics to their advantage. He had learned in Philadelphia that he enjoyed fighting in front of a large, boisterous crowd. He found the experience exciting.

But his quarterfinal bout, on Monday, was a mismatch. At 192 pounds, Norvel had the weight and arm length on his opponent, Charles Black of San Antonio, Texas, who was five feet, ten inches tall and weighed 177 pounds.

From the opening bell, Norvel knew he outclassed Black. But in spite of every powerful blow he landed on the smaller man, Norvel couldn't put him down on the canvas. The referee, mercifully, stopped the fight in the second round, awarding Norvel the victory and scoring it as an "RSC" or "referee stops the contest."

In another one of the quarterfinals, the favorite, Coley Wallace, knocked out New Yorker Charles Norkus in the second round. Wallace won the Amateur Athletic Union (AAU) national championship at this same venue in April, after winning the national Golden Gloves.

That Tuesday afternoon before a near-capacity crowd at Boston Garden, Norvel met Coley Wallace in the semifinal match. Properly briefed, Norvel conducted a strategic fight by simply trying to land impressive punches to score points with the judges. The bout was not particularly exciting, but it was successful for Norvel. The *Boston Globe* simply said, "Lee won all three rounds."

Coach Barnes was among the spectators who watched Norvel defeat the "man to beat" for the Olympic spot. Norvel now had one more person to face in order to earn the heavyweight slot on the 1948 Olympic team. It was Jay Lambert of Salt Lake City, Utah, who made the finals by a decision over Jim Motley of Nebraska in the other semifinal match.

When Norvel realized that Coley Wallace had beat Lambert on his way to the AAU heavyweight national championship and that he, Norvel, had taken Wallace out of the competition, he felt confident about his chances of becoming the heavyweight on the Olympic boxing team. At the beginning of the competition he hadn't even been mentioned as a possibility.

It was a boisterous standing-room-only crowd at Boston Garden for the final match of the 1948 Olympic trials: Jay Lambert versus Norvel Lee.

The bell signaling the start of round one sounded faint against the noise of the crowd. Norvel felt fortunate to hear it. He moved to the center of the ring and met Lambert, who immediately started jabbing and throwing aggressive punches that found their mark. Norvel was aware that the aggressive moves left Lambert vulnerable to Norvel's counterpunch. Both men kept brutally finding their respective targets on each other's body and head. When the bell ending the round sounded, the referee had to break them apart. Lambert's lip was bleeding.

During the second round, Norvel found himself at the receiving end of Lambert's hard left jabs and perfectly timed right crosses. Norvel felt his lips swelling from the attack. Then a barrage of body punches and a quick cross to Norvel's jaw sent him to the canvas. Norvel sat for a moment as the referee counted, but was back on his feet by the time the count reached six.

For the third round, Norvel found himself on the defensive as Lambert continued taking the fight aggressively to him. Mid-round, Norvel tried moving his focus inside Lambert's stance but could not inflict any significant damage. When the bell sounded, Norvel knew that was it. The judges generously awarded Norvel the first round, but it was obvious Lambert had dominated rounds two and three.

*Well, that's that*, he thought. *That man could really hit, and I wasn't prepared. I wasn't supposed to get this far anyway, so nothing really lost. At least Mama and Dad will be glad to have me home for the summer. And in the fall I can get myself back to the books.*

Just then, as Norvel stepped away from the ring, holding a towel to his lips, Drake, Barnes, and a third man approached Norvel and congratulated him on his efforts. Barnes in particular said how proud he was of Norvel's determination, and yes, for sure, he would be a member of the Howard boxing team the following year. "No tryout required," he said, laughing.

The third man stepped forward, smiling, and introduced himself. "Norvel, I'm John Walsh, one of the coaches of the Olympic boxing team."

Norvel smiled and shook his hand, curious as to why Walsh would present himself at this point.

"Let me be the first to congratulate you," Walsh continued. "You have been selected as the heavyweight alternate on the team going to London in a few weeks." Walsh paused and then added dramatically, "Young man, you are a member of the United States Olympic team."

*My goodness!! I am an Olympian! Goin' to England, yessiree! Guess those popcorn fields back home are going to have to get along without me this summer. I'll have some explaining to do.*

Norvel had only fought in seven official bouts over a five-month period, establishing a near-perfect record except for the loss against Lambert.

And now, here he was a member of the U.S. Olympic team.

That evening, Norvel wrote a letter to his family breaking the news that on July 14 he would be sailing to London from New York as a member of the U.S. Olympic team. He also told them he would not be able to get home because the selected boxers were required to spend the next two weeks at West Point, training. He promised to come home as soon as he returned.

Norvel did think it ironic that he would finally be going to West Point, just not as a cadet.

During training at the military academy along the Hudson River, Norvel received a letter signed by all the members of the Rising Mount Zion Baptist Church wishing him Godspeed while overseas.

# CHAPTER 6

## *XIV Olympiad—London, England*

The Summer Olympics were last hosted by Berlin in 1936, prior to the outbreak of World War II. The planned 1940 Helsinki and 1944 London Games were canceled because of the war. It was unknown at the time if there would ever be another Olympics. But when the war ended, Great Britain insisted on hosting the Games, knowing they were doing so in the face of continuing world political tensions, major financial constraints, and ongoing infrastructure rebuilding efforts. In spite of those hurdles, five thousand athletes from fifty-nine nations traveled from every corner of the globe to London to celebrate, on a world stage, the onset of peace.

Norvel was among the six hundred athletes and support staff from the United States who boarded the *SS America* on July 14, 1948, on their way to England. Norvel had last been at sea when he returned home from Manila during the war. That journey was a miserable experience as Blacks were confined to the overcrowded bowels of military transport ships. Now Norvel shared a comfortable stateroom with another boxer, Washington Jones, from St. Louis. A festive spirit was felt by all throughout the modern ocean liner.

During an evening meal in the grand dining room, with the ship rolling back and forth while navigating the swells of the North Atlantic, Norvel sat with several members of the track-and-field team. He recognized one of the athletes at the table—a thin, wiry man about Norvel's age who exuded a pleasant, confident demeanor. After observing the man for a few minutes, Norvel recalled where he had first seen him.

Norvel said, "If I'm right, I saw you at Tuskegee. Right after I got there, I believe you were the one I watched get flight wings pinned on."

The man immediately stood up, reached across the table to shake Norvel's hand and said, "Great to meet a fellow Airman. I'm Mal Whitfield."

"Norvel Lee, the pleasure, uh, uh, is mine."

"I got my wings in late '43," Whitfield said. "How about you?"

"February, '44. Eventually ended up in the South Pacific involved in ground support."

Whitfield said, "I was a gunner for the 99th Pursuit Squadron in Europe."

"Whew, I bet you've got stories to tell," Norvel said.

"Don't we all," Whitfield chuckled. "I'm still in the Army, I mean, Air Force now. What about you?"

"No, got out and enrolled at Howard University."

"The Air Force is supporting me in classes at Ohio State," Whitfield said. "You may want to look and see if they have a ROTC program there at Howard. It will help pay your way and give you some choices after you graduate."

"Thanks, Mal. I'll check it out."

One of the other trackmen at the table remarked, "I find it remarkable that two Tuskegee boys are on the same Olympic team. Has to be one for the books, I'd think!"

On July 18, two nights before arriving in England, entertainment was organized and staged by the athletes and other members of the Olympic party. Norvel enjoyed the fashion show put on by the women's swim team and a beautiful rendition of *Without a Song* performed by Bernice Robinson, a woman hurdler. For the grand finale, everyone in the ballroom sang a loud, enthusiastic rendition of *God Bless America.*

London didn't have the time or resources to construct an official Olympic Village. So as the athletes arrived in England, they were accommodated in barracks and tents left over from the war. The austere environment provided a unique setting for the camaraderie and celebratory atmosphere prevailing in postwar England. The American boxing team comprised sixteen members, half of whom were Black. The Blacks were expecting to be assigned segregated quarters, as was the custom. But to their surprise, their bunks were assigned alongside their white teammates.

Coach Walsh made sure that the eight alternates who backed up each weight class would help get the team ready for the upcoming matches, still several weeks away. After the Olympics were completed, the boxing team would travel to Dublin, Ireland, for the Duals Matches, an annual competition between selected European countries and the United States. This year it would be America's top amateur boxers versus Ireland's. Walsh made it known that each of the alternates would get a turn in one of the matches, implying their conditioning was important also.

Norvel mostly sparred with the heavyweight who beat him for the Olympic slot, Jay Lambert. During the days of training with him, Norvel discovered that Lambert was a smart, thoughtful person instead of the rogue bruiser that gave him a lesson the previous month. Norvel also sparred with the light heavyweight, Chuck Spieser of Michigan.

When the boxing team began to practice, Coach Walsh also encouraged Norvel and several other alternates to visit the practice sessions of competing teams and report on what they learned. Norvel was glad to spend his time contributing something useful to the team. He looked in on several teams, and while observing the Canadians one afternoon, he struck up a conversation with Adam Faul, the Canadian heavyweight champion.

"Are you spying on us?" Faul asked, when Norvel came upon him.

"Not really," Norvel said, smiling. "Uh, uh, I'm an alternate on the team, and coach asked me to go pick up some tips."

Faul, slightly shorter than Norvel, had wavy dark hair. Norvel thought he looked like the actor Guy Madison, whom he recently had seen in the movie *Till the End of Time*. It was about veterans returning from the war.

Faul smirked, saying, "Well, we don't have nothing to hide here, except our strengths."

Just then one of the Canadian coaches, Ken Goff, joined them.

After introductions, the three men watched Canadian bantamweight Fred Daigle dance around a boxing bag. He was focused, intent on inflicting serious damage to the defenseless apparatus.

Goff hollered over to him, "Hey Daigle, lighten up and save it for the bout!"

Faul and Norvel chuckled. Then it was Faul's turn at the bag.

Faul did not dance around the bag like the bantamweight. He stood flat-footed, delivering powerful punches and jabs.

Goff looked at Norvel and explained, "Faul always relies on his sheer power against his opponents. I've been trying to work with him on moving around more, but he is having some trouble doing so. Looks like you won't actually have a match since your team's heavyweight boxer, Jay Lambert, looks ready. I was wondering if you might be available to practice with Adam. We don't have another person who can go up against him. I want him to have a little more practice against the kind of competition he might potentially face."

Norvel simply said, "I would be happy to, but you'll have to ask Coach Walsh."

When the American boxers had free time on their hands Norvel, Washington Jones, and alternates James Mitchell and Frank Daniels— both from California—got together. Norvel taught them the card game pinochle, which they spent many hours playing in the tented dining area. They also went into London to explore the large, smoky city. Occasionally other boxers, most notably Lambert and Spieser, joined them. When crossing a street at one point, Spieser looked to his left instead of his right for traffic and might have been hit by a car, were it not for Norvel grabbing his arm and yanking him back to the sidewalk.

One muggy overcast day, when the group of boxers strolled by the Tower of London, a young boy walked up to Norvel and asked in a strong cockney accent, "Are you with the Olympics? Why's your skin so dark?"

Norvel laughed, while his companions were taken aback by the youngster's brashness. "Why, young man, that's the way God made me," Norvel responded, displaying a broad smile. Then he asked, "Why aren't you in school?"

"It's summer time and it's the Olympics," the boy said excitedly. "Do you run real fast?"

Lambert, holding his hand in a fist, said, "No, son. We are fighters, not track men."

Just then the boy's mother came up, saying sheepishly, "I'm sorry gentleman. He's just so curious at this stage."

The men tipped their hats as she shooed her son away.

Lambert glanced at Norvel and the others, saying, "It's like he's never seen a person with dark skin before. Pretty much like where I'm from, Utah."

Daniels, the Californian, said prior to coming he had wanted to know what Blacks might be facing in London and was surprised to learn that in England only 1 percent of the population was Black. But the numbers were increasing because of an influx of refugees from Africa, forced to flee their homelands.

Daniels looked at Norvel and said, "I understand you're from Virginia—yes?"

"Sure am," Norvel said, looking out at the murky Thames River.

"And aren't there rules about where you shop, go to school, and sit on a bus?"

"Yes, they, uh, uh, are called Jim Crow laws."

"I must say, I've heard about them, but I'm not sure I could put myself in that position," Mitchell joined in. "Although in California there's an unofficial agreement on what neighborhoods we can live in."

Spieser chimed in, adding, "Same thing in Michigan."

*I wonder what's worse*, Norvel thought. *Putting the rules out in the open like we have them back home, or having to figure out on your own where you're not welcome.*

One day Irv Mondschein, Floyd Simmons, and Bob Mathias, the three decathletes on the American team, dropped in to see the boxers. Several of the boxers, including Norvel, introduced themselves to the trio. Mondschein and Simmons, appearing to be about Norvel's age, looked to be well-conditioned, self-confident athletes. But Norvel thought the starry-eyed Mathias not old enough and much too frail in stature to be effective in the grueling two-day decathlon.

On Tuesday, July 27, most members of the American team were sparring, working the punching bags, and shadowboxing during the mandatory team training sessions. While Norvel was toweling off and talking with Lambert, Jones came hurriedly into the room, out of breath.

"Fellas," he said in a loud voice. "This bulletin just came in! It says that President Truman issued an Executive Order last night."

The team members stopped their individual workouts and came over to hear what Jones was so excited about.

"Come on, man," Mitchell said. "What's it say?"

Jones said, "There's a lot of legalese here, so I'll just read the important words. It says: 'It is hereby declared to be the policy of the President that there shall be equality of treatment and opportunity for all persons in the armed forces without regard to race, color, religion, or national origin.' It goes on to say that this order will start now, immediately."

The men all stopped, somewhat stunned, silent. Then Lambert put one arm around Norvel and another around Mitchell.

Coach Walsh observed the scene quietly for a moment before saying, "Well, I'll be. I think the President is using us as an example of how it's all going to work. Now let's get back to work, men!"

Two days later was the Opening Ceremony. The event was a perfectly orchestrated show from beginning to end. The Americans were the fifty-sixth country in the long line of nations making their way into the stadium. But that didn't stop them from clapping loudly as each competing team entered the procession. When it finally became the U.S. team's turn to walk up the tunneled ramp leading into the great stadium, Norvel was filled with awe when he looked up to the eighty thousand people cheering, accompanied by blaring marching music playing on and on. Norvel felt proud to be an American, living during these exciting times, marching with the team as an equal.

Jay Lambert leaned over to Norvel while they marched and shouted above the noise, "I'll never forget this as long as I live. This is the biggest thrill of my life."

Norvel enthusiastically agreed.

After the nations were assembled on the field, a runner carrying a torch emitting silver light entered the stadium. When the runner lit the Olympic Flame, Norvel felt as if electricity had filled Wembley Stadium and bolted out energetically to all the athletes on the field and the spectators alike.

Norvel, aware that there were goose bumps on his arms, thought: *I will never forget this: the soaring pigeons, the Royal Family—and just look at all these colorful teams from all over the world with me here. Wow!*

As the boxers continued to train, Walsh informed Norvel that Goff had asked his permission for Norvel to be a sparring partner for Adam Faul and that he had agreed. Norvel thanked the coach for the opportunity, and joked with him he would not teach Faul any new tricks in the ring. Faul was not scheduled against any of the U.S. boxers in the early rounds. Based on the strength of the field, it was unlikely there would be a matchup between the Canadian and U.S. boxers.

On Thursday, August 5, two days before Faul was scheduled to fight his first opponent, Victor Bignon of Chile, Norvel practiced in the ring with him while Goff and others looked on. It became clear that Norvel was much quicker than Faul. Etiquette dictates that during a practice round no damaging punches are to be delivered since it was only a training session, not a competition, but it was apparent that Norvel was the superior boxer. He danced around, anticipating and avoiding Faul's moves by dodging and bobbing.

Goff hollered, "Move your feet, Faul!"

On the other hand, Faul would have been difficult to knock around, as his stance suggested he was firmly anchored to the ground and nothing could take him down. He could absorb a punch and come right back to his opponent with a heavy blow. Taking his cue from Goff, Norvel kept pointing to his feet and suggesting Faul move more. When Faul tried to move his feet he looked over to Goff for approval. While doing so, Norvel faked a blow to the head that would have caught Faul undefended if Norvel had struck him. The onlookers laughed, including Faul.

Later, after Faul had gone off to cool down and clean up, Goff said to Norvel, "You look like you know what you're doing there in the ring."

"Yes, sir," Norvel said, wiping perspiration from his eyes.

Goff straightened the gray tie he was wearing and said, "I am organizing an event in Canada that I would like to include you in. Are you interested?"

"What kind of event?" Norvel asked.

Goff said, "It's a boxing exhibition sponsored by the Canadian Police Association in Regina. Both Adam and I live there."

"Where's Regina?"

"It's the capital of Canada's Saskatchewan province out on the north western plains. Because you're a member of the U.S. Olympic team, your participation would help me promote the event."

"When is it?" asked Norvel.

"The end of September."

"Uh, uh, I will need to get the okay from Howard University," Norvel said, wondering how this might affect his sophomore academic year.

"You're sure a dedicated young man," observed Goff. "What's your major there at Howard?"

"Engineering."

"I know how demanding a curriculum that can be," Goff said, and then continued, "I'll discuss it with your coaches to see if we can find funding sponsors for you."

"Okay," Norvel said. He was excited about the possibilities but didn't want boxing to take over his life. After all, he initially took it up for the physical exercise and as a break from his studies.

On August 7, the first round of preliminary matches was held at the Empire Exhibition Pool House, located at Wesley Park. The previous week the same venue had hosted the swimming and diving events, but was now reconfigured with a boxing ring. There was a lingering aquatic odor in the dank, cavernous facility. Norvel and the other alternate boxers assembled in a section of the aged grandstands set aside for athletes.

The first American in the ring to fight was Bill Bassio, a bantamweight from Pittsburgh, who lost on points to a French boxer. Norvel thought the fate would be the same for the American flyweight, Ed Johnson, who was clearly losing the point count in his bout. But near the end of the third round Johnson suddenly landed a right cross to the head of his New Zealand opponent, knocking him out. The Americans cheered loudly at the unexpected outcome. Walsh looked relieved that he didn't have two boxers knocked out of the early competition. Walsh's smile increased as he watched his reclusive welterweight, Hank Herring, dispatch his Belgium opponent. Herring was a Navy man from St. Petersburg, Florida, who kept mainly to himself.

There were no events on Sunday, August 8. Norvel attended the non-denominational services held in the makeshift Olympic Village. He enjoyed the mix of international cultures attending the event. He thought of his family at home, at services in Gala. Later he wrote a long letter to his parents describing his time in England and his plans for visiting them.

The first round of preliminaries continued on Monday, including American lightweight Wally Smith and light heavyweight Chuck Spieser. They both won their matches. Next up was Lambert facing his first opponent, Vicente dos Santos of Brazil.

Santos was shorter in height than Lambert but looked intimidating, his taut body coiled to inflict damage. In the first round the two boxers traded punches, sizing each other up. Although no damage was inflicted, it appeared that Lambert's late-round flurry may have swayed the judges his way. In the second, however, Santos saw that Lambert stayed away from him by keeping his weight on his right leg and then coming forward to attempt a jab. Santos waited for his chance, and by timing his approach was able to quickly move in and let loose a succession of undefended punches, sending Lambert to the mat. The noise of the crowd echoed throughout the steamy arena.

Norvel reflected, *That's all I had to do and if I had, it would have been me up there.*

The American boxers were now on their feet for the beginning of the third round. Lambert went right at Santos and immediately floored him with a determined right cross. Santos got back up on his feet but spent the rest of the match protecting himself from any more damage. The judges awarded Lambert the victory, 2-1.

Later that evening the next session of preliminary matches got under way with the eight heavyweight matches. The first one involved Norvel's Canadian sparring partner, Adam Faul. Daniels, sitting next to Norvel, nudged him and said, "Let's see what kind of instructor you've been."

"Uh, uh, I've been more of a punching bag than an instructor."

From the outset of the fight it became apparent Norvel's practice sessions with Faul were working in the Canadian's favor. Although he didn't appear light on his feet, Faul kept them in motion. And while he moved, mostly to his right, he worked jabs and punches into Victor Bignon's midsection. In the second round the Chilean landed several solid punches in return, but in the third Faul was able to avoid any further attacks while continuing his strategy of working the Chilean's body. Faul won the bout, 2-1.

The last fight of the evening again involved Lambert. His opponent was Fernand Bothy of Belgium, who was in his first match at the Olympics. Norvel was worried that his teammate might have been worn out from his grueling ordeal earlier, but he didn't have any issues. Although the Belgian fought a respectable fight, he didn't land enough jabs or punches to earn a point. Lambert won, 3-0.

On Tuesday morning, August 10, the second round of preliminary matches continued with American flyweight Frank Sodano knocking out his opponent from India in the opening seconds of the first round. Walsh hoped for another stellar day for his boxers because the winners of this day's matches would advance to the quarterfinals.

Eddie Johnson easily handled his opponent from Uruguay, winning 3-0, and Wallace Smith was again victorious in his bout against Argentinean Manuel Lopez, 2-1. And Herring took care of his Irish opponent. Walsh now had four entries for the quarterfinals.

But then the momentum changed. In the second round of Washington Jones's bout against Belgium's Auguste Cavignac, the referee disqualified Jones for slapping his opponent with an open glove. Jones was crushed. He didn't feel that he had done anything wrong yet there he was, DQ'd. Then Chuck Spieser, who was expected to be a medal contender, lost a close, grueling slugfest against George Hunter of South Africa.

That evening Norvel and the others consoled a distraught Washington Jones, who was still in a state of disbelief that he was disqualified for a move he often made in the ring. Lambert said he had learned the Olympic judging rules were much stricter than those for the amateur levels at home.

The next day, Wednesday, the quarterfinals kicked off. Four bouts of each weight class would determine which boxers would represent their countries in the semifinals. The Americans had entries in flyweight with Solano, featherweight with Johnson, welterweight with Herring, and heavyweight with Lambert. The Canadian, Adam Faul, was also in the heavyweight quarterfinal competition.

Norvel felt excited about seeing these matches, although he wished he was one of the boxers instead of a spectator. But both Solano and Johnson lost decisively. Then Herring was victorious over Douglas du Preez of South Africa, 2-0. Herring's victory now assured the Americans of at least one medal for the boxing team.

The last chance for Walsh to see another one of his boxers make it to the semifinals was riding on Jay Lambert. Norvel and the other boxers squeezed into the overflowing crowd to watch the four heavyweight matches. Large electric fans had been set up in each corner of the cavernous arena in a vain attempt to provide relief from the heavy, wet air.

A trainer in Lambert's corner toweled the damp London air off Lambert, even though a punch had not yet been thrown. At the bell Lambert's opponent, John Arthur of South Africa, jabbed and moved forward on Lambert, who stepped back. Arthur was landing twice as many jabs for every one of Lambert's, earning points with the judges. Arthur was known to have a powerful knockout punch, evident in his previous bout when he sent his opponent to the floor halfway through round one. Lambert was trying to avoid that fate and was surprised at Arthur's change of tactics. In the second round, Arthur kept moving forward and jabbing, practically chasing Lambert around the ring.

Norvel wanted to yell, *Stand your ground and go at him!*

Arthur forced Lambert into the ropes, where Lambert grabbed him around the neck and held on. The referee broke them apart about the time the bell sounded. For round three, Arthur went at Lambert, who just kept trying to hang on. But Arthur then landed a hard punch to Lambert's mouth, bloodying his lips. Lambert backed up and spat, and fortunately Arthur missed his next swings at Lambert's head. He remained hunched over until the final bell sounded and Arthur was awarded a unanimous victory. Norvel was unsure whether he would have fared any better against the aggressive, hard-charging style of the South African.

Faul performed better than anticipated in his Olympic matches. Two days later, he took his highly ranked opponent, Gunnar Nilsson of Sweden, the full three rounds. Nilsson, known for knocking down his opponents, could not get Faul to fall. But the judges fairly judged Nilsson the winner by decision. Goff was pleased with Faul's performance. He finished fifth overall in the London Olympics, tied with Jay Lambert and two others.

In the end, the American boxers wound up with the silver medal being awarded to the quiet, unassuming welterweight Hank Herring. The team was disappointed with the overall results when Walsh called them together before their trip to Ireland.

"Okay, men," Walsh began. "Let's first congratulate Hank, our silver medal winner. Very well done, Mr. Herring!"

Herring waved at them while the men applauded. It was the first time any of them had seen him express much emotion, but now he wore a big grin.

Walsh continued, "I am proud and your country is proud of each one of you. No matter the outcome of your individual matches, I'm sure that these last few weeks will be remembered by each of you as a momentous occasion in your lives. I know they will for me. It's been an honor and privilege to be your coach. But this isn't the end. Right after the Closing Ceremony tomorrow, we will be moving on to Dublin for the Duals Matches."

The boxers applauded Walsh and thanked him for his leadership.

The final medal tally of the 1948 Olympics showed the Americans were the top medal winners, earning a total of eighty-four medals, of which thirty-four were gold. Mal Whitfield, the Tuskegee Airman, took home two gold medals: one for the 800-meter run, and the other for anchoring the winning 4x400-meter relay team. But the event that would always be memorialized by all was the decathlon, in which seventeen-year-old Bob Mathias, the decathlete Norvel thought too frail to amount to much, set a new world record. Everyone at Wembley Stadium was on their feet, including Norvel, roaring their approval as Mathias sprinted home in a driving cold rain, falling to the muddy ground after he crossed the finish line.

After the Closing Ceremony, the American boxing team took the train and the ferry to Ireland to compete in the Duals Matches. The Duals teams were made up of the national amateur champions for each weight category, determined in the United States by regional Amateur Athletic Union competitions. Many of the 1948 national champions were also on the Olympic team, but not all. For the heavyweight category, the national amateur champion was Coley Wallace, whom Norvel defeated in the semifinals for the Olympics slot. Since Norvel was already in Europe and had proved his abilities, it was decided he would be the heavyweight on the U.S. Duals Matches team.

Two evenings of matches were scheduled, both at the National Boxing

Stadium on South Circular Road near downtown Dublin. Unlike the facilities at Wembley, this venue was built specifically for boxing. It was filled to capacity, about two thousand people, each night.

During the first evening, August 17, for the seven bouts preceding the heavyweight contest the Americans were victorious in five. Surprisingly, Hank Herring lost, but Washington Jones, with a score to settle, knocked out his welterweight opponent in the first round. His teammates cheered his efforts enthusiastically.

It was finally Norvel's turn to display his skills. He looked at his burly opponent, Eugene Walsh, in the opposite corner.

*Got to settle down. What do I need to do? He doesn't look in good condition; maybe I can wear him down.*

As soon as Norvel moved to the center of the ring at the sound of the bell, it was clear to all who the superior boxer was. Displaying a classic stand-up style, he moved fluidly around the Irishman, landing jabs and punches. The fight itself was not particularly exciting, but those who were there appreciated Norvel's calm, confident poise. For the entire three rounds Norvel landed jabs and punches while Walsh chose to stay protected and preserve his energy, hoping for an opening to counter. By the third round, Walsh was quite fatigued, but instead of going in for the knockout, Norvel continued to weave, bob, and jab. The judges awarded Norvel a unanimous victory, 3-0.

The next day, a Wednesday, the team was free. Many of the boxers visited the legendary pubs off Grafton Street, while Norvel and several others, including Coach Walsh, toured the grounds of historic Trinity College, founded by Queen Elizabeth I in 1592. Norvel enjoyed the time away from training and being a tourist for a day.

The following evening, the second round of bouts took place. Olympic alternates, middleweight Frank Daniels and bantamweight James Mitchell, each drew an opponent. Daniels won, but Mitchell lost. And, in spectacular fashion, Washington Jones again knocked out his opponent with a massive flurry of punches midway through the second round. The Americans had won five bouts heading into the heavyweight and final fight of the evening.

Norvel drew the same opponent, Eugene Walsh. Norvel simply moved around the ring scoring hits, while Walsh tried to avoid the knockdown or getting pummeled.

Norvel was glad for the experience; his confidence buoyed knowing he could compete on an international stage. He was now looking forward to finally getting home to visit his parents and friends and regaling them with tales about his travels before beginning the fall term at Howard.

Norvel arrived in New York on the *USS Washington* on August 28. The boxers parted ways after again thanking Coach Walsh. Norvel boarded a train at Penn Station that took him to D.C., where he stayed two days before going home. On Wednesday, September 1, he took the Sportsman, C&O Railroad's daily train to Cincinnati. One of its many stops included Clifton Forge. Norvel made sure to sit in the section of the train that was designated "colored" when the train traveled through Virginia.

Norvel arrived at the train station in Clifton Forge at 5:30 p.m. that day and was relieved to see his parents waiting at the station. His sister Edna and brothers Jimmy and George were standing alongside them. He was worried that they might not have received the message about his travel plans. They ran to him when he came out of the train, taking turns hugging him. Even Jack Lee, who wasn't prone to overt displays of emotion, wrapped his arms around his oldest son. It had been over six months since Norvel was home.

The next day, Norvel felt relaxed being with his family. He helped his father tinker with a car before Jack was asked to go help repair a nearby railroad track. The railroad work was sporadic, but when Jack was called he felt obligated to go right to it.

Norvel, after his recent experiences, sat down on an old porch chair looking at the hills, knowing there were deer, squirrels, rabbits, and the occasional bear foraging among the trees and shrubs. Robins, bluebirds, and doves were everywhere, noisily chirping and cooing. Norvel reflected on how routine his family's day-to-day existence was compared to life beyond this part of the world. There was something comforting about knowing it was here if he decided to eventually return.

Georgiana and Jimmy joined him out on the porch. His mother sat down in the chair next to her son, while Jimmy remained standing.

She said, "We wanted to wait until you got home to tell you the good news."

"What's that?" Norvel asked.

"Jimmy has been accepted to Howard and will be starting the same time you will be going back."

Norvel stood up and wrapped his arm around his brother, exclaiming, "That is fantastic news! Congratulations! Uh, uh, I can't believe you kept that from me until now."

"Oh, baby," Georgiana said. "You're so busy doing important things. We are proud of you, you know. We really are. But you know this Olympic fame will be short-lived, and I worry boxing will keep you from your studies."

"Mama," Norvel said, "I know. My priority is getting through college. It's not boxing. But you must know I've done real good with it. Howard is supporting it and my education. It's a good fit for me."

He turned to Jimmy and said, "You, of course, are going to be living with me up there."

"He's already planning for it," Georgiana said.

Norvel's accomplishments regarding the Olympics were either not known or ignored by local newspapers such as the *Roanoke Times* and *Fincastle Herald*, which were geared toward the white communities of Alleghany, Botetourt, and Roanoke Counties. But news spread throughout the area by word of mouth at the Black churches and other community gatherings. The white population who knew of it didn't accept or acknowledge the significance of the achievement. But every day people came by the Big Hill family home to talk about the Olympics with Norvel.

On Sunday, September 5, the church services at the Rising Mount

Zion Baptist Church included a prayer of thanks for watching over Norvel on his journeys and for his safe return to the community. The pride on Georgiana's and Jack's faces was apparent.

Jimmy left for D.C. a few days after informing Norvel of his acceptance as a freshman at Howard University so he could register for classes. Before he returned to campus himself, Norvel was urged to visit his second cousins, the Byrds, in Covington. On Monday, September 13, Jack and Georgiana drove Norvel up to Clifton Forge so he could catch the daily C&O 303 train for the thirty-minute ride west to Covington.

Norvel boarded the 303, with its two cars—one for baggage and one for passengers—with one other passenger, a white man. Norvel didn't think it mattered at that time of day where he sat, so he simply took a seat, ignoring the sign indicating Colored and White sections of the passenger car. There were only two of them on board and Norvel didn't think the other man cared where they sat.

The train began its journey, clanging through the Allegheny Mountains over to Covington. After they were moving the conductor came into the passenger car to collect the two tickets. He took the white man's ticket and came over to Norvel, took his ticket, and then pointed to the sign. Norvel shrugged his shoulders, and the conductor simply shook his head and returned to the front of the train.

*I will not move from this seat. He knows it isn't necessary—I know it isn't necessary. I've been to places where there is no division. I helped defend and represent my country, with honor. I was in the war and the Olympics. The military is now integrated. I'm not going to move from this seat!*

The next morning, after visiting his cousins, Norvel boarded the 310 to Clifton Forge and was arrested for refusing to sit in segregated seating.

# CHAPTER 7

## *September 23, 1948—Regina, Saskatchewan, Canada*

After arriving by train from Winnipeg, Norvel walked to the nearby field house to meet with Ken Goff. On that train, unlike the one he had taken a few weeks previously in Covington, Virginia, he was able to sit anywhere. The other passengers greeted him cordially, just as they had in London the previous month.

It was two days before the Canadian Police Association boxing event was scheduled. With Norvel's status in the international boxing community on the rise and support from the AAU, Howard University agreed that he could be absent at the beginning of the new term so he could participate in the program.

Goff, talking with workers preparing the facility, spotted Norvel when he entered and exclaimed, "Well, if it isn't the great Norvel Lee."

"Yes, sir," responded Norvel. "I finally made it here, uh, uh, a few days later than I was planning to."

"I was getting somewhat concerned," Goff said. "Your fellow boxer, Willie Davis, said you were supposed to be with him, but that you had an unexpected personal matter to attend to."

"Yes, sir."

"Well I'm glad you made it because I wouldn't want to refund all the tickets we've sold for this event. We already had one change. Unfortunately, you won't be going up against Adam. He injured his leg at his family's farm a few days ago, so we are going to match you up against our national light heavyweight champion, Ed Zastre. He's very popular here and is expected to give you a good match, perhaps even better, but please don't tell Adam that."

"I'll just have to get a different mindset then," Norvel said. "Just like when I got back home to see my family."

"Did something happen?" Goff asked, now curious.

"I was arrested for sitting in the white section of a train that had separate sections for white and colored folk."

"I'll be damned! I've heard about those laws, but this is outrageous. Why would anyone arrest a member of the United States Olympic team, especially a nice, respectful man like yourself?" Goff paused and added, "But surely you knew they would do something about it if you sat where you weren't supposed to, didn't you?"

"I've sat there before and they didn't do anything," Norvel said. "I thought things might be changing. Some folks have jumped in to help me fight it. I don't expect much to come out of it, and they said they would pay for everything, so it's no skin off my back."

"Even if your skin is a little darker than theirs," remarked Goff, with a gleam in his eyes.

Norvel smiled and said, "Guess so. I live in Washington, D.C., now where the 'separate but equal' laws are more permissive. My mother was very upset and disappointed with me that I got in this kind of position. That's what bothers me the most about it."

Goff put his hand on Norvel's broad shoulder and said, "It appears you're dealing with it the best you can, Norvel. I'm glad you made it here."

Just then a young woman walked up and looked anxiously at Goff. Her hair was jet-black and her skin was dark brown.

She said, "Mr. Goff, the mayor just called and said he'd like to come over to see how the plan is coming for this weekend."

"Thanks, Matisa," he responded. "Norvel, I'd like you to meet the person that keeps everything on track around here, Matisa Wascana. Matisa, please meet Mr. Norvel Lee. As you know, he is the star from the United States Olympic team we've been promoting for our headline event."

"Oh, Mr. Lee, I have heard all about you from Mr. Goff and Mr. Faul. I am so glad to meet you."

"The pleasure is mine," responded Norvel, finally happy he had left the troubles at home and was in a new city and in the presence of a beautiful woman.

Later that evening, after he worked out on the punching bag, showered, shaved, and cleaned up from his travels, Matisa showed Norvel the small town of Regina and told him about the history of the region.

Matisa explained, "Regina was a planned city that was founded in 1882 as the seat of the Northwest Territories of Canada. Boundaries were redrawn since then, and now Regina is the provincial capital of Saskatchewan. Prior to that, however, the area was called Wascana, meaning Buffalo Bones in Cree."

Norvel said, "It's interesting your last name is the same as the original name of the area."

"I'm Cree," she said. "My ancestors were from here."

Norvel said, "I'm part Indian also. My mother is half Arapaho."

They were delighted to discover a unique connection between them. Norvel asked Matisa if she'd have dinner with him the next evening, and she said she'd enjoy his company. When Friday evening arrived, Norvel was dressed in a suit, Matisa in evening clothes, and they ate at a popular downtown restaurant. Norvel reflected that at home they would have needed to be much choosier selecting a restaurant that would accommodate two dark-skinned people.

On Saturday, the main event of the exhibition, Norvel Lee versus Ed Zastre, was scheduled for 8 p.m. The field house could hold about 2,500 people, and it looked as if every seat was taken by 6 p.m. There were several preliminary fights between Canadians from different regions. But the crowd was there to see the two men from the United States take on their local heroes. The first pitted welterweight Willie Davis against Stoker Alford, the Canadian welterweight champion from Saskatchewan. Davis easily outlasted his opponent.

The crowd was buzzing with excitement when Norvel stepped through the ropes and into the ring. Norvel looked across at his opponent and could see why Goff thought he would be a good match. Zastre almost reached Norvel's height of six feet, two inches, but was leaner, just under the weight limit of 178 pounds for light heavyweights.

The announcer came to the center of the ring with a microphone and, after introducing the referee and the judges, addressed the audience: "Ladies and gentlemen!" His voice reverberated throughout the arena. "This is the final contest of the evening. It will be a five-round event. The judges will award one point to the winner of each round. The opponents will be," said the referee, pointing to Zastre's corner, "Canada's national light heavyweight champion, Eddie Zastreeeeee!"

The crowd cheered loudly for the boxer from Manitoba Province.

The announcer pointed toward Norvel, saying, "And from the United States of America, Olympic boxer Norv-elll Leeeeee!"

The crowd again cheered enthusiastically, this time for Norvel, who enjoyed their excitement.

When the announcer left the ring, the referee came forward and called both boxers to him. He gave them the admonishments; then Norvel and Zastre tapped their gloves together and went to their corners. The bell rang and the boxers came out. Norvel assumed a classic boxing stance—left foot forward, hands up, elbows down, and weight evenly distributed, moving elegantly around his opponent. He directed long flowing jabs to the lower ribcage exposed under Zastre's elbows. Norvel's jabs didn't appear to hurt Zastre, nor did they cause him to lose his balance, but Zastre wasn't able to counter Norvel's attack.

Rounds two and three were similar, but in the fourth Zastre appeared to be tiring. Norvel nailed Zastre with a right, sending him bouncing off the ropes. Zastre tried to counter and Norvel hit him again; while Zastre was trying to move away, Norvel connected with a right cross. The crowd was on its feet, filling the arena with a deafening roar. Norvel won them over with his poise. They were waiting for him to put their boxer on the mat. But the bell clanged, ending the round.

Norvel returned to his corner and thought, *I can try to put this fella down, but why? I've probably won all the rounds and the fight. Don't be a showboat.*

For the fifth and final round, Norvel continued to dance fluidly around

Zastre, connecting with jabs to his body, while Zastre was determined not to be knocked down.

After Norvel was announced the winner and exited the ring, several fans came down to meet and congratulate him. While he was answering their questions, he realized that Goff, Willie Davis, Matisa, Adam Faul, and Zastre were waiting for the fans to leave. When they finally did Faul, on crutches, was the first to shake his hand and greet him. Davis slapped Norvel on the back, and Zastre shook his hand and left to go shower. Then Matisa came up and gave him a slight hug and pat on the shoulder. Finally, Goff stepped forward, congratulated him, and told him again how much he appreciated Norvel making the trip.

Norvel turned to Faul, asking, "What did you do to your leg?"

"Oh, I jumped off the tractor and landed wrong. Doctor says it was a fracture and that it should heal okay."

"How long do you have to wear the cast?"

"Another few weeks, and he told me to watch out for those tractors."

Norvel laughed and noted, "He didn't say anything about boxers, did he?"

Faul put his arm on Norvel's shoulder and said, "No. In fact, he said this injury will help me move around the ring better."

Faul then limped over to commiserate with the other Canadian boxers.

Goff turned to Davis and Norvel and said, "Boys, my wife and I would like the two of you to come over to the house for a Sunday dinner. Matisa will drive you over."

Matisa invited Norvel to attend church services with her in the morning, and Willie Davis also wanted to go. The First Baptist Church was within walking distance of the hostel where the men were staying. They told Matisa they'd walk over in the morning and meet her there.

Norvel and Davis arrived outside the grand old church, one of the many architecturally beautiful structures in Regina, built in 1911. Matisa was not a member of this congregation, but she knew from talking with Norvel that he would choose a Baptist church. She thought by taking them there they could have a genuine Regina experience.

The interior of the First Baptist Church featured a huge domed ceiling and chandelier. A beautiful resonant pipe organ was the highlight of the service for Norvel. Especially moving for him was the congregation singing robustly "How Great Thou Art." Norvel told Matisa that this place of worship was so much grander than the rustic church he attended in Gala. He added that much of his social life revolved around the little church and the segregated schools.

Many members of the congregation recognized the two American boxers from the prior night, and some of them greeted them after the service. Several teenage boys especially gravitated to Norvel, who posed in a boxing stance while showing them how to protect themselves against an opponent. The young men looked at him in awe until their parents came over to shoo them away. Matisa reminded him of their dinner with Ken Goff.

The Goffs lived in the northern part of Regina on several well-kept acres in a former farm house. Matisa took them on a brief tour of the countryside before pulling into the driveway of the Goff home. The men, having shed their coats and ties, stepped out of the car on a sunny autumn day.

Ken Goff's son greeted them and escorted them into the backyard, where there was a long farm table covered in a colorful tablecloth. Mrs. Goff, who insisted on being called Marge, came onto the back porch, smiled, and welcomed the two men. She explained, while pointing to a row of trees, that her husband was chopping some wood.

Matisa followed Marge back into the house to help her finish preparing the food. Norvel and Davis strolled back behind the trees, where they found Goff standing over a log with an ax in his hands, taking a breather.

Norvel took off his shirt, took the ax from Goff's hand, and proceeded very quickly to expertly drive the ax into the log. In a matter of minutes, it was split into neat pieces of firewood.

"Next!" Norvel exclaimed, smiling, his muscular upper chest glistening in the sun.

"You are a man of many talents," observed Goff.

"Uh, uh, yes, sir," said Norvel. "Chopping wood was a constant chore for me and my brothers while growing up. We had a lot of trees around us. They're what kept us warm in the winter."

Davis stood smiling, never having seen a spectacle like this before. He hadn't left his hometown of Philadelphia until he started his Golden Gloves ascent in his mid-teens.

"Men, since it's just the three of us here—and this is between us," Goff said looking at Davis. "You are both impressive young men. I don't know why you're still subjected to prejudices that should have been retired decades ago. Norvel, and you too, Willie, are always welcome here in Regina or anywhere in Canada. I could especially use your help in starting the boxing club I'm planning."

"Thank you, sir," said Norvel.

"And as a further incentive, I believe Matisa is smitten with you," Goff added. "I've known her for a long time and have never seen her so happy to have met someone."

Norvel hesitated a little, while Davis nudged him teasingly.

Norvel finally said, "Well, she's, uh, uh, a nice person and I like being around her."

Goff said, "Well, good, I hope you can get back up here to see her again. I'm trying to arrange another exhibition that would pit you against Adam. And Willie, I'll see if I can get you a match also. It should be a good way to promote the new boxing club."

Norvel said, "I'd enjoy that very much. It will need to be scheduled when I'm on break from Howard."

The men returned to the table after Norvel put his shirt back on. A platter of roast chicken, freshly harvested vegetables from Marge's garden, homemade sourdough bread, and a plate of deviled eggs were laid out, along with two pies. The meal was devoured, the conversation stimulating.

The next day Norvel and Davis walked over to the station for the train ride to Winnipeg, where they'd take a plane back to Washington. Matisa came to say goodbye. Norvel promised he would be back to see her, perhaps at Christmas.

As soon as he returned to Howard, Norvel focused on making up the classes he had missed in Geometry, English Composition, Sociology, and French. He became aware that his day-to-day life and how he spent it was once again entirely up to him. For the past several months, it seemed, a coach or team manager was planning each moment. Those times were exciting, but he was energized about once again being in charge of his life.

French was the most challenging class he was enrolled in. It was his first experience at learning a foreign language.

The first day Norvel walked into the class the professor, Dr. Mercer Cook, asked, "Est-ce le pugiliste dont nous avons tant entendu parler?"

Norvel looked at Dr. Cook quizzically.

"Is this the pugilist we've heard so much about?" Cook repeated, waving his arm around the classroom.

Norvel looked at Dr. Cook and said, "Oui!"

The classroom erupted in applause.

Norvel quickly caught up with all his classes, including French. However, Dr. Cook insisted that his students recite an assignment in French each week. Each time when it was his turn, Norvel was determined to be correct in his pronunciation, trying hard to overcome his frequent stammering episodes. With patience, Dr. Cook and the other class members helped Norvel get through the exercises.

Several weeks after returning to Howard, Norvel received a letter from the AAU. He had been invited to compete in the Canadian Police Association boxing exhibition in Regina, Canada, on December 27. His opponent was expected to be Adam Faul. The letter stated that his travel arrangements were being coordinated between the Canadian Police Association and the AAU.

On October 22, 1948, Howard University's student newspaper, *The Hilltop*, finally recognized Norvel's accomplishments with a brief article about him.

# CHAPTER 8

## *October 26, 1948—Howard University, Washington, D.C.*

Inside the brightly lit Frederick Douglas Memorial Hall at Howard University, Norvel patiently stood in line with twenty-seven other undergraduates, waiting to talk with one of the two uniformed men seated at a table at the far end of the large room.

The U.S. Air Force, in its second year as an independent branch of the U.S. Armed Forces, was recruiting young men for its Reserve Officer Training Corps (ROTC). Although he had not been selected as a pilot and had been denied entry to West Point during his service in World War II, Norvel remained interested in career options that might be available to him in the military. This interest was furthered in August, when President Harry Truman ordered the racial integration of all branches of the Armed Forces. Norvel was also motivated by the $50 per month he would earn as a ROTC member, which would double the stipend he currently received from the G.I. Bill education benefits.

While standing in the queue awaiting his turn to talk with the recruiter, he felt a nudge on his shoulder. Norvel turned and looked at the man smiling broadly at him.

"Uh, uh, Robert Jackson—is that really you?" Norvel exclaimed.

"In the flesh!"

"Are you enrolled here?" Norvel asked.

"Sure am," Robert said.

"Must have been recent, 'cause I've not seen you until this moment."

"I just started last month, as a freshman," Robert said. "The Army finally got my paperwork in order. Since that's the case, I thought I'd better join up here, like I told you I would."

"I started a year ago. I'm a sophomore now," Norvel said. "Now that I think of it, you're the reason I decided to come here."

"Last week I saw an article in *The Hilltop* about a person with the same name as yours being on the Olympic team for boxing," said Robert. "I was thinking that couldn't be the Norvel Lee I knew, but I guess it is. Very impressive, my friend! How'd you get into that?"

"Oh, I just stumbled upon it with some guys overseas. It just kind of happened on its own."

"Well, you should be a big man on campus," Robert said.

"I'm getting a lot of chances to represent the school in amateur events, but I'm just trying to keep up with my classes," Norvel admitted

Just then Norvel was called up to the table. He turned to Robert and said, "I'll wait for you outside if you have time to talk."

The captain asked Norvel to sit down and said, "Good morning. It's an honor to meet an Olympic athlete who represented the United States at last summer's London Games."

"Yes, sir, thank you," Norvel responded humbly, wondering how the officer already knew about him.

"So you're interested in joining the military too?" asked the officer, who was white.

"Yes, sir," said Norvel. "This will be my second time signing up. I joined after high school and served in the U.S. Army Air Corps in the South Pacific."

Norvel handed the now even-more-impressed captain his discharge paperwork.

"Son, I'm very proud of you for taking this initiative, especially after all you've been through. You understand that colored and white are now serving together, don't you?" inquired the officer.

"Yes, sir, it's one of the reasons I want to join. I wanted to be a pilot and was trained to be one at Tuskegee, but never got the chance. Now maybe there, uh, uh, will be more opportunity for me to help serve our country," explained Norvel. He added, "That man standing there, Robert Jackson, also served overseas during the war. We were both assigned to colored units."

The captain enlisted both Norvel and Robert with no further inquiries necessary.

Later, with leaves scattering about the quad from a crisp fall breeze, Norvel and Robert sat down on a bench to talk. The last time they had seen each other was in San Diego, where they received their overseas assignments.

Robert told him about his time spent in Guam. Nothing too exciting happened at the Army Air Base where he was stationed on the island, but racial tensions ran high between Black and white soldiers. The Army was able to keep control over the situation. But at the Marine Corps Base near the town of Agana a race riot erupted on Christmas night, 1944. Afterward, a court of inquiry consisting of military officers and an officer of the NAACP investigated the incident and found evidence of pervasive racial harassment at the station. Both whites and Blacks were among those court-martialed. Robert noticed an effort among the officers to make sure Blacks were treated fairly after tensions settled. He added that the work itself was boring and that he was glad when the war ended and he could return home to Leesburg. Norvel listened to him and said there was a lot of sitting around at his base in Bougainville Island also.

"Hey, let's go get a hamburger," suggested Norvel. "I know a joint just outside the campus gates that caters to Howard students."

Robert said, "Instead of that, let's go over to where I'm staying at 5th and Florida Avenue, unofficially known as Lillie's boardinghouse."

Norvel looked at him quizzically.

Robert continued, "I heard about it through the Howard grapevine and went over there to inquire. Lillie Walton, who runs the place, found room for me. Everyone there is associated with Howard. She's also a real good chef and serves us breakfast and lunch. She'll serve you too, as long as you go to Howard."

"Okay, anyone who wants to give me a meal sits right with me."

Robert introduced Norvel to Lillie, a petite, energetic woman in her forties, who served them lunch. Afterward, they went upstairs so Robert could show Norvel the room he was sharing with a couple of other freshman students.

"This looks comfortable," Norvel said, "even if you have to share the space."

"You could ask 'Mother Dear'—that's what Lillie is called here—to put you on the waiting list for any rooms that come up," suggested Robert.

"Someday maybe, uh, uh, I will. My brother Jimmy and I have an apartment near the campus. We seldom see each other except as strangers passing in the night."

Norvel noticed a photograph on the table next to Robert's bed and asked, "Isn't that the same photo of your family that I saw in Mississippi?"

"Sure enough," Robert said, handing the picture to Norvel.

"I believe you told me that your older sister is about my age," Norvel said. "Little Napoleon is what I think you called her."

"Yes, 'cause she's a fireball, a take-charge person. Yes, we all have nicknames. My younger sister is called Weekie and I'm called Bubba at home."

"If any of them get over here, I'd like to meet them."

"I'm sure we can make that happen when the stars are aligned," said Robert. "My pops is a boxing fan. I know he would enjoy talking with you. And since Leslie is nearby, perhaps we can have lunch with her one day soon. I'm not trying to be a matchmaker or anything, but I believe you will really like her."

"In the photo she looks very pretty and from what you have said about her, I'm sure I would like her," said Norvel. "But I don't have near enough time in my life to get involved right now."

Several weeks later, Norvel and Robert were beginning their weekly ROTC classes. Other than waving to each other from across the quad on the way to or from classes, this was the only time the men saw each other.

As they were leaving the ROTC class, Norvel said, "I look forward to this break from engineering studies. The instructors tend to be reserved and serious. The colonel's style is much more interesting."

"I couldn't agree more," said Robert. "By the way, if you're free over the Thanksgiving weekend, I'd like to invite you to come over to Leesburg to meet my family. I know you'll like it out there."

"Thanks, I'd enjoy that very much," Norvel said. "I don't have any commitments then except to continue my studies of pugilism, but I can do that from anywhere so I will enjoy the break."

"What's pugilism? I haven't heard of that class."

"It's the original Roman name for boxing."

"Hmm, you're a clever man," Robert observed. "I don't know the specific plans yet, but you should plan to stay a couple of nights."

"I'll look forward to meeting everyone," Norvel said. "Thanks for inviting me."


The Friday after Thanksgiving Day, Norvel rode with Robert to a stately mansion under a canopy of trees on Dorset Avenue in Chevy Chase, Maryland, not far from the border with Washington, D.C. As they slowly moved down the leaf-strewn narrow road, they saw a slight young woman standing curbside. She was restlessly looking down the street and then waved impatiently as the car approached.

Robert pulled the car to the curb, and both he and Norvel got out.

"Norvel, I would like to present my sister, Leslie. Leslie, this is Norvel Lee, a friend of mine I met in the service and, again, at Howard."

Leslie looked at her brother and said, "You didn't tell me you were bringing anyone else. I wouldn't have dressed like a housekeeper if I'd known that."

She then turned to Norvel and said, "Pleased to meet you. I'm used to people being taller than me, but you're much taller."

Norvel reached out his hand and said, "Robert has told me a lot about you. I'm glad to put a face to the stories now."

Leslie looked up at Norvel appreciatively as he opened the front passenger door for her while Robert got in on the driver's side. Norvel got into the back seat.

The one-hour drive took them from the Chevy Chase area to the Clara

Barton Parkway, where they crossed the Potomac River, and then into Virginia. Norvel took in the beautiful mid-fall scene rolling by the country road. This way was a change from the train route through Alexandria and past Arlington National Cemetery to points south. State Route 7 meandered through rolling hills. He watched an organized flock of geese in a V-formation heading south.

Leslie turned around in her seat and asked Norvel, "I think I heard a southern accent in your voice."

Norvel replied, "Uh, uh, I'm from a small farming community called Gala. Very quiet area compared to here. Closest larger town is Covington, where my mother's cousins live. We'd go and visit them at times but, uh, uh, it took about an hour over some mountain roads."

"Are you nervous?" Leslie asked. "Is that why you are stumbling around with your words?"

"No," Norvel said. "It's the way God made me."

"Good answer," Leslie observed.

Robert said, "Leslie, be gentle with our guest!"

The car continued to travel past the farms and fields.

"I hear there's not a lot of opportunity for colored people in an area like where you come from. What do people do with themselves there?" asked Leslie.

Norvel said, "They pray a lot."

The three of them laughed and Robert retorted, "Well, we all do that. It doesn't hurt."

"My father, uh, uh, and others did whatever we could," Norvel continued. "Certain times of year everyone was into farming, for our own food and selling at local markets. He and my mother are real industrious, and would always come up with something to do. She would take in clothes and help out the other church ladies. My father also would go up to Clifton Forge and do whatever the railroad needed done. My mother's main objective was to make sure all her children were educated. She is very happy that my brother Jimmy and I are at Howard and our sister, Edna, is over at a teacher's college."

"Very impressive," said Leslie. "And after you graduate, what do you plan to do?"

"My mother wants me and my brother to come back home and become teachers. My major is engineering, and I'm thinking about electrical engineering. I believe many things involving new technology will come to pass during our lifetimes. I may want to be a part of all that. My home place may not have enough opportunities."

"I understand," said Leslie. "Leesburg is likely more open to us than where you're from, but D.C. has many more opportunities."

"We're almost home," Robert announced as houses began to appear out of both sides of the car. SR-7 became Main Street, and then he turned right onto Ayr Street.

Leslie and Robert saw their father in the front yard, raking up some leaves. He waved at them as Robert stopped the car. The next-door neighbor was in his yard doing a chore and also waved at them.

Norvel was the first to get out of the car so he could open Leslie's door. She again appreciated the gesture, smiling and flashing her dark brown eyes at him.

Robert said, "Dad, please meet my friend, Norvel." Turning to Norvel, he said, "My father's name and mine are the same."

Leslie joined them and, while giving her father a kiss on the cheek, said, "Hi, Daddy, taking care of the yard, I see."

"Hi, sweetheart," said Mr. Jackson, then turned to Norvel. "So glad you can join us at Thanksgiving for a few days. We delayed the feast for a day so we could all enjoy being together."

The three of them walked into the large, inviting home and past a parlor where three middle-aged men were engaged in conversation. They looked up but were too engrossed in their discussion to pay attention to them. A woman walked into the room, smiling at Robert and Leslie. A young girl of about ten was with her.

Robert turned and said, "Mom, I'd like to introduce you to my friend,

Norvel Lee. Norvel, please meet my mother, Margaret Jackson.'"

Norvel held out his hand to her and said, "Very nice to meet you."

"The pleasure is ours, Norvel," Mrs. Jackson replied. Turning her attention to the girl, she added, "Weekie, please know Mr. Norvel Lee. This is our youngest, and believe it or not, her name is also Margaret, but we all call her Weekie."

Norvel smiled and said, "It's a pleasure to meet both of you."

They made their way into the kitchen, where three women were preparing the turkey and fixin's.

Mrs. Jackson motioned to the other three ladies and said, "And these are my friends Carrie, Ellen, and Diane. They work with me over at the hospital. Their husbands are in the parlor. We'll let you know when it's time for the feast."

Leslie stayed in the kitchen to help out, while Norvel and Robert joined the men. They introduced themselves as Jacob, Palmer, and Sam. Having known them for many years, Robert was happy to see the men. In the corner was an expensive standup radio playing an Eddy Arnold tune. It reminded Norvel of some of the mountain music he heard as a youngster at home. Another family of relatives entered the house, including a young man introduced as Mervin Jackson, a second cousin.

Norvel mostly listened to the light talk between the men, nodding and adding a comment when expected. After a while he stepped out to the front porch into the brisk November air. The neighborhood was quiet except for two teenage boys tossing a football back and forth in the street.

Robert joined him on the porch and said, "Those are our neighbor's boys. Nice kids, good family."

Norvel said, "And you have a very nice family and a comfortable home. I was pleasantly surprised by the music on the radio. It reminded me of the sound we used to hear around home."

"My mother loves country-and-western music, and the rest of us put up with it," Robert said, and then paused. "Did you enjoy meeting Leslie?"

"Your sister is very attractive, smart, and feisty. I don't think she has much interest in me, especially when I started to stumble over my words," Norvel said.

"Who knows with her, but I could tell my mom was taken with you," said Robert. "Expect her to invite you back. She enjoys having guests around."

Leslie then stepped out onto the porch and told them it was time to eat. Everyone took their seats and Mr. Jackson said grace.

Mr. Jackson looked across to Mervin and asked, "You likin' your new position at Whitmore's helping the customers find what they're looking for?"

Mervin said, "Sure am, sir. I enjoy talking with people instead of being stuck in back moving boxes around."

Leslie noted, "You've been there several years now. It's about time they gave you some responsibility."

Mr. Jackson said, "Now, Leslie, you know Mervin's young. They want him to understand the business before putting him in front of customers. Now that he's twenty, they figure he can address any issues responsibly."

"Daddy, they should have known that from working with you all these years. I think they held back 'cause he's colored," Leslie said emphatically.

"It might be some of that," said Mr. Jackson, "but that's just the way it is. Mr. Whitmore is a fair but realistic man."

Robert changed the subject, saying, "I guess you know Norvel is a Howard University Bison like I am. What you may not know is we met in '44 at Keesler Field in Mississippi before being shipped to different places overseas."

Leslie glanced up at him, attentively.

Mr. Jackson said, "That's interesting. You must have stayed in touch with each other."

"No," Robert said. "It was hard to stay in touch, but when I was signing up for ROTC I saw Norvel in line and we got reacquainted. I've been tryin' to get him to visit us, being a fellow Virginian and all, and I finally got this busy fella to come."

Mrs. Jackson smiled and said, "We're sure happy you could make it, Norvel. We hope this won't be the only time."

"Thank you, ma'am," Norvel said. "Uh, uh, I'm enjoying this very much. It's nice to have a family sit-down meal."

Mr. Jackson asked, "What keeps you so busy on weekends, Norvel?"

Norvel shrugged and said, "Oh, a little of this and a little of that. I have a lot of studies to catch up with."

Robert said, "Norvel, you are infuriatingly low-key. You have so much to brag about, but you don't do any of that."

Weekie asked, "Mr. Lee, what aren't you bragging about?"

Norvel said softly, "I represent Howard University in some boxing tournaments."

Mervin said excitedly, "You're a boxer!"

Robert exclaimed, "Look here. Norvel is a highly ranked championship boxer. And he was a member of the 1948 Olympic team that went to London. One of the few colored men on the team. In September, he was in Canada at the invitation of their Olympic coach. He's going back up there in December again, at their invitation and expense."

Weekie said, "You must be a real hero at your home. You're probably in all the newspapers!"

Norvel shook his head and said, "My little community knew about it, but the wider area, no."

Leslie said, "Again, it's probably because he's a Negro. Not 'knowing his place.'"

Mr. Jackson turned to Norvel and asked, "You were on the Olympic team?"

Norvel nodded his head, "Yes, sir, but I didn't get into a bout. I was an alternate."

Weekie said, "You went to London to be in a boxing match? I've never met anyone who went that far away before!"

Norvel smiled. "It is a long way away. I went back and forth on an ocean liner. It took about a week each way."

The conversation moved on around the table, involving mostly local Leesburg issues and church items. Whitmore's, the general store Mr. Jackson had worked at for many years, was also where friends and neighbors would encounter each other and exchange local gossip. Mr. Jackson was an important person at the store. He could repair anything and was trained as an appliance repair person, one of the few Black men in the area trained in the skill. He was often sent to different areas of Washington, D.C., to deal with a critical repair issue. Because of this, the Jackson clan was well respected in Leesburg, even during the Jim Crow era.

Mrs. Jackson rose from the table, and the other women helped clear off the dishes and bring out the dessert.

Palmer asked Norvel, "How was London compared to Washington, D.C.?"

Norvel said, "It was very civilized there. They're still rebuilding some parts because of the bombing during the war, but I enjoyed myself very much. There was much optimism, and they were excited about hosting us."

Mr. Jackson asked, "What's next in boxing for you?"

"The most important thing for me at Howard is my academics," Norvel said. "Robert and I are also part of the ROTC program, which will give us the choice of being career military people or at least permanent members of the Air Force Reserve. Both of these activities are more important to me than boxing. But I'm proud to represent the school at some national events as long as they pay for it, which they do."

The women brought out six pies. Norvel tried a slice of apple pie so he could compare it to his mother's. It was similar and made him miss his family.

The next day Norvel wanted a conditioning workout. He was going back to Canada in a month for an exhibition match, and wanted to make sure he made a good showing. AAU officials were encouraging him to go up against a variety of other opponents so he could gain some experience for other upcoming international events.

In the morning, when he came down the stairs in athletic clothes and running shoes, he found Weekie at the kitchen table with a coloring book. Sitting next to her was a white boy, about her age.

She greeted him, "Good morning, Mr. Lee."

"Good morning, little sister, who's this?" Norvel asked, looking at the boy.

"Oh, this is Michael Huff, my next-door neighbor. I told him we had an Olympic boxer in the house and he wanted to see you."

Norvel squatted down and said, "Good to meet you, young man. Who's your favorite boxer?"

The boy said, "Joe Louis."

"Me too," said Norvel, laughing. "I'd like to sit and color with you, but right now I'm going to get some exercise."

"Can we come too?" asked Weekie.

"I'm going to run about five miles. It may be too far for your little legs."

"Five miles! Wow!"

"You can come with me up to the corner."

"No, I think we'll stand on the porch and wave!"

"Okay, then. I'm setting out now."

Weekie and her friend walked out the front door with Norvel, who then pulled a jump rope out of his pocket and started moving it around his body. His feet lightly stepped over the rope each time it swung around. He continued for about five minutes, with Weekie and her friend watching him, mesmerized. Leslie, with a cup of coffee in her hand, joined them on the porch and Norvel noticed she was smiling.

As Norvel placed the rope on the porch steps, Leslie said, "Mr. Norvel Lee, there's more to you than I first realized."

Norvel replied, "Thanks, Miss Jackson, I think."

Then he was off and running up the street toward the farm fields in the distance, shadowboxing along the way.

Norvel returned to Regina in time to celebrate Christmas 1948 at the Goffs' house, where he stayed until his room at the hostel near the field house was available. Matisa joined them on Christmas Eve and presented

Norvel with a traditional Cree neck warmer. Norvel was touched by the gift and the Goffs' hospitality. But he was glum about missing the holidays at home with his family. He also found himself thinking of Christmas with the Jacksons, where he knew he would also be welcome.

On December 27, the field house was again packed with spectators. Everyone wanted to see their premier heavyweight champion, Adam Faul, take on this American rising star. Willie Davis couldn't make this trip, so Norvel was the only guest from the States.

The undercard, made up of local Saskatchewan fighters, was appreciated by members of the audience who followed the local boxing scene. Each of these fighters was known to them, but the big draw was the six-round event between Norvel Lee and Adam Faul. Neither had been involved in a fight of this length.

As the contest got under way, Norvel knew he had Faul from the start. Faul had not improved on his flat-footed ways, even though Goff had been working with him. Previously Norvel had encouraged him to practice with a jump rope to learn to keep his feet active. But if Faul had been using a jump rope, its benefits hadn't transferred to the ring yet.

Even though Norvel was quicker and always in motion, constantly dancing around his opponent, Faul lived up to his reputation of not easily being knocked off his feet. By the time the sixth round started, however, it had become clear the only way Faul would win would be to knock Norvel down and out. As hard as Faul tried to land a knockout punch, Norvel was ready for it, dodging it deftly. By the time the bell sounded, ending the match, Norvel had won every round and secured a unanimous decision.

Adam Faul came up to Norvel and put his arms around him, congratulating him on his performance. He also told Norvel that he hoped he would be back in September so they could have a rematch. He promised he would not get tangled up in any farm equipment this time. The crowd, although disappointed in the outcome, was appreciative of the skills Norvel used to defeat his opponent. They also enjoyed seeing the camaraderie between Faul and Norvel.

Norvel stayed long enough in Regina to celebrate the dawning of 1949 with Matisa and her friends. Some of them viewed Matisa and Norvel as a couple. Matisa may have as well. Norvel left on January 1 to return home and resume his studies at Howard University.

# CHAPTER 9

## *Thursday morning, September 15, 1949—*
## *Winnipeg, Canada*

N orvel stepped into a bright autumn day from the lobby of the Fort Gary Hotel. He walked a short block and went across a bridge. A half mile farther, he continued on a path overlooking the large flowing river.

He moved slowly with slumped shoulders, lost in his thoughts, occasionally looking out at the famous Red River of lore.

*Oh Mama. You gave so much to me. You were my foundation, my life's compass. Why now?*

Norvel stopped and pulled from his pocket the folded Western Union telegram, delivered to him the previous hour. He read it again:

CLIFTON FORGE VA SEP 14

NORVEL L LEE

MOTHER WENT TO BE WITH THE ANGELS TODAY BURIAL AT CHURCH SAT JAMES

Norvel wiped a tear from his eye and continued walking along the path. Birds were flitting around the river, diving into the swiftly flowing water, hoping to grab a morsel.

He just wanted to be home with his father, Jimmy, Edna, and George. But it was impossible for him to be home in time for Mama's funeral, even if he were able to afford to fly back to Washington. The train service from Washington to Clifton Forge was sporadic and likely wouldn't get him there in time. Plus, the conductor might recognize him and find a reason not to let him board.

He would have to remain in Winnipeg and muster up interest in the highly anticipated second match against Adam Faul. The Lee–Faul bout was the highlight of the widely promoted boxing tournament.

*She just told me to make her proud. She expects me to follow through with this, no matter what. That's what we do!*

When Norvel had returned to Washington in January 1949, the AAU notified him that the Canadian Police Association had invited him to their annual September event. Norvel accepted it immediately upon learning that the AAU would sponsor his participation. This time, however, the event would be held in Winnipeg, an easier destination to access with its regularly scheduled airline service.

With his boxing acumen well established at Howard, evidenced by his acceptance as a member of the Howard boxing team, he would not have any difficulty missing a week or two of the new term. At the end of the last session he had declared his major to be physical education instead of engineering, at the suggestion of the athletics department. As an enticement, they told him he'd be encouraged to represent Howard University at AAU boxing events, and they would financially support his Golden Gloves pursuits.

Furthermore, the classes he had completed during the first two years were general and would qualify for credit in either major. His rising athletic prominence could potentially open the path to a much-needed scholarship and opportunities for recognition outside Howard University.

Soon after returning home in early 1949, Norvel had received several letters from Matisa, to which he always responded. But their frequency fell off in a few months. Then in August, a month before the start of the boxing exhibition, he received a letter announcing her engagement to a man from northern Canada who was recognized as a chief in the Cree Nation. She said she would remember fondly the special times they spent with each other and would always consider him a treasured friend. Norvel was somewhat taken aback, but knew he shouldn't have been surprised, especially with the recent lack of letters.

Now, grieving for his mother, he continued along the river path. He lost track of time but eventually noticed the sun was high above him and the buildings of downtown Winnipeg were off in the distance. He found a rock and sat down. Norvel hummed the tune from a haunting new country song he'd heard "I'm So Lonesome I Could Cry" by Hank Williams. After what seemed like an eternity, a feeling of resolve came over him and he walked back to his lodgings.

That evening the Crescent Boxing Club, local sponsors of the event, held a dinner for organizers and participants in the exhibition. Norvel was invited to sit at Ken Goff's table, where his opponent was also seated. Norvel and Adam Faul had enjoyed each other's company socially the several times they both participated in boxing events. To each of them, athletic competition was one thing and being friends another. There did not appear to be any hard feelings on Faul's part that Norvel had beaten him nine months ago.

Goff inquired about the legal situation regarding the segregated train car that he'd faced the previous year. Norvel simply told him it was resolved, without elaboration.

As the evening progressed, Norvel made small talk with Goff and the others. No mention of Matisa came up, nor did Norvel mention his mother's death. Goff once again extended his offer to Norvel to help him manage the boxing facility in Regina that he had opened earlier in the year. Norvel thanked him graciously for the offer, but said he wanted to pursue his education.

Saturday, the day of the bout, Norvel walked around Winnipeg getting his body loose and his mind focused. He wanted this day to be over soon, so that tomorrow he'd be able to return to Washington. He knew that this experience and the genuine people he encountered in Canada would stay with him for a lifetime. But he also sensed he had many dreams to pursue and that they would not be realized in Canada.

By the time he entered the massive, wooden Winnipeg Amphitheater on Colony Street, a few blocks from the Fort Gary Hotel, he felt renewed, with a sense of direction about where his life was heading. He sensed his mother's presence, knowing she was being laid to rest back in Gala, Virginia, that very day. His time strolling around included another pass by the Red River for personal reflection. He was thankful he could envision the beautiful little cemetery at the Rising Mount Zion Baptist Church that was so much a part of his childhood.

*You will be proud of me, Mama. You will be proud of me.*

The main event of the exhibition was scheduled for 8:30 p.m. As was the case for his match against Faul in Regina, the five-thousand-seat arena was fully populated with excited fans who wanted to see their Canadian heavyweight finally beat the "American Negro from Washington, D.C.," as promoted in the *Winnipeg Tribune*.

Norvel went into the locker room, where an attendant showed him to his locker. Norvel noticed Faul on the other side of the room.

Norvel went over and said, "Good evening, Adam. How are you feeling?"

"Good to see you, my friend," Adam said. "I'm feeling quite good, and you?"

"Uh, uh, I'm okay," Norvel said. "Let's you and I have a good showing for these folks. Best of luck to you."

"You, as well, Norvel."

Norvel's routine was straightforward. He changed from his street clothes into his boxing shorts and shirt. His gray athletic shirt for this fight displayed "Howard" in navy-blue red-tinged letters with a caricature of a bison, the school mascot, on the front. He took his jump rope to an area outside the locker room with a high ceiling. First he twisted his torso back and forth, left and right, increasing the intensity of his twist during each iteration of the exercise. He then widened his legs to a stance with his feet in their usual inward-pointing direction, and leaned over to touch his toes. Up and down he went, making sure he could feel the back of his thighs stretching. Finally he picked up his jump rope and started easily moving it around his body. He continued to jump for several minutes until he broke into a light sweat. Afterward, he found a mirror and shadowboxed.

When he finished his short warm-up, he saw Ken Goff smiling at him in the mirror. Goff came over and placed his hand on his shoulder.

"I wish you best of luck out there, even though I'm Adam's coach," he said genuinely. "I hope we can stay in touch with each other. You are a good man, and I'll always be curious about how things are for you."

"Thank you, sir," Norvel responded. "Best of luck to you as well. I appreciate everything you and Mrs. Goff have done for me and all your support."

Norvel was the first to enter the main arena, the spotlight highlighting his dark purple boxing robe with his name stenciled on the back. The crowd came alive, cheering him as he walked down the aisle.

Then Adam Faul entered the arena, and the crowd came to its feet with thunderous applause. He turned and waved at the fans, smiling and looking around the entire arena.

The announcer stepped to the middle of the brightly lit boxing ring, pulling along a microphone. He said in a loud, resonant voice, "Ladies and gentleman. The Crescent Boxing Club, with the support of the Canadian Police Association, is proud to present tonight's main event. This is a five-round matchup of heavyweights, both of them Olympians!"

The spectators roared in anticipation.

"In the corner to my right," the announcer continued, "from the United States of America, a student at Howard University in Washington, D.C., and a member of the United States 1948 Olympic team—Norvel Lee!"

Norvel, who was standing, turned and acknowledged the crowd. The spectators again cheered respectfully. It was clear from his demeanor that he was focused on the task at hand.

"And in the corner to my left is the Canadian heavyweight champion, a member of the Canadian 1948 Olympic team, from Regina, Saskatchewan—Adam Faaaaul!"

Faul rose up from his chair, assumed a boxing pose, and punched at the air around him. The Canadian audience was on its feet, cheering and clapping wildly. He smiled and waved to the throng of spectators.

The announcer introduced the referee and then went to the side, stepping through the ropes. With a wave of his hands the referee invited the two boxers to meet him in the center of the ring.

The referee took the nearest gloved hands of each boxer and said, "Gentlemen, you know the rules. Let's have a clean fight. Now touch your gloves, get back to your corners and wait for the bell."

The two boxers touched their gloves together and then retreated to their corners. Goff gave Faul a few last-minute instructions. Norvel didn't have a personal trainer with him, but the Crescent Boxing Club provided a corner man to towel him off between rounds.

The bell sounded and both men sprang out to the center. Faul was dancing around better than he'd done last year. It was obvious Goff had convinced him that being lighter on his feet would help overall. They danced around each other, both getting a feel for their opponent's reach by extending their hands to tap the other's body. Then, about a minute into round one, Faul unleashed two powerful punches that missed their mark because Norvel moved away. Right after the second one, Norvel sent a right and then a left into Faul's body, straightening him up somewhat but doing little damage. The crowd groaned.

They danced around each other a little more, and with about thirty seconds left in the round, Norvel landed several powerful body punches that caused Faul to utter, "Oomph!"

Although he tried to get his hands up to protect himself, he wasn't quick enough, and Norvel landed two more hard punches. Faul staggered, but the bell sounded. He went back to his corner, where Goff was waiting. Faul sat down on his chair.

In the other corner Norvel remained standing, looking at the timer, waiting for round two. When it rang, Norvel quickly regained the center of the ring, dancing, waiting on Faul. Norvel started right where he left off, sending equally powerful rights and lefts toward his opponent. This time Faul danced away, keeping his guard up, causing Norvel's strikes to glance off him. Clearly, he was following Goff's instructions. But while doing so,

Faul was unable to take an offensive position. He was constantly retreating or moving away, keeping his body protected. As in the first round, with about thirty seconds remaining, Norvel moved in and was able to score several forceful punches to Faul's body.

The third round followed the same script. Faul was on the defensive and Norvel danced around, flirting with opportunities to strike. He found them near the end of the round as Faul started tiring. After the third round, Norvel realized that the only way he'd lose was if Faul somehow scored a knockout against him. In his brief boxing career, no one yet had been able to score a knockout, technical or otherwise, against him.

In the fourth round, Faul, realizing he needed to knock out Norvel, came out aggressively. But Norvel danced away, keeping his distance and occasionally punching back when he had the opportunity. Faul was clearly becoming frustrated, and at one point stood his ground in the middle of the ring, taunting Norvel to come get him. The crowd noise was deafening at this point, but neither fighter was aware of it. Norvel moved in close before the end of the fourth round and scored a couple of powerful strikes to Faul's body.

During the break between the fourth and fifth rounds, Norvel realized he could probably go after Faul and knock him down. He decided it wasn't really necessary at this point. He didn't want to embarrass his friend and certainly not his unexpected mentor, Ken Goff. So at the start of the final round five, Norvel simply kept moving back and forth and, with restraint, jabbed at the Canadian.

Faul, on the other hand, was desperate, and his fans knew it. They were trying to urge him on. They wanted to see him knock Norvel down, but it was clear the American had this fight well under control. Faul did try to land some big knockdown punches, but Norvel just batted them away.

Finally the bell sounded, and the fight was over. Faul and Norvel embraced at the center of the ring while the crowd remained on their feet, appreciating the good sportsmanship. The two men retired to their corners.

When the announcer and referee came back out to the center of the ring, the referee motioned for the two boxers to join him.

The announcer said, "Ladies and Gentleman. I have the results of the just-completed main event boxing match between these two great Olympians, Norvel Lee and Adam Faul. By a unanimous decision, the judges have found that Norvel Lee is the winner!"

The referee held Lee's hand in the air, and the crowd cheered enthusiastically.

Faul then leaned over to Norvel and said, "Norvel, you're one helluva boxer. The best I have ever faced, even in the Olympics. I hope you'll continue to pursue boxing. Let's keep in touch."

"Thanks. I'll always have fond memories of my time spent in Canada, getting to know you and the other athletes. If you come to Washington, please let me know."

Across the ring, Ken Goff smiled and doffed his hat to Norvel.

# CHAPTER 10

## *Thanksgiving, 1949—106 South Ayr Street, Leesburg, Virginia*

N orvel was again invited to join the Jacksons for Thanksgiving. He was warmly welcomed by the family and their friends when he arrived at their Leesburg home.

In September, when he returned from Canada, Norvel had traveled to Gala to mourn his mother. He prayed alone at her simply marked grave in the cemetery next to the Rising Mount Zion Baptist Church. Afterward, he immersed himself in his studies at Howard. The process renewed his psyche and confidence, restoring his vision of a future. He contemplated dropping out of competitive boxing, feeling that it distracted from his education and the long-term objective of graduating. But he kept in top physical shape by running, jumping rope, and working the punching bag.

After the Thanksgiving dinner Norvel went out to the porch for some fresh air. In a few minutes Leslie joined him.

"Another very nice Thanksgiving at the Jacksons," Norvel said, smiling down at her.

"Yes, it was," she agreed. "And it's nice to see you here again this year. Robert tells me you lost your mother in September. I'm so sorry."

"It, uh, uh, was a shock for the entire family," said Norvel solemnly. "I was in Winnipeg, Canada, when she literally dropped dead. Everyone says she's in a better place now, but I think she was too young to leave this world."

"Tell me about her," Leslie said, looking up at him sympathetically.

"She was part Arapaho," said Norvel. "She was very involved with our church. Her most valuable possession was the family Bible, which she read to us every night. She was the only one allowed to touch the Bible. She expected a lot from all of us, including my father. Making sure her children were educated was very important to her."

"And how is your father taking all this?" she asked.

"He doesn't know what to do with himself," Norvel said, with a look of concern. "She was like a mother to him also, doing everything for him, nurturing him. She was six years older. And our youngest brother, George, is only twelve. I believe my father is going to send George up to Covington to live with family."

Leslie stepped forward and gave Norvel a sympathetic squeeze on his arm, letting him know things would work out the way they were supposed to. Norvel looked her in the eyes and saw genuine caring.

A month later, Norvel was invited back to Leesburg, this time by Mrs. Jackson, to enjoy the Christmas holidays with them. He was now comfortable on Ayr Street, sharing Robert's bedroom with him. The entire Jackson family and a collection of cousins and guests were also there. The house was decorated both inside and out, a new experience for Norvel. He stayed in the Jacksons' Leesburg home for most of the holidays leading up to the new year. Norvel divided his time between talking with Leslie, and listening to Mrs. Jackson's many stories.

He also spent some time showing the teenage boys, including next-door neighbor Michael Huff, the fundamentals of boxing. He showed them how to jump rope and demonstrated shadow-boxing techniques and he went for long runs, with the boys tagging along for part of the way.

A few days after Christmas, Mr. Jackson, or Emmett as he preferred to be called, joined Norvel and the boys in the front yard. The weather was unseasonably warm. "I see you are helping those young fellas learn how to train for a fight," he said.

"Yes, Lester was watching me work the rope a few days ago, so I gave him some tips. They all now have jump ropes and are imitating my routine," Norvel said.

"You're a good example to them," observed Emmett. "You planning to keep with the boxing this coming year?"

"Yes, sir," said Norvel, "at least for this year if I can also concentrate on my studies. They always come first, not boxing.

Emmett said, "From what I hear, you are recognized by the AAU as someone who has a chance at being a national champion. I imagine the Howard coaching staff is pushing for that."

*Where did he hear that from?* Norvel asked himself. *I suppose if I work hard enough, I'll have a shot at it. It's exciting to think about, anyway.*

Michael Huff came up to the two men and started twirling his jump rope, then handed it to Norvel to show him how to do it again. Norvel took the rope and started whirling it around. The other boys and Mr. Jackson watched him in awe. Norvel looked up and saw Leslie standing on the porch watching as well. She smiled broadly at him.

The weather held for the rest of the week with the temperature falling slightly on Saturday, New Year's Eve. The Jacksons hosted a large gathering at their home to welcome 1950. The group included Black and white employees of Whitmore's, including Mr. Whitmore, and fellow worshipers from Providence Baptist Church and from the Mount Zion Methodist Episcopal Church. Mrs. Jackson preferred Methodism, but on Sundays she yielded to Emmett's Baptist preferences, where he was a deacon. The Jacksons were known and welcome in both denominations.

Norvel socialized with many of the guests at the gathering and noticing that Leslie stood next to him most of the evening. A number of people asked him about his experiences on the Olympic team two years ago.

The music consisted of Mrs. Jackson's favorite country-and-western albums, mostly from the popular Eddy Arnold. There were champagne bottles in the kitchen waiting for the midnight hour so they could be opened, although imbibing alcoholic beverages was not the custom at the Jacksons' house. It was only for celebrations that required a toast. Many of the men smoked cigarettes and cigars outside in the crisp air.

As midnight approached Weekie and her cousin Mervin began to serve crystal glasses of champagne. Norvel found he was standing alone with Leslie, each holding their glass of champagne. He turned to her and said, "You know, Leslie, I'd like to see you more up in Washington. Do you think we could go have dinner, maybe see a movie some evening when the people you work for give you some time for yourself?"

She smiled and said, "I would enjoy that very much. Mrs. Henry will surely give me some time. She's also interested in my efforts at the library."

"What efforts are those?" Norvel asked.

The noise in the room picked up as they watched the second hand on the grandfather clock begin its last time around for 1949. When the hand showed ten seconds to go, Emmett said loudly, "Ten!"

The other people at the party joined in unison, "Nine, eight, seven, six, five, four . . . !"

Norvel and Leslie looked directly into each other's eyes and said together, "Three, two, one, Happy New Year!"

They each took a quick sip from their champagne glasses and then kissed, and held their kiss.

The moment was not missed by Mrs. Jackson, who nudged her husband. He discreetly peeked at their daughter. They both smiled. Their oldest child finally seemed to be interested in someone and they thought it might be a good match. They were pleased that Norvel was mature and ambitious. They knew Leslie would help him smooth over his social awkwardness if he allowed her to.

# CHAPTER 11

## *January 5, 1950—Howard University, Washington, D.C.*

N orvel, working up a sweat as he pounded away at the bag, didn't notice Coach Barnes standing by and watching him. When he did he stopped, leaving the bag swinging back and forth.

"Hey, Norvel," Coach Barnes said, greeting him with a solicitous smile. "Looks like you still have it, after the holiday break."

"Hi, Coach," Norvel said.

"I'm sure you realize we have big plans for you this year," the Coach volunteered.

"And, uh, uh, what would those plans be?" asked Norvel, having an idea of what was coming.

"We believe you have a shot at getting into the national tournaments for both the AAU and the Golden Gloves. And, of course, there are the regular season CIAA events our team is scheduled for."

"A lot expected from me, then," Norvel observed.

"I believe you're the quality contender of this bunch," Barnes explained. "If that turns out to be the case, then you should expect to be in the Golden Gloves finals in March in New York and the national AAU championship in April. Those will be in Boston. But first we've got to start locally. Next Tuesday we've got you over at Fort Meade going against a serviceman, Army I believe."

"What about my studies," Norvel asked, "and ROTC? If I miss classes, they might drop me from the program."

"That's the other piece of news I have for you. Howard University will be providing a scholarship to you. You are representing the Bisons spectacularly at the national level. In exchange, they are willing to make sure you eventually get the education you came here for. Your classes and ROTC will be flexible about your schedule."

Norvel was elated, profusely thanking Coach Barnes for the opportunity.

The next morning, before either of them needed to be in class, Norvel met Robert for breakfast at the boardinghouse. Norvel told him what Coach Barnes had said about the scholarship, and added that he thought he shouldn't pass up this opportunity, but he wanted to see if Robert saw any pitfalls looming.

As they were waiting for their breakfast, Robert said, "What's the worst that could happen? You're getting your education paid for, man!"

Norvel said, "I know. That's what my mother wanted."

"I'm sure she'd be very proud of you," Robert said.

"By the way, I'm planning on asking your sister out on a date," announced Norvel. "I told her I would when we were in Leesburg celebrating the New Year."

"It's about time," Robert said. "Everyone's been wondering when you might do that."

"I plan to very soon after I finally get my own car," Norvel said. "My mother left me some money she'd stowed away, and now with the scholarship, I think I can buy one. I just hope I don't get my nose broken in one of the matches Coach Barnes and Mr. Drake have lined up."

"I see. I can't do anything about a broken nose, but don't let not having a car stop you from asking Leslie out. You can borrow mine," Robert said.

"Okay, I appreciate it. But won't Leslie think it's strange to come out in her brother's car?"

"It's no matter!" said Robert. "She don't care about any of that showmanship. What are you thinking of getting?"

"Uh, I'm thinking about a Mercury Eight, maybe last year's model. They have a good reputation."

Robert said, "That's a good idea if you can afford it. I can come with you and help you get a good deal. You should be able to get one if you're coming in with cash."

"Yes, I'm going to. I learned from my father that people sometimes try to take advantage of us, thinking colored people don't know what we're doing," Norvel said emphatically. "Borrowing money is never good except for a house or in an emergency."

"For a pugilist, you're pretty smart," Robert teased.

Then Robert looked over at Lillie, who was cleaning up the dishes, and said, "Mother Dear, could you bring Norvel here a mimeographed copy of 'The List,' if you have any left?"

Norvel looked at him curiously.

"Lillie handed these out a few weeks ago," explained Robert. "The All Souls Church over on Harvard Street puts out a list of restaurants where all races are seated. I thought if you were thinking of taking my sister out, you might want to avoid any incidents."

Lillie came back with a copy and handed it to Norvel.

RESTAURANTS IN THE DISTRICT OF COLUMBIA
which are reported to serve meals
to well behaved persons irrespective of race

**LOWER CONNECTICUT AVENUE, NW**

AVC Clubhouse, 1751 New Hampshire NW
Ben Bow, 1636 Connecticut Ave. NW
Istanbul, 1742 Connecticut Ave. NW
Fan & Bill's, 1132 Connecticut Ave. NW
Harvey's, 1107 Connecticut Ave. NW
Jade Bowl, 1018 Vermont Ave. NW
Linda's Buffeteria, 1819 M Street NW
Mayflower Hotel, Connecticut Ave. NW
McReynolds Pharmacy, 18th & G NW
New Athens, 1741 K Street NW
New Bagdad, 1733 Eye Street NW
New Smorgasbord Rest., 2641 Conn. Ave. NW
Normandy, K between 16 & 17 NW
State Drug, 1901 Pa. Avenue NW
Statler Hotel, 16th & K Streets NW
YMCA, 1736 G Street NW
YWCA, 17th & K Streets NW

**NEAR ALL SOULS' CHURCH**

Bronaugh's Drugs, 3401 14th St. NW
Judd's Pharmacy, 2750 14th Street NW
Kresge's 5 & 10¢, 3116 14th Street NW
Murphy's 5 & 10¢, 3128 14th Street NW
New Amsterdam Drug, 2701 14th St. NW
Smith's Pharmacy, 2518 14th Street NW
Woolworth's 5 & 10¢, 3200 14th NW
Zoo Park Restaurant, ZOO

**NORTHEAST**

Alhambra (Weber's), 402 H Street NE
Dailey's Drugs, 1324 Florida Avenue NE
Gallaudet Pharmacy, 1000 Florida Avenue NE
H.L. Green, 1121 H Street NE
Kresge 5 & 10¢, 1107 H Street NE
Mayfair Drug, 1800 D Street, NE
Montello Pharmacy, 1609 Montello NE
McBride 5 & 10¢, 700 H Street NE
Woolworth's 5 & 10¢, 1113 H Street NE
Woolworth's 5 & 10¢, Minn. & Benning NE
Rhode Island Plaza, 2705 13th Street NE

**SOUTHEAST AND SOUTHWEST**

Stadium Pharmacy, 130 19th Street SE
Kresge 5 & 10¢, 666 Pennsylvania Ave SE
Triangle Restaurant, 1125 Maine Ave. SW

**DOWNTOWN SHOPPING AREA, NW**

A-1 Restaurant, 1003 E Street NW
Executive Pharmacy, 909 Pa. Ave. NW
Globe Pharmacy, 1133 11th Street NW
Greyhound Terminal, 1114 N.Y. Ave. NW
Kresge's 5 & 10¢, 1101 G Street NW
Mayflower Donut Shop, 1309 F Street NW
Murphy's 5 & 10¢, 1214 G Street NW
Nanking Restaurant, N.Y. at 9th NW
Neisner's 5 & 10¢, 1120 G Street NW
Pa. Drug Co., 1301 E Street NW
Trailway Depot, 1201 N.Y. Ave. NW
Willard Hotel Coffee Shop, 14th & Pa.

**MID CITY AREA, NW**

China Cafe, 1336 You Street, NW
Elks Raw Bar, 1104 You Street, NW

**7TH STREET SHOPPING AREA**

Balanis, 602 F Street NW
Goldenberg's Dept. Store, 7th & K NW
F & W Grand, 5 & 10¢, 400 7th Street NW
Hecht's, 7th & F Street NW
Hood Rexall Drug, 443 7th Street NW
Jenner's Sandwich Shop, 402 9th NW
Kann's, 7th and Pa. Avenue NW
Kresge's 5 & 10¢, 7th & E Street NW
Lansburgh's, 7th & E Streets NW
McCrory's 5 & 10¢, 826 7th Street NW
Super Cut Rate Drug, 1110 7th NW
Woolworth's 5 & 10¢, 406 7th Street NW

**ALL FEDERAL BUILDING CAFETERIAS**

**CAPITOL HILL AREA**

Union Station Gateway Restaurant
Methodist Bldg. Cafeteria, 110 Md. NE
Parker Pharmacy, N. Cap. & Rhode Island
Rhode Island Pharmacy, 1830 1st NW

(In addition to the restaurants listed
above, a number of restaurants have said
they do not refuse to serve anyone because
of race, but for various reasons do not
wish to be placed on this list.)

Please report the names of other restaurants which should be included, after checking,
in subsequent lists.

If service is refused at any of the above, please inform us at once.

*Robert's right* Norvel thought. *No way do I want an "incident" with his sister. When's this going to end? Our military accepts us. Why can't everywhere in the capital?*

Later that day Norvel worked up the nerve to meet Leslie at the market where she bought groceries for the family she worked for as a governess. She was surprised when he appeared at her side in one of the shopping aisles.

"Norvel!" Leslie exclaimed. "What a coincidence to find you here."

"It's not a coincidence," Norvel said. "Knowing I might run into you here gives me the chance to ask you something."

"And what might that be?" Leslie asked.

"Would you like to go to a movie with me?"

"Norvel Lee! Are you asking me out on a date?"

"Yes, ma'am, I suppose I am," Norvel said, glowing.

On Saturday, Norvel, in a charcoal gray suit and dark tie over a white shirt, drove Robert's old Ford over to the house where Leslie worked. She was wearing a dark full skirt that hung just below her knees. It had a tightly cinched waist that Norvel found very appealing on her small frame. Beneath her wool coat she wore a tan blouse. On her head was a stylish hat, and her hands were covered with black wrist-length gloves.

They left the car in the parking lot next to the Savoy Theater on 14th Street in the Columbia Heights area, not far from Howard University. Norvel had not been there to see a movie, but he knew from talking to others that colored were permitted in the theater as long as they sat in the rear portion. The movie they saw was *Adam's Rib*, starring Spencer Tracy and Katharine Hepburn. It brought amused laughter from both of them.

Afterward, they walked one block up to the diner inside G. C. Murphy's Five and Dime, Norvel towering over her as they strolled down the street. The List said that Murphy's seated all "well behaved persons." He led them to a table, pulling her chair out for her as she sat down. Leslie ordered strawberry ice cream, and Norvel had a banana split.

"Did you enjoy the movie?" Leslie asked.

"Uh, uh, I thought it was funny and clever, but I haven't seen many movies," he admitted. "The first time I saw one was in the service. They showed us several Westerns, I suppose to help with morale. I like the scenes of the Wild West. Do you like movies?"

"Yes, for an escape from the everyday," she said. "I saw a lot of movies in Leesburg. We had to sit in the back, but sometimes it's better for viewing the movie."

"Robert tells me you like libraries," said Norvel.

"Yes, because it's where all the books are," she said, laughing. "Books are what you learn from, and the library has them for free. I started a program at our library for donating books to children who didn't have access to them. I try to do the same thing here. The Mrs. I work for supports what I'm doing. She's a nice person. She lets me have every other weekend off, so I can go to Leesburg to be with my family."

"Your family are good people," Norvel said. "It seems like there is always some activity going on there."

"Yes, I miss that. But the reason I need to be there more now is because my grandmother is not doing well. I can help them take care of her when I'm able to get out there."

"You like helping folks, don't you?"

Leslie said, "Yes, I do. You know, my mother told me you are welcome any time. Even if Robert doesn't come, you can use his room. It would be especially nice if you would come out on the weekends I plan to be there. And just so you know, the Jacksons are accepted in all the eateries in Leesburg."

Norvel laughed and said, "That's very nice of your mother to make me feel welcome. Your parents are in the perfect location for me to get my road runs in. It looks like I'm going to have to be in tip-top shape these coming months."

After finishing their coffee and dessert, Norvel took Leslie back to the house and escorted her to the gate. They kissed, and he watched her walk over to the side door of the mansion. Just as she opened the door she looked out toward the gate, saw Norvel standing there, and waved at him before she went inside.

On January 10, Glenn Drake drove Norvel to Fort Meade, Maryland. There Norvel took on the enlisted Army man known as "Hammerin' Hank" Ebron. In front of a small group of onlookers, Norvel wore him out and easily won a unanimous decision.

The following Saturday, Robert drove Norvel to a Mercury automobile showroom in Bethesda, Maryland, where an older salesman approached them. Plastering a condescending smile on his face, he said, "I'm betting you boys would like to be driving something like this if only you could figure where to get the money from."

They were standing next to a brand new maroon Mercury coupe. Norvel and Robert walked around the automobile, and then Norvel asked, "How much are you asking for it?"

The salesman said, "Boy, this is way out of your price range. Now out there," he pointed to the parking lot, "we have some older gems which we might be able to set up a payment program for, if you qualify for the terms."

Norvel looked down at the man and said, "This is the car I want. How much is it?"

The man looked at some papers in his hand and said, "Its $1,850, but I don't think we can get anyone to lend you the money to buy it."

Norvel said, "I don't want to borrow any money, I don't believe in buying stuff I can't afford, and you're right, this is a little steep for me."

Robert stepped in and said, "Mr. Lee will give you $1,500 in cash right now for this beauty."

The salesman said, "You know you'll have to buy insurance too."

Norvel said, "I'll get my insurance through the U.S. Air Force, of which I'm a member."

The salesman went to talk to his manager. After about fifteen minutes he came out and said, "Here is what we'll do. We can't let this one go at that price. But we have one in the back that our manager has been using as a demonstrator. It has low mileage on it and if you boys are going to pay cash, we can let you have it for $1,400 if you buy it today. I'll get the paper work ready if you can give me a $250 deposit and then go make arrangements for the insurance. When you come back with the proof of insurance and the rest of the money you can drive off with the car."

"Thank you, sir," said Norvel, shaking the salesman's hand. "Let's go take a look at it."

They went back behind the building and inspected the automobile. It looked identical to the one in the showroom. Norvel indicated his approval.

Just then, Robert interrupted and said, "Norvel, $1,400 seems a little steep for a used car—$1,200 would be fairer."

Norvel looked at the salesman, raising his eyebrows.

The salesman looked at the two young men and said, "I will take $1,300 for it. That's my final offer."

Norvel completed the paperwork, and the manager came into the office to check it. He looked at Norvel and said, "Norvel Lee. Are you the boxer everyone is talking about?"

"Possibly. I'm on the Howard University boxing team."

"Oh, the word in the papers is you're potentially more than just another collegiate boxer, although they're saying you are going to lead your school team to another championship for the colored schools, like you did last year. I saw you in last year's Golden Gloves match at Uline. I have to admit, I was troubled about opening it up to everyone, but when I saw you I changed my view. Those start again this coming week, I believe. Are you entered?"

"Yes, sir, I am."

"Well, I am a fan of the sport. You have a very nice style, and I will be rooting for the best for you, Norvel."

"Thank you, sir, I hope it works out as well this year."

On January 19, at the Uline Arena, Norvel scored a technical knockout against John Sullivan when the referee mercifully halted the match in the first round.

The next evening, Norvel and Robert drove to the estate on Dorset Street in Norvel's new Mercury coupe, surprising Leslie, who was expecting to see Robert's old Ford. She congratulated Norvel on his purchase and commented how nice it was to see him in his new car.

That weekend in Leesburg, was a continuation of the uncommonly warm weather. When they arrived at the Ayr Street home, not only Mr. and Mrs. Jackson but also neighbors up and down the street, including several of the teenage boys, came out to admire the shiny auto.

During dinner, Norvel described his anticipated schedule for the next few months' boxing events, and added that he had the full support of Howard University. Leslie smiled when he said he thought Leesburg was the ideal place for him to get his training runs in. He told them how important it was to build up and maintain his endurance while keeping his legs strong and limber.

That evening when Norvel went to the room he shared with Robert, he saw a container lying on his bed labeled Dial Roll-On Deodorant. He was looking at it when Robert entered the room, and Norvel held up the item up with a questioning look on his face.

Robert simply said, "You know, with women, it's always something. My advice to you, my friend, is to just start using it before you dress and not say anything about it to anyone."

Norvel said, "Okay, will do."

The next day, after breakfast, Norvel sat in the front parlor reading his social studies textbook, preparing for an exam the following week. When he finished, he got ready to go out for a long run. Leslie said the family would like to follow him in their automobile, so they could all see how he trained.

Twenty minutes later, Norvel, dressed in shorts and a sleeveless white shirt, came down to the front porch. Waiting for him were Robert, Leslie, cousin Mervin, and Weekie.

"Okay, Norvel, we'll follow you in the car," Robert said. "If you get tired, you can get in or take a rest."

"I won't get tired," Norvel said confidently. "But I'll enjoy the company."

He took off running and, with the Ford following, kept going for about five miles. When they got to the intersection of SR-7 and SR-9, Norvel put his hand up in the air and made a circle, indicating this was the turnaround point. The Ford made a turn and fell back in behind him.

It was a beautiful winter day. The farm fields were dry and golden brown. The sky was clear, and the riders were enjoying the scene of Norvel running and shadowboxing. When they returned Norvel showered, making sure he used the deodorant, and then he and Leslie walked over to the Leesburg cinema.

On Sunday morning, Norvel and Leslie walked, while the other Jackson family members drove, to Providence Baptist Church. The family and Norvel entered the simple white wooden structure through the double-door entry and chose pews near the front. They were excited about hearing what the dynamic young preacher, Reverend Huston Brooks, had to say. Reverend Brooks moved to Leesburg from Alexandria after the previous preacher resigned. As the sermon progressed, everyone, including Norvel and Leslie seated in the pew behind her family, appreciated the new preacher's vibrant energy.

Norvel enjoyed being with Leslie and her family, so much so that, when their schedules gelled, it became his routine.

During the next two weeks, Norvel competed in two local weekday Golden Glove matches at Uline. The first was against Edgar Smith from the local YMCA, where there was a boxing program. Drake assured Norvel that he didn't expect him to run up against any significant competition from Smith, who was seventeen.

But as the first round got under way, Norvel saw a youngster who boxed with unexpected maturity. He moved with experience, flicking short jabs and landing several to Norvel's jaw and one to his nose. Near the end of the first round Smith went at Norvel with a flurry, catching him on the side of his head with a powerful right cross that caused Norvel's legs to buckle, almost sending him to the mat.

While wiping Norvel down between rounds, Drake said, "He's just trying to intimidate you. Don't take the bait. Just maintain your poise and when the kid lets loose, coolly counter. You hear me?"

Norvel nodded. He looked out at the half-filled arena and spotted the manager for the Mercury dealership several rows back. He encouraged Norvel by shouting something unintelligible and waving his arms in a boxing motion.

When he went out for the second round, Norvel focused on maintaining a classic stance while bobbing and weaving. Nevertheless, Smith was able to land some inside hits and nearly connected with another cross to the head. By the time the round ended, Norvel thought the judges could call it either way. But in the third round Norvel finally found his stride and caught the youngster off guard by landing many undefended jabs and punches.

Norvel was worried the judges might award Smith the first two rounds. But they gave the second round point to Norvel, resulting in a 2-1 victory. The following week, however, he had no difficulty against Eddie Grant, 3-0.

Norvel immersed himself in training for his upcoming matches in New York. In spite of the intensity of his schedule, which included his academic studies, he found time to accompany Leslie out to Leesburg three more times in January and February.

The national Golden Gloves championship was officially called the Intercity Golden Gloves Championship. Held each year since 1928, it was first established as a competition between New York and Chicago, with the venue alternating between the two cities. It soon became a national competition between east and west as the Golden Gloves became a nationwide organization. The eastern team consisted of competitors from the Eastern Time Zone, while the west included everyone else. The New York Golden Gloves was the governing body of the eastern team, and Chicago oversaw the west. The championship, however, retained the original moniker.

On March 4, Norvel met Glenn Drake at D.C.'s Union Station, where they boarded the Congressional to Penn Station in New York City. Drake wanted to arrive early to attend to some Golden Gloves business with his cohorts, and he thought it would be a good opportunity to accompany Norvel and help him assess his competition. From Penn Station it was a short walk to Hotel McAlpin.

As the two men carried their suitcases down the street, Drake said, "It's been an interesting two years since you showed up at my office at Apollo. From the streets of D.C. to Manhattan."

"Yes, it has," Norvel said with a laugh. "For me, it's more like from Gala to Manhattan. Not something, uh, uh, I anticipated as a young boy."

"What's Gala?" asked Drake.

"Oh, it's where I grew up in Virginia," Norvel said.

"You know if you're successful here, which I believe you will be, we'll be coming up here again in a few weeks," explained Drake. "The organizers, specifically Pete Mello, will get the eastern team that's going up against the west together at a state park north of New York City, called Bear Mountain."

The Hotel McAlpin, at the corner of Broadway and 34th Street, was chosen not only for its proximity but because it was one of the few in Manhattan serving all races. Three years earlier, it was where Jackie Robinson, who was residing at the hotel, received the phone call from the Brooklyn Dodgers making him the first Black to play in Major League Baseball.

On Sunday, Norvel went out walking. When he looked out of the window of his room on the eighth floor he saw a sunny day, but the people walking along the streets were hunched over in overcoats. The flags at the front of the hotel were flapping wildly in the stiff wind. Norvel wanted the fresh air and the exercise, so he wore the long johns he'd brought with him beneath his loose-fitting workout apparel. Fortunately, anticipating the brisk weather, he'd also brought a ski cap and winter gloves with him. He invited Drake to go, but he declined. So Norvel strolled through the impressive Italian Renaissance–style lobby into the invigorating city air.

Norvel walked down 34th Street toward the East River. As he approached Fifth Avenue, he looked up at the Empire State Building, now twenty years old and still the tallest skyscraper in the world. He wished Leslie was with him so they could enjoy the scene together.

After a while Norvel ambled over to 42nd Street, past storefronts, theaters, and street vendors, until he came to a large open area bustling with automobiles and pedestrians. He knew without asking that he'd reached Times Square. Even midday on a blustery Sunday, it felt like he'd entered a carnival for adults. He shook his head and wondered what Mama would have thought of these people out on a Sunday walking by establishments meant to entice adults, mostly men, to enter.

On Monday he went to Madison Square Garden. Before he went to the gym for a workout, he walked into the empty arena and looked with awe at its three levels of seating.

*What a place!*—Norvel said to himself. *This morning's newspaper expected that all eighteen thousand seats here will be taken. I can't imagine how much noise they'll make. I suppose they'll all be rooting for the hometown boys and not this kid from D.C.*

The next evening Norvel faced Sonny Jones of the Bronx in the eastern region Golden Gloves quarterfinals. The crowd was as boisterous as predicted, but Norvel had promised himself to concentrate on the task ahead of him. Jones, about twenty, was the same height as Norvel, but at the outset it became obvious he was too slow to counter Norvel's jabs and punches. The crowd quieted down as Norvel went about his business, which was simply to maintain his classic stand-up style for the three rounds. He easily won 3-0.

Wednesday, Norvel's semifinal opponent was Gilmore Newkirk, also of New York City, this time from Harlem. He was the crowd favorite. Two years prior, in 1948, Newkirk had made it to the finals but was knocked out in the first round by Coley Wallace. Last year he had lost in the preliminary matches but made the finals in the national AAU, losing in a decision. He was heavily favored to once again make it to the finals.

Norvel said to himself, *Just maintain your cool. Score points with your jabs and punches and watch for those headshots he's known for. Stay calm and concentrate.*

When the first round got started the crowd, expecting Newkirk to put Norvel away quickly, was cheering wildly. But Norvel took immediate control of the pace and deftly outmaneuvered Newkirk. Midway through the second round the crowd had quieted, with some booing the lack of action. But the judges were counting each hit by Norvel. The slow pace continued through the third round, resulting with Norvel winning another 3-0 decision.

Thursday night, in front of a capacity crowd, Norvel faced Nick Vasquez of Fort Bragg, North Carolina. Norvel had watched him in the quarterfinals and then in the semifinal match the previous night, before his own bout with Newkirk. He noticed Vasquez was free swinging, paying no attention to defensive postures. As the bout started, Norvel exploited Vasquez's defensive vulnerabilities and easily knocked him to the mat with a solid right to the head, a little over two minutes into the first round. Vasquez wasn't able to get up after the referee counted to ten. Norvel was awarded the eastern regional championship, earning him a spot on the eastern team, and a trip to Chicago in a few weeks for the Intercity Golden Gloves tournament that, in spite of its name, was for the national championship in each weight class.

He and a proud Glenn Drake arrived back in D.C. the next evening. Leslie met him at Union Station in Robert's car. Norvel wanted to tell Leslie about the trip, so they decided to have dinner at the Union Station Gateway Restaurant, which was on The List.

"Uh, uh, Leslie," began Norvel.

Leslie smiled patiently as Norvel struggled to get the words out. The echoing clamor of passengers and trains were ever present in the energetic station.

Norvel continued excitedly, "Uh, uh, I'm going to Chicago in a few weeks to fight for the heavyweight Golden Gloves championship."

Leslie said, "Congratulations! I'm proud of you, and the rest of the family will be also. Do you think we can get out to Leesburg to see them?"

Norvel said, "Uh, uh, I won't be able to go for an entire weekend, but maybe for church on Sunday."

Leslie, taking her time, said, "When I was in nursing school, I learned some methods to help people with speaking difficulties like stammers and stutters. Yours is a stammer, and when we have some time, we can work on it together."

Norvel said, "Okay, I've had it my entire life. My high school in Virginia tried. But if you want to, we can give it a go."

Leslie said, "Okay, I'd like to. Someday you may need to speak as a champion or an educator. You don't want people making fun of you."

"Oh, they won't make fun of me for long," Norvel said, laughing and showing his clenched fist.

Leslie laughed too, and added, "I've noticed that when you're excited or anxious about something, the stammering gets worse. When you find yourself in such a situation you might try taking a deep breath and then pause before you try speaking. It's just a suggestion."

Norvel spent Saturday washing his clothes, doing school work, and jumping rope, along with doing some bag work. Early on Sunday they went out to Leesburg, with Leslie nestled up next to Norvel while he drove the Mercury. In Leesburg they went to church with her family and visited for the afternoon.

Then on Monday Norvel went to the gym at Howard to talk with Coach Barnes, who congratulated him on his success in New York. The Howard University boxing team was undefeated so far, and had one more regular league match on Thursday, March 16. Barnes wanted to make sure Norvel would be available for it.

Norvel felt that the interleague match would be a good workout before going to Chicago. Barnes suggested he could view it as a sparring match.

At the match Norvel so far outclassed his opponent that instead of going for a knockout, he used the event to work on his conditioning against a live opponent.

On March 22, Norvel arrived for the second time that month at Penn Station, this time alone, and again spent the night at the Hotel McAlpin. The following morning the entire eastern Golden Gloves team met at Madison Square Garden, where all sixteen champions and alternates took a bus to Bear Mountain State Park. Norvel got to know his fellow boxers and the affable, charismatic coach, Pete Mello. Norvel learned that Mello headed up the Catholic Youth Organization's boxing programs in New York City.

The eastern Golden Gloves team stayed in camp-like barracks at the park, training and working out. Mello called the team together to talk about how to prepare for a match. He encouraged them to observe other matches in their weight class to get a feel for a potential opponent's style. He told them he thought many tactical boxers would simply commit to a routine and follow it, no matter what their opponents did.

Norvel realized that since the scoring was based on landing punches, a sound strategy would be to identify the tactical moves, find the vulnerabilities, and keep connecting with hard punches when the opportunities presented themselves. Mello was impressed with how quickly Norvel took his advice to heart.

On March 23, for reasons Norvel did not completely understand, Mello paired him with a light heavyweight, John Boutilier, for a two-round exhibition.

The other boxers, several onlookers, and a reporter watched Norvel use his tremendous reach advantage on Boutilier. Norvel used an effective left jab, causing Boutilier difficulty in getting inside with his own punches. In the second round Boutilier landed several solid punches, but Norvel's jabbing ability gave him the unofficial match in the eyes of the onlookers.

The next morning at breakfast Norvel made it a point to sit next to

Boutilier, who was known simply as "Bout," pronounced "boot."

When he sat down Boutilier turned to him and said, sporting a broad smile, "Thanks for the lesson last night."

They shook hands as Norvel responded, "Well, there was a weight and size difference. Uh, uh, I thought you held your own pretty well."

Boutilier was taken aback by the stammer, but said in his clipped Massachusetts accent, "You have quite the reputation preceding you. I understand you may be in Boston next month for the national AAU matches."

"Sure am," said Norvel. "How about you? Will you be there?"

"I didn't know about it until recently, so I didn't get signed up. My school, Boston University, doesn't have a boxing program. I do this to get away from campus. I learned it while I was in the Navy. I guess I picked it up from my father, who was an amateur boxer of some renown. I'm on a football scholarship at Boston University."

"Football and boxing, that's impressive. What are you studying there?" asked Norvel.

"Education," said Boutilier. "I plan to be a teacher someday. How about you?"

"My original plan was to be an engineer, working in technology, but Howard now has me on an athletic scholarship because of my boxing and moved my major to physical education. But I haven't given up on the technology path yet."

The two men chatted a little more between themselves and the others at the table. The team representing the eastern region spent the remainder of the days at Bear Mountain working out. Boutilier and Norvel sparred a little with each other. Both men were impressed with the other's quick, tactical moves in the ring. Boutilier stopped at one point during their sparring, laughing when he realized Norvel had deceived him with an apparent move in one direction while directing a punch that would have hit its target had he not pulled it back. He realized that Norvel in his own way was giving him a valuable lesson in strategy.

The eastern team took a train from New York to Chicago, arriving

March 28, the night before the scheduled matches. Norvel had breakfast at the hotel with Glenn Drake, who had come up from Washington. Early that afternoon Norvel went to Chicago Stadium, carrying a satchel containing his competition clothes. He warmed up for his match by performing his ritual of jumping rope for about ten minutes and then shadowboxing in front of a mirror for another five minutes. He left the workout area and watched several of the bouts scheduled before his, the final of the night. The heavyweight bout traditionally anchored the program.

He was out in time to see the welterweight bout in which Richie Anderson of the eastern team won on points over his opponent of the same last name, Albert Anderson. But then Chicago's Freddie Manns beat Junior Perry of New York City. Next up was his new acquaintance John Boutilier. John's opponent was Jesse Brown, a glass plant worker from Toledo, Ohio, known as a free-swinging tough competitor.

Norvel watched the two men literally slug it out. Boutilier traded blow for blow with Brown, forgetting the strategy Norvel had shown him the day before. Boutilier squeaked out the victory in the final seconds, landing a solid punch on the side of Brown's head, almost knocking him down. When the bell ended the match, the two boxers could barely stay on their feet as they made their way to their corners. The match easily could have been a draw had it not been for Boutilier's final blows hitting their mark.

*Don't let me do that*, Norvel told himself. *Bout's a brawler. It's just the way he is.*

The finale of the tournament was Norvel's match against a late substitute, Kirby Seals of Los Angeles. The first contender was disqualified because he was suffering from the flu. It was fortunate that Seals, the reigning U.S. Navy heavyweight champion, was available and willing to take on Norvel.

As soon as the bell sounded and the players met center ring, Seals went on the attack, smashing Norvel with two rights that hit their mark. Norvel knew he couldn't leave himself open to Seals, so he spent much of the round clinching. The referee frequently broke them apart. When he did, Norvel, taking advantage of his longer reach, scored points with the judges by landing inside jabs, avoiding counters from Seals.

In the second round Seals tried to keep Norvel off guard by occasionally switching from his normal right-handed stance to his left. Both boxers went into frequent clinches. The crowd, restless for some action after the preceding Boutilier slugfest, groaned when Norvel and Seals hung on to each other. Near the end of the round, Norvel realized Seals blows weren't hurting him and moved in for the attack. He landed several punches to the head and body, tangling Seals in the ropes. Norvel then became more aggressive until the bell sounded.

Waiting for the start of the third round, Norvel said to himself, *I believe I've got him. I definitely won this round and probably the first. I just won't let him get me now!*

Norvel maintained his aggressiveness in the third round, keeping Seals on the defensive. Whenever Seals wanted to hang on, Norvel let him, waiting for the referee to break them apart. The crowd wasn't pleased, but Norvel knew time was now on his side. And it was. The third round sounded, and Norvel was awarded the championship, 3-0. He was now the national Golden Gloves heavyweight champion!

Drake was the first to get to him, shouting above the crowd noise, "I knew you could do it. I knew it!! Congratulations!! This is such a fantastic time for the D.C. Golden Gloves."

Norvel maintained a humble, respectful demeanor, but inside he was churning.

*I don't believe it myself. I'm a national champion. I can't wait to tell Leslie and the family. It'll make Dad proud too, and George.*

Norvel returned to Washington on Sunday. On Monday, while he was training in the Howard University gym, Coach Barnes approached, saying, "Congratulations, Norvel. Everybody here is proud of your accomplishment. Wish you could go with us on Wednesday down to Raleigh for the CIAA championship."

"Thank you, sir," said Norvel. "And, uh, uh, I'm sorry I'll be missing them too. That's the day I'm heading to Boston for the AAU bouts. You'll do okay without me, I believe."

Barnes said, "I think so too. We've got a good solid team, but they look up to you for their inspiration."

"Oh, Coach," Norvel said humbly. "They're ready for this."

"Well, we're leaving today for Raleigh. I'll let you know what happens. Best of luck to you up there in Beantown. I know you'll represent the Bisons superbly."

# CHAPTER 12

## *April 7, 1950—Boston, Massachusetts*

Norvel arrived in Boston at midday on Good Friday. Carrying his suitcase, he walked the mile from South Station to the hostel near Boston Commons.

In the newspaper he saw a small article announcing Howard University had again captured the CIAA championship. Even though Norvel wasn't able to participate, he was credited in the article with leading the team to its second straight CIAA title.

Norvel spent Easter weekend touring Boston's historical sites, including Faneuil Hall, the Old North Church, and the Paul Revere House. He was due to write a term paper for his American History class and decided, during this self-guided tour of Boston, that he would write about the impact of the revolution on the day-to-day lives of Bostonians.

It was early spring in New England. The weather, while still crisp, was invigorating. Norvel enjoyed the colonial-style buildings of Boston and the energy of the people. However, Norvel did not see any Blacks among the people enjoying the day.

At one point he went into a small grocery store, hoping to find a soft drink. A couple who saw him looked at each other and immediately stopped their shopping and left the store. The middle-aged man behind the counter also looked at him but quickly turned away to talk with another store worker. Norvel found a bottle of RC Cola, but when he went to purchase it he was ignored. The counterman did not acknowledge Norvel and just continued to talk with the other worker.

*I don't know what's worse*, Norvel thought. *A sign on the door saying they don't serve us, or just pretending we don't exist.*

After an uncomfortable few minutes, Norvel left the RC on the counter and walked out the door.

Norvel attended Easter Sunday services at Park Street Church near his hostel and afterward went on a conditioning run. Later, he sent Leslie several tourist postcards with photos of the sights he'd seen.

The AAU preliminaries took place on Monday, April 10. A crowd of over 3,700 fans were in attendance at Boston Garden when the heavyweight matches finally got underway that night. Norvel's bout was up second. His opponent was a chubby boxer from Atlanta, Bunn Pitts, who was not up to Norvel's skill level. Norvel knocked him down in the second round, and Pitts allowed the referee the ten count, ending the bout.

On Tuesday evening Norvel faced off against Nick Vasquez, the opponent he had met a month ago at the eastern Golden Gloves finals in New York. Norvel maneuvered around the ring with speed not normally seen in a heavyweight, leveling Vasquez with a steady set of straight rights and lefts. In the second round a volley of straight rights and lefts to the head sent Vasquez to the mat, where he remained, giving Norvel his second KO of the matches.

After the fight Norvel showered and cleaned up at the Gardens facilities. He spoke with some of his teammates, including Jerry McGuigan of Cambridge, Massachusetts, who scored an upset over his opponent.

"That was quite the slugfest you had there, Jerry," Norvel said.

"Yeah, yeah," McGuigan said. "I like to do that against those who think they can trade punches with me. They got another think coming when they do."

"Must be something you New Englanders want to do," Norvel said. "I met John Boutilier last month and he just wants to slug it out also, even after I gave him some strategy tips."

"Oh, you know Bout," McGuigan said. "He's a feisty one for sure."

Norvel walked the two miles back to his hostel, wrote another postcard to Leslie, ate the sandwich he'd made up earlier in the day, and went to sleep. The next morning he ate a large breakfast consisting of six fried eggs, sausage, potatoes, and toast. He took a leisurely walk over to Boston Harbor to see if he could imagine the Boston Tea Party, seeking fodder for the term paper. He also saw the USS Constitution, whose permanent home is the Charlestown Navy Yard in Boston Harbor. He learned it was the oldest official U.S. Navy vessel and that it was seaworthy. He was put off, however, by the unpleasant odors coming from the waters in the harbor.

After returning to the hostel, Norvel went over to the Gardens in the early afternoon to concentrate on his upcoming matches. First, the semifinal put him up against Louis Packer, a tactician in the ring like himself. Norvel remembered Mello's view on tacticians, which was that many of them stubbornly stick to the same game plan. The key to this match was to work the vulnerabilities he'd observed the previous day when he watched Packer's quarterfinal match.

Norvel's planning worked. Before 8,500 Boston boxing fans, Norvel danced around during the first round to see what he could confirm about Packer's moves. Then near the end of the round, he landed several hard punches, one disabling Packer for a moment, just as the bell sounded. Then, as expected, Packer came out in the next round with the same moves. Norvel landed many more punches and felt he'd easily won the second round as well. For the third round, Norvel simply avoided getting hit by Packer and landed a few blows of his own. When the final bell sounded, the judges awarded all three rounds to Norvel.

For the finals, he faced Stan Howlett, known as "Slugger Stan," a former U.S. Army heavyweight champion and perennial St. Louis Golden Gloves champion. Like Norvel, Howlett was known as a savvy fighter, but with a more powerful knockout punch than Norvel. He was also larger physically. Norvel knew he had to be cautious and, as in his plan with Packer, do what he could to score more points with the judges. For the entire fight Norvel employed a clinching strategy, which caused the fans, expecting a slugfest, to jeer. He moved in close, giving Howlett little room to maneuver into a position where he could launch a powerful onslaught. Norvel, for his part, continued to work jabs to Howlett's body while inside, scoring points with the judges. The entire three rounds played out slowly in this fashion, with boos from the spectators increasing in intensity. But the strategy worked.

Norvel was awarded all three rounds and the AAU heavyweight championship. He was now the national champion for both the Golden Gloves and the AAU.

Norvel looked around into the stands, where the spectators were on their feet, jeering.

*It don't matter*, he thought. *The record won't show the jeering and the fans will soon forget. But the record will show I won and that I'm the title holder.*

News of Norvel capturing the title reached D.C. the next morning when the *Washington Post* published a brief article in its sports section. Norvel returned to Union Station on Friday evening to find, as he stepped off the train, Leslie, Robert, Coach Barnes, and members of the Howard boxing team waiting for him. Also present was a Howard University welcoming group to congratulate a rare athletic luminary from their alma mater. Howard University's reputation was that of an incubator for rising Black intellectuals. The institution was not accustomed to having one of their own reach athletic prominence.

The next day, while they drove to Leesburg, Leslie said to Norvel, "I was so proud when you came off the train last night and your fans were there waiting for you. My man: on top of the world!"

"Yes, Les, it was pretty exciting for me too," Norvel said. "But the only person I really wanted to see was you. And there you were."

Leslie leaned her head against his shoulder.

After arriving in Leesburg, while Leslie went to another part of the house to visit with her mother and sister, Norvel sat down in the parlor with Emmett.

"Congratulations, Norvel. It doesn't look like anyone landed any punches on you," Emmett observed. "How are you feeling?"

"Uh, uh, pretty good actually," Norvel answered. "I really didn't have any problems there. They were all good boxers, but I planned my strategy before each bout, and lucky for me, it all worked out."

"I'll bet Howard now realizes they have a national champion," Emmett said, smiling.

"Oh, I know they do. I just haven't been back on campus yet. But Coach Barnes, some of my teammates, and a group of, I guess you could call them fans, were there to welcome me home."

"Anything else coming up with boxing for you?"

"Every year there's what's called the Duals Matches. They pit the U.S. against Europe, and they alternate where it's held. This year the matches will be in two cities in the States, Chicago and here. Next year, they'll be in Europe."

"You'll be going up to Chicago?" asked Emmett.

"Oh, no, the U.S. is fielding two different teams. I'll be on the Washington team. The matches will be Friday next."

"And how are your studies coming?"

"My professors have been flexible with me," said Norvel, "so I've been able to keep up. I'm working on a history paper that's due in a few weeks."

"Well, keep it up, son. You're showing everyone around here how to get it done."

On Friday, Washington, D.C., boxing fans filled Uline Arena to see their newly crowned AAU heavyweight champion take on his counterpart from Europe, Teemu Kuusela of Finland. But Norvel quickly dispatched the slow-moving Finn without even breaking a sweat. The referee stopped the fight in the second round, crediting Norvel with a technical knockout. The fans were pleased Norvel had a good showing, although they were hoping for a better matchup.

Norvel's win over the Finn brought the Duals Matches for 1950 to an 8-8 draw. He represented Howard in several more exhibition events, but significant amateur boxing events were finished for the year. Now he could finally concentrate on his studies and spend time with his girlfriend.

During the remainder of 1950, Norvel and Leslie saw each other whenever their busy schedules allowed. Leslie continued living in the Chevy Chase mansion as the governess for the Henry family. The Henrys' had three children: eight- and nine-year-old boys, and a six-year-old girl. Mrs. Henry was an engaging and active socialite, and Mr. Henry worked for the government and was often out of town on what was described by Mrs. Henry as an assignment. Leslie knew not to ask questions.

Through her society circles, Mrs. Henry was an active booster of local charities, especially those involving children and their education, causes that interested Leslie. She mentioned to Mrs. Henry the project she had started in Leesburg, collecting books at libraries and providing them to schools and churches. Mrs. Henry, with Leslie's help, started a similar program in Chevy Chase and the surrounding areas. It gave Leslie access to and knowledge of a wider circle of like-minded people, mostly affluent and influential in the greater D.C. area. She knew these connections could potentially help her socially in the future.

During the remainder of the spring semester, Norvel played baseball on the Howard team as an outfielder, occasionally pitching. Although he wasn't a starting player, he enjoyed the opportunity to participate in a sport while concentrating on his classes, excelling in them all.

Norvel and Leslie continued to date during the spring and into the beginning of the summer. At one point during a weekend in Leesburg, Norvel and Leslie were sitting in the front parlor. Emmett was working at Whitmore's, and Mrs. Jackson was in another part of the house helping her invalid mother, who was now living with the family.

While they sat talking Leslie placed a jar of small stones on the table.

Norvel asked, "Are you collecting some rocks?"

"Sure enough," Leslie said. "I'm collecting them for you."

"What would, uh, uh, I need a bunch of rocks for?" Norvel asked.

"It's to help you with your stammer," Leslie said. "I learned a technique in my nursing school. Put them inside your cheeks on each side."

Norvel emptied some pebbles onto his hand, looked at them curiously, and then put them in his mouth, lodging them on both sides against his cheeks. He tried talking, but it came out garbled.

"I'm sorry, Les," Norvel said, after spitting the stones out onto his hand. "Are you playing with me? Nobody will be able to understand what, uh, uh, I'm saying."

"You're only supposed to use them to practice by yourself, not when you are with people. When you practice, say vowels out loud over and over again. Then when you're talking, take the deep breath you've been practicing and imagine those rocks in your cheeks. After a few weeks, you should notice a difference."

Norvel put the stones back into his mouth and said very loudly while holding each vowel, "A, E, I, O, U." He paused for a moment, looking at a smiling Leslie. He added in a garbled voice, "And sometimes Y."

They both started laughing. Norvel spit out the pebbles into his hand and kissed her.

On the weekends they didn't go to Leesburg, Norvel helped Leslie with her library charity efforts, especially those in Southeast Washington, D.C. Mrs. Henry was actively promoting their efforts among members of her various associations. They would accept the boxes at locations in Northwest D.C. and then transport them to schools, libraries, and churches in impoverished areas where they were needed. Norvel's admiration for Leslie grew as he observed her determination to improve the lives of young people.

In June, while having lunch at a Woolworths on 14th Street, Norvel said to Leslie, "Soon, I'll be going back down home to see my father and help him work in the fields. My brother, Jimmy, will be coming with me."

Leslie said, "When will you be returning?"

"Probably not until a week before next term starts in September. But I was thinking—" Norvel began.

"You're always thinking about something, Norvel," Leslie teased. "What's it about this time?"

"I'd like to see you around your birthday. Maybe you could come to my area and meet some of my kin, at least my father and younger brother George."

"Where would I stay?"

"You'll be able to stay at our family home in Gala. I'll have my car there and can run you around, show you my home turf. It's not as sophisticated as Leesburg, but I'm sure you'll like it."

# CHAPTER 13

## *July 1950—Gala, Virginia*

Norvel and Jimmy, in the Mercury, stopped in Leesburg for a visit and a midmorning meal before beginning their drive to Gala. They drove along the country roads that meandered through southwest Virginia, finally reaching their home at Big Hill in the late evening on a pleasant summer day.

As they emerged from the car, road-weary, both men stretched out their long legs. Norvel raised his arms into the air and rolled his shoulders several times. Just then their father came out of the home, walked over, and greeted them somewhat sternly, although he had a hint of relief on his face. They shook hands.

"Nice car, son," said Jack Lee, walking around and looking at it. "Looks like you're takin' real good care of it."

"Just like you taught me," Norvel acknowledged. "But it's a bit dusty from today's drive."

"Oh, we'll get it cleaned up tomorrow," Jack said. "Y'all ready fir some work in the fields this summer? I could sure use your help."

Jimmy said, "Looking forward to it. Norvel doesn't need the exercise, but I sure do. I've been cooped up in the Howard library too long. Where's George?"

"He's finishin' up," Jack said. "Be along in a few minutes."

"I thought Edna was to be here," Norvel said.

"She was here two Sundays ago for a few days to see Miss Meadows, but she's done gone back to Emporia for a summer session at school. I also think she has a beau over there."

A few minutes later, a lanky teenager came strolling up, carrying some fish on a string. George Lee was living in Covington with his cousins, but came back to Gala to help his father in the fields. George was thirteen, born in November 1936 along with a twin brother who died during the birth.

George revered his older brothers, who were both now living legends in the area. Except for the teacher, Miss Meadows, they were the only people from their segregated community who'd attended a four-year college. Furthermore, Norvel was a national boxing champion. But George was finding it difficult to live up to his older brothers' legacy.

"How are you, brother?" asked Norvel, putting his arm around him. "You getting along okay?"

George shrugged and smiled sheepishly.

"How's that school up in Covington you're going to?" asked Jimmy.

Again, George shrugged his shoulders and simply said, "its okay." Then he added, looking at Norvel, "All my friends want to fight me to see if I'm anything like you."

"Are you?" asked Norvel, ruffling George's hair.

"They mostly get the best of me," George mumbled, with his head down.

Norvel said, "Look at me."

George looked up at his older brother.

Norvel said, "By the end of this summer, you won't have any trouble with those fellas anymore. I'll show you how, just like Dad did for me when I was about your age."

George smiled appreciatively and nodded.

Jack Lee looked at his three boys and smiled. This was a somewhat rare event, and usually occurred when he was proud of something he claimed as his own.

Jack said, "I've made some rabbit stew. Let's go get us some."

Norvel and Jimmy looked at each other, astonished. They never knew their dad could make something like a stew. They'd heard the women at church were keeping him fed. They all walked into the house, sat down, said grace, and consumed a very savory stew.

That Saturday, Norvel drove to Clifton Forge, where he was to meet

Leslie's train. Norvel paced on the platform. The train could be heard in the distance as it rumbled up the long grade to Clifton Forge. As it came in, slowly losing speed, steam billowing out and around the large black engine, it finally squealed to a stop, the steel wheels grinding against the rails.

He spotted her before she saw him. She was dressed casually in a light brown skirt. Her slight figure cautiously stepped onto the platform, carrying a small suitcase. She looked up and saw Norvel smiling as he walked toward her.

"What a beautiful area of the world you're from," Leslie said, while he greeted her with a hug.

"Uh, uh, I ordered up this weather just for you," Norvel said. "Your train trip went well?"

"Oh, yes," she said. "It was very comfortable."

"And Mrs. Henry was okay with you taking a few days off?" Norvel asked.

"Yes," Leslie said. "She said Mr. Henry would be home, and he and the kids had some plans for family time."

When they got to Norvel's car, she said, "My goodness, did you paint your car?"

Norvel laughed and said, "Oh, no, our father insists we take very good care of our cars, so we give it a thorough scrubbing every few days."

"And how is he getting along with the loss of your mother?" asked Leslie.

"It's hard to tell," said Norvel. "He doesn't show emotion, but he seems to not know what to do. The church is looking in on him. Although this is home, uh, uh, I think it would be good for him to maybe go live in Covington, or even up to D.C. if he can find work there. He needs to keep busy."

They arrived back at the family home, where Jack Lee was in the yard wiping off his old car. He looked up when he saw the Mercury pull up, wiped off his hands, and walked over to them.

"Leslie, I'd like to introduce my father, Jack Lee," said Norvel. "Dad, please meet Miss Leslie Jackson."

"Nice to finally meet my boy's girlfriend," Jack said. "Your name, Jackson, is the same as my mid-name. It's for the two rivers near here: The James and Jackson."

"There's a river here named after my family?" Leslie joked.

Her remark made Jack smile. Norvel took a deep breath, relieved. It looked as if Leslie and Dad were going to get along fine.

"You're gonna stay with Mrs. Cline down by our church," added Jack, smiling. "The church ladies thought it might be more comfortable for you than staying in a house full of men."

Leslie looked at Norvel questioningly as he said, "Welcome to the real South, Les. Mrs. Cline is a sweet, nice lady and she'll enjoy your company. Let's go get you introduced."

Several hours later the church ladies put on a potluck dinner. Many of Jimmy's and Norvel's friends from school joined them and stayed until the skies darkened and the Milky Way became visible. Norvel knew it would be several hours before the rising half-moon would start peeking through the trees.

Among their old friends, both men and woman, they whiled the evening away, listening to Jimmy tell stories of Washington, D.C., and occasionally lamenting the plight of the Negro. Norvel and Leslie sat holding hands and mostly listened to the conversation, although some questions were directed to Norvel about his future boxing exploits. He simply said time would tell.

The next day Norvel and Leslie attended church services at Rising Mount Zion Baptist Church. Norvel wore a dark suit just as his mother would have expected. Leslie wore a bright-green-and-white summer dress. The preacher was a popular local farmer who knew everyone. All the parishioners carried their Bibles to the church, although many of the older attendees couldn't read. Leslie took in the simple, basic ambience of this country worship experience. It made her understand and appreciate even more this man whom she had to admit she was in love with.

After the services Norvel took Leslie by the hand, and they walked over to the graveyard next to the church. He showed her where his mother was buried. His father had placed fresh flowers at the grave, as he did each Sunday morning.

"There's no inscription here," Leslie noticed.

"We all know this is where she's buried," Norvel said.

"You need to mark it, Norvel."

Norvel explained, "Her birth name was George Anna Ray, after her father and mother. But once she settled in here, everyone called her Georgiana. She had a way about her that made you always want to do the right thing."

Leslie said, "Someday I want you to honor your mother with a plaque that won't erode away in later years. Something that will last an eternity."

Norvel said, "Maybe, although she would rather see that money given to the church or a family that needed food for the winter."

They walked down to nearby Sinking Creek.

"This is where, uh, uh, I was baptized," said Norvel, pointing to the little stream. "This is where everybody around here gets baptized."

"A beautiful place to feel God's presence," said Leslie, wiping a tear from her eye.

That afternoon Leslie said her goodbyes to the Gala community, and she and Norvel began their drive over the mountains to Covington. The humidity was up and as they drove raindrops began to splatter the windshield. They drove south and turned onto Craig Creek Road, which paralleled the stream by the same name.

Leslie took a deep breath. "Norvel, it is so beautiful here. I'm surprised you ever left it."

Norvel nodded and said, "Uh, uh, I want to show you something special."

The rain stopped and the sun poked through the clouds as Norvel parked the car. He and Leslie, holding hands, got out and started walking up a path into the woods. Off to the side was a gurgling flow of water running over some rocks. They could hear a rumble growing louder as they walked up the short trail. After about a half a mile, they stopped when they saw water falling from a cliff.

Norvel said, "We would come up here and play as kids. It's called Roaring Run, aptly named. We were quite the sight, a bunch of colored kids jumping from rock to rock, occasionally falling in the water. One of the local farmers, when he caught us, would run us off using some words I won't use now."

"I wonder if he would've done that if you were a bunch of white kids," Leslie said, taking Norvel's arm. "This spot is for all of God's people. It's so peaceful here."

Norvel leaned down and kissed her. They stood there for a moment taking in the serenity.

They returned to the car and continued on country roads, which became unpaved at a few spots as they came upon the old mining crossroads of Rich Patch. Norvel told Leslie that from time to time, some of the men in Gala worked in the mine there.

They finally made it into the normally bustling town of Covington, but it was Sunday afternoon and quiet. Norvel stared at the Alleghany County Courthouse as they drove by it. Leslie commented on Covington being a little bit like Leesburg, except it was rougher.

They reached the home of Norvel's second cousins, the Byrds, near the paper mill.

Mr. and Mrs. Byrd, who had known Norvel all his life, welcomed him warmly and were charmed by Leslie. After a delicious Sunday meal, Mrs. Byrd went into the kitchen. Leslie rose to go help her, but they asked her to stay seated.

In a few minutes a cake with twenty-five candles was brought out. Her birthday was the next day, July 25, but the family thought it easier to celebrate today. They all sang "Happy Birthday." Leslie was surprised, and thanked everybody for the celebration. It started raining again, so they sat inside and shared stories with each other.

Norvel and Leslie spent the next day driving to nearby Hot Springs, where the Homestead Resort was located. Founded fifty years earlier by a group of investors led by J. P. Morgan, it had hosted many U.S. presidents. Blacks were not permitted to enter the property, but they had fun seeing it from the outside when they pulled into the parking area before being shooed away by a Black security guard. When he did, Leslie waggled her finger at him while shaking her head with disappointment. They noticed many of the caddies at the golf course were Black, too. They spent the remainder of their time in Hot Springs driving around the beautiful countryside, stopping to enjoy the picnic they'd packed. Norvel then drove Leslie to the Covington train station.

After hugging him Leslie said, "I really like your family and friends. And they are watching after your father when he lets them. Thank you for everything. I'll look forward to your letters, and I'll be happy to see you when you come back to Washington for next term."

Norvel said, "I'll miss you too. Make sure you sit in the section set aside for special people like you."

She blew him a kiss as the train doors rattled shut.

# CHAPTER 14

## *February 1951—Washington, D.C.*

At the beginning of 1951, on January 5 in Kansas City, Norvel defeated another ranked heavyweight, Bob Miller, to qualify for the heavyweight slot on the U.S. Pan American Games team. This team would be going to Buenos Aires, Argentina, for the very first time pitting the countries of the Americas against one another. Originally, these games were to be held in Buenos Aires in 1942, but World War II caused their cancellation.

The local Golden Gloves championship took place during the first half of February at Uline Arena. Norvel's ranking automatically qualified him for the semifinals, where he was again matched against Edgar Smith, with whom he'd had a close match the previous year. And, as he did then, Smith came right at Norvel, pummeling him with a flurry of powerful lefts and rights. Norvel took a defensive position, absorbing the onslaught effectively.

Between rounds he thought, *This guy has my number! What's he doing that nobody else can? I've just got to hang in there and see if I can land something the judges like.*

At the start of round two, Norvel got into a crouch and went inside, absorbing Smith's attacks. Each time he found an opening he landed jabs to Smith's lower ribs. He heard Smith groan with some of the strikes. Norvel sensed Smith was tiring. Norvel thought it time to go on the offensive, but the bell sounded, ending the round.

*That one was very close. Could go either way. Got to knock him down and out now!*

For the last round Norvel continued to attack Smith's body, wearing him down. Smith's counters were ineffective and easily dodged. The judges awarded Smith the first round, but gave Norvel the second and third for a 2-1 victory. Some of the spectators jeered the decision.

Two weeks later, before 4,500 fans at Uline Arena, Norvel faced Eddie LaCovey of the local Catholic Youth Organization in the regional finals. The fans, remembering the Smith bout, were rooting for the underdog LaCovey.

*Don't make this complicated, Norvel! Just go for him!*

The bell for the first round sounded and Norvel came out of his corner, assumed his stance, and immediately launched a hard right and then a left, catching LaCovey off guard. Norvel exploited his advantage and landed a hard left to LaCovey's chin, putting him down for nine counts. LaCovey got back up and took a defensive position, while Norvel danced around him, stalking. Just before the round ended, Norvel draped LaCovey over the rope with a thunderous right to his midsection. The round ended before Norvel could go at him again. The fans were on their feet, making a cacophony of noise. At the start of the second round Norvel sprang to the center of the ring, expecting his opponent to do the same, but LaCovey was still hunched over in his corner. The referee called the fight. Norvel was again the local heavyweight Golden Gloves champion.

Norvel was told that because he was representing the United States in the Pan American Games, which were scheduled for the same week as the eastern Golden Gloves Championship, they would fit him into the national championship somehow, but probably in an alternate bout. Although Norvel was disappointed he wouldn't be defending his national championship, he felt that representing his country and experiencing another part of the world was the better opportunity.

On February 17, Norvel and Leslie went on a movie date in Leesburg. Afterward, they had dessert and coffee.

Norvel said, "It's so nice to have an evening for ourselves."

"It sure is," Leslie said. "You aren't the only one who's been busy. Mrs. Henry has been active too, giving me very little free time. Also, Mr. Henry was reading the paper a few days ago and said that he read about you in the sports section. Your boxing exploits are being followed by a lot of people. I believe that clerk behind the soda fountain recognized you. I feel like I'm with a movie star."

"If, uh, uh, I were a movie star, we wouldn't be sitting in a drug store," Norvel said. "We'd be in a fine restaurant having a New York steak."

"You haven't been doing your speaking exercises, have you," Leslie chided him.

"I couldn't find any pebbles up there in New York City," Norvel said, smiling. "But, uh, uh, I will look for some in Buenos Aires."

Leslie giggled and said, "I know both of us are busy, but I miss your company when we are apart."

"Me too, Les," Norvel said.

After spending the weekend in Leesburg, Norvel flew from Washington to New York where he boarded a Pan American Airways flight, which was carrying many members of the U.S. Pan American Games team, including the boxers. The plane stopped in Miami and Bogota, Colombia, before finally landing in Buenos Aires.

Boxing in Argentina rivaled soccer for the enthusiasm of their fans. They were known to physically confront officials if a particular match did not go the popular way. To make sure there weren't any uncontrolled incidences during the games, the organizers had strung barbed wire between the general spectators and the reserved section of Luna Park, where the bouts were being held.

Something was amiss when the Americans arrived at Luna Park for the March 5 semifinals and encountered a hostile, stone-throwing mob. The team required a police escort to get from their bus to the inside of the arena. Thirty-two thousand zealous boxing fans packed into an arena designed to hold twenty-four thousand to watch the action. Five of the eight Americans on the team had qualified for the semifinals, including Norvel. The other three had been eliminated in the preliminary bouts a few days earlier before a polite, near-capacity crowd.

On this day, before each match, the Argentine president and first lady, Juan and Eva Peron, would greet each contestant and shake his hand. But when a bout involving an American was up, the Perons remained seated. Eva, or Evita as she was popularly known, tried getting up several times, but her husband gently held her back. Norvel assumed the snub was because of some ongoing political tension between Argentina and the United States.

Norvel's semifinal was the last of the day. The four other semifinals were against Argentineans. While the standing-room-only crowd roared for their nation's team, the Americans lost each one by decisions rendered by three Argentinean judges. The American coach, Pat Duffy, became more incensed with the officiating as each decision was announced.

Duffy asked the American light heavyweight semifinalist, John Stewart, and Norvel to huddle with him.

"Well, guys, if either of you lets your bouts go to the judges, you're gonna lose," Duffy said. "This thing is rigged against us."

"Can't we protest and ask for new judges?" asked Norvel.

"I already tried," Duffy said. "There's only one way either of you is gonna win. You need to knock your man out!"

Duffy angrily slapped his towel on the chair next to him.

Stewart, a member of the Air Force, faced a formidable opponent, Lucio Grottone of Brazil. Stewart fought a good, aggressive fight trying to knock Grottone out and was fortunate not to be knocked down himself. But he was clearly outclassed by the highly touted Brazilian.

It was now up to Norvel to salvage a shot at a championship for the Americans. His opponent was Victor Bignon of Chile. He remembered Bignon from the London Olympics, where Adam Faul outpunched him. Norvel knew that unless Bignon had significantly improved his style since 1948 that he could take him.

The crowd was on its feet screaming vehemently when the first round got under way. Norvel sprang out of his corner and approached Bignon. The big Chilean smiled wryly at him and backed up, without swinging or attacking. Norvel kept approaching him and Bignon continued to move away.

*Very strange behavior for an Olympic boxer. Maybe he's wanting me to let my guard down and then he'll come at me.*

Norvel maneuvered Bignon into a corner and landed some right and left body jabs. Bignon deftly ducked a head shot by Norvel and got away from the corner, back to the center of the ring. For the remainder of the round, he kept avoiding contact with Norvel. The same routine continued in the second round until mid-round, when Bignon moved forward and connected with a right cross. Norvel immediately countered with two punches that easily found their target.

*At least now he seems to want to actually box. Let's see what he's got.*

But for the rest of the round, Bignon went back to his retreating mode. The third round was worse. Bignon avoided all contact with Norvel. The fans let their opinion on Bignon's performance be known by jeering loudly.

At the sound of final bell, the boxers retired to their corners to wait for the judge's decision. Everyone knew that Norvel had easily won the fight, earning him a spot in the finals. But in a shocking decision, all three rounds were awarded to the Chilean. The crowd booed and jeered loudly for fifteen minutes. Some tried cutting through the barbed wire separating them from the ring and the judges. Duffy also had to be restrained by the American boxers. Police were again called in to restore order. They escorted the judges and boxers safely out of Luna Park.

Two days later, the bouts for third place and those for the championship were held. The lightweight American, Willie Hunter, outpointed his Brazilian opponent, and John Stewart had an easy time against Juan Melias of Chile.

It was now Norvel's turn. His opponent was Arlindo de Oliveira from Brazil.

Norvel wore a hostile look as he peered across the ring at his opponent. *Gonna get this anger out now. Not going to leave it anywhere but right here. I will not be shown up this time.*

The bell sounded and the two men danced to the center of the ring, where Oliviera made an initial sizing jab at Norvel. As he did Norvel unleashed a furious right and then left to Oliviera's head, and the Brazilian went down. After a nine count, Oliviera, still woozy, got to his feet, but the referee stopped the fight. It lasted thirty seconds. Norvel went over to his opponent to make sure he was going to be okay. The Brazilian smiled, appreciating the gesture, while the crowd gave Norvel a standing ovation.

The Closing Ceremony was scheduled for March 9, so Norvel spent the day before with his fellow bronze medal winners, Willie Hunter and John Stewart. But everyone was fuming over the outcome. In all eight weight categories the Argentineans won the gold medal.

As they strolled along the grand 9 de Julio Avenue, Hunter said, "I wish we were leaving today. This whole thing was a setup."

Stewart nodded, "Amen to that."

"We should've known something was up when President Peron snubbed us," Norvel said.

Stewart said, "His wife seemed nice. I noticed she looked right at me."

Hunter said teasingly, "Just your imagination, my man. I'm sure you're not her type. She was looking at me."

Norvel interrupted and said, "No guys. She was looking at Coach Duffy. You know she's more popular than her husband is here."

Norvel enjoyed seeing new places, even if it was just for a day, to get a sense of the local culture. They admired the landmark Obelisk, Buenos Aires's version of the Washington Monument. They explored the tango venues and lively street market of San Telmo. Norvel felt comfortable with the multiethnic culture of the large, dense city.

Norvel bought a postcard along the route, wrote Leslie, and put it in the mail. He did this each day, hoping she would eventually get them, even if it was after he was home.

He returned to Washington on Sunday, March 11, feeling travel-weary but relieved to be home for a few days. The next weekend he planned to return to New York to represent Washington, D.C., at the Golden Gloves national championship. During the short week, he focused on catching up on his studies and conditioning for his upcoming bout. The only time

Leslie was able to be with him since mid-February was to meet him on Saturday for breakfast at Union Station to see him off to New York.

Norvel arrived in New York City that evening. On Sunday he took a long walk and then used the impressive training facilities at Madison Square Garden.

The next evening, in front of ninety-four hundred spectators, Norvel took on Toxey Hall of Chicago. Norvel, wearing dark blue shorts with a white stripe down each side, came out looking confident, focused on when to throw a punch. Hall was a classic stand-up boxer like Norvel. During the first round they danced around, sizing each other up.

*I'm in control. I can feel it. Just need to take my chance when I get it.*

The second round started the same way, with both boxers dancing around each other. Then suddenly, Norvel saw his opening and dropped Hall with a lightning-fast right.

The following day Norvel came back to Washington, arriving late that night. He wanted to spend time with Leslie. Norvel began to appreciate the expression "absence makes the heart grow fonder." But he knew he needed to attend to his studies and other matters before heading up to Boston for the AAU championship, where he would defend his national AAU heavyweight champion title. Unlike in the Golden Gloves, he would be required to fight his way back into the championship round with four straight days of boxing. To be successful, he needed to make sure he would be in top physical and mental shape for what could be a grueling four days.

# CHAPTER 15

## *Spring 1951—Washington, D.C.*

On March 24, a misty but warm early spring day, Norvel drove to Chevy Chase to pick up Leslie in the usual location, the curb in front of the estate. When he arrived there was a teenage boy at the entrance gate who waved at him and motioned for him to enter the driveway. As he pulled in, he saw a distinguished man in his mid-fifties, a woman, and Leslie, all standing in front of the house and smiling.

Norvel stopped the car, got out, and walked up to them.

Leslie said, "Norvel, please meet Mr. and Mrs. Henry. Ma'am, sir, this is Norvel Lee of Howard University."

Mr. Henry stepped forward and said, "Hello, young man, Larry Henry. I am pleased to meet you."

Norvel shook Mr. Henry's hand and said, "Very nice to meet you, sir, and Mrs. Henry."

"I have been following your phenomenal boxing successes," Henry continued. "You have a fantastic talent. Any chance you'll be a pro at some point?"

Norvel replied, "No, sir, I have no plans to go that route. I'm hoping to be involved in the local educational system."

Mrs. Henry touched her husband's arm and smiled, saying, "We are so pleased to have Leslie's help here and, because of her, we feel like we know you."

Norvel said, "Thank you, ma'am. Your support of both of us is greatly appreciated."

"Best of luck to you in all of your pursuits," Mr. Henry said. "Please know you have fans here in Chevy Chase."

"Thank you, sir."

After the unexpected meeting, Norvel and Leslie drove out to Leesburg. They visited with her family, and at one point Norvel went for a run while Leslie followed in the car with Weekie and a friend.

Robert also returned home that day. Norvel hadn't seen him since he had transferred to Morgan State University in Baltimore. In the evening Mr. and Mrs. Jackson, Leslie, Weekie, Robert, cousin Mervin Jackson, and Norvel, sat down at the dining room table and played a long game of Monopoly. Norvel tried to own all the railroads, while Emmett was occupied with the utility companies. But in the end Mervin quietly acquired enough cash where they had to admit he was the winner.

In the morning Leslie and Norvel walked to church together. Leslie noticed that Norvel was more restless than usual, but did not say anything, thinking he was just concentrating on what he needed to accomplish during the upcoming week before going to Boston for the AAU championship. But when they returned, he asked to speak with her father alone in the parlor.

Standing nervously in the parlor of the large home he now knew well, Norvel was facing the father of the woman he intended to marry. The room was comfortably appointed with family photos, a shelf with books, and a painting of Jesus Christ. Although Emmett Jackson was very comfortable with his eldest daughter's suitor, he did not invite Norvel to sit down.

Emmett Jackson stared at Norvel patiently, sensing what was coming.

"Uh, uh, sir," Norvel said. "Excuse me, but I need to take a deep breath, as Leslie has taught me, so I can say what I need to say."

Emmett nodded, his demeanor serious.

"Sir, I want to, uh, uh, say I'm going to ask Leslie to marry me," Norvel said. "I'm telling you this because I respect and admire you, sir, so before I ask her I'd like to have your blessing."

Leslie's father looked directly into Norvel's eyes and asked, "Do you love my Leslie? Do you promise to care for her through the good times and the bad? Will you honor and respect her as our Lord will want you to?"

"I love her with all my heart," answered Norvel, his eyes glistening. "She and I are made for each other, and I will always cherish her."

"Then I bless your marriage to her," Mr. Jackson said, smiling. "I will be honored to call you my son-in-law. And I have to say that during this past year, you have become a member of the family. I, Mrs. Jackson, those boys outside, and the entire Leesburg community are very proud of your accomplishments."

"Thank you, sir," Norvel said humbly.

The two men shook hands as Norvel let out a deep breath. Jackson reached out and patted Norvel's shoulder.

"I've known Leslie a lot longer than you have," Jackson added, chuckling, "so let me give you some man-to-man or, if I may say, some father-to-son advice. I'm sure you know by now that your Leslie is no namby-pamby girl. She wants and expects certain things from people and life itself. She wants to be involved with the social circles in her community, and she needs culture in her life. She wants to be an active participant in the life around her. You come from a different background than her. Culture, status, and acceptance are important to her."

"Yes, sir, I know what you mean," Norvel said. "She's been grooming me like she has some plans. When I met her brother in the Army Air Corps he told me her nickname was 'Lil Napoleon.'"

"Oh, yes, she is, yes indeed," Jackson said, laughing again. "So I just want to let you know that she'll expect you to be more than just an educated boxer. She and I both know that athletic ability is a young man's game, and there will come a day when you won't be able to do that anymore. She'll expect you to capitalize on the fame you have right now to get into a position where you can be a respected member of your social circle."

"Yes, sir," said Norvel, "and thank you."

Soon after, Norvel told Leslie that instead of staying in Leesburg for the customary Sunday dinner, he needed to leave to return to Washington. She looked questioningly at him, disappointed she could not spend more time with her family. Instead of changing into casual clothes, Norvel remained dressed in his dark suit. After they said goodbye to her family, they drove down a country road along the Potomac River. They crossed the bridge and to their right after entering D.C. was the Lincoln Memorial, anchoring one end of the Washington Mall. Norvel parked the car and asked Leslie to come with him.

"I thought you had to get back to Howard?" Leslie asked, somewhat perturbed.

"I didn't say I needed to get back to Howard," Norvel told her. "Uh, uh, I said I needed to go do something."

"At the Lincoln Memorial?" Leslie asked. "Should I wait here?"

"No, I'd like you to come with me," Norvel said.

Norvel opened the passenger door, took Leslie's hand, and together they walked across the pavement to the expanse of granite stonework leading to the monument of Abraham Lincoln. Still holding hands, they climbed the steps with the other Sunday afternoon visitors.

When they reached the top Norvel asked, "Have you been here before?"

"Many years ago, my school in Leesburg arranged a field trip here," Leslie said. "But I hardly remember it."

Norvel said, "This is my favorite place in Washington. I come and run the mall for conditioning, which includes running up these steps."

"We've known each other for a couple of years now, and you never told me this before."

"Well, you're just going to have to stick with me a little longer because I'll have stories to tell that haven't happened yet."

"That's an interesting way to put it," she said.

They walked to the left of the large chamber where the Gettysburg Address was carved into the stone wall.

"So, Les, if you look up there you'll see the greatest set of words ever spoken by mortal man. President Lincoln used them to consecrate what he called the hallowed ground where the Battle of Gettysburg was fought and won by the Union."

"Fourscore and seven years ago," Leslie said. "I will have to go read those words again, as an adult, and absorb them."

Norvel guided her to the other side of the large chamber where more words were carved.

"And here," Norvel said, pointing to the wall, "is Lincoln's second inaugural speech, the "with malice toward none" speech. His words were the vision of what he saw for the country after the civil war, but a bullet from an assassin changed the course of history."

Leslie remained quiet as she read the immortal words.

Norvel took Leslie's arm and they walked over to the front of the sculpture of Lincoln. He reached into his pocket and pulled out a small box that he had kept hidden. To her surprise, Norvel dropped to his knees.

Leslie put her hand to her mouth. The people at the top of the monument looked at them, smiling.

"Leslie Ellen Jackson, I want to spend the rest of my life with you, and the only way I can figure out how to do that is to be married to you. I love you. Will you marry me?" Norvel asked, smiling broadly.

Leslie stood there stunned. She looked around and then back at him, staring right into his eyes.

She said, "Norvel LaFollette Ray Lee, yes!" Then she burst into tears.

Norvel opened the box and produced a beautiful diamond ring. He stood up, took her hand, and slid the ring onto her finger.

The people at the monument burst into a round of applause. Several of the women dabbed at their eyes.

After recovering from the emotion of the moment, Leslie asked, "Can we have a June wedding? That is what I have always wanted."

Norvel said, "Of course we can. Maybe at Rankin Chapel at Howard University."

Leslie said, "Oh, yes, that's the perfect place!"

Norvel and Leslie hugged and then kissed passionately. Leslie was crying, the tears running unabashedly down her cheeks. Norvel wiped them away with his handkerchief.

The couple walked back down the granite steps while some of the onlookers waved and applauded again.

Norvel requested a formal Christian wedding because it was what his mother would have wanted. The Jacksons asked their Leesburg pastor, Reverend Huston Brooks, to conduct the ceremony. The planning of the wedding was left to Leslie and Mrs. Jackson, with advice and suggestions from their wide circle of friends.

Norvel's one assignment was to reserve the chapel at Howard University. The following week he told the administrator he could provide a cash deposit to hold the building, but the administrator said it wouldn't be necessary. The administrator shook Norvel's hand and said the school would be honored to host the wedding of such an exemplary Bison. Norvel was now free to focus on his upcoming schedule, packed with boxing events and academics.

# CHAPTER 16

## *April 1951—Lillie's boardinghouse, Washington, D.C.*

Norvel and his brother, Jimmy, continued to share a room, but they didn't see each other very often. Recently, they had taken to meeting at Lillie's boardinghouse for breakfast. Even though Robert was no longer there, Lillie welcomed all Howard students for meals. "Mother Dear" was always happy to see Norvel.

"I saw in the paper how you won the Golden Gloves again, Norvel," Lillie said when she saw the two brothers walk in on Friday, April 6. "I also saw in this morning's news that your opponent from Europe for last night's match withdrew at the last minute."

"Yes," Norvel said. "Uh, uh, Ingemar Johansson is his name. Everybody is real high on him, but he's just a baby still, seventeen or eighteen."

"The paper is suggesting he didn't want to get his pretty face beaten in by you, Norvel," Jimmy said. "Apparently you've become pretty intimidating. Isn't that right, Mother Dear?"

"Not my Norvel!" Lillie said, smiling and lightly pinching his cheek. "How can anyone be afraid of this nice, handsome, polite man here? And smart, too, I understand."

"His trainer said he was sick," Norvel said. "Uh, uh, I don't hold it against him. I may get an opportunity to meet him again this summer in Sweden."

Lillie returned to the kitchen, and Jimmy said, "You've got a lot going on. Aren't you leaving for the AAUs tomorrow?

"Yes, I am," Norvel said.

"Boston again, right?" Jimmy confirmed.

"Yes, my first bout is Monday, and there will be one each day through Thursday if I keep winning."

"Have you met any of the fighters before?" Jimmy asked.

"I probably know of them," Norvel said. "The heavyweight category is having a changing of the guard, except for me, I guess. Some of the fellas I know have turned pro. I may know a few in the other weight classes."

"How are you keeping up with everything?" Jimmy asked. "How are your classes and grades doing?"

"I'm keeping up," Norvel said. "Not taking a full load helps. Are you all ready for your graduation in June?"

"It's going to happen, ready or not," Jimmy said.

"I believe it's going to be the weekend before Leslie and I tie the knot."

"You are getting married? Wow, Norvel. What made you want to get hitched now?" Jimmy asked. "Especially with everything else you have going on?"

"She's a real good person for me," Norvel said. "I love her, and she'll help me keep my feet on the ground."

"I think it's because with all of your traveling around, you're afraid someone else might snatch her up," Jimmy said.

"Well, there's that too," Norvel said. "You know if I retain the title, I'll be involved in the Duals Matches again this summer. They're going to be held in Europe."

"My brother is getting married," Jimmy observed. "We must be growing up."

"You've done real good, Jimmy," Norvel said. "Everyone's proud of you, but Mama would especially be. Still worried about Uncle Sam?"

"Afraid so," Jimmy said. "ROTC had its benefits, but I committed to serve if called up and I'm led to believe that's what'll happen. Apparently Korea is heating up."

Norvel said. "At least you'll get to be an officer and give out orders."

Jimmy laughed. "How much do you think anyone's going to listen to an inexperienced colored officer?"

Lillie brought the food over.

"Thank you," Jimmy said.

"Y'all are very welcome, boys," Lillie said.

"Have you been in touch with George?" Norvel asked.

"He's struggling with school," Jimmy said. "He's not like you and me in terms of disciplining himself to hit the books, and he doesn't have Mama to get after him. Dad is still in the dumps, working odd jobs."

"Hmm," said Norvel, thinking. "I should pay more attention to George. Maybe we have to get him out of there and up here eventually. Maybe Dad too."

Jimmy nodded, but both men knew neither of them had the time to take that on right now.

On Monday and Tuesday at Boston Garden, Norvel fought his way through the preliminary bout and quarterfinals without much difficulty. Each opponent, James Craven of Alabama and Joe McFadden of Philadelphia, went the distance, but neither of the matches demanded much of him physically.

The light heavyweight boxer from Boston Norvel had become friendly with last year, John Boutilier, was also competing in the tournament. Norvel saw him pound out a victory in Monday's preliminary match, and then caught up with him in the locker room before his match on Tuesday.

"Hey, Bout, you got in this thing this year," Norvel said.

"Hi, Norvel," Boutilier said. "I took your suggestion and approached Boston College, so they sponsored me in here. What do you think your chances are?"

"Who knows?" Norvel said. "Just taking it one match at a time. I've got something more important going on."

"What's that?"

"I'm getting married," Norvel said smiling.

"Congratulations!" Boutilier said. "Is the bride the same gal you told me about last year?"

"Sure is," Norvel said proudly.

Boutilier said, "I've got to go get loosened up. Good luck to you out there."

"And good luck to you, Bout," Norvel said.

For the semifinals, Norvel faced Peter Rademacher, a twenty-two-year-old senior from Washington State University. Rademacher was purported to have a devastating knockout punch with either hand, but like many of the heavyweights Norvel encountered, he had not mastered the strategic side of boxing. Nevertheless, Rademacher had knocked out both his opponents in Seattle to qualify for this national tournament. In the quarterfinal match, Rademacher easily dispatched his opponent Hank Ehron of the Great Lakes Golden Gloves.

Norvel, as defending AAU champion, was considered the man to beat. It was expected that other heavyweight contenders, like Rademacher, would be gunning for him. Knowing this, Norvel established a strategy of "come get me if you can" in the ring. His goal was simply to outpoint his opponent.

Boston Garden was at capacity. Although neither boxer was a local, this was a highly promoted match between a touted up-and-comer and the reigning champion.

At the outset Norvel looked invincible. He was tall and broad, with taut muscles rippling from his shoulders down to his calves. He danced around Rademacher, intimidating him with experienced moves and a look of intense confidence. The younger boxer came at Norvel, occasionally jabbing, but left his body open to Norvel's jabs. Each time Norvel launched a flurry of punches, Rademacher started to backpedal. Just when Norvel had him set up, though, the round ended.

When the second round, started Norvel continued where he had left off. He jabbed and stepped forward, while Rademacher went into reverse. Norvel landed two punches to each one flung by Rademacher, scoring points with the judges.

In the third round, Rademacher's fatigue was on display for all to see. The gleam was gone from his eyes, and his movements became more deliberate instead of fluid. Norvel went right at him, launching a flurry of punches that moved Rademacher against the ropes, where he wrapped his arms in a clinch around Norvel. The referee split them up. Norvel knew he had the fight at that point and danced around Rademacher, daring him to attack. The bell sounded, ending the match.

Norvel went to his corner maintaining his composure, waiting for the judges to tally their cards. When they did, Norvel had won a unanimous decision.

The finals, the next night, would determine which boxers would represent eight weight categories on the national AAU boxing team. The other two spots would be filled by AAU team coaches. That team would go to Europe in a few months for the annual Duals Matches.

An enthusiastic standing-room-only crowd filled Boston Garden for the annual event. The AAU championship, staged in Boston each year since 1940, was a highly anticipated event. This year's fervor was amplified by the presence of local boxers McGuigan and Boutilier in the finals.

Norvel finished his warm-up in time to be surprised by McGuigan getting knocked out of the lightweight contest in the second round by Len Walters of Canada. The nineteen-year-old Walters not only knocked the wind out of his opponent but also deflated the audience expecting to celebrate a local champion.

When it was time for Boutilier's light heavyweight match, Norvel found a spot ringside to take in the action. Boutilier's first three matches had been tough slugfests, with the boxers trading blow for blow. Boutilier just plain liked to go for the kill shot, paying little attention to strategy. This trait was on display from the outset of his championship bout against Ned Hicks of New York, who was also of the same ilk. Boutilier went at Hicks, who immediately countered and sent the Bostonian to the floor.

Norvel tried hollering above the frenzy, "Come on, Bout. Get your hands up and move away from him!"

Boutilier got back up after the referee, Tommy Rawson, counted to eight, and stayed covered, recovering from the knockdown for the rest of the round.

For the next two rounds, however, Boutilier went back to his slugfest style and eventually wore Hicks down. In the end he won a unanimous decision. But the noise from the crowd made it almost impossible to understand what the announcer was saying.

Now it was Norvel's turn. He was up against seventeen-year-old Albert Schlimm of Baltimore. Few expected Schlimm to have made it this far in the tournament. Norvel, the heavy favorite, was cheered appreciatively when he entered the Gardens and took his position in the corner of the ring.

Schlimm, with closely cropped blond hair, looked very much like the youth he was. Norvel thought he looked as if he were ready for a high school track event more than a boxing championship. But Norvel knew not to judge an opponent strictly on appearance. Schlimm looked across the ring at Norvel, nodded slightly, and quickly glanced away.

*He's just a kid. Unless he has something I'm not anticipating, I'm gonna go just for the points.*

The fight got under way. Norvel danced around Schlimm as if this were a sparring match. It became obvious early to everyone that Norvel far outclassed the inexperienced youngster. Norvel was impressed at how game Schlimm was, however. He tried to find a way around Norvel's classic defense and occasionally landed some punches. Norvel decided to demonstrate some classic boxing moves, hoping Schlimm would learn to read them in the future. As he danced around Schlimm, occasionally blocking a wild swing, Norvel rotated his hips counterclockwise while pivoting on his right foot, allowing the rest of his body to follow. As he did Norvel exhaled sharply and extended his right arm on a level with his chin, catching Schlimm on the cheekbone, practically knocking him down.

*That, young man, is a proper right cross. Get used to it 'cause we all use it. Here are a few more for you to practice with.*

In round two, Norvel began by circling Schlimm and then pivoted both feet in a clockwise direction, simultaneously lifting his left heel while dropping his right. His body rotated as a solid block, and he swung his left fist into the side of Schlimm's head. Schlimm was staggered but gamely stayed up.

*And that was a left hook. Here are a few more.*

Schlimm's resilience was still impressive throughout round three. The crowd thought Norvel should have put him away by now, but Norvel stuck to his plan, bobbing and weaving and landing many more scoring hits than Schlimm.

At the sound of the bell Norvel put his arm around Schlimm, who finally looked defeated, and said, "You should be proud of yourself. You did very well. It's remarkable you took second in this national tournament while still in high school."

The ring announcer came to the center ring and said, "Ladies and Gentleman! Thank you for supporting the annual Amateur Athletic Union's national boxing championship. I'm going to ask each champion to come up here when I call their name."

The crowd was on its feet, applauding.

"Here are this year's national amateur boxing champions: the flyweight champion from Philadelphia, Willie Peacock; bantamweight champion from Hawaii, Ernie DeJesus; lightweight champion from Vancouver, Canada, Len Walters; welterweight champion from Philadelphia, Jim Hackney; light middleweight champion from Cleveland, Rudy Gwinn; middleweight champion, again from Philadelphia, Tommy Nelson."

Before the announcer could continue, a large roar began in the stands. The announcer smiled broadly and added, "Ladies and gentlemen, you all know this young man. From the great city of Boston, Massachusetts, voted the outstanding boxer of this year's tournament, the light heavyweight champion, John Boutilier!"

The crowd went wild, stomping their feet on the floor and yelling at the top of their lungs. Boutilier sprang into the ring, doffing his cap at the fans, and joined the line of other boxers.

When the stands quieted the announcer said, "And for the second consecutive year as the AAU's heavyweight champion; from Washington D.C., Norvel Leeeeee!"

Norvel climbed into the ring, smiled at his fellow champions, clasped Boutilier's hand, and stood proudly. He absorbed the scene at Boston Garden, relishing it.

*I wish Leslie was here with me to see this. This moment will be in my head, forever!*

When Norvel returned home, Leslie, Jimmy, and many of his Howard boxing and baseball teammates, including Coach Barnes, greeted him at Union Station. All were proud to know him and feel a part of the celebration. Other people in the station, realizing they were looking at the reigning boxing champion, came over to congratulate him also.

Later in the clear, warm spring evening Norvel and Leslie went for a walk on the Mall, near the Smithsonian Institution Building, known as the Castle.

"Your fame as a boxer keeps building," Leslie said, taking his arm. "I'm so proud of you."

"Thank you," Norvel said. "I was approached by a boxing promoter who tried to convince me to become a professional."

Leslie turned and looked at Norvel, concerned.

"Don't worry, Les," Norvel said. "He offered me $10,000 just to sign up with him, and I have to admit, it was tempting. It would sure come in handy after we're married. But I told him I had other plans for my life."

"Good. We can make it without that dirty money," Leslie countered. She paused and said, "The wedding plans are coming together nicely. Everyone is excited about it."

"Me too," Norvel said. His arm, around Leslie's waist, gave her a slight tug. "You know that I will be going to Europe in August as part of the AAU team."

"You're going to leave your new wife at home, alone?" Leslie teased. "I guess I'll just have to read about you in the newspaper."

On June 14, Norvel's father, his sister Edna, and his brother George came to Washington to attend Jimmy's graduation, and planned to stay until after the wedding the following weekend.

The next day, the 1951 Howard University graduating class, along with their families and friends, gathered on the Upper Quad, bordered by many signature buildings of the eighty-plus-year-old campus, including the Founder's Library and Frederick Douglass Memorial Hall. Chairs for the graduates and spectators filled the manicured lawn on the open space in front of a temporary platform set up at the north end, with the section closest to the platform reserved for the approximately four hundred graduates.

Jack Lee, accompanied by his two sons, Norvel and George, and his daughter, Edna, arrived early and secured a section of seats. They were together to witness his son and their brother become the first in their family to receive a college degree. Each recognized what a momentous occasion this was. Individually, they gave their silent praise to George Anna Ray Lee, wife and mother, whose relentless pursuit of educational opportunities for all her children had made this moment possible.

The Lees were joined in the same section by Leslie, Robert Jr., and their parents, Emmett and Mrs. Jackson. The senior Lees and Jacksons had not previously met, so Norvel took advantage of this event to introduce them.

The commencement address was delivered by William Henry Jernagin, the well-known pastor of nearby Mount Carmel Baptist Church, whose lifelong pursuit was to engage his congregation when Jim Crow issues confronted them. Norvel had occasionally, with Leslie, attended services at Mount Carmel to hear the eloquent pastor speak. He was curious to know what topic Pastor Jernagin would speak of in this commencement setting, and was not disappointed.

At one point Jernagin motivated the new graduates with these words:

"In this age, we must be aggressive or perish. We must be progressive, and we must seize every lawful opportunity to sustain ourselves as individuals and sustain ourselves as a race. You, the future leaders of our race, are obligated to collaborate on the best possible means for obtaining the unity and harmony that will result in outstanding success for all. Progress should be the password and byword of every Negro. It is his salvation in a chaotic and war-torn world."

*There it is, right out in the open. He said it so plainly. Inspirational!*

Finally, after several other traditional commencement events, including a choir and a short speech by the 1951 Class President, the graduates were called to the platform alphabetically to receive their individual diplomas. Leslie, seated next to Norvel, nudged him, whispering that she noticed about a quarter of the graduates were women.

Then the announcer said, "James F. Lee, Bachelor of Arts, History. Mr. Lee is a staff member of the *Hilltop* student newspaper, a member of Kappa Sigma, and a Letters and Key awardee earned as a member of the Howard University Debating Society."

Jimmy said, "Thank you, sir," as he accepted the diploma from Dr. Johnson.

Norvel and Leslie began applauding with the others. Many of the graduates were clapping, demonstrating Jimmy's popularity among his classmates.

When the lengthy commencement was over, the Lees, Jacksons, and many friends of Jimmy's gathered at the boarding house, where Lillie hosted a reception. She gave Jimmy a hug while the two families became comfortable with each other, expressing their excitement about the wedding the following weekend.

# CHAPTER 17

## *Friday, June 22, 1951, 10:30 a.m. —Andrew Rankin Memorial Chapel, Howard University*

At the altar inside the red-brick chapel stood the national AAU heavyweight boxing champion, Norvel Lee. He appeared relaxed and confident in his striking navy-blue suit with matching tie, and a crisp white shirt and silver cufflinks. Norvel was absorbing every moment, proudly, in front of their invited guests. Reverend Brooks was standing at the pulpit smiling at the congregation, the men dressed in suits and ties, the women in bright formal dresses. His bride would soon be walking down the aisle, escorted by her father, Emmett Jackson.

The Andrew Rankin Chapel, a two-story structure, is set into the side of a hill. Norvel reflected on what he knew about the spiritual center of Howard University. The building was dedicated in the 1890s in honor of its namesake, the deceased brother of abolitionist Jeremiah C. Rankin who was then president of Howard University.

Norvel estimated there were about two hundred people in Rankin Chapel. He saw his father and Edna, Mr. Jackson, Robert Jackson Jr., Mr. and Mrs. Byrd from Covington, Coach Barnes, Glenn Drake, Lillie Walton, Mrs. Henry and her three children, and many of the Jacksons friends, neighbors, and parishioners from Leesburg. Several of Norvel's boxing companions from the Golden Gloves and Howard University, as well as members of the Howard baseball team, were there. A reporter from the *Evening Star* was also present, standing in the back with camera and notepad. Norvel was thankful the wedding had been planned for the morning, because the afternoon was looking to become hot and muggy.

While they waited, the chapel's thirty-seven step pipe organ provided background music. There was a moment of silent expectation when the music stopped. Then the organist began to play a medley of familiar tunes while Jimmy, Norvel's best man, entered the chapel from the side and stood by his brother. The audience then turned and looked to the rear of the chapel. Leslie's little sister, Weekie, and Norvel's brother, George, led three other pairs of bridesmaids and groomsmen down the center aisle, followed by Leslie's maid of honor, her cousin from Leesburg. The bridesmaids wore off-white dresses, while the groomsmen wore navy-blue suits like Norvel's. The flower girl and ring bearer, Leslie's young cousins, walked nervously down the aisle and took their positions, as they had learned at the rehearsal.

Suddenly the organ and the room became silent, except for a slight shuffling at the rear of the chapel. Leslie appeared, standing with her father, who was dressed in a black tuxedo. Norvel's breath was taken away by the image he saw before him.

*She looks like a princess, glowing in a halo of light.*

The organ began playing "Here Comes the Bride." Leslie, her hand tucked into her father's arm, walked slowly down the aisle, smiling, her eyes looking forward toward Norvel. Norvel noticed she was limping slightly, which was unusual. She took her place next to him and they both turned to face Reverend Brooks, who smiled at them.

Reverend Brooks looked out into the crowded chapel. In a loud, resonant voice he said, "Friends, we are gathered together in the sight of God to witness and bless the joining together of Norvel LaFollette Ray Lee and Leslie Ellen Jackson in marriage. Norvel and Leslie come to marry one another in this holy covenant."

The couple recited their vows. After a prayer, they exchanged rings.

Releasing their hands, Reverend Brooks looked out at the congregation and said, "Now that Norvel and Leslie have given themselves to each other by solemn vows, with the joining of hands, and the giving and receiving of rings, I announce to you that they are husband and wife."

The Reverend nodded, giving his blessing for them to kiss, which they happily did.

Reverend Brooks said to the congregation, "I introduce to you, for the first time, Mr. and Mrs. Norvel Lee."

The congregation rose from their seats, applauding loudly.

As Norvel and Leslie made their way back up the aisle, Norvel noticed she was holding his arm tightly and limping.

"Are your shoes bothering you, Les?" Norvel asked. "You seem to be having a hard time walking."

"Yes," she said. "I dropped the iron on my foot this morning when I was ironing my slip. It's a big bruise. But I'm not going to let it stop me from enjoying myself."

They walked out of the front doors of the chapel and were greeted by well-wishers with a hail of confetti. As Leslie, holding on to Norvel's arm, gingerly made her way down the path in front of the chapel, Weekie ran up giggling with a handful of rice, which she deposited inside the back of Leslie's wedding gown. Leslie screamed and made a face as her sister continued giggling.

The wedding party walked over to the nearby Frederick Douglass Memorial Hall for the reception. Norvel and Leslie greeted each visitor in a receiving line. The visitors found their assigned seating and served themselves a buffet-style meal. Jimmy got the room's attention by clanging a fork on his water glass.

"Alright, everyone, listen up!" announced Jimmy to the several hundred people in attendance.

The room grew quiet as everyone looked at the head table.

"Here's to a groom with a bride so fair, and here's to a bride with a groom who is so rare. May the two of you be poor in misfortune and rich in blessings. Here's to a wonderful wedding day, and an even more marvelous marriage for Mr. and Mrs. Lee," proposed Jimmy, as he raised his glass of champagne.

The clinking of glasses and words of approval could be heard throughout the packed room. A trio with an upright bass, piano, and violin had set up in a corner of the room to provide renditions of familiar tunes. They began with Louis Armstrong's popular tune, "A Kiss to Build a Dream

On," with the piano player also serving as vocalist. Jimmy motioned for Norvel and Leslie to take the floor and to begin the dancing. The guests broke into a loud applause as Norvel and Leslie, still limping, rose from their seats to take the floor, smiling broadly at each other. Several pieces of confetti floated around Leslie as she stepped gingerly onto the dance floor.

*Leslie Jackson and Norvel Lee on a date in Norvel's Mercury.*
Ebony, 2/1/1951

*Leslie Jackson on her wedding day.*
Norvel Lee family archives

*Norvel, Edna, and James Lee.*
Norvel Lee family archives

*Norvel and Leslie Jackson Lee.*
Norvel Lee family archives

*Edna Lee, Norvel Lee, and Leslie Jackson.*
Norvel Lee family archives

*Norvel Lee at Howard University.*
Howard University Bulletin

*1948 U.S. Boxing Team on board the S.S. America (Norvel Lee is back left).*
Report of the USOC 1948 Games

*Norvel Lee on the way to a Golden Gloves Championship, March 29, 1950.*
Washington Evening Star

*Norvel Lee keeping in condition.*
Norvel Lee family archives

*Norvel Lee demonstrating his style to onlookers.*
Norvel Lee family archives

*Norvel Lee awarded a national AAU championship.*
Norvel Lee family archives

*Norvel Lee receiving an achievement award at Howard University.*
The Bison, Howard University yearbook, 1953

*Norvel Lee working with boys in Washington, D.C.*
Ebony, 2/1/1951

*Norvel Lee showing his left jab.*
Ebony, 2/1/1951

BOXING 1951

Kneeling left to right: L. Williams, S. Neverson, C. Strickland, J. Benson, C. Turner, W. Lewis. Standing: S. Barnes, Coach: A. Julian, Trainer; V. Adegbite, W. Keyes, W. Diggs, H. Cochrane, J. Land, W. Duru, C. Hoover, Norvel Lee, J. Jackson.

*Howard University Boxing Team.*
(The Bison, Howard University yearbook, 1951)

167

# CHAPTER 18

## *Thursday, August 31, 1951—Gothenburg, Sweden*

"Rise and shine, Bout!" Norvel said to the body under the bundle of blankets on the bed opposite his own. "Today's the day!"

A groan emitted from beneath the blankets.

He and Bout had been assigned this room when the U.S. Duals team arrived in Sweden's west coast seaport city, Gothenburg. They had been roommates on each stop of the team's three week European tour.

Norvel's highly anticipated match this night would be against the popular local favorite, eighteen-year-old Ingemar Johansson. Many of the ten boxers on the U.S. team were exhausted, not so much from the boxing events but from exploring the social opportunities in each city they visited. Norvel was well rested, having spent his free time helping coaches Ted Hollands and Charlie Geveke remind the team to focus on maintaining their physical conditioning.

When the team left New York on the *RMS Queen Elizabeth* on August 15, Norvel realized this was his third Atlantic crossing, after the first two going to and from the 1948 Olympics. He was the only member of the 1951 team who had been to Europe before.

One afternoon, while out on the Atlantic Ocean, Coach Hollands took Norvel aside. Standing at the deck rail, Norvel felt small next to Hollands, who was several inches taller and fifty pounds heavier. Hollands was a football coach who emphasized conditioning as the path to superior performance. The slow undulating up-and-down motion of the ship was apparent.

"Norvel," Hollands said with a smile, "you are the most experienced and mature member of the team. I could use that experience and your positive attitude in helping your younger teammates accept the unfamiliar conditions they will likely encounter. They respect you and will find your presence reassuring."

"Yes, sir," Norvel said, glad that Hollands trusted him. "Uh, uh, I'll do my best."

*The 1951 AAU boxing team on board the RMS Queen Elizabeth. From left to right, standing: Charlie Geveke, Norvel Lee, John Boutilier, Tommy Nelson, Rudolph Gwinn, James Hackney, Ted Hollands. Bottom row: Willie Peacock, Len Walters, Jerry McGuigan, Ernest DeJesus, Randy Sandy.* John Boutilier family archives

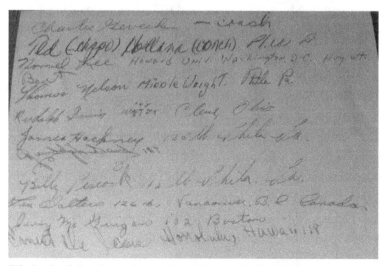

*The back of the photo above, signed by each individual.*

They arrived at the docks in Liverpool, England, on August 20. London's *Daily Telegraph* published the following article upon their arrival:

### U.S. BOXERS GET THEIR DATE MIXED

What is claimed to be the strongest amateur boxing team ever to represent the United States

in this country arrived in London today 16 hours late owing to delay in docking the Queen Elizabeth . . .

. . . A surprise awaited the team. They thought the match against Great Britain at the Empire Pool, Wembley, was fixed for Wednesday and not tomorrow.

A colourful party in every sense, they knelt on the platform at Waterloo and obliged with songs. Seven of the 10 are coloured boxers—the only three white men being James [*sic*] Boutilier, light-heavy-weight who has won 58 out of 60 bouts, John Mc-Guigan, a bus-boy and light-weight who has won 27 out of 30, and Len Walters, from Vancouver, feather-weight who has won 111 out of 119 bouts at the age of 19.

Nearly all the Americans wore zoot-suits. They wore the widest variety of hats from coloured trilbies to somber black berets—their ties were of the brightest hue. One man was eating an orange.

This afternoon the team went to weigh-in.

The team was put up at a former Royal Air Force camp in Uxbridge, the same location where Norvel and the U.S. Olympic team were lodged for the 1948 Olympics. By now many of the rooms had been converted to apartments for the population at large, but some were still used for athletes and performers visiting London.

On Tuesday morning, Hollands and Geveke gathered the team together and reminded them who they would be facing and what the scouting reports said about each opponent. Norvel looked at the faces of the excited team to see if he could sense any apprehension. All seemed to be in good spirits, ready to begin their tour of Europe.

Hollands held a stack of envelopes in his hand. Handing an envelope to each boxer, he said, "Men, inside you will find some spending money and something that may be even more valuable, a Rail Pass."

Several of the men opened their envelope, looking curiously inside at the contents.

"A Rail Pass?" Sandy asked.

"Yes," Hollands said. "We'll be traveling by rail while here, and this is your ticket to ride. It allows you to get on almost any train in Europe while you're visiting."

"Wow," DeJesus said. "Thank you."

"Thank the AAU sponsors," responded Hollands. "This afternoon we're expected to be at a formal welcoming feast with our opponents and their Amateur Boxing Association (ABA) benefactors. Keep in mind, this is a proud bunch who have never lost an international competition on their home turf. We're aiming to change this, but please be courteous during these opening festivities."

A.B.A. v. A.A.U. of U.S. LONDON, 21ST AUGUST, 1951

John Boutilier family archives

After the gathering of competitors and dignitaries, the team went to their quarters to prepare for the evening boxing events. Later, they arrived at Wembley Stadium and found it filled with a capacity crowd of eleven thousand avid boxing fans.

The first bout of the evening involved flyweights Willie Peacock and steelworker Richie Jenkins. At the outset Peacock went to work on Jenkins with right hooks. But by the end of the second round, Jenkins found his rhythm and went on to win a very closely contested bout. Likewise, bantamweight Tommy Nicholls outpointed Hawaii's Ernest DeJesus. The spectators in the packed stadium were on their feet, cheering loudly.

But in the next bout the Canadian, lightweight Len Walters, showed off his lightning-fast hands and readily dispatched his opponent, Percy Lewis.

Boutilier looked at his teammates and said, "Canada was originally part of the British Empire. They will likely claim Len as one of their own."

"They can't have him," Hollands countered. "He won the spot on our team."

The others laughed in agreement.

Next up, now fighting as a light welterweight, was Jerry McGuigan, who was fighting a classic stand-up boxer, Freddie Reardon. Reardon outboxed McGuigan who, as usual, was trying to instigate a free-for-all. McGuigan often let his guard down, allowing Reardon to rock him with well-placed rights to the chin. When Reardon was announced the clear winner, the spectators knew that their team year would win the tournament yet again. They had won three of the first four matches.

However, welterweight Jimmy Hackney quieted the crowd by knocking out his opponent one minute fifty-five seconds into the first round. And light middleweight Rudy Gwinn subdued the fans further by using long, raking lefts on Johnny Thurgood. With that win, the Americans and British were tied.

Next up was New York middleweight, Randy Sandy, against Alf Lay. The first two rounds were even, with the boxers moving around each other trading jabs. Then in the last round Sandy let loose a whirlwind of punches and right hooks that put Lay on the canvas. The Londoner managed to get back on his feet but wasn't strong enough to inflict any damage for the rest of the fight.

The Americans now had the lead, but the British got even when the referee stopped the next bout because Tommy Nelson was being pummeled by Arthur Howard.

It was time for the highly anticipated match pitting Jack Boutilier against Tony Smith. Both boxers were reputed to be the stars of their respective teams. The local press referred to Boutilier as "colorful." Arguably, the people who packed the stadium were there to see this contest.

When Boutilier settled in his corner he was sporting a plaid tartan cap. He tossed it to the ground and shadowboxed for a moment. Smith, on the opposite side, also jabbed at the air, anxious for the fight to begin. The crowd was on its feet, in a frenzied state.

Surprisingly, Boutilier assumed a classic boxer's bearing when the first round began, as move that was and out of character for him. It proved to be of no use as Smith had his way with him for the first two rounds. Smith landed jabs and several punishing punches with little cover coming from the Bostonian. Knowing he was losing, Boutilier became the brawler his teammates were expecting him to be all along. At the sound of the bell for round three, Boutilier practically sprinted from his corner and began to pound Smith with heavy rights to the head and body. Smith went down three times from the onslaught, causing the referee to halt the match. Boutilier then casually picked up his tartan, doffed it to the spectators, placed it on

*"Bout" dispatches his opponent.*
John Boutlier family archives

173

his head, and left the ring. The gesture brought scattered appreciative laughter and applause from the fans.

The Americans were up by one match.

*No need to do too much here. Just don't lose. This will be more about how I appear before the judges. These boys don't have the tournament experience we do.*

Norvel stepped into the ring, appearing confident and at ease. From the outset he maneuvered around his opponent, Peter Toch. As Toch sought opportunities, Norvel easily countered with hits that scored points. In each round, the clear differences in the skill of the two boxers were apparent to all. Norvel easily outpointed the Englishman.

The team stayed in London another day before traveling to the next event. Norvel was curious as to how London had changed since 1948, when it was rebuilding from the damage from the war.

Norvel informed his teammates that he'd be going on a self-guided tour of London; Boutilier, DeJesus, Walters, and Sandy decided to join him. They wore colorful USA regalia and were welcomed warmly everywhere. Norvel took them to the Thames River and the sites along it, including the Tower of London. As the day wore on, they walked the streets, rode the trolleys, and saw Buckingham Palace, St. Paul's Cathedral, and the London Bridge. The weather was good and the city was alive with energy.

At one point they walked by a popular pub and saw their teammate Jerry McGuigan with a mug of beer, talking to several of the locals crowded in the bar. Hollands had cautioned them on making sure they stayed healthy during their free time, but he knew the young men might take in some of the pubs. McGuigan waved them in, and Boutilier looked at Norvel.

"Not for me, fellas, but if any of you want to join him, go ahead," Norvel said.

But instead, they all decided to continue Norvel's informative tour.

On Thursday morning, Norvel and the team got together for a training session at the Wembley facilities before catching the train up to Manchester. Norvel worked with the quiet, reserved, and serious Rudolph Gwinn, the nineteen-year-old light middleweight. Norvel saw a move while Gwinn was sparring that he wanted to call to his attention. He thought an opponent might be able to anticipate his moves, because Gwinn was telegraphing the moment of his attack.

Norvel interrupted the sparring match by saying, "Hey, Rudy, I'd like to show you something, if I may."

Gwinn nodded.

Norvel motioned for Gwinn's sparring partner, Randy Sandy, to step aside. The much larger Norvel entered the practice ring.

"Don't hurt me now, Norvel," Gwinn said, with a rare display of humor.

Hollands and the others laughed as Norvel continued, "Okay, try to punch me hard with your left hand. Rest assured you won't hurt me."

Gwinn tried to deliver a hard left to the body as Norvel pulled away, pointing to Gwinn's left knee.

"See what you do with your knee before you throw the punch?" Norvel asked. "It juts out. That may work okay for you at your home club, but it won't on this stage."

"Good observation, Norvel," Hollands said.

Gwinn looked at Norvel and said, "Thank you, man. I'll see what I can do about that. Get back in here, Randy."

*"Bout" catching Norvel off guard.*
John Boutilier family archives

Sandy reentered the ring, and the two boxers resumed their sparring.

Norvel then went against Boutilier for a while. At one point during their sparring, Boutilier caught him off guard and landed an explosive punch to Norvel's face. A photographer's camera caught it at the moment of impact, and the photo was widely distributed by the press the next day.

There was not a lot do on Friday in the industrial city of Manchester, still rebuilding after the damage caused by German bombers during the war. Norvel and Boutilier strolled around the city, stepping around piles of rubble and talking about the upcoming second round of matches against England that evening.

Norvel was pleased with the strategy Boutilier had devised for himself. He simply wore down his opponent in the end. Norvel's experience had led him to believe that as long as a boxer possessed basic skills and was in a match with someone of equal skills, the key to winning was having the endurance to last to the final round.

The second of the matches against the ABA occurred at Belle Vue Stadium, normally used as a greyhound racing park. Five thousand boxing fans from around the area streamed in to see if their team could make up for the unexpected loss incurred three days before.

Peacock, DeJesus, McGuigan, and Sandy lost their bouts on points. But Walters, Hackney, and Gwinn won theirs, closing the score to 4-3, still in favor of the ABA.

Tommy Nelson, appearing no worse for being KO'd during the first round at Wembley, confidently tossed lefts at England's Eric Ludlam. Ludlam at times would emerge from his crouch and land a right to Nelson's head. When he did, however, Nelson countered with hooks to the body. In round two, Nelson trapped Ludlam in a corner and inundated him with hooks and swings to the head and body. In the third, Ludlam tried getting to Nelson with his left but was very quickly covered in blood. The referee stopped the fight. The English fans applauded Ludlam's resilience.

The matches were tied 4-4. The American team gathered ringside, waiting to see if Boutilier could again give them the lead. They yelled words of encouragement to their lively teammate still sporting his tartan cap. He faced a youthful Peter Bates, who appeared nonchalant, considering the importance of the bout.

Bates opened with a string of strategically selected lefts to Boutilier, who tried again to be patient and mount a defense, but couldn't find an effective balance. At the start of round two, to the delight of the Americans, Boutilier shot out of his corner and immediately took the English boy to the ropes. Boutilier kept boring in and landed a hard blow to Bates's jaw. Boutilier continued his attack into the third round, until he tired and backed off. At that point, against, the backdrop of a roaring crowd, Bates rallied, pummeling Boutilier with a barrage of punches and hooks, causing his face to show signs of swelling. But in the end, it wasn't enough and Boutilier was rewarded with a win.

It was up to Norvel to secure another victory for the American Duals team.

Just before stepping into the ring, Hollands encouraged Norvel, saying, "You know what to do."

Norvel nodded confidently.

In his corner Norvel looked striking. His dark, flawlessly proportioned body, glistening brown eyes, and long, muscular arms gave him a look of cool invincibility. The crowd became subdued when the fight got under way against their hometown heavyweight, Arthur Worrall. Norvel moved easily around Worrall, who tried courageously to keep up with Norvel. But Norvel landed jabs at will, stepping back from the wild hooks launched by his opponent.

Standing in his corner, between rounds, Norvel said to himself, *I'm not even working very hard here. Just need to keep my guard up and keep landing hits.* Norvel smiled confidently at his teammates, who were huddled just below him in the corner.

The second and third rounds played out the same, with Norvel moving fluidly around Worrall, who was unable to inflict any damage. The Americans were awarded the championship against Great Britain.

The next Duals event for the Americans was scheduled against West Germany, in Wiesbaden. The team left in the morning by train to Harwich.

After exploring the small medieval town, they caught the ferry to Amsterdam. It was a rough four-and-a-half hour journey across turbulent seas. Most of the boxers were sick to their stomachs.

The men spent Saturday night in Amsterdam at a hostel in the De Wallen area, also known as the Red Light District. Walking through the area by himself to stay loose, Norvel thought this section of the Dutch city made Times Square appear docile.

The next day, during the eight-hour train ride, most of the men dozed. They were tired, catching up on the sleep they'd missed. They awakened long enough to change trains in Brussels, but went right back to sleep as soon as they settled into their new seats. Except for Norvel, Gwinn, and the coaches, the other team members missed catching a glimpse of Cologne when they stopped for twenty minutes in the idyllic German city.

Norvel was worried that many members of the team weren't staying in top physical condition. He made his concern known to the team, but when they arrived in Wiesbaden on Sunday, Boutilier and his fellow Bostonian McGuigan went to a biergarten.

Come Monday, neither of them was in any condition to seriously contend in their matches against the Germans. McGuigan had not been successful in any of his matches so far, and now it seemed he found a companion in Boutilier. Boutilier had told Norvel earlier he wanted to experience as much of the culture as possible while in Europe. Even though he was the national light heavyweight champion, he wasn't serious about boxing. His main athletic pursuit was being a member of the football team at Boston University, for which he was on a scholarship. And, like Norvel, he had his eyes on achieving an academic education.

The U.S. team's performance against the Germans was awful. They lost the first five matches, flyweight through welterweight. Then Gwinn stopped the Germans' winning streak, and Randy Sandy and Tommy Nelson won their matches. Boutilier lost his match in a lackluster performance. Norvel blamed their predicament on fatigue and a failure by some of his teammates to pace themselves mentally and physically for their matches.

He attempted to encourage them by reminding each one what they were there for. Time to experience Europe would occur after their boxing mission was completed.

As for Norvel, he faced the undefeated German heavyweight, Abraham Rosenberg.

Norvel glanced across the ring at the German. He looked tough, not intimidated by the frenzy around him, or that he was up against a reputed formidable opponent. From the clanging of the first bell Norvel ascertained that Rosenberg would be another easy match. The German had potential, but not the experience of an opponent of Norvel's skill. But during the first round, Norvel changed his assessment. Norvel landed many solid shots that should have taken Rosenberg down.

*This guy can take a hit. He won't go down, refuses to.*

For all three rounds, Norvel gave Rosenberg everything in his arsenal. Combination punches, crosses, uppercuts, rapid flurries. Rosenberg absorbed them all, even with what likely was a broken nose. Norvel won the match easily.

After the bout the boxers mingled with each other during the Closing Ceremony. Norvel learned through Rosenberg's broken English that he had survived the Holocaust by miraculously escaping to Scotland while the war was on. He thought he was the only member of his family who survived. Norvel nodded sympathetically, patting him on the back as he reflected on his own personal experiences. He concluded, rightly, that this man would not ever go down, under any circumstances.

The coaches were also concerned about their team's readiness. They had barely come out on top in their matches in England, and in Wiesbaden they won only four. Their total wins going into the matches in Gothenburg were sixteen out of thirty. Coaches Geveke and Hollands wanted to be able to return home with an overall winning team. They had to win at least five of the ten matches against the tough Swedish team.

The U.S. team's record on this trip going into the matches against Sweden's team was:

| Boxer | Weight Class | Wins | Losses |
|-------|-------------|------|--------|
| Willie Peacock | Flyweight | 0 | 3 |
| Ernest De Jesus | Bantamweight | 0 | 3 |
| Len Walters | Lightweight | 2 | 1 |
| Jerry McGuigan | Light Welterweight | 0 | 3 |
| James Hackney | Welterweight | 2 | 1 |
| Rudolph Gwinn | Light Middleweight | 3 | 0 |
| Randy Sandy | Middleweight | 2 | 1 |
| Tommy Nelson | Super Middleweight | 2 | 1 |
| John Boutilier | Light Heavyweight | 2 | 1 |
| Norvel Lee | Heavyweight | 3 | 0 |

Hollands was glad Norvel was on the team, not only for his boxing prowess but for his calm presence. Norvel kept his quiet, confident demeanor in spite of the widely promoted buildup of the past several days regarding his bout with Johansson. Johansson's hand, damaged before their scheduled matchup in Washington, D.C., in early April, had apparently healed. The Swedish press was expecting their touted young heavyweight to give the "Negro from America" a lesson, especially after the American press had suggested the Swede was squeamish about facing Norvel.

The Duals competition was scheduled to commence at seven o'clock with the Opening Ceremony, and then immediately lead off with the flyweight competition. When the boxers left their accommodations at about five o'clock for the short walk over to Ullevi Stadium, excited spectators were lined up around the stadium eager to secure the best seats at the eleven-thousand-seat arena.

At seven o'clock the national anthems of both countries were played by Sweden's national band. The boxers lined up in front of the ring in their respective colors. The matches began before a standing-room-only audience.

Willie Peacock, the flyweight from Philadelphia, won his first match of the trip against Reino Nyberg, unanimously. Hollands was ecstatic about the result. Next up was Ernesto De Jesus of Hawaii who, so far, found himself on the losing end of three very close matches. He was frustrated and wanted to win at least once, but again was denied by Sweden's Roy Swedeberg by a split decision. He just could not land enough punches to sway the judges. Hollands, nevertheless, told him his contributions to the team were appreciated.

Then the Canadian lightweight Len Walters battled Sweden's Jens Helander to a three-round victory.

But Jerry McGuigan's light welterweight match against an unknown local, Bernt Johansson, became a bloody pounding of McGuigan's face causing the referee to halt the match about two minutes into the first round. McGuigan, whose late-night exploits were becoming legendary, was in no shape to box anyone. He did not win one match on this European trip.

Settling the score for McGuigan's embarrassing outing, Philadelphia's James Hackney scored a technical knockout when the referee again had to stop the fight in the second round of the welterweight match against Sweden's young newcomer Gert Groendahl. Then Cleveland's Rudolph Gwinn easily won a decision over Conny Blom in the light middleweight bout. Although he kept mostly to himself, Gwinn smiled broadly at the others at the completion of his bout. After he left the ring, he thanked Norvel for his coaching. Gwinn won all four bouts during the tour.

Next, New York's Randy Sandy dispatched Gert Strahle as expected. But Sweden's Stig Sjoelin, the European middleweight champion, won a decision against the super middleweight from Philadelphia, Tommy Nelson.

By this point of the night, coaches Hollands and Geveke were relieved. The United States had won the five matches needed for an overall winning record for the team. They were guaranteed at least a tie with the Swedes. But the coaches thought if either John Boutilier or Norvel won at least one more match, it would make for a highly successful trip.

Boutilier was expected to win his bout against Rolf Storm, who had taken bronze in the light heavyweight European amateur championship. But Norvel knew his friend had been experiencing all Sweden had to offer. Consequently, Boutilier had another lackluster outing against Storm. Norvel thought it was an accomplishment, however, for his friend to have stayed in the fight for the full three rounds. So did Hollands, who thanked him for his efforts.

Norvel again had the opportunity to give the United States an edge in the matches against Sweden and a two-up advantage overall for the tour. Norvel had not seen the highly publicized Johansson fight, but had heard he was primarily a stand-up fighter who held his ground and didn't move around much.

Johansson certainly was not polished or flashy. He was known to paw at his opponent with his left hand, and when an opportunity presented itself, he'd unleash a powerful head-busting right. Norvel planned to keep moving and let Johansson paw away all he wanted. Norvel believed his own quickness and awareness would keep him away from Johansson's right hand.

The ring announcer introduced Norvel Lee and Ingemar Johansson, first in English and then in Swedish. The crowd greeted Norvel politely while cheering with unabashed enthusiasm for the native Johansson. The referee then called them both to the center of the ring. Norvel bounded eagerly over from his corner. Johansson, with short blond hair and blue eyes, rose from the chair in his corner and walked slowly over, smiling at the referee and Norvel. He did not look particularly concerned about the fight while acknowledging his hometown crowd.

The referee gave the customary admonishments to both boxers in English and then sent them back to their corners, Norvel standing and moving his feet while Johansson sat back down. In a few seconds the bell sounded, signaling the start of the first round. Norvel stepped out smartly from his corner, while Johansson lackadaisically strolled to the center of the ring.

Both boxers assumed the stance normally taken by right-handed boxers, with their left foot forward and arms up near their chest, with their left hand near their face, ready to jab. Norvel moved by shifting his weight and rocking from his right to his left foot and back, while Johansson stood flat-footed, his arms moving slowly.

Norvel went right at him and punched Johansson hard with a left-right-left combination. Johansson started to backpedal, throwing a left-handed jab or two but not causing any damage. It was a classic Norvel Lee fight. He kept himself protected from Johansson's devastating right while keeping his opponent backpedaling throughout most of the bout. Johansson, who was sweating profusely, avoided being backed up against the ropes. The noise at Ullevi was deafening as the spectators bellowed their encouragement to Johansson. At one moment in the second round Johansson attempted to land his right, but Norvel expected it and deftly stepped away, causing the normally nonplussed Swede to yell during an awkward stumble. Norvel tried attacking him, but Johansson had recovered his balance. All three rounds were similar, consisting of Norvel punching and jabbing and Johansson backpedaling and moving around the ring, not landing many return punches.

*Norvel Lee and Ingemar Johansson duking it out in Gothenburg, Sweden.* Norvel Lee family archives

By the end, and before the judges rendered their decision, it was clear that Norvel had won a decisive victory. The crowd had known what the outcome would be from about the middle of the second round. Their cheering became more and more subdued, and some exited the arena as soon as the fighting ended, not waiting to hear the ring announcer deliver the final unanimous decision in Norvel's favor. The evening ended civilly, with each of the Swedish boxers congratulating the U.S. team during the Closing Ceremony.

With the Duals events over, the team still had a week in Europe before the Queen Elizabeth was scheduled to depart for the United States from Southampton. Randy Sandy let it be known he planned to go to Paris to experience the underground jazz scene, where many talented Black American musicians and artists found the French culture more supportive of their creative pursuits. Norvel, Boutilier, and Walters decided to accompany Sandy on his quest. They traveled by train, making connections in Copenhagen and Brussels and arriving in Paris late at night.

The next day, the four men explored Paris. Norvel found Paris was truly a walkable city, with nooks and crannies housing small cafés and stores. He was surprised at the mix of people he encountered. He and Sandy, also Black, were not subtly shunned, and he didn't feel they were a curiosity, as they were in Sweden.

*It's very comfortable here. I can go anywhere and be myself.*

The next day, Sandy led his teammates to the Tabou Club on rue Dauphine, where they saw the New Orleans–born saxophone master Sidney Bechet. Unbeknown to his teammates, Randy Sandy was a respected saxophonist. One of the musicians with Bechet was from New York and asked Sandy to sit in, which he did. Even though Norvel grew up listening to jug bands in rural Virginia, and more recently the country-and-western music of his in-laws, he enjoyed the complicated saxophone play of his teammate. He wasn't sure he appreciated the cacophony of sophisticated jazz, but he felt stimulated and energized from the sights and sounds.

On September 5, Norvel and his companions climbed aboard a Golden Arrow boat train in Paris. It traveled to the docks at Calais, France, where the six Pullman cars were pulled onto a ferry sailing to Dover, England. From there, the train went to Southhampton, where they boarded the Queen Mary for its return to the United States. Norvel spent much of his time walking the decks and looking out at the sea. He was anxious to get home to Leslie and to resume student life at Howard.

Leslie and Norvel embraced and snuggled as soon as he stepped off the train from New York. Norvel smiled broadly when Leslie said she was excited to show him how she had decorated the 16th Street NW apartment they had leased soon after marrying.

When Norvel entered the apartment he was genuinely surprised. "Les, where did this couch, table, and chairs come from? How did you get it all in here?"

"Daddy and one of his friends brought them. It's just some old odds and ends he and Mom had stored away."

"They're perfect for us," Norvel said. "It makes our home very cozy." He put his arms around her again.

Leslie said, "I enjoyed your postcards. Looks like I have one each day from you, sometimes more."

Norvel reached into his suitcase and pulled out some more. "These are the ones I wrote while onboard ship."

"You're such a dear, dear husband," Leslie said. "Here's an article in the *New York Times* that Jimmy saw. You aren't the headline like you should be, but they close the story with you."

Norvel opened the paper and read the headline at the bottom of the page: "Hackney, with Knockout in Third Round, Leads U.S. Boxers to Victory in Sweden."

"Interesting they featured a boxer from Philly instead of Randy Sandy, who's from New York. He won the match that put us ahead for the tour. I guess it's because they can sell more newspapers if they feature the knockouts."

"But you beat Johansson. They should have reported on that more."

"It wasn't that exciting of a fight. I just landed more hits than he did."

"You're exciting to me," Leslie said, her eyes sparkling.

# CHAPTER 19

## Thursday, March 6, 1952—Washington, D.C.

When Norvel and Coach Drake returned to Union Station from New York after Norvel won his second eastern Golden Gloves championship, Leslie, Robert, and Jimmy were there to meet them, along with a group of local boxing fans and news reporters. Norvel answered questions from the reporters and posed for several photos while the family waited.

Robert drove Leslie and Norvel back to their apartment on 16th Street. Once they were finally alone, Leslie turned to him and pulled him to her tightly.

"Congratulations," Leslie said. "Looks like all that dedication to conditioning paid off."

"Yes it did, Les," he said. "But I didn't face much competition. But, uh, uh, I sure encountered a lot of bluster coming from the opposing camps."

"What's next on your fight card?" she asked.

"I will be going up against the Chicago region champion," he said. "The Chicago region includes everywhere west of the Eastern Time zone. I believe I will have a formidable opponent from Los Angeles, Ed Sanders."

"Then that means you've got to keep up the hard work," she said. "But hard work could include a little romance, couldn't it?"

"It just might," he said, chuckling. "What's that you have in your hand?"

"It's a letter addressed to you, but I opened it myself," she said.

"Like you usually do. What's it say?"

Leslie said, "It's a request for you to attend a commissioning ceremony on March 20. I believe it is for your swearing in as a United States Air Force officer."

"It's going to be quite the year, isn't it?" observed Norvel. "Where's the event?"

"It's at Howard," she said.

"So we can go, but then the next day, or Saturday at the latest, I have to head up to Boston."

On a sunny March 20, in a meeting room at Frederick Douglass Memorial Hall, a gathering of family, friends, and military personnel met to witness the commissioning of three Howard University ROTC cadets. Lieutenant Colonel Daniel James was there to conduct the public presentation of the commissions.

Norvel and the other two cadets had acquired U.S. Air Force "Uxbridge blue" dress uniforms, which they were required to wear at ceremonial events like this. Norvel wore his medals from his World War II service: the Asiatic-Pacific Campaign Medal and the World War II Victory Medal.

When Norvel walked into the room with Leslie on his arm, he immediately recognized Lieutenant Colonel James, except he looked far more distinguished than in those days at Tuskegee when he was a young, newly commissioned second lieutenant. His uniform was crisp and impressive, especially with the several rows of colorful medals.

James saw Norvel and approached him, bringing Norvel to attention and causing Leslie to release her hand from Norvel's arm.

"At ease, Captain," instructed James, smiling. "I believe I know you. Weren't you one of my students while I was an instructor at Tuskegee?"

"Yes, sir," Norvel said.

"I understand you've established a name for yourself in the boxing world."

"Yes, sir," Norvel said again.

"And will you be representing the United States at the Helsinki Olympics this summer?" James asked.

"If I qualify, sir," Norvel said. "Uh, uh, I'm giving it my best."

"I'm sure you are, Captain, with the same stuff that brings you to this commissioning event. I see from your medals that you were in the war. Where were you stationed?"

"In the Pacific theater," Norvel said.

Lieutenant Colonel James called the cadets to the front of the room, which was filled with family, friends, and people associated with the Howard University ROTC. He thanked the onlookers for their support of the U.S. military and, in particular, these three men. He then addressed the men, congratulating them for qualifying for one of the most important jobs in the country, serving it. He proceeded to pin Captain Bars on each of the new USAF Reserve Officers.

Two days later, Norvel took the train to New York to compete for the national Golden Gloves championship that he relinquished in 1951 because of the scheduling conflict with the PanAm Games. He would be going up against Ed Sanders, the western champion from Los Angeles and a member of the U.S. Navy Boxing Team. He was again accompanied by Glenn Drake. They both knew Sanders would be a challenging foe. They had not seen him box yet but had heard that he, like Norvel, was smart and took a classic approach to the sport. More concerning, he had two inches in height and fifteen pounds on Norvel.

While warming up in the training room, Norvel met Sanders and his trainer, another Navy man. Norvel learned that this particular day, March 24, was Sander's twenty-second birthday. He found Sanders to be a humble, polite guy, a rare occurrence when meeting someone for the first time before an important bout.

As he entered his corner of the ring before a capacity crowd at Madison Square Garden, Norvel saw Sanders across the ring sitting in his chair with his head bowed, saying a prayer. When referee Frank Morris called them to the center of the ring, he introduced Norvel, whom he knew from previous fights, to Sanders. Sanders gave Norvel a big smile, explaining to the referee that they had met in the locker room.

It was clear from the beginning of the contest that both men respected the other's abilities. They spent much of the first round carefully dodging each other's jabs. Norvel landed the majority of hits, which, he found out later, earned him the point for the first round. At the start of the second round, Norvel's main concern was neutralizing Sander's raw, devastating power. He knew it would be difficult because Sanders employed a classic defense, allowing him to remain balanced, move left and right, and up and back, while keeping his body protected. As the round began, Norvel deceived Sanders for a moment by planting his feet instead of moving them. While Sanders processed Norvel's new tactic, Norvel put slightly more weight on his left foot, pivoted his back foot by forty-five degrees, which subtly rotated his body, and then lifted and extended his right elbow, plowing his right hand into Sander's momentarily unprotected chin. Sanders went down with a thud.

Morris hovered over the fallen boxer and conducted a full nine count before Sanders was back on his feet and the bout was allowed to continue. He recovered quickly, and both boxers resumed their cat-and-mouse game. After the start of the third round, Norvel figured he had it won and continued to jab and stay out of the way of anything Sanders might have tried to throw at him. In the end, Norvel was awarded a unanimous decision.

Sanders immediately came over and congratulated Norvel. He said he appreciated the birthday lesson Norvel gave him. Norvel smiled as the two boxers shook hands. The New York crowd was pleased the eastern Golden Gloves had once again prevailed, and approved of the good sportsmanship on display.

# CHAPTER 20

## Saturday, April 5, 1952—106 South Ayr St., Leesburg, Virginia

Norvel and Robert set out from the Jacksons' Leesburg home in the early morning for what they estimated would be a twelve hour drive up to Boston. Norvel was going there to participate and hopefully win his third national AAU title. The previous weekend, while Norvel and Leslie were visiting her family in Leesburg, Robert suggested they ride together in Norvel's Mercury.

Leslie and her mother, with Weekie's help, prepared a substantial breakfast of eggs, sausage, and pancakes for the men. The women also packed food to take along on the road. This way they didn't have to risk being turned away at any eateries with policies of not serving Black people. They didn't expect to have any issues with filling their car along the main highway, but they also brought along a five-gallon can of gasoline in the trunk. After fourteen hours they made it to the Stuart Street hostel in downtown Boston where Norvel had stayed the previous year.

Norvel gathered his suitcase and boxing gear, leaving his car parked on a side street around the corner from the hostel. He didn't expect to need it again until his matches were finished. Norvel asked if it would be legal if he left his car parked there for several days. The clerk at the front desk recognized Norvel, wished him well in the tournament, and gave him a cardboard parking pass to place on the dashboard.

On Sunday Norvel awakened about 8 a.m., very late considering he was usually up and about by 6. Both men felt well rested after the long drive of the day before. After eating breakfast Norvel took Robert on a walking tour of the places he had seen the previous year, including Faneuil Hall, the Old North Church, and the Paul Revere House.

While walking, Robert, who was studying history, gave Norvel a brief description of each place they visited. As they walked through Faneuil Hall, Robert said, "It's interesting to note that this place is called the Cradle of Liberty, a phrase coined by a Black man, a Massachusetts legislator who gave a speech there using the phrase. What's ironic about that is Peter Faneuil made his money in the 1700s from the slave trade. At one point there were thirty slaves here waiting their disposition. I wonder how they felt about being in the Cradle of Liberty?"

Norvel asked, "How do you retain all this information?"

Robert said, "That's the difference between you and me. You want to know where we are going next, and I want to know how we got here."

"Speaking of next, I'm going to a local boxing gym a friend recommended over on Boylston Street. I'll be preparing for my bout there. Then tomorrow I'm going for a jog. Feel free to join me."

"Yes, I will, but I may slow you down," Robert said.

"Oh, I'll take it easy on you," Norvel said. "Just want to feel loose against Scheberies on Tuesday."

"What do you know about him?" asked Robert.

"Not too much, except that he beat the fella I beat for the Golden Gloves, Ed Sanders. Like Sanders, he's from California. I feel lucky to have beaten Sanders," Norvel admitted.

"I'm sure you'll do fine," Robert assured him.

On Monday, in the crisp early spring New England air, the men jogged the same route Norvel had taken the previous year.

On Tuesday morning, after breakfast, Norvel went around the corner to where he had parked his car to check on it, as he did each day. But now, as he got to where it was supposed to be, he could see it wasn't there.

*Where's my car? What's happened to my car!*

Norvel returned to the hostel and told Robert of the circumstances. They contacted the police, who told them to come to the station and file a report. The officer who took the information saw Norvel's name and address and realized he was talking to the national heavyweight amateur champion, and that he was there to defend his title later that night. The policeman said they would do their best to locate the car, but it could take some time. He then told Norvel he hoped it wouldn't affect his bout.

When they left the station, Robert said, "Instead of worrying about the car, you know you need to concentrate on your fight tonight."

By the time Norvel and Robert arrived at Boston Garden, it was only thirty minutes before fight time. All told, the men had walked seven or eight miles during the day, including the trip to the police station.

Norvel put on his boxing clothes, performed a quick warm-up, and headed down the aisle to the ring before an excited Boston Garden crowd. Jack Scheberies had already made his entrance and was standing in his corner. As Norvel approached the ring, he saw his friend from the past few years, John Boutilier.

Norvel broke into a big smile and put his arms around him.

"Hello, Norvel, I came in to watch you. Hope you can do it again!" said Boutilier.

"Me too, Bout!" said Norvel smiling. "You're looking good. Not fighting this year?"

Boutilier shook his head and said, "No, I had my day in the sun; now it's time to buckle down."

Norvel nodded his understanding, and turning to Robert, said, "Bout, I'd like you to meet my brother-in-law, Robert Jackson. Robert, this is John Boutilier."

Norvel hustled up to his corner of the ring. He peered across to Scheberies, who nodded at him. Norvel estimated his opponent was an inch or two shorter and likely weighed about the same. Scheberies looked confident.

The referee, Tommy Rawson, was a boxing legend in his own right. He was the national amateur lightweight champion in 1929. He was also a professional fighter until 1941 and then became a popular boxing coach at nearby Harvard College. Rawson called the two boxers to the center of the ring and gave the instructions while reminding them this was the quarterfinals for the national AAU championship.

At the sound of the bell, both boxers danced to the center of the ring, circling each other, bobbing and weaving. Each delivered a few trial jabs. Scheberies was surprisingly quick, and was able to land jabs inside Norvel's defenses. Norvel tried some combinations of two quick jabs and then a cross to the head, but Scheberies moved out of the way and then came back inside with body punches. For most of the first round, each boxer continued to test the other for vulnerabilities.

*He got me that round with his inside work.*

In the second round Norvel came out more aggressively, trying many combinations of jabs and crosses, jabs and punches. Finally he scored with a complicated jab—right uppercut, left hook, and right cross—that caught Scheberies off-balance. The remainder of the round found the two boxers back to their jabbing, but this time Norvel effectively fended off the inside moves.

*I got him that time. Got to keep it going.*

At the start of the third round, Norvel came out jabbing with his left and punching and throwing the occasional cross to the body or head. Some landed, but Scheberies was able to avoid them by deftly pivoting away. Scheberies continued to work Norvel's body with jabs and punches, landing many.

*He was tough, but I believe I got him. My hits were more forceful.*

But Rawson and the judge, Joe Harris, disagreed with Norvel's assessment and awarded the first and final rounds to Scheberies, giving him a 2-1 split-decision victory over Norvel. This was Norvel's fourth defeat since he began boxing.

When the result was announced to the packed stands by Rawson, several boos were heard. But Norvel immediately congratulated Scheberies on a well-fought bout. Scheberies graciously accepted Norvel's gesture and said he would look forward to a rematch in the future, possibly in next month's Olympic Trials. The next morning's newspapers speculated that Norvel won the fight, but admitted the referees could have called it either way. The *Lowell Sun* reported, "We figured Lee won the fight, but Referee

Tommy Rawson and Judge Joe Harris favored Scheberies."

In the morning Norvel splurged on a long-distance phone call home to tell Leslie what a bad day April 8 had been for him. She was philosophical about the car being stolen, telling him that it was just a car while acknowledging how much Norvel loved it. Regarding the fight, she reminded him he was still the national Golden Gloves champion, and he now needed to concentrate on the Olympic qualifying trials. Norvel asked her to look up his automobile insurance policy. He wrote down the policy number and the particulars of the policy. He took the information to a nearby USAA insurance office and filed a claim. Later, he and Robert boarded the Congressional for the long train ride back to Washington, D.C.

Norvel's life continued to be a whirlwind of activity. While catching up on his classes at Howard, he also stepped up his training for the next round of matches, still hoping to qualify for the 1952 Olympic team. Being realistic, though, he had to acknowledge there were many talented heavyweight boxers who were younger. He had just encountered two of them, Ed Sanders and Jack Scheberies, winning in a close match against one and losing against the other.

Knowing that his boxing and college days were numbered, Norvel accepted an interview request, orchestrated by Glenn Drake, from the National Training School for Boys. A week later, he accepted a position as an assistant at NTS. Norvel explained he was only interested in taking the position if, when he graduated from Howard, he would become an instructor. He also explained that there would be occasions throughout the summer when he would have to be away for a boxing event, but come fall he would be available wherever he was needed. The administration accepted him on that basis, initially assigning him weekend shifts.

On Monday, May 19, an Olympic fundraising boxing event promoted as "D.C. vs. All Navy" took place at the Uline Arena. Norvel was invited to participate. He agreed, knowing it would be an excellent tune-up for the upcoming Olympic trials. His match was against the Navy's heavyweight champion, Kirby Seals. Norvel had previously defeated Seals for the national Golden Gloves championship in 1950. Seals recovered from that defeat by capturing the Navy championship, a title he had held since then. D.C. boxing fans turned out in large numbers to see their local champion take on the top boxer from the Navy. To their delight, Norvel easily handled Seals, winning all three rounds.

The next day, when he returned home to their apartment Leslie met him at the door, smiling with a gleam in her eyes. "Look what arrived a little while ago," she said, handing him a Western Union envelope.

Norvel opened it. It was from USAA. It stated that the police had found his car and they'd apprehended two suspects, juveniles. The car needed some minor body work, which the USAA had arranged. The telegram provided options for claiming the Mercury after the work was completed.

"Well, I'll be," Norvel said happily. "Uh, uh, I never thought I would see that car again."

"How are you going to retrieve it?" Leslie asked.

Norvel hesitated for a moment, scratching his head, and then said, "They say the work will be completed on Friday. I need to be in Albany next week for the start of the Olympic Trials. Albany isn't that far away from Boston. "Maybe . . ."

Leslie interrupted, "I see where you're going with this. You're thinking you can go pick it up and drive over to Albany, and then drive it back down here."

Norvel said, "That's exactly what I'm thinking."

A few days later, Norvel took the train up to Boston. The next morning, after he retook possession of the newly repaired car, Norvel learned the two juveniles suspected of stealing it were from an influential Italian family residing in the Old North End district. Norvel hoped, by getting apprehended, that the two young men learned a valuable life lesson.

On Monday, May 26, after a five-hour drive along U.S. Route 20 from Boston, Norvel arrived in Albany, New York. The Olympic Trials for the eastern region were held at the Washington Avenue Armory, a large red-brick building built in the 1890s. It was originally designed for the Tenth Battalion of the New York National Guard, including storing the unit's equipment and housing the troops during training. But since the building was often not in use for its intended purpose, the New York National Guard rented it to other organizations. Its large spacious interior, able to accommodate around four thousand spectators, made it ideal for boxing. Over the years, many regional boxing events took place there, but these regional U.S. Olympic Trials were to be its most prestigious.

The boxers stayed in a dormitory inside the Armory. Norvel was known by many who were bunking there, including those from the D.C. Golden Gloves such as Joe Gilchrist, Aubrey Greenhow, Jimmy Hanbury, and Billy Hill. Each had earned the right to represent the city in their respective weight categories by way of their local club selection process. Norvel, the most experienced and mature of the Washington contingent, organized their arrangements such that they all bunked in one section of the spacious sleeping quarters. The dormitory reminded Norvel of the barracks he was in during the war.

The semifinals for the eastern region were scheduled to be held the next afternoon, and the finals in the evening. The winners would go to Kansas City for the national Olympic Trials. Norvel kept his group relaxed by playing cards.

The matches began at 12:30 p.m. with the flyweights, the lowest weight category. In one contest, which Norvel was able to see before getting warmed up for his own bout, was an impressive youngster from New York named Floyd Patterson.

For Norvel's heavyweight semifinal, he met Julius Griffin of Brooklyn. In spite of Griffin's size advantage, Norvel impressed the referee and judge with his classic boxing style and form. Norvel easily won a unanimous decision, along with praises from the appreciative spectators. The other semifinal included Norvel's opponent from last week's fundraiser, Kirby Seals.

The finals began at seven o'clock in front of a capacity crowd. The last bout was Norvel versus Seals.

*I know him and he knows me. I learned he can't handle my jabs. I just need to keep with them. Maybe a few combos now and then will work too.*

When the bout got started Seals used the same tactic that he had in D.C.—try to land a knockout punch to Norvel's head. Norvel simply danced away when he saw the punch coming and worked his jabs inside when Seals raised his arms. Occasionally, Norvel's jabs were able to find Seals' head, but the Navy champion was able to absorb them in stride. In round two Norvel continued mostly to jab but occasionally would deploy a right cross by rotating his hips in sync with his upper body, with his right arm following the motion. Norvel landed several such right crosses to the left side of Seals' face, one almost knocking him down. The round ended before Norvel could inflict any catastrophic damage, however.

*I've got him now. Doubt that he can knock me out, 'cause he's tiring. Don't need to perform any heroics at this point.*

During the third round Norvel focused on landing jabs and moving away from any desperate crosses or hooks Seals attempted. Norvel focused on exhaling and maintaining his balance when he extended his left hand to jab at either Seals' body or his head. Norvel moved smoothly, with confidence, around his tiring opponent.

By the end of the round the crowd was on its feet, convinced they were watching the future heavyweight representative for the U.S. Olympic team.

*I can't let my emotions go just yet. Here I am again. Kansas City, here I come!*

The next day, Norvel and the four other D.C.-area boxers rode back to Washington in Norvel's sparkling "like new" Mercury. Norvel was the only one of the five to have qualified for the final Olympic Trials. After dropping the other boxers off, Norvel arrived home at 9 p.m. By that time, the news he would be competing for the heavyweight spot on the Olympic team in a few weeks had reached Leslie. For the first time she thought excitedly her husband might actually represent the United States at the Helsinki Olympics.

# CHAPTER 21

## June 15, 1952—Municipal Auditorium, Kansas City, Missouri

After arriving in Kansas City, Norvel saw many boxers he knew and was thrilled to learn that Pete Mello, the 1951 Duals team coach, would be one of the coaches for the Olympic squad. During the intervening weeks since qualifying for the trials Norvel had completed his current term at Howard, continued working at the National Training School for Boys, enjoyed his time with Leslie, and made sure he was in the best physical condition possible.

Among the boxers he knew were Ed Sanders, Jack Scheberies, and the young middleweight, Floyd Patterson. But his first opponent in the Monday preliminary bouts, Lloyd Willis, an Army corporal, was unknown to him. When Norvel asked Mello about him, he learned that Willis was a local favorite. When the western region Golden Gloves championship was contested in Omaha, Willis scored an upset knockout against Ed Sanders. Willis was known to have devastating power in both his left and right hands. It was important to know that a punch could come from either side.

On Monday afternoon, Norvel went to the Kansas City Municipal Auditorium ninety minutes ahead of his scheduled bout time. He felt relaxed, rested, and confident. He went through his well-honed warm-up of jumping rope, doing bag work, and shadowboxing. There were other boxers getting ready, including his opponent. Willis looked tough and ready to go.

Norvel was surprised to see there were several thousand fans there to watch the preliminary bouts. Normally, at this stage of a tournament there would be only a few avid fans attending. But these were the Olympic trials.

Settled in his corner, Norvel looked across at Willis, who continued to seem confident. When the bell sounded, Willis came out aggressively. It became clear to Norvel that Willis was going to rely on his left and right lethality. Norvel employed all the defensive tactics he knew and was able to blunt most of Willis's attempts with his left arm while punching and jabbing away with his right. Norvel felt it was working, even though Willis did land some very hard punches to Norvel's body. But mostly they glanced off his arm. Each round took the same form, with Willis staying on the attack and Norvel fluidly bobbing and counterpunching. When the bell sounded ending the bout, Norvel knew it would be close but felt the two judges and referee would decide in his favor.

Instead, the announcer came to the center of the ring and announced a unanimous decision in favor of Willis.

Norvel put on the best smile he could muster and congratulated Willis on a good fight.

*Well, that's that. I'm the better boxer but got put away in the prelims. No Olympics for me. No more boxing either. Nothing more I can do.*

The *Kansas City Star*, reporting on the day's events, stated, "There were only rare complaints over the judging. The one bout which drew some criticism from the ringsiders and a few team coaches was the decision awarding Lloyd Willis the victory over Norvel Lee."

Norvel considered taking an earlier plane home but decided to stick around to support the remaining contestants, especially Ed Sanders and Floyd Patterson. He was genuinely interested in how they each would fare over the next few days. The next day Ed Sanders, whom Norvel had beaten two months earlier, surprisingly knocked out Lloyd Willis in the first round of their quarterfinal match. And Patterson scored a technical knockout (TKO) in the second round of his bout with Bill Tate. On Wednesday, in the semifinals, Sanders beat Bob Ranck on points while Patterson scored a first round TKO against Willie Finney.

The finals were held on Thursday afternoon and evening before a capacity audience of fifteen thousand boxing fans, some coming long distances to see who would be on the U.S. Olympic Team. Ten final matches were held from flyweight to heavyweight. Seven of them were decided on TKOs, including Sanders versus Scheberies for the heavyweight slot and

Patterson for middleweight.

On Friday morning when Pete Mello returned from a meeting with the boxing committee, he put the word out he wanted to see Norvel immediately. He was pleased when he looked up from the desk at the sound of Norvel's tapping on the door a few minutes later.

He rose from his chair, smiled and said, "Norvel, thanks for coming right up. This is important, and you need to know this immediately so you can make your plans. You need to include a trip to Helsinki in your travel plans next month. I've received permission from the boxing commission to include you on the team."

"Why me?" asked Norvel, puzzled. "Uh, uh, I didn't qualify."

"Officially, you will be going as an alternate," said Mello, "as you were for the London Olympics. I argued, and I mean argued, with the committee. Since they will only allow four alternates, they wanted each one to be available for two weight classes. They felt that the Scheberies kid was the better choice, especially since he beat you for the AAU. But I wanted you."

Norvel found out later that Mello argued persuasively that the team was representing the country on an international stage and he thought it important for the members to possess natural poise, confidence, and intelligence in addition to the necessary boxing skills. Mello told the committee he had selected the four alternates he wanted to take with him and that none were runners-up in Kansas City, but three of the four had been there trying to qualify. His fourth member was an eighteen-year-old from his New York neighborhood he personally knew, Ernest Anthony. Although Anthony was only eighteen and hadn't competed in Kansas City, he had previously won the national AAU welterweight title. Mello knew Anthony exhibited a maturity well beyond his years.

His other three choices were the featherweight Edson Brown, another New Yorker Mello knew, who had lost on points in the quarterfinals; lightweight Charles Adkins from Indiana, who also lost on points in the quarters to the eventual winner, Joe Reynolds; and Norvel, the reigning Golden Gloves champion and, until this year, the national AAU champion, who had lost in a very close match on points in the prelims. The committee went along with Mello when he suggested they might want to choose someone else as coach if they didn't approve his recommendations.

Norvel left the office, silently saying to himself proudly, *I am going to represent the United States of America in the Olympics, once again. Leslie and the whole family, hers and mine, will be so excited!*

# CHAPTER 22

## *July 8 to July 27, 1952—XV Olympiad, Helsinki, Finland*

The three hundred seventy-five athletes, coaches, and advisors of the United States Olympic team began arriving at the newly opened Helsinki-Malmi airport on July 8. Over the next several days, departing from New York, chartered DC-6Bs ferried the team across the Atlantic. With refueling stops in Gander, Newfoundland, and London, the entire trip took nearly twenty-four hours.

The boxing team was assigned the third of the five flights, Pan Am Flight 62, departing Tuesday evening at 9:30. Leslie and her brother, Robert, drove Norvel the ten hours to the Hotel Paramount at Madison Square Garden, where the team and their guests were treated to a lavish kickoff party on Sunday evening, July 6. Robert and Leslie stayed with Norvel at the iconic hotel for two nights until the team members left for the airport, a crowd of well-wishers applauding them as they climbed aboard the bus to Idlewild. Leslie told Norvel, again, how proud she was of him, and that she would be looking for his name in the newspapers every day. Norvel reminded her he was an alternate and didn't expect to be noticed by the press.

On board the flight were the fourteen boxers, their coaches Pete Mello and James Owen, also know as J.T., and team manager Dr. Barry Barrodale. Also on the flight were ten weightlifters, eighteen wrestlers, ten men gymnasts, ten women gymnasts, eleven members of the women's track-and-field team, one cyclist, and three other coaches.

The mix of young athletes made for a lively flight. In spite of air turbulence and noise from the engines, most of the travelers were on their feet getting to know one another. Many of the men positioned themselves so they could interact with the women athletes.

Norvel spent his time reacquainting himself with several teammates from the 1948 London Olympics, including the only returning boxer, light heavyweight Chuck Spieser, along with weightlifters Peter George, Norbert Schemansky, and John Davis. Davis introduced Norvel to a heavyweight weightlifter named James Bradford who, although now serving in the U.S. Army, hailed from Washington, D.C. Norvel and Bradford immediately felt comfortable with each other, knowing they were the only ones from the nation's capital.

The Olympians eventually settled into their seats and went to sleep as the flight droned on into the night. Norvel awoke at one point and glanced out the window to see a colorful glow in the northern sky. A stewardess whispered, "Aurora borealis!"

The plane arrived in Helsinki at 2:30 a.m. and was met by buses that transported the men ten miles to the Olympic Village in Käpylä, on the outskirts of Helsinki. Although it was the middle of the night the orange light of dawn was quickly appearing in the southeastern sky. The women boarded a separate bus and were taken to the Nurses Training College that had been converted to an Olympic Village.

The main Olympic Village consisted of thirteen buildings with accommodations for up to forty-eight hundred participants. The United States and the nineteen-member team of the new self-governing territory of Puerto Rico shared the ample, comfortable space of building number three.

The building was organized into many large rooms, each furnished with four to eight beds and a lavatory. Spacious communal showers were at the end of the hall on each floor. Next to each of the showers was a Finnish sauna. The rooms were assigned such that each sport had a specific area of the building. The boxing team and coaches occupied four of the rooms. Mello, Owens, and Barrodale took one, while the boxers spread themselves out in the remaining three. On each bed the boxers found the following leaflet:

## Olympic Competitors!

THIS is the village where you – the competitors in the XV Olympic Games are going
to reside together with your leaders and assistants
during your brief sojourn in Helsinki.
Without the disturbing influence of the outside
world you will here have the opportunity of gathering congenial impressions and of storing away
pleasant recollections; and also to enter into friendly relations with your neighbours, who are inspired
by the very ideals you are devoted to.
This village will be your home for the duration of
a few summer days. Out of the discipline and spirit
of true sportmanship radiating from the teams,
there will be born the cosy atmosphere of social
unity that will constitute an indispensable asset
in helping you to concentrate your physical and
mental faculties upon the ultimate mobilization
of strenght on the Olympic arenas.

*We wish you a hearty welcome*
*to your village!*

XV OLYMPIAD HELSINKI 1952

From the Official Report of the XV Olympiad, Helsinki 1952

Pete Mello made sure Norvel would be in the same room as seven-teen-year-old Floyd Patterson. Implied in the arrangement was that Nor-vel, an alternate on the team and the most experienced team member, was to be Patterson's mentor and unofficial chaperone. But Mello also ex-pected Norvel to stay in top condition so that he would be ready if he was needed. The team spent Thursday and Friday resting and becoming famil-iar with their temporary home. Norvel wasn't anticipating getting into the competition, but he was committed to Mello and to being ready to fight if the situation presented itself.

The Olympic Village contained a large sports field where the athletes could run and practice the skills required for their particular sport. It was also expected that adequate boxing training facilities would be located at the Olympic Village, but Mello, Owens, and Barrodale were disappointed with what they found. There was no formal boxing ring, and the equipment was in rugged condition. They were also concerned about having to share what was available with boxers from other nations. The team, however, was very impressed with the Finnish baths located in each building, a large communal pool and sauna, and the quality and variety of food available at the large tented dining hall.

Late Friday afternoon Norvel, Floyd Patterson, Ed Sanders, and Joe Reynolds decided to explore Helsinki. As they came out onto Forsbyvagen Road bordering the Olympic Village, they found a bustling modern city. In addition to the pedestrians there were many late-model automobiles, including a number of Fords, driving about on the busy streets.

Norvel and the others looked around and saw that they were attracting stares and waves from the pedestrians. Sanders immediately knew why and said, "Fellas, this may be the first time any of them have seen people like us before. I guess people with dark skin don't live here. They appear happy to see us, so everything will be okay. At least they don't have to guess where we come from with that big USA on the back of our jackets."

Just then three children, two boys and a girl, all about ten years old, came running up to them holding notebooks. Norvel looked down and smiled at them. The girl handed the notebook to Norvel, looking questioningly up at him. An adult man, following the children, said something in Finnish and, using hand gestures, indicated they wanted the men to sign their autographs. The men wrote out their names for the youngsters, who each said, "Kiittos," which the men assumed was "Thank you" in Finnish.

On Saturday, at noon, the Olympic Organizing Committee held a formal reception for the American team. Each of the seventy countries competing in the Games was required by protocol to be formally received by the host country. The ceremonies began at noon for the countries arriving the previous day. They were conducted at the entrance to Olympic Village, where the flags of each nation were displayed after they were officially hoisted during the reception. The ceremony for the United States was next in size to the Soviet Union, which had been held the previous Saturday. The Soviets brought a six hundred eighty-member team with them by buses across their shared border with Finland. Because of their numbers the Soviets were expected to capture the majority of the medals available at the games, gold or otherwise.

As Norvel was getting ready for the event, two very tall young men walked up to him. One of them was wearing a big smile.

"You are Norvel Lee, aren't you?" the man said. "I believe I remember you from the 1948 team. Am I right? Were you on that team?"

"Yes, uh, uh, I was, and of course I remember you," Norvel said. "You're the one everyone's talking about. You were just a teenager when you won the decathlon last time."

"Yes," he said, offering his hand for Norvel to shake. "I'm Bob Mathias, glad to see you here again."

"The pleasure is mine," Norvel responded, looking up at the other young man.

Mathias said, "Sim, I would like you to meet the boxer Norvel Lee. Norvel, this is my friend Simeon Iness, although everyone just calls him Sim."

Norvel and Sim Iness shook hands.

Mathias continued, "Sim is here for the discus competition. We met at Tulare Union High School in California and have been friends ever since."

"Two Olympians from the same high school?" Norvel observed. "That's got to be a rare occurrence."

"I suppose so," Mathias said.

Just then a lean man slightly shorter than the rest of them at only six feet joined in and said, "Norvel, I keep running into you in the most interesting places: first London, then Buenos Aires, and now here in Finland."

Norvel smiled back and responded, "Good to see you again too, Mal. Bob and Sim, this is Mal Whitfield, a half-miler among other things."

Whitfield said, "We already know each other. We Californians watch out for each other, don't we, Bob?"

Mathias and Iness laughed and Whitfield continued, "Have you told Norvel about your idea, Bob?"

"Not yet." Turning to Norvel, Mathias said, "There are a number of us here who were in London in 1948. I'm thinking since we will be here for three weeks, we ought to band together to help spur each other on and give the new guys the benefit of our previous experiences. We can start our own gold rush for the U.S.A. and not just for California."

Norvel smiled broadly and said, "That's a great idea. Several of us '48ers were on the plane ride here. Uh, uh, I'm an alternate again this time, like I was in '48, so I need to keep busy with something. I'm expected to show my experience with this young group of boxers, but I might need some other things to do."

"Hey, Mal, we've got another L.A. boy on our boxing team," Norvel said. "Do you know Ed Sanders?"

"I do," interrupted another one of the young boxers who had joined them. "I'm Ellsworth Webb, grew up on 103rd Street in Watts. Originally from Tulsa but moved to L.A. when I was young."

"You and Sanders must know each other because he's also from Watts," Whitfield said. "He's five years younger than me. But everyone here looks younger than me and Norvel."

Whitfield gestured to the other athletes and observed to Norvel, "You and I are the oldsters here, I believe. I'm gonna be twenty-eight in October—you?"

"I've got you by a month," Norvel said. "I'm turning twenty-eight on September 22nd."

Whitfield turned to Mathias and Iness and said, "And these two are barely out of their teens. They will benefit from our collective experiences."

The five men laughed. Then Norvel motioned to his own teenage charge to come over.

"Men," Norvel said, "this young fella here is Floyd Patterson, a middleweight boxer from New York. He can really do some damage with those quick hands and arms of his. And, unlike the rest of us, he's a real teenager and still putting meat on those bones."

The men shook hands with Patterson, who smiled shyly. Then Mathias said, "Sim, let's go locate the rest of the '48ers."

The reception took place on a sunny, temperate day at the entrance to the Olympic Village, where seventy thirty-foot flagpoles were standing in rows and columns. Only half had flags, while the others stood empty, waiting for their teams to be formally received. A podium was set in front of the flag display and next to it was a twenty-piece brass band.

*A reception welcoming Japan and Ceylon at the Käpylä Olympic Village.*
From the Official Report of the XV Olympiad, Helsinki 1952

Dressed in official Olympic attire, with "USA" prominently displayed on the back of their smart blue blazers, a festive U.S. team gathered in front of the podium. Norvel fell in near Mathias and the twenty other athletes who had competed four years earlier in London. He encouraged a nervous but excited Patterson to stay by him.

At precisely noon, the brass band began to play the Olympic fanfare, and then the opening chords to "The Star-Spangled Banner." The Americans removed their headwear, placed their right hands over their hearts, and sang as the flag was hoisted.

The president of the organizing committee, Erik von Frenckell, stepped to the podium and welcomed them to Finland. Next, Avery Brundage, head of the U.S. Olympic Committee, greeted his team, telling the athletes their great nation was very proud of them for representing the United States. After several other people spoke, the ceremony ended. An hour later, a flag was also raised at the women's quarters.

Later in the day, the word went out among the athletes that the Velodrome, the venue for track cycling, housed a dance club to be opened each night. The Velodrome was a half-mile walk from the Olympic Village down Mäkelänkatu Street. Its easy access motivated many members of the various Olympic teams to experience its social possibilities in the evening, but Norvel decided to stay back and write a letter to Leslie.

On Sunday morning Norvel went to church as he promised Leslie he'd do. He learned there was a Methodist church called Kristuskyrkan nearby. He chose it, believing the services would be more in line with what he was accustomed to at home.

He asked several others if they were interested in joining him for church services. In the morning Floyd Patterson, Davey Moore, James Bradford, and the three Los Angeles teammates, Ed Sanders, Mal Whitfield, and Ellsworth Webb, all wearing summer suits and ties, climbed into a small van provided by the Olympic Village services. The men rode three miles to the neo-Gothic building with the distinctive spire that was visible throughout Helsinki.

Upon entering the church, Norvel didn't notice the gawkers and then the welcoming smiles from the parishioners because he was mesmerized by the pipe organ overlooking the nave of the spacious interior. Norvel counted fifteen pipes and was hoping it would be used during the service.

The services were more staid than what was usual at Leslie's family church, with its rousing gospel choir. But the sound of the pipe organ filling the cavernous space was stirring just the same. The welcoming prayer of greeting and the structure of the service was similar to what he was accustomed to, except it was in Finnish. But then for the benediction the pastor smiled directly at the seven men and offered in English the church's blessings for a successful Olympics. Upon leaving church, the men walked back to the Olympic Village in the pleasant sunshine, greeting people they encountered along the way.

*This is the way it should be,* Norvel thought. *Walking in the city openly, not wondering who's thinking we don't belong here because of our skin color. We belong here because we are Americans in the Olympics.*

The U.S. Olympic boxing team was made up of the following men:

| | |
|---|---|
| Flyweight | Nathan Brooks—Cleveland, Ohio |
| Bantamweight | Davey Moore—Springfield, Ohio |
| Featherweight | Bobby Bickle—Hoisington, Kansas |
| Lightweight | Archie Slaten—Chattanooga, Tennessee |
| Light Welterweight | Joe Reynolds—St. Louis, Missouri |
| Welterweight | Louis Gage—San Francisco, California |
| Light Middleweight | Ellsworth Webb—Los Angeles, California |
| Middleweight | Floyd Patterson—Brooklyn, New York |
| Light Heavyweight | Chuck Spieser—Detroit, Michigan |
| Heavyweight | Ed Sanders—Los Angeles, California |
| Alternates: | |
| Featherweight | Edson Brown—New York, New York |
| Lightweight | Charles Adkins—Gary, Indiana |
| Welterweight | Ernest Anthony—New York, New York |
| Heavyweight | Norvel Lee—Washington, D.C. |

On Sunday afternoon, Mello asked the entire fourteen-member team and the other coach, J.T., to gather in his room so he could lay out the plan for the next few weeks. The boxers sat where they could or stood.

"Hello, men, did you enjoy the Sunday services here in Helsinki?" he asked, ever the Catholic youth coach.

Norvel and the others who'd gone to services with him nodded yes, while a few did not respond.

"I'd like for us to talk about how we're going to prepare for our competition," Mello said. "As you know, we have almost two weeks before the boxing starts, but I don't want us to get fat and lazy waiting, especially with the real good food they are serving us here."

Rubbing his belly, Ed Sanders said, "You got that right, Coach!"

The men laughed as Mello continued, "You've seen the state of the nonexistent boxing faculties here. So I've made arrangements to use a local facility that has everything we need to keep our conditioning up. Every morning, except for Sunday, we're going to meet out front at 9 a.m. and go through our workout. This will start tomorrow morning. Understood?"

"Yes, sir," the men said in unison.

"One more thing I want all of you to understand," Mello said. "We have a very talented team. Perhaps the most talented we've ever brought to the Olympic Games. When the time comes, I want to field the best team possible for bringing home as many medals as we can. So even if you're one of the designated weight class winners, the final determination of who goes into the competition will be up to me. We've got four alternates here who will be ready, willing, and able to step up if any of you aren't at form."

Chuck Spieser asked, "Who will decide who gets to fight?"

Mello, smiling affably, pointed to himself and said, "If you train every day, temper your appetite, and don't stay out all night, I'm sure everything will be fine. But I'll be watching. Now, let's go get some chow."

As the men filed out, Mello discreetly asked Norvel to wait. When it was only Owens and him left, Mello said, "I'm concerned about a few of the guys and their approach to the competition. Some are acting more like

Olympic Games Helsinki 1952, Boxing. USA men's boxing team. Front, left to right: co-coach J. T. Owen, co-coach Pete Mello and trainer William Fallon. Middle, left to right: manager Barry Barodale, Edson Brown, Joe Reynolds, Robert Bickle, David Moore, Louis Gage, Charles Adkins, Archie Slaten and Nathan Brooks. Rear, left to right: Edward Sanders, Ernest Anthony, Ellsworth Webb, Charles Spieser, Floyd Patterson and Norvel Lee.

*The 1952 U.S. Olympic Boxing Team.* United States 1952 Olympic Book, page 156

they're on holiday than here to represent their country. I'm hoping that will change, but I want you to be ready to go down a weight class or two. That means you'll have to shed some pounds on you."

"Coach, uh, uh, I may be able to lose fifteen pounds in two weeks to get to light heavyweight, but it would take a thirty-pound loss to go down to the next level," Norvel said.

"I want a backup for middleweight because I'm not sure that Patterson kid is going to be able to stand up to the pressure," Mello said. "Don't know if he's got the maturity."

"I'll have him ready," Norvel said confidently. "And if you're looking for a backup, you can always see if you can get Chuck to lose enough pounds to get down to middle."

"I may mention it to him," Mello said. "In the meantime, just eat protein and vegetables. Stay away from spaghetti and those Scandinavian desserts. I'll be weighing everyone every day as soon as I get my hands on a scale."

"Yes, sir, Coach."

"But that doesn't mean don't eat anything. You still need to be strong, so let's go get some chow," Mello said.

The three men proceeded to the large tent that served as the Olympic Village's restaurant.

Beginning the next morning and throughout the following week, the fourteen boxers, coaches Mello and J. T., and athletic trainer Billy Fallon met at the entrance to the Olympic Village, where a white Mercedes coach would be waiting. Fallon was the athletic trainer at the U.S. Naval Academy. His function was to help members of the boxing, wrestling, and field events team keep in top physical conditioning. The manager, Dr. Barrodale, was rarely seen by the team.

It took about fifteen minutes to get to their destination, an ancient granite castle. Its official name was Paasitorni, but the local Finns called it "the People's House" because it was the home of Finland's social democratic association. It also housed Helsinki's main boxing club, Tarmo.

It was clear that the Tarmo Club was very pleased to have the Americans use their facility. It was reserved completely for the U.S. team, and the staff was accommodating. This large facility was equipped with all the team would need to maintain their conditioning. There were two standard-size boxing rings, several punching bags, and assorted weights.

While encouraging each team member to proceed with his own workout routine, Mello also wanted to arrange specific sparring matchups. As the week progressed he made sure the flyweight, bantamweight, featherweight, and lightweight boxers—Brooks, Moore, Bickle, Slaten, Brown, and Adkins—paired up with one another. Likewise, he wanted to see how Reynolds, Gage, Webb, and Anthony looked in the ring against each other. He left Patterson out of that group, feeling the young prodigy needed to get some experience against the larger, tough Spieser and the larger but fluid technician Lee. He also wanted Sanders to spar with them.

Each morning, a mix of young men and women waited to see the six white and eight Black boxers arrive at and enter the People's House. Several hours later, when the team emerged, the cluster of onlookers was still gathered. They, especially the women, wore admiring smiles while they waved at the boxers as the bus took them back to Olympic Village.

The Opening Ceremony for the XV Olympic Games was held beginning at 1 p.m. on Saturday, July 19, 1952. For the Parade of Nations, each country would enter the stadium in formation and parade around the track in front of the Olympic Organizing Committee and the spectators. Tradition dictated that Greece would lead off the Parade of Nations and Finland, as the host country, would anchor the spectacle. The remaining teams would march in Finnish alphabetical order. That put the three-hundred-seventy-five-member U.S. team next to last, just before the three hundred athletes from Finland and right after the fourteen men from Vietnam.

Norvel was mesmerized by the cacophony of the scene before him at the staging area of Elaintara athletic grounds near Olympic Stadium. Unfortunately, the beautiful climate of the past week had become cool with intermittent rain, but the change in weather did not dampen the festive mood of the spectators. They came to Finland from around the world to enjoy the spectacle that would play out over the next several weeks. The noisy throng of young athletes was organized around large signs displaying in colorful letters the name of their country next to their flag. The signs and flags were placed around the field in the order in which each nation would enter the stadium.

Norvel was standing in the middle of the American team, next to Mathias and most of the other '48ers but also with his fellow Washingtonian, Bradford, his heavyweight rival, Ed Sanders, and Patterson, who was under his watchful eye. There was a slight drizzle in the air. A few minutes before 1 p.m. applause emanated from the stadium.

Sanders said, "Looks like things are finally about ready to get started."

Mathias said, "Not us for a while yet." He waved his arms around and added, "All these other countries get to go ahead of us."

Norvel looked at Bradford and asked, "Does this remind you of anything?"

Bradford said, "Sure does. Hurry up and wait, as we say in the Army."

"You're still involved with the Army, aren't you?" asked Norvel.

"Oh, yeah, still am," said Bradford. "My four years will be up next year. Competing here got me out of Korea, so it hasn't been all bad. Did you serve?"

"I'm ROTC," said Norvel. "Air Force. I was also in the South Pacific during the war."

"Really!" said Sanders. "You don't seem old enough."

"That's what my mother said," Norvel joked.

"I bet things were segregated then," interjected Bradford. "Colored unit?"

Norvel nodded and then said to Sanders, "I know you're still in the Army. Any plans to stick with it?"

"Nah, I'm going to use those GI Benefits for college, maybe go pro. I've got some pressure to do that. Did you think about going pro?"

"No," said Norvel. "This is it for me. I'm getting too old. I'm going to raise a family and go earn an honest dollar."

Just then another man walked up next to Mathias, who'd been listening to the conversation. He turned to him and said, "Hi, Frank. Do you know these gentlemen?"

"I've seen them around," he answered, and then turned to the others and said, "Frank Havens, another '48er."

Norvel, Sanders, Bradley, and Patterson all introduced themselves. Music, loudspeaker announcements, and cheering fans could be heard from the stadium.

Norvel asked, "What's your sport, Frank?"

"Canoeing," he answered, and then, looking at Norvel and Bradford, said, "Bob tells me the two of you are from D.C., the only ones on the team from there."

"That we know of," Norvel clarified.

"I'm from Arlington, born and raised. I can see the Washington Monument from my home there," Havens said.

"Then you're one of us," Norvel said, smiling. "I bet you're one of those rowers out on the Potomac we sometimes see."

Sanders said, "This really is just like being in the Army, a lot of standing around talking until we get lined up and start marching."

Norvel continued the conversation with the others as they paced restlessly. The music from the stadium was surprisingly clear, considering it was coming from a half mile away. He could hear the cheers ebb and flow, assuming it coordinated with the arrival of each new nation. After about forty minutes he heard a huge roar from the crowd, and guessed that the Soviet Union and their six hundred eighty men and women had entered. More rain began to fall, but the spectators didn't seem to care.

The U.S. contingent was finally told to get into formation. Norvel helped Mello get the boxers all together so they would march in as one squad. He found Reynolds and Spieser cavorting with the women gymnasts they met on the plane and pried them away. Norvel and Sanders, the tallest of the boxers, stood in the middle of the three rows they formed. They began to move forward to the northern entrance behind the Olympic flag-bearer for the United States, Norman Armitage, a fencer from Albany, New York. Norvel hadn't noticed who led the parade in 1948, but learned from Mathias it was also Armitage, making him one of the '48ers. This was his fifth Olympics, having first competed in 1928 in Amsterdam. His only medal came in London, when he captured the bronze.

As Norvel entered the stadium, he beheld a spectacular sight. He thought providence may have intervened because as soon as the United States entered the stadium the rain suddenly stopped and the sun shone directly onto them when the field came into his view. He heard the band transition from the march they were playing to the opening of "The Star-Spangled Banner" before returning to the Olympic march. He looked across to the opposite end of the stadium, the south end, where he saw a very large choir dressed in white and the orchestra. The crowd in the stands was on their feet applauding and cheering madly. The moment caused him and the entire team to stand straighter and square their shoulders. Norvel got goose bumps as they marched around the field. Right behind the Americans were the Finns, who moved the crowd into a higher state of frenzy.

*The United States marches into the stadium.*
The XV Olympiad Official Report, Helsinki, 1952

After marching around the track, the Americans settled into their designated place on the field. Erik von Frenckell, the same man who'd welcomed them to Helsinki, took the rostrum to address the fifty-eight hundred sportsmen on the field, the seventy thousand spectators in the grandstands, and the world listening on the radio. He moved his address through four languages, first directing his attention to his fellow Finns and thanking them for their patience as their hosting of these events had been originally planned for 1940, until World War II interrupted those plans. He switched to Swedish, then French, and finally English, in which he concluded: "If the Olympic spirit and international understanding will have grown among the youth, then the organizers will have been granted the gold medal they have currently aspired to earn."

Norvel tried to keep his emotions under control.

*I hope the world is listening. I hope our leaders at home are listening. Here we all are on the world's biggest stage—black, white, Asian. Jim Crow is nowhere to be found. No bigotry here either. We're all equal. We all care about and want the best for each other.*

Frenckell then asked the eighty-one-year-old president of Finland, Juho Paasikivi, to come to the rostrum. Paasikivi leaned into the microphone and said, in English, "I declare open the Games of Helsinki celebrating the XV Olympiad of the modern era."

As soon as the words reverberated throughout the stadium, Norvel watched the Olympic Flag rise to the top of the flagpole while the Olympic fanfare was played, this time by a sixty-piece brass band. Simultaneously a twenty-one-gun salute commenced from cannons mounted on a rock at the north end of the stadium. Upon the twenty-first barrage, thousands of pigeons were released from the north end of the stadium and flew west toward Sweden.

Norvel became aware of the crowd turning its attention to the electronic scoreboard and heard them begin to cheer ecstatically. Norvel looked at the words displayed in both Finnish and English: "The Olympic Torch is being brought into the Stadium by Paavo Nurvmi." The roar of the crowd became even louder as all eyes turned to the north entrance. In came a lone runner carrying the Olympic Torch.

Norvel recalled from 1948 that the torch began its journey in Olympia, Greece, several months before, where eleven women representing the Vestal Virgins lit the flame by focusing sunlight onto arranged kindling. This year it was subsequently carried by a relay of

*Paavo Nurvmi ignites the Olympic Flame.*
The XV Olympiad Official Report, Helsinki, 1952

runners from Greece to Finland. Norvel was not familiar with the name Paavo Nurvmi, but clearly he was someone well known to the spectators in the stadium.

Nurvmi ran around the track once, holding the torch high with his right hand. Upon completing his circuit, he trotted up to a large vessel sitting on a pedestal in front of the rostrum. He raised the torch high next to the vessel where, in a brief flash of light, it erupted into flame. The crowd was on its feet, cheering.

Norvel looked at the faces of his fellow Olympians, especially those of the boxers who, besides himself and Chuck Spieser, had not before experienced the elation of such a huge crowd. Patterson, standing next to Norvel, jumped up and down when he saw the torch light the Olympic Flame. Norvel watched Whitfield discreetly wipe tears from his eyes.

Then Norvel saw an older man emerge from the assembled dignitaries and run out to the flame wearing running shorts and an Olympic shirt. The announcer introduced him as Hannes Kolehmainenn, obviously another very popular Finnish athlete. Kolehmainenn carried an unlit torch to the flame and set it on fire by reaching into the flame. He then trotted in the direction of the stadium tower, whose height of 72.71 meters was set to commemorate the Finnish javelin thrower, Matti Jarvinen, winning the gold medal in the 1932 Olympic Games with a throw of the same length.

All eyes were on the top of the tower, where another vessel had been placed. In a few minutes Kolehmainenn appeared at the top and placed his torch in the vessel as another mass of flame erupted. The spectators clapped and cheered loudly. This flame would stay lit for the entirety of the games, only to be extinguished during the finale of the Closing Ceremony.

That night, the dance club at the Velodrome hosted many members of the international Olympic teams. Mostly the celebrating was carried on by those whose events were not going to start until later in the games, like the boxers. Norvel was encouraged to come along. Mello seemed to indicate he'd like Norvel to help police the behavior of the young team. So Norvel went, and he had a great time dancing with the Finnish girls and female Olympians.

For the next week Norvel involved himself with four activities: his own conditioning, including monitoring his weight, just in case; keeping Floyd Patterson focused; and watching other Olympic events.

The small white bus met the team and took them over to the Tarmo Club, where the boys, young ladies, and newspaper reporters waited outside each morning for their arrivals and departures. The team took the time to engage in casual conversation with the group, sign some autographs, and be available for brief interviews with newspaper reporters. After arriving at Tarmo and changing into boxing clothes, Norvel kept to his routine. He started with some stretching and moved to jumping rope, and then to light shadowboxing. After the warm-up he worked the bag, getting more aggressive until he was perspiring.

Then, at Mello's request, Norvel would take Patterson into the sparring ring to show the young boxer what he could expect from experienced boxers if he continued with his unorthodox style. Patterson had a unique boxing style that Mello didn't think would work very well against the more experienced competition. Mello knew Patterson's trainer, Cus D'Amato, quite well. Both men were from New York and involved in Catholic youth programs. But Mello, a proponent of traditional boxing style, was not fond of the style D'Amato taught his boxers, called a peekaboo stance. It involved putting the hands up to the face and employing head movement to put the opponent off his guard. Mello felt it left the body vulnerable to undercuts. But Patterson had become quite proficient at the style.

Norvel was fond of Patterson. He was born in North Carolina, the youngest of eleven children. When he was seven, he moved to Brooklyn and caused a lot of trouble for himself and those around him, so much that he was sent to a reform school, where he learned he was smart and a superior athlete. Norvel quickly saw that Patterson was passionate about becoming a championship boxer. He had his eyes on becoming a pro, even at a young age. It was also obvious Cus D'Amato had had an extraordinary impact on Patterson.

Norvel sensed that Patterson would not abandon the peekaboo style, so instead of trying to change it, he decided he would show how experienced boxers might try to exploit it. But he wasn't too successful because of Patterson's quickness and natural abilities. When they got into the sparring ring Norvel moved around in the classic style, moving his feet from side to side and landing jabs. But Patterson's head-bobbing was deceiving, and more than once Patterson could have caught Norvel by surprise with a left hook had this not been a sparring match. Mello watched the men intently.

Mello also requested Norvel spar with Sanders and Spieser, not so much to instruct but to keep them fresh against a quality, experienced boxer. Norvel and Sanders had formed a collaborative friendship since the time they'd fought a few months earlier. Norvel noticed that Sanders's boxing style had improved considerably since their bout, and expected him to be a formidable opponent to whoever faced him.

When the squad returned, even though they had showered and changed into their street clothes at Tarmo, Mello insisted they change back into their workout clothes and continue their conditioning on the Olympic Village running track. Most days Norvel would run from five to ten miles around the track, take another shower, and dress again to go be an Olympic spectator.

On Monday, July 21, after Norvel showered he looked over at Patterson. "Hey Floyd, you feel like heading over to the stadium with me to see if we can catch any of the '48ers?"

"Sure do," Patterson said enthusiastically. "I think Ed was going to go also—might as well wait for him too."

They took a shuttle to the stadium and found seats in an area of the grandstands set aside for participating athletes. The seats were wet from the intermittent rain of the past few days. There were clouds in the sky now, but no rain. They had an excellent view of the finish line on the track, albeit at an angle, and also of the interior field where field events were conducted.

Several minutes later, Mathias came into the stands and sat in a seat behind the three boxers.

"Hey, Bobby," Norvel said. "Where's Sim?"

"His discus event is tomorrow," Mathias said. "So he decided to stay put and rest up."

"Good idea," Norvel said.

Mathias leaned forward, pointed out to the field, and said, "Looks like the shot put finals have started. Three of our boys are in it."

Sanders started counting. "Sure enough, I think you're right, Bob. I see thirteen finalists, and three of them are ours."

"Any '48ers in the group?" Norvel asked.

"One of them," Mathias answered. "Jim Fuchs. He took bronze in London in this event, and he's back again."

"In a few days, you have to throw that thing, don't you?" Norvel said.

"Sure do," Mathias said.

"How will you do compared to the others?" Patterson asked.

"It's one of my better events," Mathias said. "It makes up for the ones I'm weak at, like the javelin throw. But I've been listening to Fuchs," Mathias added, pointing at his friend. "He shouldn't even be here because of his football injuries. So instead, he developed a whole new way of throwing that sixteen-pound hunk of lead. The standard way is for the thrower to step up, cock his hand under his chin and then give it the heave-ho, while letting out a loud grunt. Jim's legs wouldn't support that method, so he developed a glide forward in the circle and while maintaining his balance and not cocking the put, he'd just let go. He's dominated the shot-putting world the last two years, setting the world record at 17.95 meters, which still stands today. I'm lucky if I can do 15 meters."

When it was Fuchs's turn to throw, the men saw what Mathias was talking about. His delivery looked like a windup a baseball pitcher would use, except the object he was delivering weighed sixteen pounds. Fuchs's first toss was 16.93 meters.

After a few more competitors had their turn, the American Parry O'Brian stepped into the throwing circle. Fuchs told Mathias that O'Brian's style was more radical than his own. And sure enough, when O'Brian launched his shot, he started with his back to the target area and spun and slid forward before propelling the put out into the field.

A huge roar was heard from the stands when it was obvious O'Brian's throw was the longest so far. When the distance of 17.41 meters was officially posted on the scoreboard, another cheer erupted from the crowd. If it held, it would be a new Olympic record. O'Brian was in the lead after the first round, followed by his teammates Darrow Hooper, a tall Texan, and Fuchs.

While the shot put event was in progress, the men also paid attention to the 100-meter sprint semifinals. The three Americans on the team—Lindy Remigino, Dean Smith, and Art Bragg—all made it to the semifinals.

Norvel said, "Uh, uh, I've seen Bones Dillard in the village. He won this event in '48, so I'm wondering why he's not here. Did he get eliminated?"

Mathias said, "No, he didn't qualify for the sprint, but he's on for the 110-meter hurdles, which is the event he's known for. He's also on the 4x100 relay team."

Norvel nodded, "Now I remember. He tried for the hurdles in '48 but had a fluke fall in the trials, so he tried for the sprint and made it."

The two races had six competitors, of which the top three from each would get to the finals. Norvel was rooting for Art Bragg because he knew him from the 1951 Pan American Games, where Bragg had taken silver. Bragg was attending Morgan State in Baltimore, where Norvel's brother-in-law Robert was also now a student.

But in the first semifinal Bragg unexpectedly turned up lame. He finished last and was limping, holding his hamstring. In the same race Smith came in second with a time of 10.6 seconds. The men continued to watch the shot put as the runners queued up for the second race. When the gun sounded, the sprinters quickly moved toward the finish line, where Remigino placed second in 10.5 seconds.

The shot put competition continued through the five rounds of throws from each of the thirteen competitors, with O'Brian's throw still holding first place. Fuchs's best came on his fourth attempt, with a 17.01 meter throw. On his last attempt, Hooper came very close to besting O'Brian on his final attempt with a throw of 17.39 meters, just two centimeters short.

The Americans swept the event, taking the gold, silver, and bronze medals. The other events taking place in the stadium were paused as the men mounted the three-level awards podium situated midfield. O'Brian took the highest platform in the middle, Hooper to O'Brian's right for the silver, and Fuchs to his left for the bronze.

Norvel looked at the men standing on the podium and saw sheer patriotic pride on their faces. He did not know them personally, but they each were representing the team, including himself and those he was seated with. An official walked over and presented the medals, shaking each man's hand. Then the sixty-piece brass band began to play "The Star-Spangled Banner." The spectators rose from their seats.

*Darrow Hooper, Parry O'Brien, and Jim Fuchs on the awards podium.*
The XV Olympiad Official Report, Helsinki, 1952

The men looked around to see what was coming up next. Mathias saw Mal Whitfield warming up, stretching, and jogging.

"Hey, guys," he said. "I think we're going to get an opportunity to see Mal run his 800-meter heat."

Norvel said, "If he's the same person he was a year ago, you're going to see the definition of poetry in motion."

"That's for sure," Mathias agreed.

Whitfield was in the first of three heats in which, as in the 100 meter, the top three of each heat would head to the finals. The race started in front of them and would go around the 400-meter track twice. The gun sounded, and the eight competitors went loping off. They watched Whitfield run near the front, keeping pace.

As they came by the stands the first time, Patterson said, "He looks like he's floating on air and not trying very hard."

"That's Mal," Norvel said. "He knows he's easily going to qualify, and doesn't have to win the heat. If he wins, he may draw the inside lane for the finals, and he doesn't like to run from there."

When they came around the second time, it looked to Norvel as if Whitfield was just pacing himself. He easily came in second and jogged to a stop."

Mathias yelled from the stands, "Way to go, Mal!"

Whitfield looked up and saw the group in the stands. He smiled and waved.

About thirty minutes later, the 100-meter final was held. The 100-meter sprint was one of the premier events of the Olympics, coming on the second day of competition. The grandstands were at capacity, and the American men were grateful for their seats.

Mathias said, "Looks like all of Helsinki is looking forward to this one. I thought Blacks were supposed to excel at sprinting, but there are only two in this race, and none of them is American."

Norvel and Sanders felt comfortable around Mathias, and to them his teasing comment meant he felt the same. Patterson frowned, not having experienced a casual comment like that in mixed-race company.

Norvel winked at Patterson and, turning around to Mathias, said, "Well, isn't that what's great about athletic competition. Everyone is equal on the playing field, and the best man always wins."

Mathias reached out and patted Norvel's shoulder.

They watched the six 100-meter finalists warm up. There were the two Americans, an Australian, a sprinter from the Soviet Union, a Black man from Great Britain, and a Black man from Jamaica.

A murmur arose from the spectators as the starter called out, "Gentlemen, take your marks!"

Each sprinter carefully lowered their bodies into a crouch, placing one leg against the forward preset block and the other against the rear. They placed each hand on the ground behind the chalked starting line.

"Get set!" ordered the starter while pointing a pistol toward the sky.

*The 100-meter starter ready to fire the pistol.*
The XV Olympiad Official Report, Helsinki, 1952

Bang!

The sprinters broke from their blocks, and their legs propelled them down the short distance. The grandstands broke into an uproar. The race seemed over as soon as it began. Norvel thought the runners looked as if they were a coordinated tidal wave as they simultaneously approached the finish line. It appeared as if they crossed it together.

"Who won?" Sanders asked.

Norvel shrugged, while Iness said, "Hope they had a camera on it like they do at the horse races; otherwise it'll be a six-way tie."

"It definitely was a photo finish," Mathias added.

The judges were trying to decide also. In about fifteen minutes a roar went up from the crowd as the results were posted on the electronic board:

| | | | |
|---|---|---|---|
| 1 | Remigino, L. | USA | 10.4 sec |
| 2 | McKenley, H. | Jamaica | 10.4 sec |
| 3 | McDonald Bailey, E. | Great Britain | 10.4 sec |
| 4 | Smith, F. | USA | 10.4 sec |
| 5 | Suharev, V. | USSR | 10.5 sec |
| 6 | Treloar, J. | Australia | 10.5 sec |

The next day the world's newspapers showed the photograph used to determine the outcome of the race. Showing Remigino's right forearm crossing the line first, it was the first time a photograph was used to determine the results of an Olympic event. The newspapers called it the closest finish in Olympic history. Later, when the official report of the 1952 Olympics was published, it stated, "The 100 metres were won for the first time in 24 years by a representative of the white races, Lindy Remigino of the U.S.A."

*The closest finish in Olympic history.*
The XV Olympiad Official Report, Helsinki, 1952

When the men returned to the Olympic Village, Mello was waiting for them. He had borrowed a scale from the American Embassy in Helsinki that measured weight in pounds. He also posted on a wall a sheet with columns and rows. At the top of the left hand column was NAME, the next column was labeled GOAL, and next was the day of the week.

Under GOAL, Mello entered a number one pound less than the maximum for the weight category he expected each boxer to be qualified for. He wasn't too concerned about the lower categories. Those boxers were within the range they needed to be, and Mello knew if he had a problem, he could swap one with another. He was concerned about middleweight and light heavyweight.

Patterson's stature was large for a middleweight boxer and, worrisome to Mello, the seventeen-year-old exhibited a youthful appetite. He entered "164" next to Patterson's name. Mello put the same number next to Spieser because he wanted a backup to Patterson in case the kid got hurt or seemed to be in over his head on the Olympic stage. He knew there was also the option of moving Ellsworth Webb up a category and filling in the opening with an alternate.

Even though Norvel was the heavyweight backup, Mello didn't believe substituting him for the talented Sanders would be necessary. So Mello entered "177" next to Norvel's name in case he needed a backup to Spieser at light heavyweight. The space next to Sanders's name was left blank.

Mello asked each boxer to step on the scale, noted their weight, and wrote it in the column next to the boxer's name. When Patterson stepped up the scale registered 163. Mello smiled at him and told him to keep up the good work. Spieser's reading was 174, good for light heavyweight, but 9 pounds above the number Mello needed him to be at for middleweight.

Then Norvel stepped onto the scale. He looked sheepish when it registered 190.

"Norvel," said Mello. "You've only lost two pounds in the week and a half we've been here. I know the food is tempting, but I really need for you to concentrate on losing those next thirteen pounds. I suggest you spend some time each day in the sauna down there, to sweat some of it off. Okay?"

"Yes, Coach," Norvel said. "And you're right. They are really trying to fatten us up with all the ice cream and hot fudge sundaes."

"You'll have plenty of time to fill up on ice cream when you get home, but for now you need to eat just enough to stay strong."

"Yes, sir, Coach," Norvel said.

*He's right. I have a weakness for desserts, and they have a lot of choices here.*

The boxers settled into a routine for the remainder of the week. Their mornings were spent at the Tarmo boxing club, training individually and sparring with each other. Norvel continued to pair up with Sanders, Patterson, and occasionally Spieser. Afterward they returned to the Olympic Village and ran on the track to work on endurance. Norvel limited his eating to breakfast and a meal before he went to the stadium. He skipped eating an evening meal and, instead, sat in the sauna for thirty minutes. On several occasions, however, he snuck in a bowl of vanilla ice cream. Patterson teased him at one point, wiggling his index finger back and forth, indicating what he was doing was forbidden. Each night he wrote a letter to Leslie, posting it the next morning before going to Tarmo.

In the afternoon, most of the boxers accompanied Norvel, Patterson, and Sanders to the stadium to take in the scheduled events, but several rested so they could go to the dance club that evening. Weightlifters John Davis and Norb Schemansky, both '48ers, and James Bradford, Norvel's fellow Washingtonian, joined the stadium group.

On Tuesday the on-again, off-again rain was finally gone. The group secured seats in the athlete's grandstands, where they observed the first heats for the 200 meter, finals for the pole vault, and the discus final that Sim Iness had easily qualified for. Sprinters from the United States won three of the twelve 200-meter heats. Bob Richards, a '48er, and Don Laz took gold and silver, respectively, in the pole vault. Mathias, who was sitting next to Norvel, was particularly interested in the pole vault since it was one of the decathlon events.

Norvel asked, "If I've converted Richard's 455-centimeter vault correctly, then it's just short of 15 feet. What height do you usually get in the pole vault?"

Mathias said, "I can't get that high, but I can usually get over 13 feet. It's one of my better events and I usually beat or come close to beating the other decathlon competitors."

He hesitated for a moment and continued, "I reached out to Richards to try and get some tips, but there was a, how do you say it, a certain superior attitude about him. I've heard rumors, just so you know."

"Oh, uh, uh, I've run into those types all my life," said Norvel. "You just learn to avoid any trouble. As my father said, just do better."

"Now its Sim's turn to compete," said Mathias. "He was in the first heat this morning and held back. He just wanted to throw far enough to beat the 46-meter qualifying distance, which he easily did.

For the next hour they watched the seventeen discus throwers go through the first three rounds of throws. On that third throw, Iness set a new Olympic record of 55.03 meters. After the three rounds, the field of competitors was cut to six. Each thrower had two more turns to beat the mark set by Iness. The closest anyone got was Iness himself, with a toss of 54.13 meters. Iness won the gold, Consolini of Italy the silver, and another American, James Dillion, took the bronze. The U.S. team in the stands cheered loudly when the results were announced.

The next highly anticipated event was the finals of the 800-meter run, in which Mal Whitfield would be defending his gold medal from the 1948 London Games. Norvel had formed a

*Sim Iness, winner of the discus throw.*
The XV Olympiad Official Report, Helsinki, 1952

good friendship with Whitfield, first in London and then in Buenos Aires at the Pan Am Games the prior year.

When the starting pistol fired, the nine runners took off in almost a sprint. Whitfield did not take the lead. Instead, he held position in the middle of the pack, easily keeping pace for the first lap with his graceful loping style. As they passed the stands and began the second lap, he moved into the third position, slightly on the outside. When they rounded the corner for the home stretch, Whitfield moved into first and went on to win, tying his Olympic record of 1:49.2 minutes. Mathias, Norvel, and all the boxers and wrestlers were on their feet, cheering. The spectators enjoyed their exuberant demonstration.

*Whitfield takes the lead during the final turn.*
The XV Olympiad Official Report, Helsinki, 1952

The men stayed around for a few more events and returned to Olympic Village, where they knew Pete Mello would be waiting. When Norvel stepped onto the scale, Mello was pleased to see it register 187 pounds, a three-pound loss in twenty-four hours.

But the next evening, Wednesday, Mello's mood was one of disappointment. Spieser had lost only two pounds, and Norvel's weight remained at 187. Mello told both men, in no uncertain terms, that he expected better results from them for the next weigh-in. Spieser and Norvel looked at each other and shrugged.

The next day, Thursday, Norvel looked forward to the afternoon's events at the stadium. He went there with Floyd Patterson, along with Ed Sanders, Davey Moore, John Davis, James Bradford, and Norb Schemansky. Mathias did not join them because he wanted to be well rested and mentally prepared for the decathlon, which began the next day.

Norvel was looking forward to watching Harrison Dillard, or "Bones" as he was known by the team, run in the finals of the 110-meter hurdle. But while waiting for Dillard's event, the 5,000-meter run took place. Along with the other spectators, Norvel turned his attention to its progress. He wasn't expecting to be captivated by it, since none of the '48ers were competing.

The favorite, Herbert Schade of Germany had set a new Olympic record in his qualifying heat the previous day. Schade led a single file of six of the fourteen competing runners for most of the way. The pack of six stayed tightly bunched until about 4,400 meters had been covered. Then Gaston Reiff of Belgium unexpectedly exited the track. By then Norvel and the others were on their feet. The noise of the crowd was such that he couldn't hear what the others were saying. As the pace quickened one of the others fell back, leaving four in the lead on the final lap. Czech Emil Zátopek took the lead at the start of the last lap, but then on the back stretch, Schade and the other two contenders—Alain Mimoun of France and Chris Chataway of Great Britain—forged past him. With 250 meters to go, Chataway moved into first. Halfway through the final turn Zátopek began a spurt that took him past the other three. Zátopek's winning time once again set a new Olympic record.

It was the most exciting track event Norvel had ever experienced. The men looked at each other, truly awed at what they just saw. But the frenzy among the spectators continued to grow. Many pointed toward the field where the women's javelin throw was in progress.

Bradford, who was sitting next to Norvel, nudged him and pointed toward the scorecard. Talking loudly so he could be heard, he said, "Look at the name of the winner of the race we just saw and leader of the lady's javelin contest."

Norvel said, "Uh, uh, I see what you mean. They're both named Zátopek."

Then the name of the javelin winner was posted: Zátopek.

Schemansky said, "Look at that! The track man, Zátopek, is running over to the javelin area!"

They all watched the Zátopeks hug each other. Norvel learned later that he'd seen an unusual Olympic moment. The Zátopeks were husband and wife. Adding to the curious event, both gold medal winners were born on the same day of the same year, September 19, 1922.

*Zátopek takes the 5,000 meter lead, Mimoun is 2nd, Schade 3rd, while Chataway trips and falls.*
The XV Olympiad Official Report, Helsinki, 1952

*Dana Zátopek takes the gold medal in the women's javelin throw.*
The XV Olympiad Official Report, Helsinki, 1952

*Mr. and Mrs. Zátopek at the reception with President Paasakivi of Finland.*
The XV Olympiad Official Report, Helsinki, 1952

After the sensational drama of the 5,000 meter, the 110-meter hurdles was somewhat anti-climactic. Norvel was interested in the story of Harrison Dillard, likely the top 110-meter hurdler in the world in 1948. He inexplicably tripped over a hurdle and fell during the Olympic trials. Instead, he qualified for the 100-meter sprint and won. Four years later, he was still the top 110-meter hurdler, and now he had an opportunity to prove it.

And prove it he did, but it was tight. The Americans took the top three spots, with Dillard winning gold for a new Olympic record. Jack Davis made almost the same time, but a fraction behind Dillard, and was award-ed the silver medal. Norvel was looking forward to con-gratulating Dillard.

Later, after spending time in the sauna with Spieser, Nor-vel weighed in with Mello, who recorded a drop to 186. Spieser was at 172. Patterson was well within the range to stay at middleweight, impress-ing Norvel with his discipline.

When he was at the Lon-don Olympics, Norvel had be-

*Harrison Dillard and Jack Davis taking gold and silver in the 110-meter hurdles.*
The XV Olympiad Official Report, Helsinki, 1952

come fascinated with the decathlon, in large part because of Bob Mathias, who was now known as the world's greatest athlete. Mathias epitomized all the event required: a balance of natural athleticism, physical conditioning, and mental fortitude. Before London Norvel did not know much about the decathlon, but during those games he gained appreciation for the grueling contest.

The ten events are conducted over two days, five on each day, with up to 1,000 points per event awarded each athlete. On the first day the order of the events was the 100 meter, long jump, shot put, high jump, and 400 meter. For the second day, the events were 110-meter hurdles, discus throw, pole vault, javelin, and the 1500 meter. A table of points was created based on the time achieved during the track events, and the distance or height achieved in the field events. Bob Mathias won the decathlon sensationally at the 1948 London Olympics as a seventeen-year-old with a total point count of 7,139. During the trials for these Olympics, he set a world record with 7,825 points.

Norvel had read in the newspapers that Mathias's chances of winning a second time would depend on how he would defend against the formidable Soviet Union team. Soviet radio declared that Mathias was an example of how America spoiled their youth. Tensions between the two powers were exacerbated by propaganda from both sides. A Soviet newspaper circulated the statement from the Soviet government that the U.S. Olympic team had been taken over by the military, while the *New York Times* and *Washington Post* complained the Soviet athletes were being compensated and therefore were not amateurs.

But the twenty-one-year-old Mathias and similarly aged Soviet decathletes were friendly with each other. So much so that while practicing the pole vault Mathias saw the Soviets struggling with their hands slipping on the pole, and offered some of his balm to them. They appreciated the gesture.

*Bob Mathias in the company of his Soviet Union competitors.*
XV Olympiad Official Report, Helsinki, 1952

When Norvel and the other boxers returned from their morning training session, they went to the large tented dining room at the Olympic Village. To their surprise they saw Mathias and his two decathlete teammates
eating steaks. With them was an older man Norvel had seen around the
Olympic Village.

Norvel and Patterson walked up to their table. Norvel said to Mathias,
"You fellas must have a long break between events."

Mathias smiled affably and said, "We do. We had the 100 meter and
long jump this morning, and now have to wait until three o'clock for the
shot put. So we thought we'd refuel ourselves. You look like you're losing
some weight there, Norvel."

"Thanks for noticing," Norvel laughed. "Coach Mello's orders in case,
uh, uh, I have to go down in weight class. I'm not expecting to, though."

Mathias said, "Always good to be prepared. Norvel, Floyd, these are
my fellow teammates, Milton Campbell from New Jersey, and Floyd Simmons from Los Angeles. You may recall Floyd was with us in '48. And this
is our coach, Jack Weiershauser." Then motioning to Norvel and Patter-

son, he added, "Guys, meet members of our boxing team, Norvel Lee and Floyd Patterson."

The men shook hands with each other. Mathias looked at Campbell and Patterson, saying, "I believe the two of you are about the same age, eighteen?"

Patterson said quietly, "Seventeen."

Mathias said cheerfully, "Same age I was in London. Milt here had a good morning, and is leading everyone after these first two events."

"Only by ten points," said Campbell, "1735 to 1725."

Norvel asked, "Who's got the 1725?"

Simmons pointed to Mathias and said, "Who else?"

Mathias, looking sheepish, said, "Well, I did have an embarrassing blunder in the 100. I mistook a click of a camera for the gun and had a false start. Everybody else was still in their blocks. If I faulted a second time I would have been disqualified, so I stayed in the gate waiting for the gun and somebody else to break first. Probably cost me a couple of tenths."

"How's your left leg feeling now?" Coach Weiershauser asked. He turned to Norvel and Patterson to explain. "During the long jump, he felt a twinge in his upper leg. Your thigh, I believe, Bob?"

"It's my thigh, but it will be okay," Mathias said.

Weiershauser said, "Chow down, men. We've got to get our asses back over there."

Norvel said, "Best of luck to you. A group of us will be over there to cheer you on."

Norvel and the entire boxing team, except for Archie Slaten, who was not feeling well, went to the stadium to see the first day of the decathlon. The weightlifters, many of whom had been joining the boxers at the stadium, could not come this day as their competition at the nearby Messuhalli Exhibition Hall was commencing. Messuhalli was also where the boxing events would begin in three days.

Once settled in the grandstands under clear skies, Norvel noticed a stiff northerly breeze beginning, likely coming off the icy glaciers several hundred miles north. Norvel looked out onto the field for the Americans. He spotted Campbell and Simmons but didn't see Mathias. Finally he saw him emerge from under the stands where, Norvel found out later, he had been napping. When Mathias came out he was wearing a blanket around his shoulders and sat down on a bench near the shot put area, while the other competitors, including his teammates, were pacing around. When the event began Mathias stayed seated while the others took their turn. When it was his turn, Mathias calmly got up from his seat and put the shot five feet beyond his closest competitor, Campbell, at 50 feet 2 and 3/8 inches or 15.3 meters. This earned him 912 points and put him in the overall lead.

Norvel wondered how Mathias maintained his tranquility in front of seventy thousand people and the rest of the world. He didn't appear to be under any stress.

The next two events were the high jump and the 400 meter. When it was his turn to jump, Mathias cleared 190 centimeters and figured it was enough to keep him in the lead. So he put on his jacket, took a seat sheltered from the wind that was now showing its teeth, and watched the rest of the field continue jumping. Only one competitor outdid him in the high jump, Goran Widenfelt of Sweden, at 194 centimeters.

It was nearing 8 p.m. in the waning sun and bitter cold wind when the three heats of the 400 meter dash were held. When it came time for Mathias to run, Norvel noticed his thigh was giving him a problem because Mathias appeared to slow his pace on the last half of the one-lap race after maintaining a world record pace during the first half. But his 50.2 seconds was the best in the field, a tenth of second better than the Finn, Reikko. By the end of the first day of the decathlon, the Americans held the top three places, with Mathias on top at 4,367 total points; Campbell in second at 4,222; and Simmons third with 3,924. The closest Soviet was Vladimir Volkov, at 3,689 total points.

Later in the evening the team cycled through the scale in Mello's room. Everyone was at the weight they were expected to be, except for

Spieser and Norvel.

Mello said to Spieser, "You are off the hook, Chuck. Patterson's looking good and I'm going to go with him. You're set for light heavyweight. Just keep doing what you're doing."

Spieser cleared his throat and said, "Thanks, Coach."

Mello said, "Okay, take care of yourself." Then turning to Norvel, he said, "One hundred eighty-four, big man. You've got seven pounds to go to get to your required weight. We are going to have to get you on a real aggressive program."

Norvel simply said, "Yes, sir."

In the middle of the night, Norvel heard commotion in the hall and went out to see what was taking place. Two men in medical uniforms were helping the lightweight boxer Archie Slaten out of his room and onto a stretcher. Slaten looked at Norvel as he was lying down and pointed to his lower abdomen. It was obvious he was in excruciating pain. Mello patted Slaten's shoulder tenderly and walked with him as they wheeled him out of the building. Norvel followed along and watched them put Slaten into a waiting ambulance. Mello also got into the ambulance as it left.

In the morning Mello called the squad together for a meeting. He looked tired and worried. "Gentlemen, perhaps you heard the commotion last night. We had to get Archie Slaten some medical attention, and it's a good thing we did. When they got him to the hospital, they determined his appendix had ruptured and they performed an emergency appendectomy. He's going to have a full recovery, but I'd like for all of us to pray to help him along."

Mello led them in a brief prayer. He then asked the team to make some time to see him at the hospital, and to keep him in their individual prayers. The squad then shuttled over to Tarmo for the last of their daily training sessions.

On Saturday when the boxers returned from their workout and went to the tented dining area, there was no sign of the American decathletes as on the previous day. Norvel and others ate quickly and caught a shuttle to the stadium to catch the final decathlon event. When they arrived most of the American team, except for those competing in other events, was in the stands to see if Mathias could make Olympic history. If he won, he would be the first to win two Olympic decathlons.

The weather was terrible. There was a cold rain that at times appeared horizontal as the winds kicked up. Overhead the clouds were dark, occasionally parting to let some of the northern sunshine through, but then closing again, casting a dark shadow on the proceedings. For a moment, Norvel flashed back to the time of his youth in Botetourt County during March and early April. He and his father, brother, and neighbors would be out planting the crops, enduring the harsh elements, just as the decathletes on the field were doing now. Several of the competitors who were performing dismally dropped out, knowing it was futile in these conditions.

The boxers arrived at their seats at 4 p.m. while the pole vault was still in progress, but halted at the moment because of the winds. Norvel was told the event was proceeding at a snail's pace. He found out that at the completion of the two morning events, the 110-meter hurdles and the discus, the Americans still occupied the top three spots. On the scoreboard he saw that Mathias had cleared 400 centimeters and was leading the event. Norvel spotted him on the field, huddled in a rain blanket. It looked like he wasn't planning to take any more turns, using the same approach he'd taken the previous day with the high jump to preserve his energy and his sore leg. Norvel learned later that, for the first time in a major competition, Mathias had used a vaulting pole made of fiberglass.

The pole vault took up a grueling five hours. In spite of the horrible weather, most of the American team remained in the stands to watch the rest of the decathlon play out. After a brief break, the remaining decathletes gathered for the javelin throw. The rain had stopped and the wind subsided somewhat.

Norvel was seated between Patterson and the bantamweight boxer Davey Moore. They were all huddled under rain blankets. Moore was also wearing a woolen ski hat.

"Where'd you get that?" asked Norvel.

"They've got them at the store in the Village," Moore said. "Some nice things there—you may want to consider taking a souvenir back to your honey."

"I'm glad our event is indoors," Norvel observed. "Can you imagine fighting in this weather?"

Moore and Patterson shook their heads. A large cheer went up from the crowd as Mathias got up to throw. It was one of those rare moments in Olympic history when the crowd was rooting for the person more than for a nation.

When Mathias threw, his javelin landed surprisingly short compared to the other competitors. He stood there dumbfounded, then looked up to the flags to see if the wind had thwarted his attempt. Just then his coach, Weiershauser, seated ten rows below Norvel, stood up and looked up toward the section full of Americans. He wasn't permitted to go onto the field to coach his team, but he'd thought of a unique way of communicating a message to Mathias from the stands.

He said in a loud voice, "Alright, everyone, listen up. On the count of three repeat after me, loudly."

Everyone got on their feet as Weiershauser began, "Oh, Bob, hey you! Don't forget to follow through!"

The chant became louder and louder as the entire stadium took it up. "Oh, Bob, hey you! Don't forget to follow through! Oh, Bob, hey you! Don't forget to follow through!"

Mathias looked up at the American section, waved, and gave the okay sign. When it was his turn to throw again, he delivered the longest javelin throw of his life, 59.21 meters, for 715 points.

By the time the javelin contest was completed and the grounds crew sopped as much of the rainwater off the track as they could, it was 10 p.m. The final event, the 1500-meter run, still had to be competed. Mathias was told by a person tracking the scoring that he needed to run the 1500, known in the United States as the metric mile, in 4:55.3 to break his own world record in the decathlon. During normal track conditions, and when he was fresh, achieving this time wouldn't have been a concern. But these were extraordinary conditions, and everyone in attendance knew it.

In the misty, cold night air, the sky the color of a solar eclipse, the Olympic Flame and the scoreboard supplied the only light. The starting gun sounded and Mathias set a comfortable pace for himself behind Vladimir Volkov and Göran Widenfelt. Norvel and all around him knew they were witnessing history and an epic display of athletic endurance. Everyone in the stadium was on their feet when Mathias crossed the finish line first with a time of 4:50.8, breaking his own world record.

*Bob Mathias completing the 1500-meter run, setting a new world record in the decathlon.* The XV Olympiad Official Report, Helsinki, 1952

*The three American decathlon medal winners listening to "The Star-Spangled Banner" on the medalist's podium.* The XV Olympiad Official Report, Helsinki, 1952

*The three Americans—Floyd Simmons (left) and Milton Campbell (right) celebrating Bob Mathias's (center) remarkable decathlon victory* The XV Olympiad Official Report, Helsinki, 1952

The Olympic Village was abuzz with the excitement of the American sweep of the decathlon and of Bob Mathias's incredible performance. Norvel had a brief opportunity to congratulate the three medal winners before they met the international press.

That night many of the athletes went to the Velodrome dance club to celebrate. But Norvel didn't think it prudent to spend the night at a party and be expected to compete in top form. Pete Mello made it clear that it was time for his boxing squad to get to work. He requested that the team meet with him at 7 a.m. on Sunday, before church services.

Norvel and Patterson were the first to arrive at the Coach's room. Both Mello and J. T. Owen were there. The team manager, Barrodale, had not been seen since they arrived. In spite of his title, his job was to represent the team at committee meetings so that Mello and Owen could work with the team without having to deal with other priorities.

When they all were gathered, Norvel saw that only twelve had showed up. He knew Slaten was still in the hospital, but one other was missing. He was trying to determine who it was when Mello started the meeting.

"Good morning, men, it's time for us to get to work," Mello announced. "Preliminary matches start tomorrow night, but weigh-in is tomorrow morning. We have a few issues to deal with. You know about Archie, but we have two other potential issues to figure out. Joe Reynolds is under the weather. I've had him quarantined in a room so he won't spread around what's gotten to him."

Sanders said, "Maybe it was brought on by some gal over at the Velo dance club who seems to have fancied him."

Everyone chuckled while Mello said, "Now, now!"

Mello continued. "Our other issue is standing right there." He pointed to Spieser.

The men looked over to the light heavyweight and noticed that his lower leg was wrapped.

"We think it's his Achilles' tendon," J. T. said. "He may have injured it while doing some sprints."

Spieser shook his head, as if he were apologizing.

Norvel felt a twinge of excitement come over him as a murmur went through the room. Several of the men looked at Norvel. He hadn't thought he'd have a shot at actually participating, but this news made it a possibility.

Mello continued, "So here's what I have, subject to change, depending on if Spieser's condition improves and the official weigh-in tomorrow morning."

He looked at J. T., who pulled out a sheet of paper and read from it in his Louisiana drawl, "Here's what we've come up with to make sure we're covered in all weight classifications: For flyweight it's Brooks and for bantam, Moore. For featherweight we're going to bring in Brown from the reserve and move Bickle up to lightweight to replace Slaten. For light welterweight, bring Adkins up from lightweight reserve to substitute for Reynolds. You're okay with that, ain't you, Charles?"

Mello looked at him and added, "You've been showing real good form at the gym this week."

Adkins said, "Oh, yeah, I am, thank you."

The other men looked at each other and nodded their agreement that the plan so far made sense.

J. T. continued, "For welterweight, light middle, and middle we will continue with the original plan with Gage, Webb, and Patterson."

Patterson beamed at this news, and several of the others patted him on the shoulders.

Mello took over and said, "Now we come to the complication. Norvel, I want you to be able to sub for Chuck if he doesn't have a miraculous recovery by tomorrow morning. But you will have to lose five pounds between now and then to qualify for light heavyweight."

Norvel nodded.

"If you can't," continued Mello, "then we will have a real mess on our hands. I'm guessing we'd move you, Floyd, up to light heavy and bring in Ernest from the reserve list to fill in somehow. So here's what I'd recommend you do, Norvel. You should fast until the weigh-in tomorrow morning, meaning don't eat or drink anything except for water for the next 24 hours or so."

"Okay, Coach," said Norvel. "If that's what I have to do, that's what, uh, uh, I'll do."

The other boxers applauded.

Mello said, "J. T. and I will help you through this, but any of you others who want to help, go ahead. And whatever any of you do, don't go near Reynolds!"

Norvel set aside his plans to watch the scheduled relays and the marathon. He spent the entire day not eating, and alternating between running on the track, sitting in the sauna, and participating in lengthy jump-roping sessions. He was also drinking what seemed like gallons of water. When the evening came he wrote a letter to Leslie, as was his ritual. Meanwhile, word spread throughout Olympic Village that the Czech, Emil Zátopek, the winner of the 5,000- and 10,000 meter runs, at the last moment entered the marathon and won it.

Norvel was hungry and tired. He went to bed, hoping his efforts had paid off.

# CHAPTER 23

## *July 28 to August 2, 1952—XV Olympiad, Helsinki, Finland*

A t 7 a.m. on Monday, July 28, the now eleven-person U.S. Boxing Team was back in Coach Pete Mello's room.

"Norvel," he said. "Let's get you on the scale."

With everyone standing around, Norvel stripped to his underwear and stepped onto the scale. Mello adjusted the weights at the top until the indicator was balanced. He and Norvel broke into a relieved smile as the indicator showed 176, two pounds under the light heavyweight limit.

The entire room broke into applause.

*I'm in! Time to focus on winning. Leslie will be so excited when she sees it in the paper!!*

Mello said, "Okay, men, listen up. Our friends Chuck Spieser and Joe Reynolds are not well enough for me to commit them to the ring. We've called for a doctor to see to them. We are going to go with the lineup we talked about yesterday. Weigh-in begins in two hours at 9 a.m. over at the venue. Let's all plan to meet at the entrance to the village in an hour. Dress for weigh-in. Some matches will start tonight, so do what you must to get prepared. We won't know who among you will be going on tonight until we get over there. Any questions?"

"I'm the only reserve left," said Anthony. "Do I stay here, or come with you?"

"Please come with us," said Mello. "If someone doesn't qualify, we will get you in. If not, you'll be a big help to me."

Anthony said, "Yes, sir, thank you."

Mello turned to Norvel and said, "Norvel, I know you're hungry, but you can't eat anything until after you've weighed in. And even then, I want you to stick to protein and vegetables. You are going to have to weigh in every day, but you also will need your energy. Capiche?"

Norvel nodded in agreement.

The weigh-in went as expected. It took place at the large building called Messuhalli Hall, the venue hosting the basketball, wrestling, weightlifting, and boxing competitions. Messuhalli, consisting of two halls, was originally built in 1935 to bring concerts and exhibitions to Helsinki. Because of the large number of boxing entries, both halls were planned to be used for the early matches.

Mello pulled the entire team off to one corner and started talking excitedly. "Here's the lineup of the first matches. We only have four matches today and tonight, involving Brooks, Brown, Bickle, and Adkins. Everybody else goes tomorrow. But I'd like everyone here to watch your teammates. It's always good to know that someone in the audience is in your corner. In the meantime, I've got a couple sheets here you can look over and see what you'll be up against."

Norvel took one and saw that he'd be going against a French boxer on Tuesday night. He didn't know anything about the man but would ask around to see if anyone knew of him. Norvel was relieved he didn't have a match that day. There were two light heavyweight matches scheduled for the first round, neither involving the United States. Norvel didn't know how that was determined; he was just happy it came out that way. He was famished from his fast of the past twenty-four hours, and wanted to have a steak and some vegetables. He would try to avoid anything that would put weight on. He was also wondering if and when the family at home would get the news that he was actually going to compete in the Olympics.

Later in the afternoon he joined his teammates in watching Nate Brooks defeat his opponent, Risto Luukkonen of Finland, in a unanimous 3-0 decision in the first round of the flyweight division. A few hours later, Edson Brown went 3-0 against Benoy Bose of India. Then Bobby Bickle fought an opponent from Ceylon and clearly outclassed him, causing the referee to stop the fight in the second round, earning Bickle a TKO. Finally, they saw Charles Adkins pummel the Norwegian Leif Hansen. Again the referee put a stop to the fight two minutes into the first round: another TKO for the Americans. Adkins, worried he had hurt the Norwegian, went to his opponent's corner after the bout to check on him.

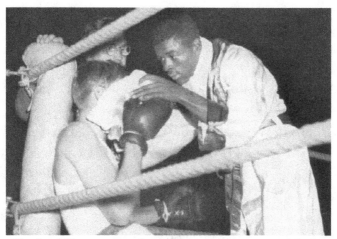

*Charles Adkins tends to Leif Hansen after scoring a TKO.*
The XV Olympiad Official Report, Helsinki, 1952

The next morning, Norvel, knowing he wouldn't have to weigh in until an hour before the evening sessions, treated himself to a large breakfast of six fried eggs, bacon slices, and toast with jam. Afterward he had a light loosening workout, went to the sauna, and ate an early afternoon meal. It was the last meal he planned to have before his bout.

Later in the afternoon Norvel joined others in watching bantamweight Davey Moore take down Egon Schidan of Germany 3-0. Then Norvel went to his weigh-in, registering 176. He rejoined the others to watch Edson Brown win his match against Illie of Romania, 3-0. Later, in a tough, closely contested bout, they saw Bobby Bickle lose 2-1 to Aureliano Bolognesi of Italy, putting him out of the competition.

During a break between American bouts, Norvel and Patterson went to the gym in the basement to begin loosening up for their upcoming matches. Ernest Anthony, the sole remaining alternate on the squad, acted as courier to keep his teammates in the gym informed as to when one of their own was about to compete, so they could come up and watch.

The matches continued into the night in both halls. Norvel was beginning to feel weary from the several days of restricting his diet. Nevertheless, he continued to warm up or watch his teammates' bouts. He saw Louis Gage knock out Ali Belkacem of France in the first round in the welterweight division. Likewise, he saw an impressive Ed Sanders easily defeat his opponent, Hans Jost, of Sweden, by knocking him out in the first round. Then, with the hour approaching midnight, they realized the next two contests would take place simultaneously. The light middleweight bout with Ellsworth Webb against the highly respected gold medal winner from 1948, László Papp of Hungary, would be in front of a capacity crowd in the larger hall. The middleweight contest involving Floyd Patterson would be in the small room. The Californians Gage and Sanders went to watch Webb, along with Coach J. T. Norvel and the others, including Pete Mello, went to see the Patterson fight.

Patterson's opponent was the French boxer Omar Tebbaka. Both the United States and France had byes in the first set of preliminaries, making this a second preliminary match. The room was at about half capacity, as everyone was more interested in seeing the Papp-Webb bout next door.

Norvel noticed a different look about Patterson when he entered the ring. He transitioned from a gangly, shy adolescent to an intensely focused gladiator. When the bell sounded, signaling the beginning of the fight, the Frenchman was taken completely off guard by Patterson's peekaboo style of keeping his gloves in front of his face while crouching. Tebbaka was fortunate to stay on his feet through the three 3-minute rounds, during which Patterson landed several hard combinations on him. The judges awarded Patterson an easy victory, unanimously giving him all three rounds.

Norvel and Mello greeted Patterson as he left the ring.

"You looked real good in there, son," Norvel said.

Patterson smiled and returned to his teenage self, mumbling, "Thanks, man. Couldn't get him down, though."

Mello said encouragingly, "But you get to do it again on Thursday."

J. T. stepped up and said, "Norvel, you'd better go get ready. They'll be starting the light heavies soon in the big room. László Papp is all he's advertised to be. He took Ellsworth out in two rounds, knocked him out cold."

Mello asked, concerned, "Is Ellsworth okay?"

"He's fine, except for his pride," J. T. said.

Norvel went to prepare for his bout, also against a French competitor.

At 1:10 a.m. the spectators in the larger hall still numbered around one thousand. Norvel looked across to the other corner of the ring and judged his competitor, Claude Arnaiz, to be peculiarly relaxed, talking with several people who looked more like friends from his social circle than the usual trainers or handlers. They were a jovial group, talking and laughing. Norvel picked out a few words he'd learned in French class at Howard.

In the corner with Norvel was Billy Fallon, the team trainer. As was his routine, Norvel was on his feet shuffling back and forth, waiting for the bell after the referee delivered the standard instructions and admonishments, in French and English. Norvel noticed that many of the officials at the Olympics were multilingual. He wondered why most Americans were not.

When the bell announced the start of the first round, Arnaiz sprang out of his corner, surprisingly aggressive. Norvel normally shut out crowd noise when involved in a match, but he became aware of French cheers of "Obtenez-le Claude!" which he translated as "Go get him, Claude!"

Norvel soon determined that Arnaiz was more of a showman than a boxer. So Norvel settled into his classic style of moving around his opponent, staying light on this feet, and looking for combinations of lefts and rights to land while keeping himself protected. Norvel consistently landed solid jabs and punches, while Arnaiz flailed away. Norvel was worried about his energy level, but in the end it didn't matter. Arnaiz couldn't match Norvel's skill and experience. The judges awarded each round to Norvel, giving him a 3-0 victory. A smiling Pete Mello was the first to congratulate Norvel.

*Sure glad he was my first draw, because I didn't need to dig deep to pull that one out. Got to get my energy back. Need some protein in me!*

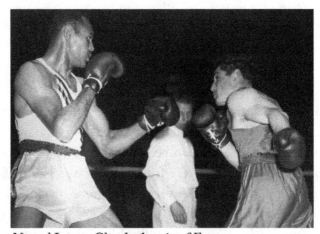

*Norvel Lee vs. Claude Arnaiz of France in a preliminary match.*
Photo by KEYSTONE-FRANCE/Gamma-Ralpho via Getty Images

The remainder of the second set of preliminary matches continued until almost dawn Wednesday morning. The U.S. team slept in, including Norvel, who was a notorious early riser. Then the group went back to Messuhalli to support the remaining preliminary matches.

They watched Brooks, Brown, and Adkins dispatch their opponents, each with 3-0 scores from the judges. Then, in a closely contested bout, Gage lost to Torma of Czechoslovakia, 2-1. Mello didn't like the scoring. Norvel thought it was fair but kept his thoughts to himself.

The quarterfinals were held on Thursday, July 31, still using both halls at Messuhalli. The Americans had seven boxers left in the competition: Brooks, Moore, Brown, Adkins, Patterson, Lee, and Sanders.

In a narrow victory, Nathan Brooks beat Mircea Dobrescu of Romania 2-1 and moved on to the flyweight semifinals. But in the bantamweight bout, Davey Moore was beaten by the Korean boxer, Kang, 2-1; and Edson Brown was easily taken out by Joseph Ventaja of France, 3-0, in the featherweight class. The next chance for the Americans was in light welterweight, where Charles Adkins met the highly regarded Grant Webster of South Africa, notorious for a devastating left hook. But to the team's delight, Adkins fought a brilliant strategic fight and outpointed Webster in each round, earning him a 3-0 win.

Norvel wanted to see Patterson's match against Leen Jansen of Holland, but he also knew he needed to loosen up for his bout, expected to take place once the middleweight quarterfinals were complete. Patterson's was the second of the four matches, so Norvel figured he could get loose before the bout and would still have time for his preparation after Patterson's event. He went down to the workout room, jumping rope and shadowboxing while waiting to be informed of Patterson's bout. Just before the start of the fight, Norvel appeared outside the ring at Patterson's corner and said, "Okay, son, you know what to do—just get in there and do it."

Patterson had again transformed himself from raw teenager to lethal weapon focused on unleashing his fury. As Norvel spoke, Patterson seemed to be in a trance. When the bell sounded he rose slowly from his seat, took his peekaboo stance, and moved to the center of the ring. Mello had taken a position right next to Norvel.

They watched Patterson and Jansen dance around each other, jabbing and getting a feel for each other's style. Jansen appeared to be well prepared for Patterson's unorthodox style, and just moved around the ring, waiting for his moment. At about the two-minute mark of the first round, Jansen appeared to decide he knew all he needed to know and attempted a series of aggressive punches. As he did, Patterson unloaded a punch and a devastating hook to Jansen's head, and the Dutchman went down for the count. Patterson would be moving on to the semifinals.

Now it was Norvel's turn. After the thankfully quick Patterson fight, Norvel returned to the workout room and completed his warm-up with more shadowboxing. His opponent would be Tadeusz Grzelak of Poland. Norvel decided that instead of strategically trying to land punches that would compel the judges to award him points, he would show his power in order to keep his opponent off guard. The strategy worked, as Grzelak wasn't prepared to take the punishment Norvel delivered. He lasted the full three rounds, but Norvel was the clear winner at 3-0.

His teammates gathered around him, congratulating him. Patterson was beaming. They were both going to the next round.

Mello was quoted in the *Washington Evening Star* as saying, "Lee surprised us with his power. He's normally been strictly a boxer. Against the Pole he was a slugger."

*A slugger? No one has called me that before. Maybe they will stop calling my matches disciplined and restrained. No matter what they call it, it's me who's in the semifinals in the Olympics!!*

Later, in the heavyweight quarterfinals, Ed Sanders knocked out Italian heavyweight champion Giacomo di Segni in the third round. The Americans would be sending five of their ten boxers to the semifinals.

Back in Olympic Village, Mello and J. T. gathered the team together.

"Men," Mello began. "Everyone on this team has a lot to be proud of. But I need to remind you that there is a time to celebrate, but it's not now. We need to concentrate on getting these five men to the finals." Mello waved his hand toward the five semifinalists who were standing together. "We are all in this together. Okay!?"

The boxing team burst into applause and cheers. Olympic Village building 3, where the American team was housed, abuzz with the news, left the five boxers alone so that they could focus on their upcoming bouts.

On Friday afternoon and evening, August 1, the twenty semifinal matches across the ten weight categories were held, now only in the larger of the two arenas. Nearly the entire five-thousand seat hall was filled to see who would, the next day, compete for the gold medal in each weight category. The Olympic Boxing Committee had decided, somewhat controversially, not to award a third-place bronze medal. It meant the losers of these matches would be finished with the competition, but both losers of each weight classification's semifinal match would still have the honor of occupying the third-place platform during the awards ceremony.

The entire American boxing squad arrived at Messuhalli at noon, two hours before the competition was scheduled to begin. Each of the five members weighed in and certified they were qualified to continue in their weight categories. Norvel was back on a normal eating schedule, and his weight held steady at 176 pounds.

The two semifinal matches for each weight class would begin with the flyweights and conclude with the heavyweights about 9:30 p.m. When they weren't warming up, the team members were cheering on their teammates.

While waiting for the Nate Brooks flyweight match to start, Norvel overheard Mello saying to J. T., "What do you think our chances are?"

J. T. shrugged, "I think this kid Patterson and Eddie Sanders will win easily. Very soon we will see if Nate can get this one our way, which I think he will. But I don't know about Adkins and Lee. It was a miracle that Adkins squeaked out his win over the South African Webster, especially with the bruising his left eye took. He's got two stitches over and one under his left eye. Plus, he's fighting a cold. And on paper he's over his head, by my estimation. Furthermore, I'm worried Norvel won't be able to handle Harry Siljander, especially since he's before his hometown crowd."

Mello said simply, "I think they all will win, guaranteeing at a minimum we'll have five silver medals."

*I'm just going to have to prove J. T. wrong. The Finn will be too worked up to mind the fundamentals.*

The featherweight semifinals started the long day with a match between Edgar Basel of Germany and Anatoli Bulakov of the Soviet Union. Basel won, 2-1. Next up was the match between Brooks and nineteen-year-old Willie Toweel of South Africa. Brooks landed enough jabs and punches during the three rounds that the judges unanimously awarded him the victory. The next match for the Americans, Charley Adkin's light welterweight bout, was at least ninety minutes away, so Norvel and several of the others went down to the locker room to change into their athletic clothing. Brook's locker was in the same row as Norvel's.

Norvel looked over at him and said, "Congratulations, Nate. You did real well out there."

"Thanks, man, he was a worthy opponent," Brooks said.

At that moment Toweel, the South African he'd just defeated, came walking down the aisle wearing a smile. Toweel was a popular, affable figure in the Olympic Village that many of the athletes had gotten to know during the past weeks. Brooks had run into him on a couple of occasions himself, and found him likable.

As Toweel approached, he said, "Nathan, I just want to congratulate you on a well-executed, fair fight. Also I want to wish you the best in the championship tomorrow."

Brooks shook Toweel's hand and said, "Thank you, Willie. That means a lot to me."

Norvel was glad to see that Toweel didn't seem to be influenced by South Africa's apartheid policy, which mimicked the segregated culture of his youth.

While they were in the gym, waiting for Adkin's match, loud cheering from the crowd vibrated throughout the building. Norvel, Patterson, and Sanders, along with Mello and J. T., went up to see what the commotion was. Upon arriving, they observed a bantamweight fight involving the Finnish boxer Pentti Hämäläinen and the favorite, Gennady Garbuzov of the Soviet Union. As the third round began, it was obvious the Finn was winning and would hold on to his match. Another Soviet boxer had lost. One of them was eliminated during the earlier featherweight semifinals, and then during the quarterfinals the highly regarded heavyweight, Algirdas Shotsikas, was eliminated by the South African Dries Nieman, who'd be facing Ed Sanders at the conclusion of the evening. The packed crowd was in a frenzy cheering their favorite son, who was awarded a 3-0 victory.

But the crowd quieted down when the time came for the two light welterweight semifinals. The first bout involved another Soviet boxer, Viktor Mednov, against Finland's Erkki Mallenius. However, Mallenius had broken a carpal bone in his quarterfinal match and couldn't fight. Mednov was required to present himself as ready to fight in order for the judges to award him a walkover victory.

Then it was the stitched-up Adkins's turn against Bruno Visintin of Italy. From the time he entered the ring, it was apparent this fight was going to be Adkins all the way. The only thing he had to watch out for from the Italian was a rogue power punch finding its mark. But Adkins stayed out of Visintin's reach and landed many punches of his own, earning a 3-0 victory.

Mello's team now had at least two silver medals virtually assured, with those possibly becoming two golds. And there were three more contests, each with the potential of an American going to the finals the next day.

While Patterson, Norvel, and Sanders warmed up in the exercise room, the remainder of the squad watched the welterweight and light middleweight semifinals. In the welterweight category, Zygmunt Chychla of Poland went up against Sergei Scherbakov of the Soviet Union in the semifinals. In the light middleweight category, László Papp again easily outpointed his opponent, the South African Theunis van Schalkwyk, eliminating another highly touted Soviet entry.

Norvel and Sanders returned from their warm-up and stood with the American squad to watch Patterson in his semifinal match against Stig Sjölin of Sweden. Patterson did not look over at his teammates, staying in his pre-bout focused state. The first round was close, with each boxer dancing around the other, probing for his opponent's potential weaknesses. Then in the second round, Patterson let loose and put the Swede on the mat three times. The thud of Patterson's powerful blows and the *oomph* emitted by his opponent could be heard throughout the arena. By the end of the round, Sjölin was groggy and hanging on to Patterson. At the beginning of the third round Sjölin had not recovered, and immediately started hanging on to Patterson again. At that point, the referee, Neuding of Poland, stopped the fight by disqualifying Sjölin, inciting some boos from spectators. Mello and J. T. thought it should have been ruled a TKO rather than a DQ but, nevertheless, they had another fighter going to the finals.

The entire team was awed at the pure power Patterson displayed. They gathered around and congratulated him. Norvel gave him a broad smile, while Sanders said, "I'm sure glad that wasn't me you were beating up. Nice going!"

Patterson's demeanor returned to his sheepish teenage self. It was quite the contrast to the lethality of a few minutes earlier.

At the conclusion of the next middleweight semifinal, they saw that Patterson's opponent in the final would be Vasile Tita of Romania.

It was time for the light heavyweight semifinals. Norvel's bout was the second one, but he decided to watch the first to see who his opponent in the final would be. He watched a free- swinging Antonio Pacenza of Argentina pummel another boxer from the Soviet Union, Perov, who could not find the right approach to defend against the onslaught. Norvel knew the Argentinian would have a more difficult time getting through his defenses. Now he needed to focus on his upcoming match against the popular Harry Siljander of the host country.

It was 8:30 p.m. when Norvel entered the ring and observed the capacity crowd. Siljander had come home with the bronze medal in 1948. They were there now to see if their favorite son could make it to the finals and compete for the gold. They cheered boisterously when Siljander was announced and politely applauded Norvel.

At the beginning of the first round, both boxers met at the center of the ring. Norvel took his stance: left foot forward, right heel slightly raised, weight distributed evenly. His elbows were pointed down and his gloved hands up, with his head behind them. Siljander took a similar stance and immediately tried to punch Norvel, who evaded the attempts and noticed Siljander was slightly off-balance and slow to regain his stance. Norvel kept his body relaxed and made sure not to telegraph his move. Each time Siljander went off-balance, Norvel straightened his left arm like a rod that connected with Siljander's head. It was a classic simple jab that Norvel was able to deliver with lightning speed. After each one, Norvel moved to his left and Siljander followed, again attempting to land a punch. At the end of the first round, Norvel noticed the noise of the crowd had subsided.

When the second round was under way, the fans began to make some noise again, hoping their boxer had regrouped. But Norvel saw that Siljander came out and went about his business in the same manner. Norvel noticed that Siljander began defending against a right cross from Norvel so instead of countering with a simple jab, as he did in the first round, Norvel began to keep Siljander off guard by employing a double jab. Siljander's face and nose began to turn red from the relentless pounding it was taking from Norvel's left hand.

By round three, the crowd was quiet. It was obvious Norvel was having his way with Siljander, even though he began to fend off the jab, but much too late in the bout. When he did, Norvel would deliver more of a tapping one with his left and began to shift his weight forward to deliver power right crosses to the left side of Siljander's face. The Finn never went down, however. By the end of the round the crowd was on its feet, applauding Norvel for his superior performance. The judges agreed and awarded him all three rounds.

When the results were announced, Norvel looked around the arena, appreciating the moment, absorbing it all. *I'm going to be in the finals. I'm competing for a gold medal for my country, my team, my family, my wife, my legacy.*

As soon as he left the ring, Mello, with the rest of team gathered around him, said, "Nice going in there. You showed tremendous control. The judges were very impressed with you."

J. T. said, "One more to go with Sanders in the heavyweights."

The heavyweight matches went as expected. The Swede Norvel had beaten last year in Gothenburg, Ingemar Johansson, squeaked out a victory over another Finn, Koski, 2-1. And big Ed Sanders put his opponent, Dries Nieman, on the mat in the second round for a TKO.

Mello was ecstatically proud of his team's accomplishment. All five Americans who fought in the semifinals were now going for the gold medal in their weight class the next day.

After dining, Norvel accepted congratulations from various '48ers, including the recovering Chuck Spieser; weightlifters Peter George, Norbert

Schemansky, and John Davis; and fellow Washingtonian James Bradford. Davis had won the gold medal and Bradford the silver in weightlifting on Sunday. Norvel then retired to his quarters, wrote his nightly letter to Leslie, and went to sleep, soundly.

The next day, the team gathered for a late morning meal, followed by a meeting at their table in the tented restaurant. When Norvel arrived, he saw a smiling Bob Mathias and Sim Iness standing at the table next to theirs. Also at their table were Mal Whitfield, Peter George, Schemansky, Davis, Bradford, and some other members of the wrestling team.

Norvel said, "Uh, uh, Bobby, Sim, good to see you here. Uh, uh, uh, I thought you were on that exhibition tour with the other track-and-field folks."

"Oh, we were, but we had to get back in time to root for the boxing team and," Mathias said, pointing at Norvel, "a fellow '48er. Mal here also couldn't miss it."

Whitfield stepped up and put his arm around Norvel, congratulating him on his success so far. He wished him the best of luck on this day of boxing and the next to last day of the Olympics. Norvel realized he was standing with three gold medalists from these games, and hoped he could be the fourth in this group of friends.

Mathias turned to the rest of the table and noticed Archie Slaten had returned and was recovering from his appendectomy. Also, a still sneezing but much healthier Joe Reynolds was there.

Mathias said, "Good to see both of you back in the saddle, so to speak." He then turned to the others at the table and said, "Men, the entire track-and-field team is proud of your accomplishments. We look forward to watching you represent the U.S.A. this afternoon."

The table of boxers erupted in applause and in unison said, "Hear, hear."

Mello stood up and addressed the boxers, who were spread across two adjacent tables.

"Guys," he began, speaking in his strong New York City accent, "I want you to know that getting to know each of you has been the experience of a lifetime for me personally. Each of you has represented your country to the highest of standards. You should all feel proud of everything we, as a team, have accomplished here. This afternoon, five of you will be competing for the highest of Olympic honors, the gold medal. But I want you to know, and I am speaking on behalf of the entire United States Olympic Committee, that you are all winners in our book. You are each guaranteed the silver medal already, so just go out and give it your best."

The three tables of boxers and supporters gave another round of applause and cheers. A strong feeling of pride came over Norvel. For a brief moment, he felt the presence of his mother's watchful eye on him, encouraging him. He was in Helsinki, in Europe, representing his country and his family on a world stage.

Mello continued, "We need to get over to the arena. At 1:30 all the boxers from all the nations and their coaches have been asked by the president of the boxing committee to attend a ringside meeting."

Arriving at Messuhalli, the squad looked dapper in their Olympic slacks, coats, and ties. The five boxers changed into their athletic wear, and then went to the arena and stood together ringside. Other teams began arriving until there were over two hundred and fifty athletes crowded into the space between the ring and the stands. Spectators were beginning to flow in for the big day. A standing-room-only crowd was expected to witness this, one of the final events of the XV Olympic Games.

At 1:30 p.m. Viktor Smeds, president of the Olympic Boxing Committee, walked to the middle of the ring with a microphone in his hand. He looked around at the boxers surrounding the ring and out to the spectators.

In precise, clipped English, he started to speak directly to the boxers although his words reverberated throughout the arena. "Gentlemen, congratulations on being a part of what will be remembered as one of the most prominent boxing events in history. Each of you has represented yourselves individually and your country honorably. Since 1936 and then in 1948, this committee has had the honor of presenting the Val Barker

Trophy to the outstanding boxer of the Olympics. As you may know, Mr. Barker was a pugilist himself, and for years was president of the Amateur International Boxing Association, or AIBA. This trophy in honor of Mr. Barker's many contributions to our sport is presented to the boxer who best exemplifies the sport. We present this trophy at this time in the competition, prior to the championship round, because it is not necessary to be the gold medal winner to receive this award. In the judgment of the AIBA the selected person must demonstrate grace, boxing style, etiquette, and sportsmanship. This year we were fortunate enough that among the two hundred fifty boxers from forty-four nations many met these criteria."

Smeds paused for a moment, looking to each side of the ring, and said, "In our judgment, the boxer among you who meets these highest of standards is the great light heavyweight boxer from the United States, Norvel Lee. Please step up here, Mr. Lee."

The boxers, representing all the competing nations, erupted in spontaneous jubilation. The American team reached out and hugged their teammate. Norvel caught a glimpse of Floyd Patterson brushing a tear from his eye. Norvel himself was stunned. He had never expected something like this. He couldn't wait to tell Leslie and his friends back home about this moment.

Norvel stepped lightly up to the ring and walked over to Smeds, who handed him a large silver trophy. Smeds said into the microphone, "Congratulations, young man, and thank you for taking our sport to the very highest of standards."

Norvel modestly thanked him, waved at the audience, and carried the trophy to a corner of the boxing ring, where a beaming Mello was waiting. Norvel handed the trophy down to him as he lowered himself out of the ring. Mello said he would take it to a secure place for safekeeping and instructed Norvel to focus on getting ready for his championship match against Antonio Pacenza of Argentina.

The first of the ten championship matches of the day was between the flyweights Nate Brooks and Edgar Basel of Germany. Brooks was the clear winner before the more than five thousand spectators packed into the hall. The American team and a large contingent of other American athletes, including Bob Mathias and his '48er group, were ecstatic that Brooks had won the first gold medal of the day.

*Brooks and Basel in the flyweight final.*
The XV Olympiad Official Report, Helsinki, 1952

The next three finals for bantamweight, featherweight, and lightweight did not involve any American boxers, but Norvel enjoyed watching each match. Doing so warded off any anxiety he felt while waiting for his bout. It was invigorating to feel the effects of the predominantly Finnish crowd cheering enthusiastically for their native Pentti Hämäläinen, who won a thrilling split-decision victory over John McNally of Ireland for the bantamweight championship. The next two bouts were also decided by split decisions, with Ján Zachara of Czechoslovakia winning the gold medal for the featherweight class and the Italian Bolognesi, who beat Bobby Bickle in the preliminaries, taking the lightweight gold medal.

Next up was one of the featured matches of the night: Charles Adkins versus the Soviet Union's Victor Mednov, who'd won his semifinal over a Finn. This match-up was hyped as the first time in boxing history that a boxer from the United States would take on a Soviet opponent. Both fighters were ready for the contest. Norvel noticed that Adkins, who possessed a friendly, empathetic personality, now wore an intent look. Whatever smiles there were earlier, were nonexistent now.

As Adkins and Mednov stepped into their corners, Norvel, who was standing between Sanders and Mathias, remarked, "Those boys look like they've already been fighting."

Mathias laughed. "Yes, at least in my sport when we get beat, nobody can see it."

Sanders said, "That's right, Bobby. And all you have to do is wrap something around that sore muscle."

The three men looked at the ring and saw that Adkins still had patches over and under his left eye. Mednov wore heavy patches covering gashes above both of his eyes. The word was that under the patch on the right were seven stitches, and the one on the left, six.

Mednov was known to be an aggressive fighter. But Adkins came out more aggressively and immediately hammered left hooks to Mednov's head, winning the first round. He also knocked the patch off of Mednov's left eye. During the second round, Adkins continued to throw damaging left hooks, with the Russian desperately trying to avoid getting trapped against the ropes. By the third round Mednov was hanging on to Adkins, who still managed to stagger him by delivering two powerful uppercuts that almost sent Mednov to the mat each time. When the bell sounded ending the bout, blood was flowing from several cuts on Mednov's face.

The bout was a controversial split decision in Adkins's favor, 2-1, but nevertheless another gold medal for the Americans. At this point, Norvel left the onlookers and went to the downstairs gym to warm up. He was informed that Zygmunt Chychla of Poland had won the welterweight, and László Papp, as expected, had won the light middleweight. Norvel was planning to finish the warm-up in time to watch Patterson's bout against Vasile Tita of Rumania, but by the time he got to the ring, the fight was over. Patterson had knocked out Tita in the first round.

*Floyd Patterson knocks out Tita.*
The XV Olympiad Official Report, Helsinki, 1952

And now it was time for the light heavyweight match. Norvel felt at ease. A feeling of quiet confidence settled over him. He reflected on how he'd arrived at this moment. He thought of a passage from Ernest Hemingway's novel *For Whom the Bell Tolls* that had stuck with him. It reminded him that this day is just one of many days in his life, but what would happen in all the remaining days might depend on what happened today. Flashing before him were images of his home, the popcorn fields, his mother scolding him, his father inspiring manhood and pride, Academy Hill, Rising Mount Zion Baptist Church, his induction into the U.S. Army Air Corps, and finally a smiling Leslie supporting him all the way.

He stood in his corner with the trainer Billy Fallon. Norvel looked across the ring at his Argentinean opponent. Antonio Pacenza had dark hair, a mustache, and a well-toned body and appeared calm, cool, and collected. Norvel remembered him from the Pan Am Games, where Pacenza was the light heavyweight winner, one of the Argentineans who swept the boxing titles.

*No political advantage this time. Not like last year in Buenos Aires.*

*Just need to watch out for a rogue punch finding its way through to me. He's not going to get me.*

When the two boxers were called by the referee to receive their pre-fight instructions, Pacenza also appeared to remember Norvel from the Pan Am Games. When the bell sounded, Pacenza discarded his calm demeanor and came out aggressively, while Norvel assumed the classic boxer stance he was known for: left foot forward, weight evenly distributed, elbows down, hands up in front of his face.

*Wow, those swings are wild. He's telegraphing them way in advance. Just keep your arms up, Norvel, and protect yourself. Then get those scoring jabs in.*

Norvel peppered the Argentinean with short scoring jabs and punches from both his left and right hands, while Pacenza failed to land anything significant in the first round. Pacenza had his fans in the hall, however, who hollered words of encouragement throughout the round, becoming more boisterous at the end as the bell sounded.

Fallon nodded at Norvel when he returned to the corner and began to towel him off. Norvel waved him off, remaining standing.

*Just don't let him surprise you with anything. Keep your hands up and jab away. This is mine.*

Round two saw Norvel moving fluidly around the ring, showing his quickness while maintaining his balance, and jabbing at Pacenza at every opportunity. Pacenza continued to flail away at Norvel, attempting to land both body and head punches. But Norvel made sure nothing damaging got through. As the round came to an end, Pacenza's fans were still offering encouragement.

*I've faced tougher at home, much tougher. I was expecting more from him. All I need to do is get through the next round!*

For the final round Norvel came out from his corner, barely sweating or breathing hard. Pacenza, on the other hand, was dripping wet and tiring. The encouragement from Pacenza's fans had finally died. Everyone's eyes were now on Norvel, appreciating the beauty of the moment.

*He's tired. I can let loose a few here.*

After a few left-handed jabs, Norvel shifted his weight to his left foot while propelling his right hand by swiveling his hips counterclockwise. The punch caught Pacenza below the rib cage, causing him to utter an "Oomph!" Norvel caught him again with a left-handed counter, causing Pacenza to emit a groan. Pacenza backed off and tried to wildly attack Norvel, but Norvel easily moved his body out of the way. The seconds ticked down until Pacenza, breathing heavily, could hardly stay on his feet. The bell sounded, ending the bout. The spectators were on their feet, clapping and cheering.

*I've won! I'm an Olympic champion! Wow! I will be bringing home the gold! A gold medal!*

Norvel was the fourth gold medal winner of the evening for the Americans. He felt a pride he didn't know he possessed when he mounted the podium. Pacenza was on his left and the semifinal runners-up on his right. Viktor Smeds came up to the podium in front of the runner-ups, shook their hands, and presented each a rolled-up parchment. He went over to Norvel's left side, shook Pacenza's hand, and congratulated him while presenting him a box containing the silver medal.

He then stood before Norvel, smiling, and said, "See, the AIBA knew you were the classiest boxer in the Olympics, and you winning this gold medal proves that class wins. Congratulations, Mr. Lee."

"Thank you, sir," Norvel said, receiving the box containing the gold medal.

When Smeds stepped away, the twenty-piece wind band played the opening chords of "The Star-Spangled Banner." Norvel squared his shoulders and felt goose bumps rise on his arms. Although he was surrounded by five thousand people in Helsinki, his mind's eye took him back to Fincastle, Virginia, and the Academy Hill School for Negroes. He recalled standing erect as a fifteen-year-old, just as he was at this moment, with his hand over his heart, reciting the Pledge of Allegiance with the seven other students in Mr. Terry's classroom.

*Things have come so far since those days. I'm standing on a world stage, but at home I still have to worry about where to sit on a train and where to take my girl on a date. But this is progress, and I'm enjoying the moment. Just take it all in, Norvel.*

As the melody of the anthem filled the arena, the words ran through his head, "Oh, say does that star-spangled . . ." At that moment Norvel noticed a white dove, likely a stray from the Opening Ceremony that somehow had found its way into Messuhalli, fly across the spacious room. ". . . banner yet wave. O'er the land of the free and the home of the brave."

*Norvel Lee accepts congratulations from Viktor Smeds for winning the light heavyweight gold medal.*
The XV Olympiad Official Report, Helsinki, 1952

*Harry Siljander, Anatoly Perov, Norvel Lee, and Antonio Pacenza on the awards podium as the "Star Spangled Banner" is performed.*
The XV Olympiad Official Report, Helsinki, 1952

*Norvel Lee proudly holding the Val Barker Trophy.*
United States 1952 Olympic Book, page 159

Ed Sanders won the heavyweight gold medal in his bout against Ingemar Johansson who, curiously, chose not to put up a real fight against Sanders and was disqualified.

*The Five American Olympic gold medal winners (l–r): Nate Brooks, flyweight; Charles Adkins, welterweight; Floyd Patterson, middleweight; Norvel Lee, light heavyweight; Ed Sanders, heavyweight.*
Bettmann collection via Getty Images

The following article ran in the *Baltimore Sun* and other newspapers around the world:

### U.S. Fighters Take Five Gold Medals

Helsinki, Finland, Aug. 2—A twenty year Olympic drought ended in a cascade of first place medals tonight as America's inspired boxers swept five championships, beat Russia in the only face-to-face meeting of the two nations in the sport and won the unofficial team title for the first time.

In matching their perfect five-for-five performance in the semifinals yesterday, the United States not only broke the Games record for individual victories but also romped off with the silver loving cup given to the outstanding boxer of the tournament.

This went to Norvel Lee, the 27-year old fighter from Washington who won the light heavyweight crown and drew rave after rave from other boxers, officials, coaches and trainers, for being the "perfect Olympic boxer."

✿✿✿✿✿✿✿✿✿✿✿✿✿✿✿✿✿✿✿✿✿✿✿✿✿

## *August 2, 1952—106 South Ayr Street, Leesburg, Virginia*

L eslie was driving to Leesburg to visit her parents when a bulletin came over the car radio. It stated that the Americans had won five gold medals in boxing. When the announcer said Norvel's name, she pulled off to the side of the road and screamed with elation.

Arriving at the house, she ran in through the door, screaming, "Daddy, Mom, did you hear the news!"

Emmett Jackson came into the room. "Les, what's going on? Why all the ruckus?"

"Daddy, Norvel won the gold medal!" she screamed.

Margaret Jackson joined them. "Oh, my goodness!" she said.

The phone began ringing and continued into the night. As the news got out, neighbors and family started dropping in. Leslie had to repeat the same story several times. She said that Norvel was writing several letters to her every day, but nothing in the letters hinted that he was going for the gold. The last one she received said he had gotten his weight to just under 180 pounds and that he felt good at this weight.

The next day, Sunday, at church Reverend Brooks structured the sermon around Norvel's Olympic performance. That afternoon a reporter from the *Washington Evening Star* came by to interview Leslie about Norvel's achievement. She told the reporter that this was likely the end of Norvel's boxing career, that it was a wonderful way to close his time in the ring, and that Norvel was going to dedicate his time to helping young boys find their way in the world.

# CHAPTER 24

## August 12, 1952—National Training School for Boys, Washington, D.C.

A luncheon was held at NTS to honor Norvel's Olympic accomplishment. The Department of Justice, Bureau of Prisons, and NTS awarded a plaque citing him for his "salient conduct and performance." The school dining room was packed with members of the staff and boys, who had donated a large cake for the occasion.

Among those paying tribute to the light heavyweight champion was Joe Louis, former world heavyweight champion. When Louis congratulated him, Norvel said, "Mr. Louis, you came to visit, uh, uh, us in the South Pacific, during the war. You put on an exhibition match with one of our boys."

"I'm glad you remember," Louis said. "I felt you fellas were doing a lot more important work than me, and I wanted to let you know that by visiting."

"Oh, your work was very important," Norvel said. "We needed our spirits raised and you certainly did that. You may have inspired some of us to take up boxing."

Later, two men came over to meet Norvel. The taller one, with wavy blonde hair, said, "Norvel, congratulations on behalf of the instructors here," the man said. "I'm Mike Mehalic and this young man here is Al Maltz."

"Pleased to meet you and thank you," Norvel said. "Haven't I seen the two of you in the lunchroom playing cards?"

"Sure have," Maltz said. "Just some gin rummy. If we had another player or two we'd be playing pinochle. Mike and I have played that game since high school. You don't happen to play cards, do you?"

"Yes I do, and pinochle is a game I play," Norvel said. "My dad played with his work fellas and taught the game to my brothers and me."

"Then you'll have to join us some time," Mehalic said.

In June 1953 Norvel received a bachelor's degree in physical educa-

tion and became a full-time instructor with NTS. Also, as a captain in the
Air Force Reserve he was assigned to be a ROTC training officer at Howard University, teaching air science and tactics. His other role at Howard
was volunteering as a coach for the boxing program. In this role, aside
from helping the boxers with basic techniques, he frequently encouraged
the young men to continue their education and for them to look at the
military as a way to expand the opportunities available. And, when their
schedules permitted, Norvel joined Mehalic and Maltz in the lunchroom
for three-handed pinochle games.

On June 18, 1953, Norvel was invited to lunch with President Dwight
Eisenhower at the White House with other prominent athletes. He and
Art Bragg from Morgan State were last-minute invitees when the organizers realized that no Blacks had been included. Norvel felt honored to be
invited to the lunch and at the subsequent photo shoot.

*President Dwight D. Eisenhower (front row, center) with prominent athletes
at the White House. Norvel Lee is second row, center. Art Bragg, sprinter from
Morgan State, is in the third row over Norvel's left shoulder. Note in the front
row, right side, Rocky Marciano is standing next to Joe DiMaggio. The golfer,
Gene Sarazen, is on the other side of DiMaggio.*
National Park Service; obtained from the Eisenhower Presidential Library

In 1954, after returning from active duty with the Air Force in Korea, Norvel's brother Jimmy also became an instructor at NTS. He occasionally joined Norvel, Mehalic, and Maltz for four-handed pinochle during his lunch break.

Edna Lee, their sister, received her teaching credentials after attending Bluefield State in West Virginia. She took a teaching position at an elementary school in Emporia, Virginia. She frequently returned to Gala to see her father, Jack, and to visit with friends. One such acquaintance was her former teacher, Georgia Meadows, who had taught her and many of the Black Botetourt County children. She also went to see her brother, George, who was attending high school in Covington. His future after high school was uncertain as he didn't show interest in academics.

On June 1, 1954, Leslie gave birth to Deborah Louise Lee. Leslie's parents were excited about being grandparents. Her mother came into Washington to help Leslie with the baby, while Norvel, proud and excited to be a father, attended to his many responsibilities.

He remained involved with boxing by continuing to coach at Howard and occasionally judging for the Golden Gloves. Then, in late 1954, he was asked if he would consider trying out for the Pan Am Games, planned for Mexico City during the summer. Although it had been assumed his competitive boxing days were over, Norvel wanted to avenge the 1951 Buenos Aires fiasco. He began to work out to see if he still had the skill and desire. He quickly returned to form and handily won the trials, becoming the heavyweight on the U.S. team. During the semifinals, however, he lost again to an Argentinean and went home with the bronze medal. But this time, the fight was fair. Norvel was proud of his accomplishment and to have represented the United States again.

On December 1, 1955, Leslie gave birth to Denise Kay Lee. A few days later, Norvel learned that while his new daughter was being born, a young woman named Rosa Parks was arrested in Montgomery, Alabama, for refusing to relinquish her seat on a bus to a white person.

He thought, *My new baby girl will enjoy freedoms that her forebears could never imagine. I will do everything I can to help her be a part of this new world of opportunity she's entering.*

Later that same month, Norvel saw on the front page of the *Baltimore Sun* that his Olympic teammate, Ed Sanders, had died from boxing injuries suffered in Boston. He was twenty-four and still in the Navy. Norvel later learned that Sanders was laid to rest in Santa Monica, California, with full military honors. Norvel was saddened at the loss of Sanders and committed to visiting his gravesite the next time he was in California.

Using the GI Bill, Norvel purchased a townhome on 8th Street NW to accommodate his growing family. It was on the southeast fringes of an area becoming informally known as the Gold Coast district of Washington, where an affluent Black community was settling in.

In the mid-1950s Al Maltz and then Mike Mehalic left NTS for other career opportunities. Maltz took a human resources position with the newly formed Federal Emergency Management Agency. Mehalic became a professor at Wilson Teachers College. When they left NTS, Maltz proposed they continue to play cards. He suggested they get together every other Friday at one of their homes. The three of them, plus several others who joined, became known informally as the pinochle gang.

In 1957 Leslie was working at the Police Boys and Girls Club, an outreach organization established for disadvantaged youths. While there she learned of a research grant that would benefit Norvel's activities at NTS. He applied for and was awarded the grant on behalf of NTS and became the program's administrator. Norvel used the funds to help the troubled boys at NTS develop basic learning skills. He set it up in a manner that would give positive reinforcement to young men who had the desire to advance. Points would be earned if they achieved preset goals. At the end of their confinement, the points were exchanged for money.

When George finished a six-year Navy enlistment, he decided to settle in D.C. near his brothers. He was hired by a large construction company. He also tried his hand at boxing, which he took up while in the Navy. Norvel helped coach him, but George didn't perform well enough in the few official bouts he was in to stay with it.

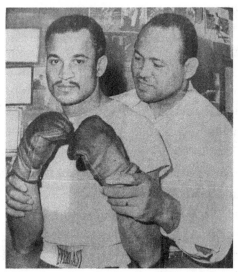

*Norvel coaching his brother George before a bout.*
Norvel Lee family archives

As a USAF reservist, Norvel was required each year to participate in two weeks of active military duty involving training and preparation exercises. This took place in the summer. For the 1959 session his unit went to Fort Campbell, an Army base in Kentucky and home of the 101st Airborne Division. The word went out that an Olympic boxer was with the visiting Air Force Reserve unit. The 101st soldiers let it be known they had a boxer of their own in their ranks, Archie Whitfield, a professional heavyweight.

The 101st Airborne troops bragged about Whitfield being a much higher-quality boxer than a washed-up amateur. Taunts ensued between the men of each unit, resulting in a match being set up for Saturday night. Norvel was reluctant at first to get involved, but his fellow reservists let him know that the unit's honor was on the line. He was informed that even if he lost, the unit would still gain a measure of respect. Norvel reminded them he was thirty-five, and that he had not fought competitively since the 1955 Pan Am Games. But he had kept up his physical conditioning by jumping rope, sparring, and working the bag. An informal underground wagering system was established between the men of both units. Whitfield became the heavy favorite because of the wagers by his fellow members of the 101st Airborne.

A boxing ring was set up on the Fort Campbell parade grounds. Practically every reservist and active 101st Airborne member came out to root for their local champion.

From the opening of the four-round contest, Norvel surprised himself with his stamina and ability to move around the ring fluidly. Whitfield, who was known to pack a powerful punch, was not able to land anything solid on Norvel. By the end of the tussle, the informal judging panel called the bout a draw. Whitfield complimented Norvel by saying he had never encountered such a competent opponent.

The 1959 bout against Whitfield was Norvel's last competitive time in the boxing ring.

Beginning in 1961, Norvel and Leslie became involved with influential D.C. social circles. On January 20, they briefly met President John F. Kennedy and his wife, Jacqueline, in the receiving line at the inaugural ball at the D.C. National Guard Armory. Norvel, who wore his Air Force uniform to the ball, found the young president warm and sincere as he thanked Norvel for continuing to serve the country. Leslie was enamored of the poise of First Lady Jacqueline Kennedy.

On May 1 Norvel was named the first Black member of the D.C. Boxing Commission. He was also elected president of the Lamond-Riggs Citizens Association, a community action group involved with improving schools and bringing libraries into the northern neighborhoods of D.C., which didn't have any public libraries, only Bookmobiles. Leslie worked with Norvel to lobby for the establishment of brick-and-mortar libraries. Norvel was also listed in the Who's Who of Black America for the first time.

Also in 1961, Norvel received a phone call from his sister Edna. She was concerned because their father wasn't taking very good care of himself and he seemed depressed. In 1959 Jack had retired from the C&O at age fifty-five. Times had changed from when he was a day laborer with the railroad, not knowing from day to day if there would be any work. His no-nonsense steadfastness and persona had finally brought him a full-time position where he became a valued employee, earning him a qualified pension. Jack decided to take the pension instead of continuing to work for the C&O because he wanted to open a local automobile repair business, but the auto shop was not making enough money to sustain itself.

Norvel and his brothers convinced their father to move to Washington, where he would be near family. Jack acquiesced when Norvel lined up a job for him as a part-time mechanic at a gas station in SW D.C. He moved in with George at his apartment in early 1962.

In April 1962, Norvel left NTS after spending nearly ten years there as a teacher and counselor. His reputation as an educator and mentor for underprivileged youth became well known to those responsible for such programs throughout D.C. Because of the funded study program he administered at NTS to motivate troubled juveniles, he was recommended for the new position of director of education for the D.C. Department of Corrections at the Lorton Reformatory in Fairfax, Virginia. In this position, he was responsible for setting up an educational curriculum within Lorton's Youth Program for eighteen- to twenty-two-year-olds who hadn't finished high school. The goal was for them to earn a high school diploma while incarcerated.

For his own family, of course, Norvel wanted the very best. On September 12, 1962, President Kennedy gave a speech announcing that the United States was going to put a man on the moon before the end of the decade. Norvel found himself drawn to technology and the sciences. He and Leslie were excited about what Kennedy's announcement could do to inspire young people like their daughters. Leslie's younger sister, Weekie, was now working for NASA as an emulsions specialist. He knew their Aunt Margaret would be an excellent example for his daughters to follow.

The same day as President Kennedy's moon speech, Norvel bought a taxi cab. The cab was orange and black and had Diplomat Cab emblazoned on its doors. His daughters were becoming more involved in activities, the house was in need of some repairs, and Leslie frequently had to spend personal funds to support her outreach cases, at times depleting their spending money. Norvel didn't believe in borrowing money except for a mortgage. If they ran short, he was confident he could always find a way to earn the difference. He also knew that lending practices for Blacks were unfairly expensive. The next night he took the cab to Mike Mehalic's home on Eastern Avenue NE, where the pinochle gang was playing cards that week. His friends could not understand how Norvel could consider adding another responsibility to his very full schedule.

On March 20, 1963, exactly eleven years after receiving his commission, Norvel was assigned to the 909th Command and Control Squadron in Amarillo, Texas. The 909th was being reactivated for the first time since World War II. The Air Force required a liaison between Andrews Air Force Base and the 909th Headquarters. Lieutenant Colonel Bill Shook, who knew Norvel through the pinochle group, had relocated with the 909th to Amarillo and recommended his friend for the role, as a reservist. The position required Norvel to handle highly sensitive and designated top secret information, requiring a clearance from the government.

Leslie teased Norvel when he told her about the arrangement. "What kind of secrets will you have to keep from me?"

"Only those involving national security," Norvel said, smiling. "Otherwise, my life is an open book to be read by you and you alone."

"Why that's beautiful," Leslie observed. "But what does this 909th do, or what can you tell me about it?"

"They, or I guess I should say we, are the guys who refuel planes in the air," said Norvel. "Please understand I won't be doing any flying around. I'm just the liaison. The reason I have to have high-level clearance is the 909th supports the Strategic Air Command. We have to be ready on a moment's notice to refuel one of their planes if the country is undergoing an emergency. Since I have to help them communicate with the powers that be at Andrews, then I need to know what's going on."

Leslie said, "Well if there's some kind of emergency going on, I would hope you will let your family know about it, clearance or no clearance."

Two days later, the television networks covered the death of another Olympian from the 1952 team, Davey Moore. He was fatally injured while boxing in Dodger Stadium against Sugar Ray Ramos. A horrified national TV audience watched Ramos pummel Moore relentlessly until the referee stopped the fight. Moore was coherent after the fight, but collapsed several hours later. Norvel was saddened once again about his former teammate, just as he was when he learned of Ed Sanders's death.

On August 28, the March on Washington took place. The Reverend Dr. Martin Luther King Jr. spoke from the Lincoln Memorial before a massive crowd. Norvel didn't actually hear the speech in person, since he was busy ferrying attendees in his cab from the airport to staging locations near the National Mall, dropping them as close as he could without getting mired in the traffic.

Norvel later listened to the "I Have a Dream" speech Dr. King delivered on that historic day and felt hope that his country was on the right path to the goal of achieving equal opportunities for all of its people. His girls would not have to encounter the same obstacles he did. But he knew there would be hurdles for them to overcome.

# CHAPTER 25

## September 15, 1963—Washington National Airport, Arlington, Virginia

Norvel parked the orange-and-black Diplomat Cab at the area reserved for taxis near the aging airport terminal building. His was the only cab parked at the curb, but Norvel expected the taxi zone would soon fill up with competing ride services looking for fares from passengers exiting the next Eastern Shuttle from New York.

Unlike the other taxi drivers, Norvel was there to pick up a specific passenger. He'd received a phone call from his Air Force Reserve commander earlier in the day asking him if he would be available to transport a U.S. Army officer over to Fort McNair, in D.C. After to the March on Washington a few weeks earlier, where three hundred thousand civil rights supporters had gathered, the Army was concerned that even though the officer was in uniform a local cab service might not pick him up because he was African American.

When the reserve commander learned of a possible dilemma, he thought Norvel, a cab driver and reserve officer, might be able to help. The commander explained that the meeting the captain was attending at Fort McNair was sensitive and important to all involved.

The Eastern Shuttle ran about every two hours. Norvel stood next to his car, awaiting the next flight's arrival.

Norvel never leaned on his car, a habit he learned as a boy growing up in Gala. Even though his father's automobile was old and always in need of repair, it was kept as neat and clean as possible.

On his way to the airport, Norvel considered stopping into the nearby Lorton Reformatory, where he was employed, to make sure his brother-in-law, Clifford Russell, was adjusting to his new position there. Previously he had been employed as a teacher in Halifax, Virginia, but when he and

Weekie married in June, Norvel had recommended him to Lorton. He was hired as an instructor and guard. Clifford's lack of seniority meant he sometimes was assigned duty on weekends. But instead of going to Lorton, Norvel decided it would be better to arrive early at the airport.

Two more taxis pulled to the curb behind him while an airplane's jet engines could be heard screaming down the runway behind the building. The driver of the Yellow Cab next in line nodded at Norvel through the windshield but stayed inside. But the taxi third in the queue pulled to the curb aggressively, and the driver opened the door, lit a cigarette, and ambled cockily over to Norvel.

The driver, much shorter than Norvel and pudgy, looked suspiciously at his vehicle and said with a distinctive accent, "Who are you, Diplomat Cab? Never seen you here before, and you know you can't work here. They don't let District cabs work here unless you have a special permit on your windshield. I don't see nothing on yours. None of your kind will be on the plane, and the others won't ride with the likes of you, so scram."

Norvel looked directly into the arrogant driver's eyes and said softly but firmly, "I am here at the request of the United States government."

Norvel kept looking directly into the driver's squinting eyes until the pudgy little man turned away in a huff and walked back to his taxi parked at the curb. Several other taxi cabs had pulled in behind him by now.

The sound of a jet plane could be heard pulling up to the terminal. After several minutes a group of harried travelers came out, a few holding the door for the next person. They scattered in different directions.

Two men dressed for business, even though it was Sunday, came through the doors. Since he was first in the line of cabs, they walked directly over to Norvel. As they approached, Norvel waved his hand toward the cab right behind him and said, "I'm reserved for a specific passenger but I'm sure this gentleman in the Yellow Cab will be glad to give you a lift."

The driver tipped his cap at Norvel, opened the door for the two men, and after a minute pulled out from the curb and drove away. The independent driver who had attempted to intimidate Norvel earlier moved his car up behind him as the rain started up again.

A Black man, also dressed in business attire, stepped through the doors and walked over to Norvel, smiling.

Norvel said, "I'm waiting for an Army officer and unless you are that person you will need to ride with one of these other fellows."

The man said, "No, I am not an Army person. I'm just here to visit my firm's Washington offices."

Norvel then said, winking at the man, "My advice is not to go to the cab right there," motioning to the car right behind. "You might not get to where you need to. The one behind that one should work, but if you have any difficulties, come back here and I will make sure you get where you need to go, even if we have to share the ride."

The man expressed his gratitude and walked past the independent cab without looking at the driver. He went on to the Yellow Cab next in line. The driver motioned for the man to get into the car. He then gave a slight wave to Norvel, who nodded at him. The driver of the cab behind Norvel had his arms crossed and glared at him.

Finally, a tall Black man in his mid-twenties, wearing a sharp Army dress green uniform and carrying a small duffle bag, came through the terminal doors. There were silver captain bars on his shoulders. He walked with a slight limp.

Norvel stepped over to him, smiled, and said, "Captain Powell?"

The man looked at him and said, "Yes, that's me."

Norvel said, "I'm here to take you over to Fort McNair. I'll put your bag in the trunk."

In a resonant baritone voice, the soldier said, "I wasn't expecting anyone to pick me up. What's this about?"

Norvel simply said, "I received the request just this morning."

He took the captain's duffle bag, opened the trunk and placed it inside while the officer limped over to open the rear door. Norvel walked back and put his hand on the door and reached into his jacket pocket and pulled out an identification card.

"You're sitting in the front with me, so we can visit," Norvel said, showing him his military identification.

"You're military?" asked the Captain as he got into the front seat.

"Yes, I'm with the Air Force Reserve here in Washington, based at Andrews."

Norvel pulled the taxi away from the terminal and onto Highway 1, or Jefferson Davis Highway.

"I'm a personal services officer, working directly for the commander of our unit," said Norvel.

"You're an officer? What is your rank?" asked the curious officer.

"I know it's hard to tell in my taxi driver outfit, but my rank is the same as yours, a captain," Norvel said. "Did you go to West Point, or were you ROTC like I was?"

"I joined the ROTC while at City College of New York, where I was majoring in geology. The Army apparently became my calling, as I received my commission in 1958. Here I am five years later, although I have to admit I'm at somewhat of a crossroads now."

Norvel said, "I'd like to hear about that, but we're very near Arlington Cemetery. Have you ever been there?"

Powell said, "No, but I'd like to some time."

Norvel said, "Well, it looks like the sun is trying to shine through the clouds, and we're coming up to the main entrance. Would you like to make a brief stop so I can show you a couple of places that I like to make sure everyone sees?"

The young officer said, "Okay. Just as long as you aren't going to charge me for the time we spend here. My time is my own this evening, as far as I know."

"Captain, I'm glad to show you this special place. And there is no charge for a veteran to pass tradition along to the next generation."

Norvel turned left onto Memorial Avenue and drove through the gates anchoring ornate twin arches for a short distance. The various sections of the cemetery were identified by signs with numbers. Thousands of white headstones could be seen in all directions.

They stopped at a small parking area with a sign stating Section 27. As they exited the car, the two men looked out across the rows of gravestones as shadows cast by the sun shone between the storm clouds, causing the gravestones to become spotlighted briefly.

Norvel began to explain the significance of this area of the National Cemetery. "This is where many forgotten souls lie who greatly impacted how our country became what it is today. About fifteen hundred Black soldiers from the Civil War are buried here. Their graves are the ones with U.S.C.T, or US Colored Troops. These are soldiers who could have been you and me, had we been living then."

The young captain nodded and said quietly, "I didn't know. My parents emigrated from Jamaica. The experiences of my ancestors were different than yours."

Norvel said, "My grandparents were born into slavery in Virginia, but were very young when emancipated. It's unclear how they acquired the land they farmed tobacco on, but they did, in Amherst, down the James River about forty miles from where I grew up. My mother was half Arapaho. Everyone knew their place, so to speak, plus the nearby railroads needed the labor my people could provide. In the colored unit I served in during the war, I began to appreciate that my experiences with segregation were far different than many in my unit."

"You must be talking about World War II," said Powell. "I must say, you don't look old enough to have been in that war. Thank goodness President Truman did away with the segregated military as soon as he took office. Were you an officer then?"

"Oh no, I enlisted straight out of high school. I was discharged after the war, enrolled at Howard University, and discovered the ROTC like you did. Had I been in it now, I may have just stayed. Why are you thinking about going with the Reserves instead of staying active? What would you do if you weren't in the Army?"

The two men walked among the gravestones. Many of them just said

"Free Man," without a name. Others showed a first name and an occupation, such as "Blacksmith."

"Sir, may I ask your name?"

"Yes, Norvel Lee." Norvel firmly shook the soldier's hand.

"Sir, a few months ago I returned from an assignment as an advisor in southeast Asia. 'Advisor' was what the politicians called my duty, but in reality there's a war taking place over there. I was smack in the middle of it."

"Is that what caused your limp?" asked Norvel.

"Yes. I was there to provide training to the South Vietnamese soldiers. But we were actually leading patrols near the borders with Laos and Cambodia where incursions from opposing forces were taking place. Several weeks ago, I was leading one of those patrols at the border with Laos and walked into a booby trap that fortunately didn't take my leg or foot off. But it caused my foot to swell up. Officially I'm on a medical leave while it heals, but unofficially they wanted me down here for a debriefing of sorts."

"Is your home in New York?"

"Yes, sir, my parents settled in Harlem, which is where they still live. My wife had been staying with them while I was overseas. And that's what is difficult for me. I was married about a year ago and in December I got shipped over to Vietnam in this advisory position. She and I missed our first Christmas together. And we want to have children. On the other hand, I don't know what I'd do as a civilian. She was very happy to see me, injuries and all, as it means we'll be spending this Christmas together. It wasn't clear that I would be home, had I not been injured. What was your war experience like?" Captain Powell asked.

Norvel said, "It was a different time than yours. I wanted to enlist when I was seventeen but my mother wouldn't let me and my father wouldn't sign the waiver. As soon as I turned eighteen I went to Tuskegee, where they had a flight school for us colored who were interested in being pilots. But I was cut from the program because of my stammer. It comes up when I get excited, and they were afraid I wouldn't be able to handle the stress. So I got sent to the South Pacific instead. It was an unpleasant situation for me."

The soldier shook his head compassionately and said, "I'm surprised that you came back into the military."

"I saw some good things too. I saw the great Joe Louis come in and put on a boxing exhibition for us. It was one of the few times that both the white and colored fellows were allowed to assemble together. Mr. Louis chose a kid from my unit to spar with. He was chosen because of his Golden Gloves experience. Joe Louis didn't have to fight very hard against him, though. I decided that Mr. Louis was a good example to follow as to how to conduct yourself when the playing cards of life are stacked against you."

Norvel paused, took a deep breath, and looked at the captain.

He continued, "It's important to appreciate that no matter what you face in life, good or bad, there is always the next thing to do. This world has a lot to offer us. We just have to sometimes work a little harder to find it. My mother and father always taught us to set the example and to be true to ourselves."

"And driving the cab?" quizzed the young soldier. "It doesn't fit with everything else you do."

"You do whatever you can to make ends meet 'cause you never know when it will get taken away. I have a wife and two young girls. Doing this brings in some extra money, and gives me a chance to meet young men like you."

"And, if I may ask, do you have a regular job also?"

"Yes, I'm with the D.C. Department of Corrections."

"In what capacity?"

"I'm the Director of Education." Norvel added, "Let's get back in the car and go to the other place I want to show you."

They went back to Norvel's taxi. Norvel started the car and drove slowly to Roosevelt Drive, where they came upon a small parking area in front of a walking path leading over to a prominent monument. Several groups of visitors were also walking along the path. Norvel parked and they started toward the monument, the captain limping beside Norvel.

He asked, "Is this the Tomb of the Unknown Soldier?"

Norvel said reverently, "Yes, it is."

The men walked up the path to a marble tomb. A lone uniformed soldier with a rifle on his shoulder marched a precise pattern back and forth along the mat.

Norvel said, "That soldier is on around-the-clock guard duty that has been ongoing nonstop since 1937. The soldier takes twenty-one steps, stops for twenty-one seconds, turns to his left and stands for twenty-one seconds, turns again, then takes twenty-one more steps and repeats his motions. Each time he turns, he snaps his heels together."

Several other people were gathered quietly to witness the proceedings.

Norvel continued, "His commander will come at some point with another guard, and there's a formal ceremony for the changing of the guard. The commander will order the guard being relieved to pass on his orders to the new guard. He'll say: "Post and orders, remain as directed." And the new soldier responds with: "Orders acknowledged.""

The captain nodded, eyes fixed on the scene.

Norvel said, "Notice that the guard does not have any rank showing on his uniform. It's because it would be an affront to outrank this unidentified hero."

The two men continued to take in the proceedings for a few moments. And then the young captain squared his shoulders, performed a crisp military salute, and kept his hand at the brim of his hat in honor of the Unknown Soldier. When he completed the salute, he turned and limped back to the automobile. Norvel joined him along the pathway, impressed at what he had just witnessed.

They drove out of the cemetery and crossed Memorial Bridge into the District of Columbia, with the Lincoln Memorial looming large to the right of the roadway. Both men noted without having to say anything that that was where Dr. King, two weeks earlier, had so passionately delivered words about his dream that someday in the future the United States would live up to its promise that all men are created equal. They drove along the National Mall quietly, the Capitol Building now filling their field of vision as they approached it.

The captain asked Norvel, "Are you taking the long way over to Fort McNair on purpose?"

"Guess I am. I didn't know if you had seen it before, and just wanted to remind you why you are in the Army and what you are protecting."

"Thank you. I have another question for you, sir. Were you ever a boxer?"

"Uh, yes, I was. Why?"

"You won gold in Helsinki! Did you ever fight in Madison Square Garden?"

"Yes, I did, on several occasions."

"I believe I saw you fight there when I was around thirteen," the captain said. "My father was interested in boxing and trying to get me interested. He took me to see the Golden Gloves championship against Chicago. I thought I recognized your name because I remember a fight with a boxer named Norvel in it who knocked down the opposing boxer."

"Yes, that was likely me, and you probably mean Toxey Hall. He was a good fighter, just not at the top of his game that night. I still see him from time to time."

"It was exciting because I saw a newsreel on it also. I made the connection when you were talking about Joe Louis earlier. Are you still involved with boxing?"

"Oh, yes, not as a fighter anymore, of course, but I work with juvenile delinquents. I try to get them into boxing, just so they have somewhere to let out some of their frustrations. My ultimate goal is to get them interested in a formal education. I also serve on the board of the D.C. Boxing Commission."

"I'm sure those young boys find that you are a real inspiration. I know I do."

"Well, Captain, I appreciate you taking notice. I just want you to know that whatever decision you make about your military career will be the right one for you. I predict you'll be successful in whatever field you decide to be in. But the military today is the most color-blind institution in the world, in my opinion."

Norvel drove to the barracks at the compound where he had been instructed to drop the officer.

The captain turned to Norvel, reached for his billfold, and said, "Thank you for the tour and especially the conversation, sir. How much do I owe you?"

Norvel got out of the car and went around to the trunk, opened it up, and handed the man his duffle bag. He looked him directly in the eye and said, "I don't charge military men. You just pass it on some day, Captain Powell."

The two men shook hands, and Norvel stepped back into his cab as the young captain turned and went into the building.

# CHAPTER 26

## November 22, 1963—Lorton Reformatory, Lorton, Virginia

A t 1:45 p.m. Norvel was sitting at his desk when the phone rang. A male voice said, "Captain Lee, sir, you are ordered to report to the 909th headquarters at Andrews Air Force Base immediately. The president has been shot and SAC is on high alert!"

Within five minutes Norvel was driving to Andrews AFB. He listened to frenzied news reports on the car radio about the presidential motorcade passing by a grassy knoll in Dallas when shots rang out. In the chaotic aftermath, the car carrying the president zoomed off to a hospital. It wasn't long until it was reported that President Kennedy had died. Norvel felt a strong sense of disbelief come over him. Fighting tears, he recalled when he and Leslie met the president and his wife.

Norvel stayed at Andrews until the next afternoon, ready to handle any crisis that came up. While there he witnessed Air Force One, carrying newly sworn-in President Lyndon Johnson, land at Andrews. When he returned home, the family watched the somber memorial and funeral services televised around the world.

Heading into 1964, Norvel and Leslie expanded their community activism. Norvel was named chairman of the D.C. Boxing Commission. Leslie continued her work with the Police Boys and Girls Club, paving the way for Norvel to be placed on their board of directors. Norvel also became a member of Toastmasters in order to help him overcome his stammer whenever he was asked to speak publicly. After completing the program, he was named to the board of directors of the Department of Corrections Toastmasters.

In April, Secretary of State Dean Rusk summoned the ambassador to Senegal, Dr. Mercer Cook, to Washington. Cook, an intellectual and romance language expert, was Norvel's French professor during his soph-omore year at Howard University.

Cook was born and raised in Washington, D.C. His paternal grandfa-ther, a former slave, was the first dean of the Howard University School of Law. Cook's father was a child prodigy who became a well-known violinist and composer. His mother, Abbie Mitchell, was an opera singer who be-came widely known for playing Clara in the premiere stage performance of *Porgy and Bess*. She was the first to record "Summertime" from the musical. As a child, Cook traveled extensively with his parents while they pursued their respective musical careers. His childhood home was across the street from a boy three years older, who went on to become the leg-endary jazz musician, composer, and orchestra leader Duke Ellington.

For several centuries most of West Africa had been under the rule of the French colonial empire. France's control over the region began to crumble during World War II until, in the late 1950s, several of the terri-tories began lobbying for their independence.

As the regions of Algeria, Sudan, Mali, and Senegal began to break away, the Eisenhower administration established diplomatic relationships with each new government. In 1961, after President Kennedy took office, he continued the policy. Kennedy, a voracious reader, became aware of Mercer Cook after reading several of his scholarly translations of books and essays by African intellectuals, most notably those of Leopold Seng-hor. Senghor, educated in France, was elected Senegal's first president when that country gained its independence in 1960. After Kennedy was assassinated, President Lyndon Johnson appointed Cook as the ambassa-dor to Senegal.

Cook's congenial personality was one of empathetic confidence. His early exposure to the theatrical world had convinced him of the value of motivating people to function as a team, like a well-tuned orchestra or theatrical company. He was successful in bringing the positive influences of these synergies to the classroom, and felt similar results could be had in the diplomatic world.

There were several immediate issues that potentially could undermine the fragile politics of the region if diplomacy was not carefully planned and implemented. Rusk believed Ambassador Cook's presence could help bring about a smooth transition. It was assumed he would be able to leverage his close academic relationship with President Senghor. When they met, Cook told Secretary Rusk that he felt a cultural exchange between France, Senegal, and the United States, if sponsored by the United States, might help ease any developing tensions.

The next day Cook was scanning the *Washington Post* and saw a brief article in the Sports section about Norvel Lee and his role as chairman of the Boxing Commission. He recalled fond memories of the motivated young man from his French class at Howard University. Norvel often needed to be away from class to compete in boxing events elsewhere. It was explained to Cook by university administrators, in no uncertain terms, that it would be beneficial to the University if Norvel's instructors would exercise some flexibility with regard to the timing of Norvel's academic assignments.

Cook smiled to himself as he recalled the challenge this presented, especially with Norvel's speech defects. Nevertheless, Cook was impressed with Norvel's determination to excel academically as well as in the boxing ring. At one point Cook, without informing Norvel, went to the Uline Arena as a spectator for one of Norvel's bouts. He was fascinated by the poise and confidence he saw in Norvel.

Now, in an epiphany, Cook thought Norvel might be exactly the person the State Department needed to help pave the way to a cultural exchange, using boxing as the exchange vehicle. Dean Rusk agreed, and arrangements were made.

# CHAPTER 27

## *August 15, 1964—Dakar, Senegal*

N ear the end of the five-hour flight from London to Dakar, Norvel
looked at the ground below as the plane circled. He saw an island just offshore from the mainland and recognized it as Goree
Island, a place he wanted to visit before returning home. He did not know
if his ancestors were taken, shackled and chained, from there, but it was a
possibility.

After deplaning and entering the surprisingly modern air terminal, he
was met by a group of smiling ebony-black people offering a potpourri
of goods and services. He had to fend off many of them. They were selling flowers, maps, an assortment of food, and transportation services. It
was a chaotic, noisy scene permeated with pleasant but unfamiliar odors.
The crowd was dressed in a variety of styles from colorful native dress to
western jeans and plaid shirts. Incongruous with the rest of the scene was
hearing Patsy Cline's "Walking After Midnight" playing through the loud-
speakers.

While determining where he needed to go to claim his luggage, Norvel
noticed a tall distinguished Black man in a gray business suit. The man
spotted Norvel and walked over to him, smiling. He stuck out his hand,
and introduced himself as Malick Diop. He explained that Ambassador
Cook had sent him to be Norvel's driver while in Dakar. As the various
peddlers saw the man introduce himself, they opened a path for him and
did not pester Norvel further.

Diop helped Norvel locate his suitcase and carried it out of the terminal into the thick, muggy, West African afternoon to the embassy limousine. Diop drove a few miles to a walled compound protected at the
entrance by a uniformed sentry. Within the walls of the compound were
several individual seaside huts. Seagulls were scavenging in groups around

the grounds. Norvel had the feeling rain had come through the area within the last hour.

Diop explained that this was where the United States put up their guests. He pointed out a larger building on the compound where a chef was on duty and available twenty-four hours every day. Whenever Norvel was hungry, he could ask the chef to prepare a meal. Norvel had the option to eat in the dining area, or they would bring it to his hut. Malick told Norvel he would return in the morning to take him to the embassy, where he was scheduled for a meeting with Ambassador Cook.

The next morning, Monday, Norvel met the ambassador in his office at the American Embassy. Both men were dressed in dark suits and white shirts. Norvel's tie was his customary navy blue, while the ambassador's was red. After personal pleasantries were exchanged, and some small talk regarding their mutual connections to Howard University, Ambassador Cook explained what Norvel would be doing the next number of weeks.

"We received the containers with what I am assuming are the props for your boxing clinics," said Cook. "It is interesting material. Will you be taking it all back with you?"

"I'm not taking any of it back," said Norvel, smiling. "I plan to leave some of it with each locality I visit. Will that be a problem?"

"No, not at all," said Cook. "That is very kind of you. I hope you are getting reimbursed for this."

"Again, it's not a problem," said Norvel. "I'm sure we could put it on the State Department's budget, but Leslie, my wife, and I are involved in many organizations. When they learned I was coming here and what I was doing, they stepped forward. As you know, back home growing up, we all learned the key to getting things done was to get as many folks as we could to pitch in. That's one of the lessons we can pass along here."

"These people may surprise you with their resourcefulness," Cook said. "Malick will be your driver and aide while you are here, accommodating your needs as required. In addition, he will also act as your liaison at the various locations scheduled for you."

"And," Cook continued, smiling, "he will act as your translator in case your French, in spite of your excellent training, fails you. You will be relieved to know Malick speaks many of the major African languages spoken in West Africa. Most of the general population speaks the native Wolof, an ancient and beautiful-sounding language. The better educated will speak French and Wolof, or a hybrid of the two."

Norvel said, "Thank you. I believe I may need some help communicating beyond *Bon jour.*"

"You do know one Wolof word that has made it to English: banana." Cook paused and then added, "I hope your back is good and strong because, when you leave Dakar and especially when you get into Mali, you will be on not-so-good roads. But the vehicle you will travel in is designed for them. Fortunately, Malick knows how to get around West Africa."

"Thank you," Norvel said. "I appreciate the hospitality, sir."

Cook then said, "We have an appointment to meet with President Senghor at the Presidential Palace in an hour. I don't believe it will be a lengthy meeting. He wants to tell you how appreciative he is of your visit."

Ambassador Cook's driver took them in another limousine, slightly more luxurious than the one Malick used to drive Norvel, down a major Dakar thoroughfare. Although the Presidential Palace was only seven miles away, it took forty patient minutes of navigating the chaotic traffic conditions. When they finally arrived at the Presidential Palace, Norvel noted the disparity between the conditions on the street and the lavish environment at the palace.

The meeting with President Senghor was brief, and exactly as Cook had advertised it would be. President Senghor graciously welcomed Norvel's mission on behalf of the nations of West Africa. Norvel witnessed firsthand the warm friendship between Ambassador Cook and the Senegalese president and African scholar.

When they returned to the embassy, Cook asked Norvel if he would like to make a phone call home. He explained phone service in Dakar and through the entirety of the West Africa region was mostly not available, but the American Embassy had its own secure lines installed.

Norvel called home. Fortunately, Leslie was there, but the girls were in Leesburg with their grandparents. He was pleased to be able to have a conversation with her, and she was very happy and surprised to hear from him. He cautioned her that it might be several weeks before he would have access to a phone again.

The next morning, Norvel came out of the hut when he heard a vehicle approach. He saw Malick and the olive drab Range Rover and said, "This looks straight out of a safari movie. Does this belong to the embassy?"

"Yes, sir, it does," said Malick. "I drive it whenever I leave Dakar. It will be very good for the roads we will be on. Also, over the next several weeks, this may be our home on occasion.

Malick explained the rugged vehicle was the preferred means of transportation to where they would be going. The back compartment was packed tightly with the items Norvel had shipped for use at the boxing clinics. Anchored to the front hood was the spare tire.

The first clinic was scheduled in the morning in order to avoid the afternoon rains. It was planned at a large park in the Hann neighborhood of Dakar. Norvel had dressed in light cotton sweatpants and a white sleeveless shirt with "USA" stenciled on the front. They arrived a half hour early, but several teenage boys were already hanging around, and others were strolling into the area.

In the center of the park stood a baobab tree with strong, sturdy branches. They tried to hang the heavy punching bag on one of them, but Malick and Norvel encountered some difficulty getting the rope to the selected branch, so one of the boys scooted up the tree and perched on it. Norvel tossed the rope up to the teenager, who wrapped it around the branch and tossed the end back down. Norvel smiled and nodded his thanks as the young man flashed a big smile at him.

By the time the clinic got started, there were about thirty boys and several older men looking on. Norvel asked them in English to gather around as Malick repeated the words in Dakar-Wolof, a French-infused dialect of

Wolof. Malick introduced Norvel as a representative of the United States and a former Olympic boxer whose mission was to conduct a clinic on the sport.

Norvel stepped forward and asked, "How many of you have ever boxed before?"

Nobody moved.

"Okay, then," he continued. "How many of you have been in a fight that required striking out with your fists and hands?"

Most raised their hands.

Norvel said, "Fighting is not the best way to resolve problems. I understand why young men have to prove themselves by slugging it out sometimes, but the better way to settle differences is to talk about them openly. Boxing, however, has nothing to do with fighting. It is a time-honored sport with rules and traditions. My job today is to introduce you to the sport of boxing."

The group of boys looked at Norvel, absorbing every word. Norvel selected five boys from the group and asked them to step forward. "The first thing you'll need to learn is how to take a boxer's stance."

Norvel chose one of the taller, more athletic-appearing boys, took him by the shoulders, and turned him to face the other onlookers. He scratched a line into the ground and said to the boy, "Stand here with your legs on either side of this line. Put your left foot forward with your toes placed on the line. Now move your right foot back behind your body. Place the heel on the center line and adjust your weight evenly across both legs and slightly bend your knees. Now get your feet a little wider than your shoulder width. Raise your back heel."

Norvel, using his hands, made some adjustments to the boy's posture.

"Now point your elbows toward the ground and hands up," instructed Norvel. "Good! Get your head behind your hands, keep your chin a little down so your eyes will see just over your hands."

Malick helped the other four boys follow Norvel's instructions and as he did Norvel double checked each one and made some adjustments in each of their stances.

The remainder of the boys looking on began to mimic those up front. "You look real good," said Norvel. "Now, relax and breathe!"

The boys laughed, and several of them said, teasing each other, "Detendez-vous et respirez!"

Malick smiled and said, "Indeed—detendez-voux et respirez—relax and breathe!"

The onlookers laughed.

Norvel took the boy he was working with and guided him over to the heavy bag hanging from the tree. He directed him to take the stance Norvel just showed him. The boy did a reasonable job of repositioning himself into the boxer's pose he had just learned. Norvel then led the boy and the gathered onlookers in the art of footwork, and afterward he showed him the various punches and defensive measures boxers need to be familiar with.

Norvel wrapped up the clinic by talking about the importance of conditioning. As he did so he picked up a jump rope and began to twirl it around himself. The onlookers were silent, watching in awe as the rope went quickly around Norvel again and again.

In the morning Norvel and Malick began the journeys that for the next several weeks would take them to towns outside Dakar and neighboring countries The Gambia and Mali.

After several weeks of conducting clinics in small villages, Norvel felt relieved when they arrived in Bamako, Mali. He and Malick planned to stay for several nights at a compound near the embassy while conducting boxing clinics in the sprawling city.

Arriving at their compound, they were informed that they would be dining that evening with the U.S. ambassador to Mali. A limousine took Norvel and Malick to an exclusive restaurant. Along the way, Norvel noticed several musicians on the unpaved streets, playing drums and exotic instruments. One had attracted enough spectators, some who were dancing, to stop the limousine's progress down the street until a policeman cleared a path for them.

Upon entering the restaurant, a well-dressed man seated at the bar walked over and said, "Welcome to Mali, Mr. Lee. I'm Bill Handley."

"Thank you, sir," said Norvel. "I'm pleased to be off the road and into the civilized world again."

Ambassador Handley laughed while shaking Malick's hand and saying, "Malick, good to see you again. I'm nursing a martini over here; please join me and our guest."

The three men stepped into the dark bar area, which had the feel of a private club. As they approached the table a slim man stood, smiling broadly at Norvel.

"Why, if it isn't Marvelous Mal!" exclaimed Norvel. "What a surprise!"

Whitfield clasped hands with Norvel, saying, "The same goes for me. The last time we saw each other was at the Pan Am Games in Mexico, I believe. Nearly a decade ago."

"Yes, that was it," Norvel said. "I heard you were in Africa but didn't expect to see you."

Over drinks and dinner, Norvel became comfortable with Handley and caught up with Whitfield's life since he last saw him. He learned that after graduating from UCLA, Whitfield went to work for the U.S. Information Agency. He was designated a goodwill ambassador, based in Kenya. He was involved in activities throughout the continent.

During the next few days, Norvel and Malick hosted boxing clinics at several locations around the greater Bamako area. Norvel also had the opportunity to phone Leslie from the embassy. He briefed her on his adventure, while she told him of the happenings at home and wished him an early happy fortieth birthday.

While exploring the city one evening, Norvel and Malick came across an establishment opening onto the street and serving local food and drinks. The crowd inside was unusually quiet, intent on listening to a guitarist playing a complex, appealing rhythm.

Malick inquired and learned a musician named Ali Farka Touré, who was revered throughout Mali, was performing. Norvel and Malick spent the evening mesmerized by what they were seeing and hearing. Touré, who looked to be in his twenties, was dressed in a traditional Malian long, flowing, colorful tunic.

Norvel marveled at a particular melody Touré sang in his beautiful, haunting voice and an intricate guitar line invoking a stark, solitary scene out on the desert sands. When it was finished, Norvel asked Malick to interpret the words. Malick said Touré was telling the listeners that trust and faith in their fellow man has no equal and that if you have experienced trust, then you will know its strength and that you must know yourself before you know others. Norvel wondered how an African from a small village along the Niger River learned to impart such powerful universal messages through music. He knew it was an experience he would never forget.

After leaving Bamako, during the 1,400-kilometer trip back to Dakar, Norvel and Malick put on boxing clinics at small towns in Mali and eastern Senegal. This part of Africa, with its many ancient customs, enchanted him. And although the different societies he encountered seemed to be organized in ways that only the locals understood, there was distinguishable charm here he was trying to absorb.

As they drove from Diourbel to Dakar, Norvel said, "Malick, I want you to know that this journey with you has had a profound effect on me. I'll carry the experiences of the past few weeks with me for the rest of my days. I've learned so much from being with you and the people here."

Malick said, "This adventure has meant much to me as well. I feel as if I have a new friend in the world. I hope that we will remain in touch."

Norvel said, "I hope you will visit Washington, and I'll show you what that city is about."

Malick said, "I will like that very much, thank you. I'm sure I will see it and find it very modern."

Norvel said, "Yes, you will, but you may also conclude the life you have here might be more rewarding."

As the drive went on, the two men reminisced about their travels and the people they'd encountered. Late in the afternoon, Malick dropped Norvel at the compound in Dakar where he had spent his first days in Africa.

The next morning Malick, now driving the embassy limousine, collected Norvel and his luggage. He told Norvel that Ambassador Cook wanted to meet him at the Ile de Goree instead of the embassy, as originally planned. Malick drove him to the dock on the southeastern shore of Dakar, where Norvel boarded a ferry to the Island.

Norvel stood facing the entrance to the Maison des Esclaves, or Slave House, on the eastern side of Goree Island, one of nineteen districts within the city limits of Dakar. As Norvel took in the surroundings he heard the crunch of feet on the gravel walkway, turned, and saw his former professor approaching.

Ambassador Cook, smiling warmly, said, "Norvel, I realize this is not the most convenient place to get to, but I thought it would be a fitting conclusion to what I understand was a very successful journey through West Africa. I'm sure, though, you're anxious to return home to your family."

"Yes, sir, I am," Norvel said. "But I want to thank you for arranging the services of Malick, and for the hospitality I was provided throughout the entire region. This was truly a stimulating and inspiring journey for me."

"I'm sure it was, Norvel—and gratitude is a two-way street," said the ambassador. "We in the Foreign Service appreciate you making your time available to us during this period of change in West Africa. I've been briefed on the aspects of your mission, but if there are any particular moments you would like to highlight with me, please do so."

Cook then smiled knowingly and said, "But before you do, I am anxious to know if any of the French you learned at Howard was useful on your journeys?"

"Uh, uh, I was a little rusty with it," said Norvel. "But that's where Malick came in, translating when necessary. I'm glad I studied the history of the area before coming over."

"Yes," Cook said. "We're fortunate to have his services. I also know he enjoyed the time he spent with you. I hope the two of you can stay in contact with each other."

"We're resolved to," Norvel said.

"What was the highlight of your trip?" Cook asked.

Norvel said, "Helping those young men I had the opportunity to counsel in the art of boxing, which for me is a metaphor for life."

"And the low point?"

"That we couldn't do more than we did. In retrospect, I would have encouraged them more about the benefits of an education."

"Maybe next time, Norvel," Cook said. "I trust you now know about this historic ground you are standing on, don't you?"

"Yes, somewhat," Norvel said.

"This site was refurbished and became a museum and a World Heritage Site just two years ago. The door in front of you is called the 'Door of No Return.' The curator, Boubacar Joseph Ndiaye, documents that more than one million souls came through this place. I have confirmed that I descended from Senegal. My ancestors were seized from the area you visited the last several weeks. Do you have any thoughts on your ancestry?"

Norvel thought for a moment and said, "I didn't know before I began this trip, but I'm now curious if I have Malian in me."

"Tell me why," encouraged Cook.

"The place resonates with my soul—the music, the people, the food, everything. I just feel it. I can't imagine what it must have been like to have strangers come to the area and yank a family apart and send them to a faraway place, never to return."

"Over half didn't survive the trip," Cook added.

Ambassador Cook put his hand on Norvel's shoulder and told him to keep up the good work he was doing in the world.

That evening Norvel was on the British Overseas Airways Corporation flight to London, returning home.

# CHAPTER 28

## *September 1964—Dulles International Airport, Virginia*

L eslie and her sister Weekie waited excitedly for the Pan American Airways flight from London to disembark. When the passengers began to stream into the terminal, they didn't recognize Norvel at first. His skin was much darker, and his hair was noticeably longer. Over his shoulder was a string holding a set of small, bongo-like drums. They knew it was him when Norvel spotted them, hurried his step, and wrapped Leslie in his arms.

Soon after Norvel returned, he and Leslie attended a lecture that she had learned of at the Police Boys and Girls Club. The lecturer was Stan Salett who, in his late twenties, was working within the Johnson administration on implementing War on Poverty initiatives. One such program developed by him was Upward Bound, in which students from low-income families who had completed the eighth grade and were potentially college-bound were encouraged to continue their studies. The program focused on those students who would be the first in their family to attend college.

After absorbing the information, Norvel brought Upward Bound up during a coordination meeting he had with the D.C. Department of Public Welfare. They asked him to consider putting together a briefing on how Upward Bound would apply to their organization. As a result, in August 1965, Norvel left the Lorton Reformatory to become the head of training for the Public Welfare Department.

In that role, not only did he implement the Upward Bound program, but also he took responsibility for training heads of households. Leslie had learned that Title 5, a provision of the Social Security Act of 1935, was set up for improving the health of mothers and children. In addition to Upward Bound grants, Norvel was able to secure funding through Title 5 for the training programs.

Around the same time Norvel expanded his taxi business by hiring two more cars and drivers and calling it the Diplomat Cab Association.

The every-other-Friday card games continued, with Al Maltz as the unofficial coordinator. They rotated from Norvel's and Mike Mehalic's D.C. homes, to Al Maltz's Maryland home, and to their friend Eddie Thompson's apartment in Alexandria. When it was Thompson's turn to host, Norvel would drive Maltz and Mehalic in his cab across the Potomac River to Virginia, humorously insisting that they sit in the back seat of the car.

In early 1966 Norvel's longtime friend from the Howard boxing team, York Van Nixon, organized a boxer's reunion at Uline Arena. There was no boxing involved. It was a gathering of older boxing luminaries to help raise money for disadvantaged youth. Van Nixon and Norvel had remained friends over the year even though they were an odd pair. Unlike Norvel, Van Nixon pined to draw attention to himself. This trait, coupled with his strong entrepreneurial instincts, made for memorable occasions.

Leslie's father, Emmett, was still an avid fan of boxing, following the sport intently. He felt he had access to that world through Norvel's continued participation in boxing through the D.C. Boxing Commission. So Norvel brought Emmett to Van Nixon's event. where he was able to meet, talk with, and obtain autographs from many well-known boxers, including Jersey Joe Wolcott and Rocky Marciano.

In the spring of 1966, the mission of the 909th, Norvel's reserve unit, was relocated to California and no longer required a direct liaison with Andrews AFB. As a result, Norvel was promoted to major, and became the chief of staff for the reserve component of the 459th TAC Wing at Andrews. The 459th's mission was also a refueling function, but in a reserve capacity. Norvel found the new position better defined and more predictable, permitting him to pay attention to his civilian career and his family.

He and Leslie remained active in their various youth outreach programs, mostly involving activities associated with the Police Boys and Girls

Clubs. Norvel and Leslie felt fortunate that the benefits of their hard work and prominence in the community could set an example for their girls, their extended family, and others around them.

Then, on April 4, 1968, while Norvel and Leslie were watching the six o'clock news, the world changed. A bulletin brought the gut-wrenching news that Dr. Martin Luther King Jr. had been assassinated in Memphis.

# CHAPTER 29

## Friday afternoon, April 5, 1968—5808 8th Street NW, Washington, D.C.

The turbulent events following the assassination impacted decisions Norvel and Leslie made about their future plans for themselves, their daughters, and their extended family. They were affected most by the destructive riots following Dr. King's murder that left Columbia Heights along the 14th Street corridor, within a mile of their 8th Street home, in shambles. During the riots Norvel stayed near home, feeling his presence would ward off any unwanted incidents.

In the afternoon he walked the few blocks over to Georgia Avenue. There, he encountered a group of angry young men in their late teens, several displaying swagger and bravado, carrying baseball bats and sticks. One was lugging a gasoline container.

Norvel, who could muster up an imposing, intimidating appearance anytime a situation called for it, shouted, "Men, where are you going?"

"We be bad news for the pigs," one of them said.

The young man with the gas can held it up. "Gonna give the devil some medicine."

Norvel walked over to the young man and yanked the can from his hands.

"Hey, where's yo soul, old man?" the young man said.

"What's your name, son?" Norvel said.

"Who wants to know?" he asked.

"I'm Norvel Lee."

The young man looked at the others and said, "This here is Mr. Lee, the boxing dude."

Norvel said, "Men, I'm not here to tell you what to do. If you want to ruin your lives and burn buildings, that's up to you. But I know who you are." Looking at one of the boys, he said, "You're Shirley's son, aren't you?" The boy nodded.

Norvel said, "Then you might know she's in my program to get trained so she can work in an office. There won't be any office for her to go to if you burn it down."

Norvel suggested the boys surrender their baseball bats and follow him back home, where he said there would be some food for them and where they could talk more. Three of them did, including the young man who brought the container. The other two said they were going over to 14th Street to see what was going on. They said they just wanted to hang out. Norvel told them to stay out of trouble, and they could come get their bats when they were ready to use them for what they were intended for.

The young men calmed down at Norvel's home. After they left, Norvel sat in the front room with Leslie, Debbie, and Denise. The television was turned off because they were tired of hearing the news about their city burning.

Norvel said, "Uh, uh, I'm so frustrated. We're not getting anywhere. Why can't they get it through their thick heads that if they burn everything down, they're going against everything Dr. King stood for?"

Debbie and Denise remained quiet. They seldom heard their father express negative feelings.

Leslie said, "They think the government is responsible for the miserable lives they're leading. It was an excuse for them to be angry."

"And what about us?" Norvel said, pointing at Debbie and Denise. "What about my daughters?"

"What about them?" said Leslie.

"They see kids not much older than they are carrying on in the streets. What will they think?" said Norvel.

Denise, wiping some tears away, said, "Daddy, we think like you do. It's scary to see them burn down all those buildings."

"I'm glad you girls think like your father and I do," Leslie said calmly. "This world has ups and downs, and you just have to go with it."

"I think two things," Norvel said. "We need to honor Dr. King by setting a shining example to those who see us every day. Education, which Booker T. Washington paved the way for, is the most important gift anyone can give themselves. And we've all been doing our best, haven't we?"

Leslie nodded, "Go on."

"You know they're opening that new Federal City College in the fall," Norvel said. "My colleagues and I have been setting up a partnership through Title 5 so some of the more qualified people in the program will get priority."

"I know," Leslie said. "There should be more publicity about that."

"Well, from the discussions," Norvel said, "I know they want to start a master's program. I told them if they needed any help with setting it up to let me know."

"You don't have a master's degree," Leslie said to him, winking at the girls. "How could you help set it up?"

"Best way I know is for you and me to be their first students," Norvel said.

"Both of us?" said Leslie. "Good gracious, Norvel, it's been a very long time since I went to school."

Denise said, "You're always helping us with our schoolwork. Just do what you've been telling us to do."

"That's why you should go with me," Norvel said, "as an example. That's how we move on from these unfortunate circumstances playing out among us. Right, girls?"

Leslie said, "That's why I love you. No matter what, you're always thinking about the next thing to do, mountain to climb, or obstacle to conquer."

After the girls had gone upstairs, Norvel said, "I also want you and the girls to feel safe. It may be time to move to a more secure area, and a bigger house."

Leslie said, "Oh, Norvel, that would be nice, but we don't have the money to do that. Someday, maybe."

Norvel said, "Where there's a will, there's a way."

*York's been telling me that a housing downturn is coming, and that it will be a good time to buy real estate. So yes, there may be a way.*

Norvel convinced the new Federal City College administrators to begin a postgraduate program during the summer quarter before regular classes commenced in the fall. Norvel and other proactive organizers in the Washington area recommended a curriculum leading to a master of arts in adult education. Norvel and Leslie enrolled in the initial graduate-level courses at Federal City College. The curriculum included classes in Trends in Education, Generic Issues, Behavioral Objectives, and Ghetto Psychology.

# CHAPTER 30

## January 20, 1969—Smithsonian Museum of History and Technology, Washington, D.C.

Norvel wore his dress Air Force uniform while Leslie donned a formal gown for the inaugural ball honoring President Richard M. Nixon. When Norvel and Leslie moved up the receiving line to meet the new president and first lady, Norvel tried to make eye contact with them. First Lady Pat Nixon smiled broadly at Leslie, but the president hastily shook Norvel's hand without looking at him and turned to the next person in line.

Norvel noticed that Nixon was not engaging many of the people in the line, as if he wished to be elsewhere. But it had been a long day for the new president, and this was only the third of the six balls he was obligated to attend. Norvel was there to acknowledge the new commander in chief. Even though he had not voted for Nixon, he felt the new president would bring much-needed order to the country following the unrest of the past two years. The assassinations of Dr. Martin Luther King Jr. and presidential candidate Robert Kennedy, whom he would have voted for, and the ongoing protests against the war in Vietnam left the nation yearning for steady leadership.

Norvel and Leslie took advantage of the dip in housing prices caused by the political uncertainty to purchase a six-thousand-square-foot home located in the northern neighborhoods of Washington, D.C. The informal boundaries of the prestigious area were 16th Street on the east, Holly Street on the south, Beach Drive on the west and the Maryland-D.C. border on the north. The Lees were one of the first Black families to purchase a home in this mostly Jewish enclave of D.C, which in an earlier time had a covenant forbidding residents of "Negro blood or of the Semitic race."

Norvel determined he could afford the $80,000 mortgage using the income from his and Leslie's education jobs and his Air Force Reserve salary. They kept the 8th Street home as a rental. He was confident in his ability to supplement his income, even though he was coming up on his fifties.

While studying for his master's degree, Norvel transferred from the Title 5 program he managed at the D.C. Department of Welfare, and took the position of director of continuing education at Federal City College. From that position, he coordinated programs of adult and continuing education aimed at evaluating educational needs for the Washington, D.C., metropolitan area. Additionally, he was responsible for establishing and monitoring equal opportunity guidelines. He selected, supervised, trained, and evaluated the work of department heads and program directors, and administered the master of arts degree program. He was also an associate professor of adult education at the school.

Norvel continued to chair the D.C. Boxing Commission and sit on the executive board for the Police Boys and Girls Club. He frequently brought a few young men to his home to mentor them about the options they had for a life beyond the impoverished urban environment of D.C. He introduced those who showed the inclination and skill to athletics, either baseball or boxing.

Meanwhile, Norvel learned that the Air Force Reserve had been charged with organizing a response capability in the event of a national disaster or social disturbance. The concern for the Air Force was for civil emergencies requiring their intervention. The paramount situation would be in the event of war affecting the civilian population, and especially if nuclear weapons were involved. The reservists needed to ensure a state of readiness.

As his security clearance was still active, Norvel was asked if he was interested in receiving training to be a disaster preparedness officer. The initial training would involve two months of classroom and field training. A few days later, he went to Fort Leonard Wood in the Ozarks of Missouri, where the U.S. Army Chemical School was located, to receive the training. The school served all branches of the Armed Forces, and specialized in chemical and radiological defense training.

Since Norvel never lost his interest in the sciences, exploring a technological field at the invitation of the Air Force was a welcome diversion. He had passed that interest along to both his daughters, who excelled at the sciences. At Norvel's urging, Debbie applied for and earned a scholarship to Drexel University in Philadelphia to study nuclear physics. Her sister Denise was following a different science path, taking an interest in animal health and their care. Although only a high school sophomore, she was already researching colleges that specialized in animal husbandry and veterinary studies. Tuskegee Institute was one she had her eyes on.

At the end of July 1971, when Norvel returned from training at Fort Leonard Wood, he took Leslie on a date into the city, just the two of them. It was rare that they didn't have other people around, like their girls or friends. On occasion, at the large Sycamore Street home, a spontaneous gathering would occur. Leslie's parents, who still lived on Ayr Street in Leesburg, visited often. Leslie kept a guest bedroom ready because they often showed up unannounced. Their son and daughter—Robert and Weekie—lived nearby with their families, and there was always a grandchild's birthday or other event bringing them into the District.

Furthermore, acquaintances from the world of boxing, the military, or education would stop by unannounced. John Boutilier, now a teacher in San Diego, made a surprise appearance at the Lee's home when he visited D.C. And Congressman Bob Mathias would occasionally drop by when Congress was in session.

Leslie was happy to have Norvel to herself on a beautiful summer evening. He drove into downtown D.C. and parked curbside, just beyond the front entrance of the Mayflower Hotel. The doorman came over, opened the door for Leslie, and greeted her cordially. The Lees were well known by the doormen at the Mayflower for the various functions they attended.

They were shown to a table in Carvery Restaurant. Many Washington luminaries, including presidents, had dined in the restaurant over the past century.

Norvel took a drink from the RC Cola the tuxedoed waiter brought to him.

"This is very nice," Leslie observed. "And we don't have to check a list to see if we can eat at a lunch counter, like the old days."

"Very true," Norvel agreed. "A lot has changed in the last twenty years, and our babies are reaping the benefits of this new world."

"Do you think they understand that?" Leslie asked. "Or do they just accept it as if it's always been this way?"

"Oh, there are plenty of obstacles still out there for them," Norvel said. "I'm convinced everyone faces some obstacles, no matter what your background. They just need to be confronted and overcome. We're teaching them to do that while enjoying each day."

Norvel paused for a moment as the waiter described the evening's fare. Norvel ordered steak for both of them with Caesar salad to start.

"I had a dream last night," Leslie said. "A woman appeared out of nowhere and said to remember her. It was very vivid, and she looked familiar. She had long black hair."

"Who do you think she was?" Norvel asked.

"I was wondering the same thing, so this morning I went into that envelope of old pictures and compared my dream woman with the picture of your mother. It was her, Norvel! I know it was."

"Dreams are interesting," Norvel said. "There isn't a day that goes by that I don't remember her."

"That's sweet," Leslie said, "but I think she was asking me personally to make sure she is remembered. Do you recall when you took me to her gravesite, and I said she should have a more prominent marker on her grave?"

"I suppose."

"The dream was telling me that now is the time to give her that larger headstone," Leslie said firmly.

"We'll see." Changing the subject, Norvel said, "Now that I've been trained, the Air Force has me reporting to Robins Air Force Base in Georgia. My new assignment will be disaster preparedness officer."

"I hope you're not going to say we have to move to Georgia," Leslie said.

Norvel laughed and said, "No. I may have to make an appearance there from time to time, like I have to next weekend, but my duties will still be out of Andrews."

"That's okay, but why do things have to be so complicated?" Leslie asked. "Why would you report to Robins?"

"The Air Force Reserve Command is based down there, and they own the charter on dealing with disasters. They plan to have someone like me at every Air Force base."

"Norvel, there is no one else in the world like you," Leslie said, lovingly.

"And you too," Norvel said. "Speaking of which, how are things going with the index system you're pushing for adoption at the library at Federal?"

"It looks as if they are going to finally adopt my system. Well, it's really not mine per se. It's a modified version of the system they use at the Library of Congress. Anything would be better than just having the books arranged alphabetically by author, the way it is now."

"Why not the Dewey Decimal System?" asked Norvel.

"I thought about it, but with the Library of Congress nearby, I thought it would be better to be aligned with them," said Leslie. "It's a lot of work to implement, but once it's set up, it will make life much easier for the users, who are mostly students. Many of these kids have had limited exposure to libraries because their schools don't have libraries."

"I didn't have any libraries growing up," said Norvel. "I just had a mother who made it clear it was expected we would get ourselves educated, however we could."

"Well, I don't have parental control over those kids. I barely have it over my own. But I can lobby the schools. Once this project is wrapped up, I am going to advocate for libraries at every one of our public schools in the District—from elementary to high school."

"Going to make the world a better place, are we?" Norvel kidded her. Leslie nodded, her dark eyes shining in the softly lit restaurant.

Jack Lee continued to work as an auto repairman. One day, a government employee from West Virginia, Ruby Jackson, took her car in for repair. She and Jack struck up a relationship and soon became engaged. She retired in September 1972 and they moved to Jack's railroad town of Clifton Forge, where they married on October 7 at the Main Street Baptist Church.

After attending the wedding, Norvel and Leslie drove to Gala to visit his mother's grave. Again Leslie told Norvel she thought his mother deserved a more prominent marker, and Norvel, busy as always, said he'd take care of it eventually. They also walked down to Sinking Creek, where on that beautiful October day the leaves were falling, their golden remains scattered on the path. They came upon the old white oak tree, now massive, where Jack Lee had hung the makeshift boxing bag for Norvel. He told Leslie about the incident, and she was touched by the story, remarking how life-defining it had been for Norvel.

On March 28, 1973, Norvel was promoted to lieutenant colonel and assumed the position of state civil defense liaison officer. He became the point of contact between the Air Force and the State of Maryland. He was still based at Andrews but reported to the Air Force Reserve headquarters at Robins in Georgia. His primary duty was to be a conduit for communications between the Department of Defense, federal, state and local governments, and non-governmental organizations, to make sure all were prepared for emergency events, and to coordinate a response when necessary. Normally, a full-bird colonel would be assigned the position, but Norvel's two years as a disaster preparedness officer and continued training in mitigation techniques for potential disasters highly qualified him for the assignment.

During his next seven years with the Air Force Reserve, Norvel served in the liaison role and established a respected reputation among Maryland officials, who not only appreciated his accessibility but used his knowledge to implement federally mandated emergency compliance procedures, especially those addressing exposure to nuclear radiation.

Throughout 1973, Norvel and Leslie continued to work in their positions at Federal City College, and to fulfill their responsibilities on various community boards, most prominently the Police Boys and Girls Club. Mid-year, Norvel was named the first African American board member of the World Boxing Association. Its annual convention, in December, was held in San Juan, Puerto Rico. The WBA covered the expenses of the board members and their spouses, and Leslie attended it with Norvel.

In March 1974 Norvel left Federal City College to take a full-time position as coordinator of adult and community education with the Baltimore Board of Education. His responsibilities included the operation of all manpower training programs in Baltimore City Schools and selecting, supervising the training of, and evaluating the work of staff members and counselors.

Inspired by the people he worked with in Baltimore, many of whom were PhDs, Norvel enrolled in the doctorate of education program at Catholic University. A motivating factor for entering the program was concern for his daughters. Twenty-year-old Debbie was at Drexel on a nuclear physics scholarship, but she had recently met a boy who worked at a local gas station she was obviously serious about. Norvel hoped that Debbie, normally pragmatic, would take note of his example and not be deterred from her goal of graduating from college. Likewise, he hoped her younger sister, Denise, was also paying attention.

Leslie's attitude toward the situation was simple. It was the way of the world, and nature would take its course. In June 1975, shortly after turning twenty-one, Debbie married Francis Ricks. On July 10, 1976, she gave birth to Francis Nathaniel Ray Ricks II. Norvel became a very proud grandfather. His pride was evident when he insisted in showing off Ricky, as his grandson became known, when it was his turn to host the pinochle gang.

In 1976 the Rockville, Maryland, Jaycees invited Norvel to help them with the local Special Olympics event they were sponsoring. This was the third year of the event, held at Montgomery High School. Norvel was asked if he would put on a boxing clinic for the young disabled athletes. For the June event Norvel set up a mat, boxing gear, towels, and a bucket of ice water. During the event, kids of all ages flailed away at him for hours. The event was widely popular, so much so that Norvel came back year after year to conduct the clinic.

During a 1977 pinochle evening, the men talked about the upswing in demand for affordable housing in Washington and Maryland. They decided that for those who had the resources to invest, the market was worth considering. Norvel listened intently. It went along with what his longtime friend, York Van Nixon, was saying about opportunities in real estate. Van Nixon, it seemed, was always adding to his growing holdings of multifamily dwellings. Norvel felt his friend was taking unacceptable risks, but that was York, opportunistic in all in which he was involved.

Leslie and Norvel decided it was worth investigating the possibilities. Since their experience with renting 8th Street had been positive, they felt that buying another one or two properties might give them additional cash flow. With housing prices forecast to appreciate, their net worth would increase. If so, they would be able to stop working traditional jobs without compromising their lifestyle.

By the end of 1977, they had purchased two properties, a four-unit apartment building in Fort Washington, Maryland, and a six-unit building on Fort DuPont Terrace in Southeast D.C. Both were financed, but the cash flow from renters paid the mortgage and upkeep.

Norvel became fascinated by the field of real estate, including the selling, brokering, financing, and ownership of it. His experience with eleven rental units showed excellent promise. He saw an opportunity to counter the predatory practices of many of the landlords present in the neighborhoods where disadvantaged people, mostly Black, lived. By establishing a reputation as a fair landlord, he knew he'd always have people interested in renting places from him. He just needed to check their references to ensure the tenants were trustworthy. He also relied on his instincts.

In April 1978 Denise married Daniel Anderson. They were married on the campus at the Tuskegee Institute where she attended school. Norvel and Leslie were proud their daughter insisted on having her wedding at the school founded by Booker T. Washington. Norvel appreciated that the campus grounds, which were constructed by the students themselves, were the same as he remembered them from 1944.

In early 1979, Norvel decided the end of the year would mark his last in a formal education role. He was ready to go for the next challenge. Al Maltz of the pinochle group was now human resources director for the Federal Emergency Management Agency (FEMA). When he learned of Norvel's plans, he asked him to consider a role at FEMA he was having trouble filling, equal opportunity director. Norvel agreed and told Maltz he would set up the FEMA EEO program but would not commit to the position for the long term. Norvel knew having FEMA on his resume would complement his experience with the Air Force Reserve.

In March 1979 Norvel was elected to the Washington, D.C., Boxing Hall of Fame.

Norvel also enrolled in real estate classes to prepare for the real estate license exam. He passed on the first attempt, was approved for a real estate license in September, and joined the staff of Century 21 in Oxon Hill, Maryland. That office was not only involved in brokering real estate but also acted as property managers for owners who didn't want to be involved in the day-to-day management of their buildings. Norvel set out to learn as much as he could about property management, with an eye to acquiring more rental properties.

Norvel's brother Jimmy, still an instructor with the federal prison system, grew distant from the family. His free time was spent writing dark essays and books. Beginning in the late 1970s, he seemed to lose some of his energy and passion for his various causes. Norvel and Leslie became concerned. While visiting him at his home in Laurel, Maryland, Norvel noticed Jimmy was having trouble with his equilibrium. Norvel encouraged Jimmy to see a doctor who eventually diagnosed him with multiple sclerosis.

By the end of the decade, Norvel continued to fulfill the responsibilities of the civil defense liaison for the Air Force. Looming, though, was his departure from the Air Force Reserve in 1980 because he was required to retire after twenty-eight years as a commissioned officer.

# CHAPTER 31

## *Friday morning, April 18, 1980—Andrews Air Force Base, Maryland*

Lieutenant Colonel Norvel Lee arrived at the 459th TAAC Wing Headquarters with just minutes to spare for what was a mandatory meeting, scheduled suddenly the day before. Making sure, one more time, his dress uniform would pass the inspection of General Dillon's critical eye, he walked quickly from his car into the foyer of the building.

The sudden scheduling of the meeting was an anomaly by Air Force standards, where every event was planned and its purpose reviewed weeks or months in advance. But late yesterday, when he arrived home from the office, he had received an urgent message ordering him to report to the offices of Major General Edward Dillon, commander of the 459th. Norvel was one week away from mandatory retirement from the Air Force Reserve. He couldn't imagine what further duties General Dillon wanted from him.

Almost thirty-two years had passed since Norvel, while at Howard University, had enrolled in the ROTC program. His primary motive for signing up had been the additional monetary compensation. He chuckled to himself, realizing how important that $50 per month has been to him. He had given no thought as to what impact a six-year commitment to the Reserves would have on the rest of his life. But over time the Air Force became an integral part of his life and served as a patriotic platform to conceive and launch new pursuits.

As he entered the 459th TAC Wing Headquarters, Norvel was still trying to figure out what General Dillon needed from him. Unexpectedly waiting for him in the foyer were Leslie, his daughters and their husbands, his nearly four-year-old grandson Ricky, Margaret (Weekie) and Clifford Russell, Robert and Hattie Jackson, card-playing friends Al Maltz and Bill

Shook, and many of his Air Force acquaintances. Something was clearly up. They were all smiling at him. Leslie walked up and gave him a kiss and a hug.

"Uh, uh, what are you all doing here?" Norvel asked. "I'm here to see General Dillon."

Just then General Dillon, a tall, burly man about the same age as Norvel, entered the foyer from a door to the right. The group turned to greet him, and Norvel and the other reservists saluted. Dillon returned their salutes, smiled at the onlookers, and escorted them into an adjoining conference room. Everyone remained standing. General Dillon walked to the front of the room.

"Lieutenant Colonel Lee," said Dillon in a commanding voice. "Please step forward."

Norvel stepped forward and stood at attention. The general said, "At ease, Colonel."

Norvel had known General Dillon for several years and had never experienced this level of formality from him. Normally he met the general and others in a meeting, where reports on incidents that could potentially evolve into civil defense crises were discussed. Those meetings, while serious, had an informal "let's resolve this issue" atmosphere.

"Lieutenant Colonel Lee," began General Dillon, "on behalf of the United States Air Force, I am here to recognize the excellent work you have performed while serving our organization. The collective achievements of our organization are shaped by individuals such as you, who are dedicated to performing their duties at the highest level of excellence. In recognition of your total commitment to excellence and service to the Unites States Air Force, I am honored to present to you the Meritorious Service Medal."

General Dillon then took the medal and hung it around Norvel's neck.

"Congratulations, Norvel," said General Dillon, smiling.

The onlookers clapped loudly as Leslie, Debbie, and Denise came forward and gave him hugs. Norvel proudly accepted their and the others' congratulations.

Flooding into Norvel's head were memories of that day in 1943 when he left home, his mother and father watching the train leave the station at Clifton Forge. None of them would ever have imagined a day like this would come.

*Wish I could bring back that moment, and have them here right now, seeing what it led to. I wish they would let me stay in longer.*

One week later, Norvel officially retired from the Air Force Reserve and enlisted in the D.C. Air National Guard, based at Andrews Air Force Base. In this role he continued performing his liaison duties. Committing to two more years of military service qualified him for full retirement benefits.

# CHAPTER 32

*April 13, 1981—1701 Sycamore Street, NW,*
*Washington, D.C.*

Norvel, up early as usual, went to the front steps and picked up the morning edition of the *Baltimore Sun*. At the breakfast table he read the front-page headline: "Winged space shuttle blasts off into orbit." The article was about the maiden voyage of the space shuttle Columbia. Norvel and Leslie had watched the NBC live television coverage of the launch the previous day. Not able to stay seated, Norvel had stood and excitedly paced the room during the countdown and subsequent liftoff of NASA's latest marvel.

Norvel then glanced at the other headline on the front page: "Ex-champion Joe Louis dies of heart failure at sixty-six."

*Only sixty-six. You were my inspiration, Joe. I'm so sorry you're gone!*

For the past six years, aside from expanding his real estate holdings, managing the cab business, working for FEMA, sitting on several community boards, and attending to military duties, Norvel had been pursuing his PhD at Catholic University. He finally completed the academic requirements, but did not give a dissertation. He was given an ABD—all but dissertation—degree in June 1981.

On April 12, 1982, Denise gave birth to Norvel and Leslie's second grandchild, Danielle Kristina Anderson. Leslie was overjoyed to have a new grandchild to dote on, a girl no less. Ricky was almost six now and couldn't be babied any longer.

Then life took a turn for Norvel. During a family getaway to Ocean City to celebrate Leslie's fifty-eighth birthday, she uncharacteristically fell asleep midday. Debbie tried to wake her, but Leslie seemed unaware of the surroundings. They called for a doctor, who determined that Leslie's blood sugar had crashed. The doctor suspected she had diabetes. When they returned from the beach, further medical tests confirmed this was the case. She was put on insulin to manage her sugar levels.

About the same time, Norvel left his position at FEMA and became the director of the new D.C. Office of Emergency Management. He was well suited for the job. It dovetailed with the various certifications he had acquired, including recent ones for emergency management and nuclear emergency operations.

Norvel and Leslie continued to invest in residential real estate. He purchased apartment buildings and duplexes. He found that as a licensed real estate agent, he could negotiate better terms by only having to pay commission to the selling agent, if there was one.

On February 26, 1983, Debbie's second child, Tiffany Alexis Mercedes Ayler, was born. Again, another granddaughter brought joy to the proud grandparents.

In April, Leslie's doctor put her on a new insulin, a synthetic variant, recently approved by the FDA. It purported to have longer lasting benefits over standard insulin, which was derived from animals. Tragically, after using the new insulin for a week, Leslie went into hyperglycemic shock. She became weak, lethargic, and uninterested in the day-to-day activities of the active household.

The unexpected turn of events caused Norvel to not accept the prognosis that Leslie would not recover. "Lil Napoleon" had always been the foundation of the family. From their early days together, she had been Norvel's confidant and life partner. She was the one that drove their community participation, while nurturing him and the rest of the family.

*I will do everything I can to get her on the mend. She will be comfortable and surrounded by this happy, exuberant family we've created. The real Leslie, locked inside, will come back. I know she will.*

Every day Leslie's brother Robert or sister Weekie stopped by the house to pitch in on household chores. Then Denise, her husband Danny, and daughter Danielle moved into the sprawling home. Shortly after moving in, Denise became pregnant. The prospect of another grandchild living there added vitality and life to what otherwise was a dire situation.

After several months Norvel finally admitted that Leslie would not be the same again. Having his daughter and her family live with him brought comfort as he coped with the loss of his lover and partner in life, even though she was still physically present. It was so unfair that Leslie's irrepressible vitality had been taken away. Norvel eventually got back to doing what he always did. He dealt with the issue at hand, and moved on to the next one.

The pinochle gang continued to meet every other Friday. Norvel looked forward to the company of his friends. Each time they got together they caught up with each other's lives, giving Norvel a welcome break from the myriad of activities occurring in his life.

On February 18, 1984, a Saturday, Norvel answered the phone, thinking it was one of his cab drivers calling. But instead, it was George calling from Clifton Forge. George had gone down to Virginia a few weeks earlier when he heard their father wasn't feeling well. Now he was calling to let Norvel know that Jack had died.

Norvel drove down to Clifton Forge to attend the February 22nd funeral, alone. He'd hoped his brother could go with him, but Jimmy's multiple sclerosis prevented him from making a long road trip. When Norvel arrived he met his brother George, his sister Edna, and Jack's wife Ruby.

The funeral was held at Norvel's childhood church, Rising Mount Zion Baptist, and presided over by Reverend Townes. At the conclusion of Jack Lee's funeral, the mourners followed the pallbearers to the adjoining graveyard, avoiding lingering patches of snow from a recent storm. Norvel thought about the last time he had been at the little church that had been the center of his family life growing up, and all that had passed since those days.

As Norvel walked with the group behind the pallbearers, he wished Leslie was there with him. She was unable to do much of anything now, let alone travel. He missed her wise counsel and the activities they'd shared.

Fortunately the recent thaw had left the ground soft enough that the grave could be dug in time for the funeral. As the fifty or so people walked with the casket to the burial spot, a soft melody rose from the group, at first low and then gaining in strength. Ruby's voice joined in and rose above the others in singing "Just a Closer Walk with Thee."

As they reached the location, the others made room for the family to stand up front. Reverend Townes led the mourners in prayers while the casket was lowered into the grave. The spot was next to their mother's gravesite, and Norvel noticed that it now had a large headstone marking it.

After the service, Norvel said, "That headstone wasn't there last time. There was just a little plaque like many of the other graves here. When we came down for Father's wedding, Leslie said Mama needed to have a more substantial headstone, and then a while back she told me about a dream she had."

Edna said, "She and I worked on it together. She wanted to surprise you with it. If she was healthy, she would have come here with you."

"How is she?" Ruby asked.

"She has her good days and bad days," Norvel said. "We are fortunate to have many people checking up and caring for her. I miss the old Leslie, the one with the nonstop energy. Now she mostly sits and watches television," he added sadly.

On May 27, 1984, Denise gave birth to Norvel and Leslie's fourth grandchild, Daryn Elena Anderson. She added further excitement and joy to the boisterous household on Sycamore Street.

In the afternoon of November 27, 1987, Leslie fell asleep in her chair and did not wake up. Norvel was devastated by the loss of his wife, but he tried to make that Christmas a time of joyful celebration of her life.

After the funeral and the holidays, the family carried on by working, attending school, and supporting each other as they continued to live together. Norvel, now retired from the government, immersed himself full-time in property management and the several community committees with which he was still involved. Leslie's sister and brother-in-law, Weekie and Clifford, lived nearby and were often over at Norvel's home helping with cooking and tending to the rambunctious household. Over many years, he and Clifford had become close friends and were often mistaken for siblings. And Norvel's longtime friend and brother-in-law, Robert, and his wife Hattie, a pastor, who also lived nearby, spent many hours socializing with Norvel as well.

Norvel went on with his life. He continued to support the Special Olympics, sit on various community boards, and enjoy his family. And he played cards with his friends from the pinochle gang.

Norvel purchased a vacation time share at Eagle Trace Resort at Massanutten in the Blue Ridge Mountains of Virginia. This area, one hundred miles north of Gala, with its dense forest, rolling hills, and variety of wildlife, felt similar to Norvel's childhood home.

He enjoyed taking his grandchildren to the mountains to give them an idea of what things were like for him growing up. He also took one or two youths from one of the outreach programs he was involved with, giving them an opportunity to experience a world away from the streets of Washington, D.C.

In 1990 Norvel qualified for a real estate broker's license. With it, he was able to purchase the Oxon Hill Century 21 office. He set up a property management operation that administrated his holdings and those of other property owners who didn't want to manage their rentals themselves. The office also employed traditional real estate agents who listed and sold properties in the area.

In May 1992 the pinochle gang gathered at Norvel's house. Norvel's business commitments had caused him to miss the past several games, so the men had not seen him for six weeks or so. When they did, they noticed his slacks and shirt were hanging very loose on his still six-foot-two-inch frame.

Al Maltz said, "You may have to get a new wardrobe, Norvel. Those clothes are looking like they are about ready to fall off."

Norvel said, smiling, "Thanks for noticing. I haven't been at this weight for a long time; I'm still not at my lowest fighting weight, though."

"Any reason for the weight loss?" Mike Mehalic asked.

"Not really. Like Leslie, I developed diabetes a few years ago, which is common for people of my race and age, from what the doctor told me. Lately my appetite hasn't been that good. The doctor I saw a few days ago thinks it's related to my blood sugar. They did some tests, which I should know more about next week."

Maltz, who was standing by the back window, said, "We'll appreciate you keeping us posted, Norvel. I see the cab is gone. Is one of your guys out with it?"

"No, I no longer have it. I sold the Diplomat Cab to a nice young fella. It's about time I got out of that business. It was good to us, though."

On August 5, Norvel asked Al Maltz to help him prepare a will. It provided for most of his estate to be equally divided between his two daughters, Deborah and Denise. It also had a provision that money be held in a trust for each of his grandchildren. Its purpose was to help support their college education. If any of the grandchildren chose not to attend college, the money would be held in trust and not released until they reached the age of thirty. At that time they would have access to the funds.

✿✿✿✿✿✿✿✿✿✿✿✿✿✿✿✿✿✿✿✿✿✿✿✿✿✿✿✿✿✿✿✿✿✿✿✿✿

Two weeks later, on August 19, 1992, at 8:40 p.m., Lieutenant Colonel Norvel LaFollette Ray Lee died of pancreatic cancer at the age of sixty-seven at Bethesda Naval Medical Center.

# CHAPTER 33

*Tuesday, August 25, 1992—Union Wesley A.M.E.
Zion Church, Washington, D.C.*

Norvel Lee's funeral services were set for 10 a.m.
Eight hundred family, friends, and acquaintances of Norvel gathered to offer their respects. Latecomers were forced to stand along the sides and at the rear of the six-hundred-capacity nave. The first three rows were held for members of the family and close acquaintances.

At ten after the hour, the pipe organ began playing "America the Beautiful." The processional began with two ministers leading the family down the center aisle. Following the ministers were Debbie and Denise and their children Francis, Tiffany, Danielle, and Daryn; Denise's husband Daniel; Norvel's brother George pushing his brother James in a wheelchair, followed by their sister Edna, her husband Hayes Hill, and Norvel's brother-in-law Robert Jackson, whose wife Hattie was one of the ministers; and Clifford and Margaret Russell. Following the family were close friends, including members of Norvel's pinochle group. After the people in the procession were seated in their rows, an eight-member chorus joined the organ, ending with a rousing "from sea to shining sea."

Reverend Harold S. Stinger, pastor of Providence Baptist Church in Leesburg, Virginia, stepped to the dais and spoke in a resonant, passionate voice the Words of Grace. He then looked across the crowded room and said, "Friends, we have gathered here to praise God and to celebrate the life of Norvel Lee. We come together in grief, acknowledging our human loss."

Several sobs were heard.

"May God grant us grace," Reverend Stinger continued, "that in pain we may find comfort, in sorrow hope, in death resurrection."

Reverend Hattie Jackson led the congregation in the Invocation prayer.

The chorus provided a moving a capella rendition of "Amazing Grace," followed by scripture readings from Reverend Stinger. After another prayer, Al Maltz was asked to step up to the dais.

Maltz rose from his aisle seat in the second row and approached the podium.

He smiled out at the quiet room and said, "A wise man once said he who finds a faithful friend finds a treasure. We who are friends of Norvel Lee agree completely."

"Amen," was the response.

"Who are we?" continued Maltz. "What does having Norvel as a friend mean? We are certainly many in number—just look around."

Maltz extended his arm and waved it across the room.

"We are old, and we are young. We are tall, and we are short. We are stout, and we are slim. Some are professional athletes, and some are college students. Some are business managers, and some homemakers. Some are executives, and some are secretaries. Some of us are still working, and some of us are retired."

"We are Christian." Maltz moved his arm flowingly across the audience.

"Muslim." He pointed toward the delegation from the embassies of Senegal and Mali.

"And Jew." He pointed at himself.

"We are Black, and we are white. We are friends who have come to honor and mourn."

"Amen," the congregation said.

Maltz paused, looked out at the room, took a deep breath, and continued. "Norvel's friendship to each of us has meant far more than the dictionary definition of 'one attached to another by feelings of personal regard' and 'a well-wisher, patron or supporter.'

"For example, to York Van Nixon, a friend of forty years, Norvel was a fellow boxer, a colleague on the D.C. Boxing Commission, a traveling companion to World Boxing Association conventions, a fellow member to the

Executive Committee of the WBA, and the person who employed him to work for the D.C. Job Training Program when Norvel was administrator of that program. Norvel was the friend who brought one hundred and twenty people to eat at York's restaurant during a period when the restaurant needed patrons.

"To David Minor, a young man who dated Denise in earlier years and who came with his wife and three children from North Carolina to visit Norvel at the hospital, Norvel was a mentor and guide. He was the one who encouraged David to continue his undergraduate education and go on to get his master's degree. He counseled David on the Air Force Reserve program, which David subsequently joined as an airman. I believe he is now a chief master sergeant.

"Dr. Judy Christian, whose father attended Howard University with Norvel, considered Norvel a second father. She gives him more credit than any other person in her life for her professional accomplishments. She was in her early twenties when Norvel hired her to the staff of the then–Federal City College, and thus gave her a start in academia. Over the years Norvel was always interested in Judy's personal and professional career. He literally drove her to Catholic University to ensure that she enrolled in the doctoral program. More recently, he participated as a speaker in a number of programs conducted by Dr. Christian and UDC."

Maltz glanced at his notes, and continued.

"Yvonne Williams, a friend of Norvel's for over twenty years, also viewed him as a second father or big brother and certainly her best friend, one with whom she could discuss serious personal problems and who would advise, but not judge. One who would always listen, counsel, hold your hand when necessary and help. Norvel was Yvonne's landlord as well as a confidante and friend. One who held an apartment for her over a lengthy period of time, on a handshake. A friend who, when Yvonne was a little short of funds, said, 'Don't worry; pay me when you can.'

"The friendship of the 'Pinochle Gang' of which I am a member started about forty-three years ago with Eddie, Mike, Bill and myself. Norvel joined with us in 1954, and Frank in 1964. We have been playing cards together every other week at each other's homes all these years. Our friendship revolved around the game, but involved many activities. Norvel, Mike, and I taught school together; Eddie, Norvel, and Mike worked part-time jobs together; Bill, Norvel, and I were in the D.C. Air National Guard together—and much more. Until Leslie passed away, we and our wives periodically went out to dinner together and vacationed together. We watched each other's families grow, and joined each other at happy times at weddings and sad times at funerals. Above all, we enjoyed having dinner and playing pinochle together every other week. Over all these years, there has never been a time when we sat down or got up angry. Although every point in a game was deemed important, a win by two points after hours of play was as great an accomplishment as a win of one hundred points. We just enjoyed the game and each other."

Maltz looked out at the mesmerized congregation, many with handkerchiefs wiping the tears from their eyes.

He went on. "I recognize that I have cited only a few of many possible examples of what being a friend of Norvel Lee means. While each of these examples is different, I found a great commonality in how we view Norvel as a friend.

"He was a person you could always count on. He came in good times and bad. If he said he would be there, he would. He was a man of tireless energy. Each of us was in awe at the extent and diversity of his activities. He was an educator, a manager, an airman, a realtor, a boxing official, a landlord, a gas station owner, a card player, a taxi driver, a fast friend, and above all, a devoted grandfather, and much more—many at the same time. He was genuinely caring and concerned about people of all ages, but especially young people. Norvel could be counted upon to encourage, counsel, and guide when asked. He would listen intently and advise occasionally. Those of us who saw his family marveled at how gentle and patient he was with his children and grandchildren. Eddie clearly remembers the pride and loving look on Norvel's face when he first showed his baby grandson to the pinochle gang. Norvel thought of others constantly. If he was in your neighborhood, he would stop in to say hello. Each time he visited his brother Jimmy, he would make it a point to stop in and visit Frank, who also lived in that part of Maryland. Mike particularly appreciated that Norvel took the time to visit Mike's father and mother in Florida when he was traveling in that area. Mike's father spoke often about how pleased he was for that visit.

"Norvel was generous and trusting. He would conclude a business deal on a handshake, and generously provide for friends in need, whether that need was for funds for home repairs or just a short vacation. He was very understanding if a tenant could not pay his rent in a timely manner, and would always say, 'Do the best you can.' He was modest and discreet. If you didn't know all of Norvel's abilities and accomplishments, you wouldn't learn them from him. Only from his friends would you find out about his academic prowess and contributions to the boxing world; his business acumen; his generosity in both money and time to family and friends; and his involvement in the total community, especially in the spheres of education and training.

"He was a perfectionist who always wanted to do well in his own work, and to be one of assistance to others in their work. He helped people find employment as well as advised them on how to succeed on the job.

"York spoke of him as 'a Jolly Green Giant,' Eddie as 'a gentle giant,' Yvonne spoke of him as 'a magnificent person,' Judy as 'a rare species,' and David said Norvel was 'special to a lot of people.'

"Obviously, the sage who said friendship is man's greatest gift knew Norvel Lee."

"Amen!" said the congregation.

Several others chimed in with, "Hallelujah!"

Maltz waited for the commotion to subside.

"I close my comments with a quote from a banner, signed by many of his friends, that was displayed in Norvel's hospital room. It said: 'Norvel, you are in our hearts and prayers. We love you. We love you.' I can only add, Rest in Peace, dear friend."

✿✿✿✿✿✿✿✿✿✿✿✿✿✿✿✿✿✿✿✿✿✿✿✿✿✿✿✿✿✿✿✿✿✿✿✿✿✿✿

Norvel L. R. Lee was interred with full military honors at Fort Lincoln Cemetery, next to his wife, Leslie J. Lee. The flag of the United States was meticulously folded and presented to his daughter, Deborah Lee Sellars. The Fort Lincoln Cemetery in Brentwood, Maryland, is at the border between Maryland and the District of Columbia where, on the D.C. side of the boundary, the former National Training School for Boys was located.

# EPILOGUE

## September 9, 1949—Howard University, Washington, D.C.

N orvel Lee was driving blow after powerful blow into the punching bag set up in the corner of the Howard University gymnasium. Several other members of the boxing team were gathered around, awaiting their turn at the bag, which hung from a crossbar. Some had jump ropes they were using for warm-up drills, but mostly Norvel's teammates looked on in astonishment at the sheer power of the punches, especially those delivered with fluid ease by Norvel's right hand.

A middle-aged man in a dark suit joined the boxers observing Norvel's exhibition. The others looked at him curiously, but he held his hand up while Norvel unleashed a powerful combination of jabs and punches.

When he finally stopped, Norvel glanced at the man standing with his fellow boxers as the punching bag swung back and forth. He reached for a towel and wiped the sweat off his forehead and neck.

The man stepped forward to shake Norvel's hand. "Mr. Lee, I'm Lester Banks with the NAACP, and I'd like a few minutes of your time."

Norvel asked, "Right now?"

"Yes, please," Banks said. "Is there somewhere in here where we can talk privately?"

"Uh, uh, yes, in the coach's office. He's not here right now, but the office is open."

Norvel and Lester Banks strolled over to an office on the other side of the gymnasium. As they left, one of the other young boxers stepped toward the punching bag and began to jab at it.

After they sat down in the sparse office, Banks said, "I graduated from Howard twelve years ago. I'm proud of this school and what it did for me. I understand you represent the school magnificently with your athletic and academic achievements. We alumni are proud to know that the next generation of students consists of strong, resilient members like you."

Norvel, trying to get comfortable in the small chair, said, "Yes, sir, thank you."

"I'm here to inform you of some information I received from your attorney, Mr. Martin. On Wednesday, two days ago, the Virginia State Supreme Court reversed the judgment of the trial court that heard your Jim Crow violation case. It found that because you held a ticket for transportation to Washington you were an interstate passenger and not answerable to Virginia's segregation laws, in spite of the fact the train was local."

Norvel, with a broad smile, said, "Uh, uh, my family will be so happy and relieved. My mother was very worried I had gotten involved with something that would hold me back. She's not too healthy."

Banks said, "Well, I hope this news makes her feel better. You can tell her there will be a press release about this truly landmark decision. Its importance cannot be overemphasized. It's the first time a state Supreme Court anywhere has held that a person on local public transportation was not subject to a state's segregation laws. One of the justices supported the decision by saying it was the character of the journey, not the character of the train.

Just within the past year, the North Carolina Supreme Court in similar cases has said that although a person is traveling in interstate commerce, if on a local train, they are in violation of the segregation laws if they choose to sit in the wrong section. This decision will now allow us to fight these unjust laws everywhere."

They spoke a little more and then shook hands. Banks found his way out of the gym, while Norvel walked back across the gymnasium floor toward his teammates, who were taking turns at the punching bag.

Norvel took a jump rope out of a nearby cabinet and positioned it behind his back. With a flick of his wrists the rope began to move around his tall body, his feet stepping over it as it flew by.

*Mama, I'm gonna be the person you always knew I was. I'm gonna*

*make you proud. I'm gonna do good.*
The rope spun fluidly around Norvel Lee, faster and faster and faster.

# ACKNOWLEDGMENTS

To create a book such as this takes much more than just me putting fingers to the keyboard. It takes extensive research, as shown by the cited references on the following pages. Getting access to the source material, interpreting it, and assembling the information could not have happened without the help and support of many people.

First, I want to thank Judith Barnett at the Botetourt County Historical Museum. She learned of Norvel Lee while researching the rich local history of African-Americans and took the story to Ed McCoy of the *Fincastle Herald*. And it was the August 17, 2016, edition of Botetourt County's weekly newspaper with the headline "Botetourt Native Won Olympic Gold in the Boxing Ring" that my wife placed in front of me at our breakfast table. A companion article told of Norvel's arrest for violating the Jim Crow laws at the time. These two articles were my motivation to pursue the story of Norvel Lee.

After meeting Judy she became a consistent supporter and source of information for this project. Her firsthand experiences of life in Botetourt County's segregated Black culture helped me understand what the conditions were like during the time Norvel lived in the area.

During the initial research I came across the website Boxing Along the Beltway. BATB is a blog about boxing in the greater Washington, D.C. area hosted by Gary Digital Williams. I found a 2012 posting by Williams entitled, "Beltway Boxing History: Norvel Lee." Through that article I found Daryn Anderson, Norvel's granddaughter. After a few emails and phone conversations, she and her sister, Danielle Anderson, encouraged me to meet with them. On the first of several visits my wife, Barbara, and I also met Norvel's sister-in-law Margaret Russell (Weekie). Her stories of growing up in Leesburg were invaluable for setting the foundation in the book for Norvel's marriage to her sister, Leslie Jackson. Each time we visited with the family they made available: scrapbooks, photos, and other treasures from Norvel's and Leslie's lives.

Betty Holland of the Botetourt County Board of Education permitted me to examine archival records from Academy Hill. She brought me a box of pristinely kept material from the late 1930s and early 1940s. Inside each box were sections labeled for Colored and White, with beautifully handwritten records for each class. It didn't take me long to find Norvel's outstanding academic records from Academy Hill. Several of the records included notes regarding his speech difficulties.

In late 2017 Daryn informed me that she had found one of the pinochle players, Mike Mehalic. Daryn and I met him at his Washington, D.C., home on November 7, 2017. That interview is where I learned how the pinochle gang was formed at the National Training School for Boys in 1953. When I brought up Norvel's Jim Crow arrest, Mehalic said he hadn't heard anything about it. That admission confirmed what his family said about Norvel: he never dealt on the past, he was always moving forward.

I spent hours of research seeking a backstory regarding Norvel's act of civil disobedience. I'm grateful for the people who came forward and helped me with this quest. Tewodros Abebe, Howard University's senior archivist, encouraged me to spend time at the archival library on the Howard University campus reviewing their documents, which I did. I received credentials from the Library of Congress to be a manuscript reader. On two occasions, I studied fascinating correspondence and memoranda from the NAACP archival files housed there. I visited the C&O Historical Society in Clifton Forge and perused their documents, mostly train schedules. I searched, in vain, for Martin A. Martin's personal archival records, hoping he had kept notes regarding the details of Norvel's case. I appreciate Margaret Edds, author of the book *We Face the Dawn,* for providing counsel on where I might find them. In the end, I decided to limit the narrative to the facts of the case, and leave the backstory speculation to the reader's imagination.

The testimony in the prologue is taken directly from the transcripts of the case, obtained from the Virginia State Law Library. Likewise, the eulogy was taken directly from a copy, provided by Daryn, of the document that Al Maltz composed for Norvel's funeral.

I contacted the D.C. Boxing Commission to see if they had any archival information about Norvel. Henry "Discombobulating" Jones, ring announcer for Washington, D.C., boxing events, responded and connected me with Adrian Davis. Davis, a prominent D.C.-area boxing trainer, told me he was a fifteen-year-old troubled kid when he met Norvel, who took him under his wing. At one point during the conversation, he said with great emotion, "My life wouldn't be what it has been if Norvel Lee hadn't taken an interest in me." I will forever be grateful for the insight both men from the D.C. boxing world provided.

I am also grateful for becoming acquainted with Lisa Telles, John Boutilier's daughter and the friendship we have since established. When Barbara and I visited with her and her husband at their Southern California home, she showed us her late father's memorabilia. It had been stored in the attic at her mother's home. That information and our ongoing email correspondence contributed significantly to the amateur boxing sections of the book, especially the 1951 Duals Tour chapter.

Perhaps the most moving experience of the journey occurred on March 11, 2018, when I had the honor of meeting Norvel's brother, George Lee. Daryn scheduled a meet up with him at a long-term rehabilitation center in Forestville, Maryland, where he was staying. Barbara and I joined Daryn, Danielle, their cousin and Norvel's other granddaughter, Tiffany Ayler, and George's son Ken Floyd for the meeting. When we met George, in a wheelchair, he wore a serious look. I initially thought he wouldn't be up for a lengthy interview but felt thankful I could at least say I met him. However, when I sat next to him to introduce myself, he looked directly and confidently into my eyes, his family looking on, and said, "You can ask me anything you want, and I will answer you." I had to contain my emotions at that point.

At the completion of the third draft, I asked several acquaintances to read and provide a critique of the manuscript. Many thanks to each of them: friends and neighbors Brian Abel, Lynn Abel, Robbie Dix, and

Robin Dix; long-time friend Bill Simpson in California; daughter-in-law Julie Conklin in Kentucky; Norvel's granddaughter, Daryn Anderson; and Andy Eisenzimmer in Minnesota. The story of Andy's and my connection is interesting, but that's a story for another time. He was the only person among the readers to not know about the subject matter. I asked him to read the manuscript from the beginning without any research and to provide his feedback. Each of the readers provided valuable critiques, which I took to heart and incorporated accordingly into the narrative.

I also want to acknowledge the impact the following people had on the development of the narrative: Michael Dixon, the C&O Historical Society Publications Coordinator; Bob Yalen, International Boxing Research Organization (IBRO); Miles Templeton, UK Boxing History archivist; and Petri Paimander, Finland's boxing historian. It was Paimander who informed me the Val Barker Trophy was awarded prior to the gold medal matches. He helped me bring those long-ago games alive.

My daughter Dale Levine helped with the search for background information on some of the characters appearing in the book. Most notably, the obituary she found on Jack Lee's second wife, Ruby Virginia Jackson helped bring her personality alive on these pages. Thank you.

When it was time to engage professional editors, I was very fortunate. For developmental editing I worked with the esteemed Leslie Wells. Leslie has worked on many bestselling books during her career. She convinced me to tell the story chronologically, rather than in the original manner I had presented it. It was my first experience working with a developmental editor. She exceeded my expectations.

While attending the Roanoke Regional Writer's Conference during the past few years I learned that it was critical, no matter how many times I had read through the manuscript, to work with a professional copyeditor. As was the case with Leslie Wells I was fortunate to have the services of top tier editor Beth Partin. She not only included the construction of the sentences in her review but she made sure the narrative adhered to consistency in names, time, and historical facts. Her attention to details was invaluable.

I can't say enough about Asya Blue, the designer of both the cover and the interior of the book. Her passion for making sure her work is the best it can be while satisfying my expectations was motivating.

The support of family and friends throughout this journey has kept me buoyed and moving toward the end goal. Your patience with me while I recounted minute details of obscure things I found in my research along the way helped me more than I let on. You know who you all are, thank you.

Simultaneously with the publication of the first edition of NORVEL, in hardcover, I was invited to speak at the kickoff of Botetourt County's celebration of Black History Month. It was also an event commemorating the 250th Anniversary of the founding of Botetourt County. I was thrilled to have in attendance from Maryland, Norvel's granddaughter Danielle Anderson and his nephew Ken Floyd, and from California, John Boutilier's daughter, Lisa Telles. Other events were scheduled but canceled as the COVID-19 pandemic took hold. I look forward to speaking at future events when it is safe to do so.

But the person I want to thank the most is my wife, Barbara, who has been a part of this project since she first showed me the headline from the *Fincastle Herald.* She patiently read and lovingly critiqued each draft. She has accompanied me down every path of this incredible journey. Without her love and support, this book would not have been possible. Thank you, my love.

To all whom I encountered and supported me on this continuing journey of a lifetime: Thank you.

# NOTABLE CHARACTERS

| NAME | BRIEF BIOGRAPHY |
|------|-----------------|
| Abbott, Judge Earl | Circuit judge who presided over Norvel's appeal. (1905–1973) |
| Adkins, Charles | Welterweight gold medalist for the United States in the 1952 Olympics. (1932–1993) |
| Banks, Lester | Executive director of the Virginia section of the NAACP. (1911–1986) |
| Barnes, Samuel | Howard University boxing coach. |
| Boutilier, John "Bout" | The 1950 Golden Gloves and 1951 lightweight AAU national champion in 1951. He retired as an educator with San Diego City Schools. (1926–2012) |
| Bradford, James | Silver medalist in weightlifting in 1952 and 1960 Olympics. Became a bookbinder and researcher at the Library of Congress. (1928–2013) |
| Brooks, Nathan | Flyweight gold medalist for the United States in 1952 Olympics. Later received a law degree from Ohio State University. (1933 -    ) |
| Brooks, Rev. Huston | Pastor of Providence Baptist Church in Leesburg when Norvel and Leslie were married. His reputation was one of a charismatic and inspiring orator. |
| Cook, Dr. Mercer | Ambassador to Niger, 1961–1964, Senegal, 1964–1966, and The Gambia, 1965–1966. Previously, he was professor of romance languages at Howard University. (1903–1987) |
| Drake, Glenn | A strong proponent of the Washington D.C. Golden Gloves, a boxing trainer, and the operator of the Apollo Athletic Club. (1917–1990) |

344

| | |
|---|---|
| Faul, Adam | Canadian national heavyweight champion. Member of the 1948 Canadian Olympic team. (1929–2016) |
| Goff, Ken | Assistant coach of Canada's 1948 Olympic boxing team and founder of the Olympic Boxing Club in Regina, Canada. (1910–1993) |
| Henderson, Edwin | A distinguished educator and a major force in the integration of basketball and other sports. Received a PhD in education from Howard University. (1883–1977) |
| Iness, Simeon | 1952 Olympic gold medal winner in the discus throw. Went to the same high school as Bob Mathias in Tulare, California. Iness became a high school athletic coach. He and Mathias remained close friends throughout their lives. (1930–1996) |
| Jackson Jr., Robert | Norvel's brother-in-law, brother of Leslie and Margaret. They were lifelong friends after meeting in the Army Air Corps. (1926–2019) |
| Jackson, Margaret | Norvel Lee's mother-in-law and mother of Robert, Leslie, and Margaret. (b?–1984) |
| Jackson, Mervin | Cousin of Robert, Leslie, and Margaret Jackson. Later became vice mayor of Leesburg. Mervin Jackson Park in downtown Leesburg is named in his honor. (1929–2009) |
| Jackson, Robert Emmett | Norvel Lee's father-in-law, a.k.a. Emmett. Father of Robert, Leslie, and Margaret Jackson. (b?–1984) |
| James, General Daniel | Known as Chappie. In 1975 he became the first African American four-star general. He began |

his military career as a flight instructor at the
Tuskegee Institute and became a fighter pilot.
(1920–1978)

Johansson, Ingemar

Former professional heavyweight world champion - see Floyd Patterson bio. (1932–2009)

Lee, Deborah Louise

Daughter of Norvel and Leslie. Mother of
Norvel's grandchildren Francis Ricks and Tiffany
Ayler. (1954–2014)

Lee, Denise Kay

Daughter of Norvel and Leslie. Mother of
Norvel's grandchildren Danielle and Daryn.
(1955–2005)

Lee, Edna

Norvel's sister. Became an educator in Emporia, Virginia. Married Hayes Hill. She became
friends with her teacher Georgia Meadows and
came to Eagle Rock often to visit. (1926–2006)

Lee, George

Norvel Lee's younger brother. Served in the
Navy and then settled in Washington, D.C.
Boxed at one point. Worked in construction.
The author had the honor of interviewing him.
(1936–   )

Lee, George Anna Ray

Known as Georgiana, mother of Norvel, Edna,
James, and George. Instilled family, education,
and community service as top priorities in Norvel's life. (1898–1949)

Lee, James Fitzhugh

Norvel Lee's brother. Graduate of Howard University and author of several books. (1928–1992)

Lee, James Jackson

Known as Jack–Norvel Lee's father. (1904–1984)

Lee, Leslie Ellen Jackson

Wife of Norvel, mother of Deborah and Denise.
Led effort to establish libraries at all public
schools in Washington, D.C. Established library

card system at Federal University. (1924–1987)

| | |
|---|---|
| Lee, Norvel | Husband of Leslie, father of Deborah and Denise and grandfather of Francis, Danielle, Tiffany, and Daryn. The subject of this book. (1924–1992) |
| Lee, Ruby Virginia | Second wife of Jack Lee, Norvel's father. (1919–2010) |
| Louis, Joe | The world heavyweight champion from 1937 to 1949. Widely considered to be the greatest boxer of all time. (1914–1982) |
| Maltz, Dr. Albert | Member of the pinochle gang, educator, director of personnel at FEMA; earned PhD from GWU. Delivered eulogy at Norvel Lee's funeral. (1929–2004) |
| Martin, Martin A. | Attorney for Norvel's appealed Jim Crow case. Graduate of Howard University. Partner in the civil rights law firm of Hill, Martin, and Robinson who joined the Brown vs. Board of Education desegregation case. (1910–1963) |
| Mathias, Bob | 1948 and 1952 Olympic decathlon gold medal winner. Considered one of the greatest athletes of the twentieth century. Elected to the U.S. Congress from California. (1930–2006) |
| Mehalic, Michael | Member of the pinochle gang, educator. Played role of Ronald McDonald in Washington, D.C., and Maryland. Interviewed by the author on 1/28/2017. (1931–    ) |
| Mello, Pete | Co-coach of the 1952 United States Olympic Boxing team. Also very active in Golden Gloves boxing as head of New York City's Catholic Youth Organization. |

Moore, Davey

Bantamweight member of the 1952 Olympic boxing team. In 1959 became the feather-weight world champion. He died from injuries in defense of his title against Sugar Ray Ramos at Dodger Stadium. Bob Dylan wrote the song "Who Killed Davey Moore?" about the tragedy. (1933–1963)

Patterson, Floyd

Mentored by Norvel, he won the gold medal as a middleweight in the 1952 Olympics. He went on to be the professional heavyweight champion, defeating Ingemar Johannson. Later he and Johannson became friends, visiting each other every year and running marathons together. (1935–2006)

Rawson, Tommy

Legendary Harvard University boxing coach, referee, and former national junior lightweight boxing champion. (19092003)

Russell, Margaret "Weekie"

Norvel's sister-in-law, sister of Leslie. Married to Clifford Russell. Had long career at NASA Goddard as an emulsions expert. In-person interviews with her conducted by the author. (1939–   )

Sanders, Hayes Edward

Known as Ed. Heavyweight boxing gold medalist in the 1952 Olympics. Norvel beat him the only time they faced each other. Died from injuries suffered during a professional boxing match. A Navy man, he was laid to rest in Woodlawn Cemetery in Santa Monica, CA, with full military honors. His younger brother, Stan, became a Rhodes Scholar, attorney, and aide to Mayor Tom Bradley of Los Angeles. (1930–1954)

Senghor, Dr. Leopold

Considered to be one of the most important

<table>
<tr><td></td><td>African intellectuals of the twentieth century as well as a widely acclaimed poet. He served as the first president of Senegal for twenty years. (1906–2001)</td></tr>
<tr><td>Terry, Roger</td><td>Norvel's teacher at the Academy Hill School for Negroes in Fincastle, Virginia.</td></tr>
<tr><td>Touré, Ali Farka</td><td>Became one of Africa's most internationally re-nowned musicians. He is ranked 76th on Rolling Stone's Top One Hundred Guitarists of All Time. (1939–2006)</td></tr>
<tr><td>Walton, Lillie</td><td>Known as "Mother Dear," operator of Lillie's boardinghouse at the corner of 5th Street and Florida Avenue NW, Washington, D.C. (1902–1979)</td></tr>
<tr><td>Whitfield, Malvin</td><td>Olympic gold medalist in 1948 and 1952 800-meter run; goodwill ambassador to Africa for forty-seven years. His daughter, Fredricka, anchors the weekend edition of CNN's News-room. (1924–2015)</td></tr>
</table>

# NORVEL LEE'S BOXING RECORD

**1948**

| | | | | |
|---|---|---|---|---|
| Feb 6 | J. Gwalthney | W 3 | Washington, D.C. | D.C. Golden Gloves |
| May 19 | Eddie Grant | W 3 | Washington, D.C. | D.C. Olympic Trials finals |
| May 25 | C. Louis Duncan | W 3 | Philadelphia, PA | Olympic Trials Region 3 semis |
| May 25 | Earl Matthews | W 3 | Philadelphia, PA | Olympic Trials Region 3 finals |
| Jun 28 | Charles Black | TKO 2 | Boston, MA | Olympic Trials quarters |
| Jun 29 | Coley Wallace | W 3 | Boston, MA | Olympic Trials semis |
| Jun 29 | Elbert "Jay" Lambert | L 3 | Boston, MA | Olympic Trials finals |
| Aug 17 | Garda Walsh | W 3 | Dublin, IRE | USA vs. Ireland |
| Sep 25 | Ed Zastre | W 5 | Regina, CAN | Canadian Police Association bouts |
| Dec 27 | Adam Faul | W 6 | Regina, CAN | Canadian Police Association bouts |

**1949**

| | | | | |
|---|---|---|---|---|
| Mar 25 | J. Gwalthney | W 3 | Richmond, VA | CIAA championship semifinals |
| Mar 26 | C. Louis Duncan | W 3 | Richmond, VA | CIAA champship finals |
| Sep 16 | Adam Faul | W 5 | Winnipeg, CAN | Canadian Police Association bouts |

**1950**

| | | | | |
|---|---|---|---|---|
| Jan 10 | Henry Ebron | W 3 | Fort Meade, MD | |

| Jan 19 | John Sullivan | TKO 1 | Washington, D.C. | D.C. Golden Gloves quarters |
|---|---|---|---|---|
| Feb 1 | Edgar Smith | W 2-1 | Washington, D.C. | D.C. Golden Gloves semis |
| Feb 9 | Eddie Grant | W 3 | Washington, D.C. | D.C. Golden Gloves finals |
| Feb 27 | Ed Knepp | TKO 3 | Cumberland, MD | |
| Mar 7 | Sylvester Jones | W 3 | New York, NY | Eastern Golden Gloves quarters |
| Mar 8 | Gilmore Newkirk | W 3 | New York, NY | Eastern Golden Gloves semis |
| Mar 9 | Nick Vasquez | KO 1 | New York, NY | Eastern Golden Gloves finals |
| Mar 23 | John Boutilier | W 2 | Bear Mountain, NY | Exhibition |
| Mar 29 | Kirby Seals | W 3 | Chicago, IL | Intercity Golden Gloves champs. |
| Apr 10 | Bunn Pitts | KO 2 | Boston, MA | National AAU trials |
| Apr 11 | Nick Vasquez | KO 2 | Boston, MA | National AAU quarters |
| Apr 12 | Louis Packer | W 3 | Boston, MA | National AAU semis |
| Apr 12 | Stan Howlett | W 3 | Boston, MA | National AAU finals |
| Apr 21 | Teemu Kuusela | TKO 2 | Washington, D.C. | International Golden Gloves bouts |
| May 1 | Harry Mazick | W 5 | Cumberland, MD | |
| Jul 25 | Jesse Lane | TKO 2 | Winnipeg, CAN | |

**1951**

| Jan 5 | Bob Miller | W 3 | Kansas City, KS | Pan Am Games trial bout |
|---|---|---|---|---|

| | | | | |
|---|---|---|---|---|
| Feb 1 | Edgar Smith | W 3 | Washington, D.C. | D.C. Golden Gloves quarters |
| Feb 15 | Eddie LaCovey | TKO 2 | Washington, D.C. | D.C. Golden Gloves finals |
| Mar 5 | Victor Bignon | L 3 | Buenos Aires, ARG | Pan Am Games semis |
| Mar 7 | Arlindo de Oliveira | KO 1 | Buenos Aires, ARG | Pan Am Games bronze medal bout |
| Mar 19 | Toxey Hall | W 3 | New York, NY | Intercity Golden Gloves alt. champ |
| Apr 5 | Ingemar Johansson | w/o | Washington, D.C. | Europe vs. U.S. Golden Gloves match |
| Apr 9 | James Craven | TKO 1 | Boston, MA | National AAU trials |
| Apr 10 | Joseph McFadden | W 3 | Boston, MA | National AAU quarters |
| Apr 11 | Pete Rademacher | W 3 | Boston, MA | National AAU semis |
| Apr 11 | Albert Schlimm | W 3 | Boston, MA | National AAU finals |
| Aug 21 | Peter Toch | W 3 | London, ENG | USA vs. England Duals matches |
| Aug 24 | Arthur Worral | W 3 | Manchester, ENG | USA vs. England Duals matches |
| Aug 27 | Abraham Rosenberg | W 3 | Wiesbaden, GER | USA vs. Germany Duals matches |
| Aug 31 | Ingemar Johansson | W 3 | Gothenburg, SWE | USA vs. Sweden |

**1952**

| | | | | |
|---|---|---|---|---|
| Jan 16 | Edgar Smith | W 3 | Washington, D.C. | D.C. Golden Gloves semis |
| Jan 24 | Barrett Kiff | TKO 2 | Washington, D.C. | D.C. Golden Gloves finals |

| Feb | Don Lee | KO 2 | Washington, D.C. | March of Dimes bouts |
|---|---|---|---|---|
| Mar 3 | Alexander Brown | W 3 | New York, NY | Eastern Golden Gloves trials |
| Mar 4 | Mike Tunney | W 3 | New York, NY | Eastern Golden Gloves quarters |
| Mar 5 | Oliver Walker | KO 1 | New York, NY | Eastern Golden Gloves semis |
| Mar 5 | Harold Johnson | W 3 | New York, NY | Eastern Golden Gloves finals |
| Mar 24 | Hayes "Ed" Sanders | W 3 | New York, NY | Intercity Golden Gloves champs. |
| Apr 8 | Jack Scheberies | L 3 | Boston, MA | National AAU trials quarters |
| May 19 | Kirby Seals | W 3 | Washington, D.C. | D.C. vs. All-Navy |
| May 27 | Julius Griffin | W 3 | Albany, NY | Eastern Olympic Trials semis |
| May 27 | Kirby Seals | W 3 | Albany, NY | Eastern Olympic Trials finals |
| Jun 16 | Lloyd Willis | L 3 | Kansas City, KS | Olympic Games trials eliminations |
| Jul 29 | Claude Arnaiz | W 3 | Helsinki, FIN | Olympic Games trials |
| Jul 31 | Tadeusz Grzelak | W 3 | Helsinki, FIN | Olympic Games quarters |
| Aug 1 | Harri Walfrid Siljander | W 3 | Helsinki, FIN | Olympic Games semis |
| Aug 2 | Antonio Pacenza | W 3 | Helsinki, FIN | Olympic Games finals—gold medal |
| | | | | Awarded Val Barker Trophy |

## 1955

| Feb 24 | Bob Ranck | W 3 | San Antonio, TX | Pan Am Games trials quarters |
| Feb 25 | Bob Jefferson | TKO 2 | San Antonio, TX | Pan Am Games trials semis |
| Feb 26 | Arthur Statum | W 3 | San Antonio, TX | Pan Am Games trials finals |
| Mar 17 | Pablo Alexis Miteff | L 3 | Mexico City, MX | Pan Am Games semis—bronze medal |

## 1959

| Sep 10 | Archie Whitfield | T 4 | Fort Campbell, KY | Exhibition |

Multiple references. Compiled by the author.

# REFERENCES

Amateur Boxing Results, www.amateur-boxing.strefa.pl/index.html.

Baltimore Afro-American.
   *U.S. Boxer Fined in RR Seat Case,* October 18, 1948.
   *Howard Athlete to Appeal Va. Jim-Crow Travel Case,* October 23, 1948.
   *Through Ticket Serves to Kill State Jim Crow Laws,* September 17, 1949.

The Bison.
   1951 Howard University Yearbook, page 64.
   1952 Howard University Yearbook, page 21.
   1953 Howard University Yearbook, page 54.

Boston Herald.
   *N.E. Lands One Olympic Berth,* June 30, 1948.
   *McGuiggan, Boutilier Win in National Ring Tourney,* April 11, 1951.
   *Boutilier Wins Ring Crown,* April 12, 1951.
   *Lee's Car Stolen,* April 8, 1952.

Boxing History.org.uk, www.boxinghistory.org.uk.

Brooks, Ken. *Ingemar Johansson.* McFarland and Company, 2016, page 21.

Chambers, Ted. *History of Athletics and Physical Education at Howard University.* New York: Vantage Press, 1986.

Cook, Dr. Mercer. Letter to Norvel Lee on American Embassy letterhead, August 10, 1964.

Ebony.
   *Lee: Amateur Champ,* February 1, 1951, page 65.
   *Lee Defeats Five Countries,* February 1, 1951, page 66.
   *Lee's Amazing Leg Work,* February 1, 1951, page 68.
   *Fight Commission Chairman,* December 1, 1963.

The Fincastle Herald. McCoy, Ed. *Botetourt Native Won Olympic Gold in the Boxing Ring*, August 17, 2016.

The Hilltop, Howard University.
Anderson, Sam. *In the Light*, October 22, 1948.
Lee, James. *HU Captures Boxing Crown*, April 13, 1949.
*Norvel Lee Was Mainstay in Dist. Golden Gloves*, April 11, 1951.

International Boxing Research Organization (IBRO), www.IBROresearch.com.

Jet Magazine.
*Boxers Win Five Olympic Championships*, August 14, 1952.
*Two Negro Athletes Attend Ike's Luncheon;* June 18, 1953.
*Norvel Lee Named D.C. Golden Gloves Judge;* June 21, 1954.
*Olympic Boxing Champ Heads D.C. Boxing Body*, November 7, 1963.

The Jewish Boxing Blog. "A Look Back: Abraham Rosenberg," http://www.jewishboxing.blogspot.com/2013/08/a-look-back-abraham-rosenberg.html, 8/22/2013.

Milwaukee Journal.
*Argentine Judges Award Bouts to Home Fighters*, March 6, 1951.
*Revenge Brings Lee Out of Retirement*, March 12, 1955.

The New Jersey Journal. *U.S. Olympic Boxing Team Chosen After Olympic Trials*, June 30, 1948.

New York Times.
*Boutilier Takes AAU Ring Title*, April 12, 1951.
*Hackney, with Knockout in Third Round, Leads U.S. Boxers to Victory in Sweden*, September 1, 1951.
*Lee Scores by Decision*, May 28, 1952.
*Webb Knocked Out by Papp in Second*, July 30, 1952.
*5 American Boxers Reach Final Round*, August 2, 1952.
*U.S. Fighters Take Five Gold Medals—Lee Wins Outstanding Boxing Trophy*, August 3, 1952.

The Organising Committee for the XV Olympiad, Helsinki, 1952. *The Official Report*, 1952.

Remnick, David. *Life Stories: Profiles from the New Yorker.* New York: Random House, 2001, page 303.

Saskatchewan Sports Hall of Fame, Ken Goff, www.sasksportshalloffame.com.

Sports Reference LLC, Norvel Lee, https://www.sports-reference.com/olympics/athletes/le/norvel-lee-1.

Supreme Court of Appeals of Virginia at Richmond, Record 3558—*Norvel Lee v. Commonwealth of Virginia*, February 26, 1949.
The United States Olympic Committee. *Games of the XIVth Olympiad*, 1948.

United States Olympic Committee. *United States 1952 Olympic Book*, 1953.

Washington Evening Star.
   *Lee, Only Capital Boy Left in Olympic Ring Tests, Faces Trouble*, June 29, 1948.
   *Lee Is Standout as 4 District Boxers Move Up in AAU Meet*, April 11, 1950.
   *Lee Rated Title Cinch After Knocking Out Two AAU Rivals*, April 12, 1950.
   *Lee and Thompson, AAU Boxing Champs, Eye World Titles*, April 13, 1950.
   *Victory Here Consoles European Ringmen for Loss in West*, April 22, 1950.
   *Lightweight Champ Davis Heads for Golden Gloves Welter Title*, February 2, 1951.
   *Heavyweight Lee Again Shows Best Punch in Golden Gloves*, February 16, 1951.
   *Eldridge Thompson Boxes Chicago Star*, March 19, 1951.
   *Norvel Lee Helps to Win Draw for East in Golden Gloves*, March 20, 1951.
   *Two Close Fights Seen When Europeans Box D.C. Amateurs Tonight*, April 5, 1951.
   *Three D.C. Fighters Lose AAU Bouts, Lee Only Winner*, April 10, 1951.

*Lee Beats McFadden to Reach Semifinals in Boxing Tourney,* April 11, 1951.

*Navy Has Pick of Two Fighters to Oppose Lee in Show Monday,* May 14, 1952.

*Crack Olympic Team Indicated by Navy Golden Gloves Bouts,* May 20, 1952.

*Lee Moves to Finals of Olympic Ring Tests with Regional Victory,* May 28, 1952.

*D.C. Ring Champions Off for Olympic Trials,* June 15, 1952.

*Lee and Hill Beaten in First-Round Bouts at Olympic Tryouts,* June 17, 1952.

*Norvel Lee Is Alternate as 3 College Boxers Make Olympic Team,* June 18, 1952.

*One American Boxer Stopped, but Sanders and Gage score KO's,* July 29, 1952.

*5 Americans in Boxing Finals; Best U.S. Olympic Showing,* August 2, 1952.

*Coach's Threat, Rigged Scales, Hot Baths Took Lee to Victory,* August 4, 1952.

*Plaque Given Norvel Lee for Olympic Boxing Win,* August 13, 1952.

*Norvel Lee Heads U.S. Team for Pan American Boxing,* February 28, 1955.

*Lee and Stewart Bow in Pan Am Boxing,* March 18, 1955.

Washington Post.

*Lillie Walton, 77, Operated Boarding House for Students,* February 6, 1979.

Murray, Edward H. *Washington's Greatest,* August 29, 1992

Williams, Gary. "Beltway Boxing History: Norvel Lee," Boxing Along the Beltway, http://boxingalongthebeltway.blogspot.com/2012/07/beltway-boxing-history-norvel-lee.html, July 26, 2012.

# ABOUT THE AUTHOR

Ken Conklin, a native of Los Angeles, lives in Botetourt County, Virginia. His essays have been published in the *Roanoke Times* as well as other publications such as the *Victoria Advocate, Easy Reader*, and *Microwave Journal*. He has received several local poetry awards. *NORVEL* is his first book.

Although always a writer, he made his living in the technology industry as a business development and general management executive. In those roles he had the opportunity to travel throughout North America, Europe, and Asia. The experiences from those journeys inform his writing.

Aside from working on his next book, Ken and his wife enjoy spending time with their family, going to live music events, golfing, and hiking the beautiful trails of southwest Virginia. Ken continues, however, to root for the Los Angeles Dodgers.